History tells of mad emperors, foolish kings, and their often tragic queens, but almost nothing of ordinary people. This is especially true of the so-called Dark Ages. But recent developments in forensic archaeology are shining brilliant beams into the Dark Ages, illuminating societies rich in colour and complexity.

I hope The Whispering Bell will transport you to 7th century England, to share the lives and loves of ordinary people. I want you to hear their chatter, smell their food and animals, and go with them into their villages, homes and farms. If my story can place you, however briefly, at their tables, their bedsides, or even in the crush and thunderous racket of the glittering shield wall, I will have succeeded.

Brian Sellars
brian@briansellars.co.uk

CW01564013

Also by Brian Sellars

Tuppenny Hat Detective

A period detective story set in Sheffield, England, in 1951.
Was the old Star woman murdered? Schoolboy Billy Perks, who found
her body, is sure she was, but the authorities disagree. Their haste to
close the case heightens Billy's suspicions. He decides to investigate,
unwittingly provoking a long hidden serial killer and unearthing secrets
of a wartime conspiracy and betrayal.

Time Rocks

Working on a dig at Stonehenge, archaeology student, Jack Shire,
uncovers an electronic gizmo in earth undisturbed since the Neolithic. It
blasts him back to a time before Stonehenge without hope of returning.
Only his girlfriend, Tori Morris, can help him, but she must first do
battle with a ruthless megalomaniac who has stolen the secrets of time
travel.

www.briansellars.com

The Whispering Bell

Brian Sellars

First published in 2009 by Quaestor2000 Ltd
Crewe CW1 3WZ

This edition
Published by YouWriteOn.com, 2011

A CIP catalogue record for this title is available from the British Library.

Photography and cover design
by Alex Parker
(alexparker.freelance@gmail.com)

For Jeanie

Glossary of Old English terms and place names at the end of book.

Sketch map shows old English kingdom of Mercia and the main locations mentioned in the book.

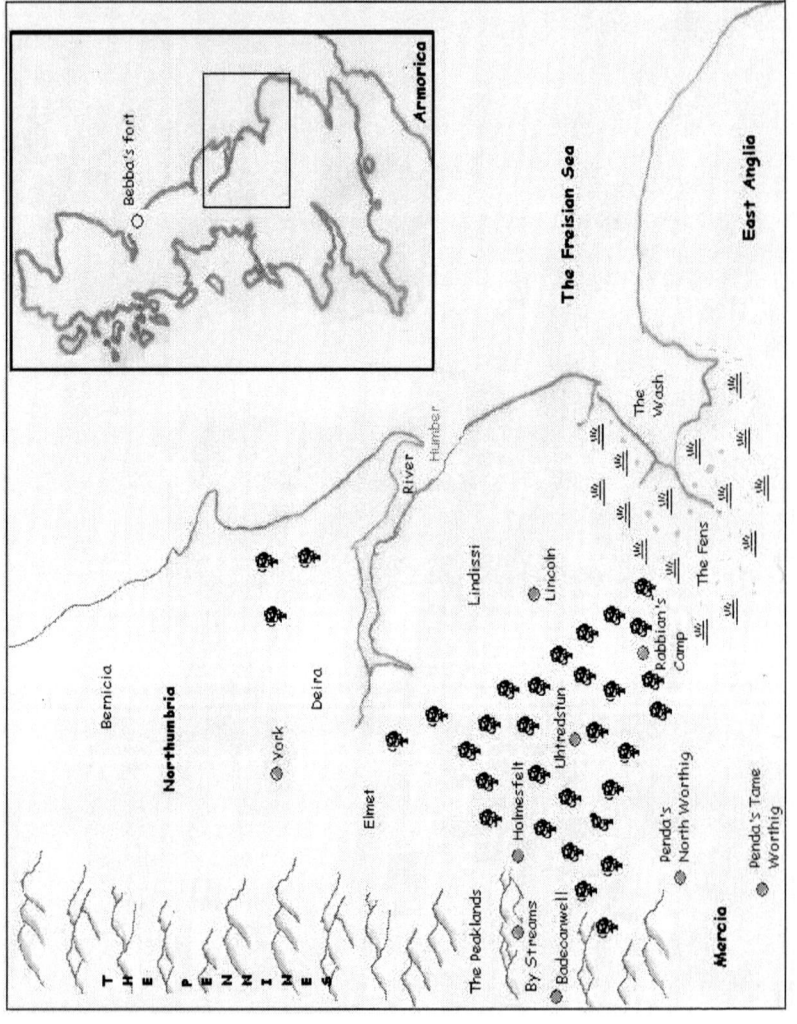

CHAPTER ONE

Mercian England circa 620 AD

After the great sickness famine gripped the land, garnishing it for riot and murder. Abandoned farms fell into ruin. Weeds shrouded rotting ploughs in neglected fields and yards. Bands of vengeful wealhs picked over their lost lands, preying on the few English incomers who had managed to save a little food. In smouldering settlements corpses lay unburied, their flesh a gruesome harvest for the dying. Beyond limp stockades and deserted city walls secretive groups of fearful refugees scoured the great shire-wood for berries and roots.

Twice Ettith had defied famine and plague. Despite the aches of her old bones she had outlived her entire family, strapping sons and daughters with their rowdy broods. She was a loner deeply suspicious of others. That was how she had survived so long and though weak from hunger and as frail as a rush-light flame her old eyes still burned defiantly in their waxy sockets.

She came upon a hamlet deep in the forest on a soft summer's morning piped with glistening dew and birdsong. As usual she hid and settled to study the place assessing its situation. Did the inhabitants have food? Might they be dangerous or hospitable? If she saw they too were starving she'd pass them by. It would not be wise to linger.

All was silent: no dogs, no smoke, no hens scratching in the road, no children playing near the pond, no men in the fields, or women hunched over the washing stones beside the well. Like so many farms and settlements she had seen it stood abandoned, stripped and ravaged by plague and famine. Already the greening haze of disuse covered its single street as the forest reclaimed the rutted earth.

"A mouse would be lucky to fill its belly in this place," she said, as if to craning onlookers.

She was about to leave when she spotted a cat cleaning itself beside the door of one of the small, windowless houses. It stopped its grooming and eyed her as she stepped from cover. "Cat is meat," she whispered, stalking it like a wolf on a lamb. "Cat is meat, good meat." Such a cat could feed her for a week or more. "Here kitty kitty."

A sound burst upon her, scaring away the cat. Her old joints froze as stiff as sticks. She tilted her head and flicked her gaze around trying to pinpoint the source of the sound. It was several moments before she recognised the sounds of the snapping crash and rip of someone forcing their way through the forest, with no care for who might hear them. She freed her joints and hobbled back to her hiding place. Moments later a man burst from the tangled undergrowth at the far side of the village. He was short and muscular with greying hair and a thick, wild beard. He wore leather armour and had a sword slung across his back. A stocky saddle pony bearing his shield, spears and a large pack trailed behind him. On the end of a long leash attached to the horse an amiable milk cow followed.

Though weary and bedraggled by his journey, the stranger's fearless bearing showed the arrogance of the warrior kind. He barged into the village, sweeping aside the vegetation, clearly expecting a deferential welcome. Though far from arrogant, the milk cow followed, equally self-assured.

Ettith had not seen a cow for months, let alone a fine, meaty horse. She imagined eating the succulent red meat they could provide. Her mouth watered, though she knew it was a foolish daydream. Without the magic of salt or a smoke house, fresh juicy meat would soon rot into a stinking flyblown mess. She had seen plenty of those.

The warrior was striding through the village searching the houses. After poking his head into several of the meaner dwellings he entered the largest where he remained for some time.

She cursed him for the loss of the fat cat. Her old body creaked as she crouched in hiding. Her stomach rumbled with hunger. Again she thought of roasted cow meat, its juices dripping over a fire. She must have food. Clasping her hands together she prayed for the man to go away and leave her to her scavenging. When at last he emerged from the house, he carried a bundle wrapped in cloth. She thought it looked big enough to be a whole ham or a side of bacon. The certainty that it was food burned into her brain, and again she cursed the warrior. If only she had arrived sooner, that ham, or whatever it was, would be hers now. But what could it be; smoked pig meat, a salted side of mutton? What was this arrogant thief stealing from her?

The man lowered the bundle to the ground and hurried back into the house. He re-emerged carrying a spade. Ettith watched him choose a spot of earth near a small shrine to Eostre, the spring goddess. He poked the spade at the ground a few times and then dug it in deep, piling his weight behind it.

"Food, he's burying the food," she told herself, before doubts dismissed the notion. No, not food, she thought, but what? She stared at the bundle, trying to make sense of the swaddled shape. Is it a little child? She shuddered as the idea that it could be grew in her mind. It could be a bairn – perhaps his own. She smoothed her palms over her cheeks and stood up, watching him work. Sadness chilled her like shadows. She pitied him. Despite her years of trouble and loss, the sight of this lone warrior digging a grave for his small child struck her deeply. She stepped out of hiding and hobbled towards him, determined to offer whatever comfort she could.

Startled, the man spun round to face her, wide eyed. "Oh gods, mother!" he said. "You scared the marrow out o' me. I didn't think there was anybody here."

She was about to reply when, from the corner of her eye, she caught a slight movement in the swaddled bundle. "It's alive!"

"Aye, just about. It's the mother who's dead. The bairn seems right enough," he said, sweat dripping off his nose and vanishing into the wilderness of his whiskers. He studied Ettith for a moment then asked, "You're not their kin are you? I don't remember seeing you before."

"No."

"Aagh — pity. She died just now while I was in there. You'd have thought she was waiting for me. She just handed me the bairn and died - never made a sound."

Ettith eyed him closely. "So, you're not kin either?"

"No, but I knew 'em. Not her so much as her man. He was a comrade, a blood sworn friend," he said. "It's the least I can do for him. He was killed."

He began digging again, but with a fierce energy. Ettith watched him, wondering where such strength came from. After a while he stopped and mopped his brow. "I know these parts well, but don't recall seeing you, old mother."

"No, I'm just passing," Ettith said, adding hopefully. "Have you any food?"

He waved a hand in the direction of his pony. "Aye, there's a pack on the horse. I brought it for the woman. Her man was killed alongside me in the shield wall. I promised him. She'll not need it now. I brought her that damned cow too. It's slower than winter honey. Can you take it off me? I've urgent duties. I can't be slowed by a stubborn cow."

Ettith could hardly believe her luck. The pack was full of such food as she had only dreamed of in months; bread, salt pig, cheese, a sack of dried white beans, some coarse flour, a block of salt, honey and a skin of ale. She sat beneath the horse's belly, stuffing her mouth as fast as she could; afraid she may be dreaming and might wake up before she'd had her fill.

When the grave was finished, the man carried out the body of the child's mother and gently lowered it into the ground. Ettith stood beside him looking down at the scrawny corpse wound in a sheet.

"She were a real beauty in her day," he said, his voice thickened by emotion. "You'd not think so now, would you?"

"Huh, so was I, once upon a time," said Ettith.

The man inspected her, unconvinced. "Aye well, that's the way of things I suppose." He shovelled earth over the corpse leaving the face until last.

Ettith left him to his task and wandered towards the dead woman's house, pausing for a closer look at the child sleeping in its bundle of cloths. It was a little girl about three years old. A pretty child, even though her tear-stained face was thin and drawn. Her tiny hands were slender and delicate. A leather thong, shiny with wear curled around one hand and threaded through a hole in a purple gemstone, about as big as a pigeon's egg. Ettith handled it, admiring its colour and river-polished smoothness.

"Is she all right?" the man called from the grave side.

His voice startled her, scattering her thoughts. "Oh, aye she's fine. She just needs a few good meals." She tucked the child in its soiled rags and left her sleeping to go and peer into the open door of the house. Of course, she did not dare enter. It was a house of death. Spirits would still be lurking inside hoping to catch another unwary soul.

The warrior finished his sad work and tossed the spade aside. Wiping his hands on his front, he approached Ettith, stopping on the way to pick up the sleeping child. Ettith watched with trepidation as he tried to gather up the infant. His clumsy struggle to balance the child safely woke her up. She began to howl with such a voice that its echo bounced around the village like the wail of some other-worldly creature. With a pained look the man came close to Ettith. "Do you want to come with me, or stay here? I'll leave you the cow if you're staying. Only, I must travel quickly. I don't want it slowing me down again. Treat her kindly and she'll milk well. Milk's better than meat in these times, old mother."

Ettith thanked him, praising him ecstatically as he mounted his pony. He barely heard her as he struggled to calm the screaming child in his arms. At the forest edge, Ettith stopped and watched him disappear into the enveloping green. A wave of apprehension swept her. Perhaps she should go with him? What was she to do? The solitude and secrecy of her life had become open and complicated. She now had a cow and a great pack of food to protect. Instead of being free to wander she would have to stay put, at least until the food ran out, or the cow died or wandered off. As she reviewed her new situation, she looked around the empty village. Its oppressive silence bore down, intensified by the distant, fading sounds of the warrior's departure.

She was alone now, but for her cow munching contentedly at the living turf roof of one of the houses. The silence heightened her sense of dread. She thought of yoking the cow beneath the pack of food and chasing after the warrior, and was on the point of doing so when a new sound chipped at the emptiness. It was a feeble cry, like a kitten's mewing. With relief, she remembered the cat and looked about for it. Now it could be company, not food.

Again, she heard the sound, but this time it did not seem quite so feline - more like a gurgling cough. It came from the dead woman's house.

"Spirits!" She backed away in terror. "Oh Holy Mother Frigg spare me," she cried, falling to her knees.

The sound grew louder, becoming unmistakably an infant's cry. Something deep inside her awakened, transforming her fears for herself into concern for the mysterious, unseen child. She edged towards the house, trembling at the realisation that she must go inside that place of death. She chipped a handful of salt from her newly acquired supply, and summoning courage, hobbled to the house. As she stepped over the threshold she scattered the sacred charm before her. Her courage stiffened as the charm did its work. Inside the large single room she met not even one lurking spirit.

It was a well-to-do house with many of the trappings of prosperity. There was a sturdy oak table with a bench and stools drawn up to it. A large bed had embroidered curtains. Against the walls were two elm-plank coffers, a shrine to the goddess Frigg, and a standing loom. Beside the loom a finely carved, ash-wood mydercan caught her eye. Beneath its polished lid she found sewing yarns, needles and pins. This she realised explained how two hangings of extraordinary quality, such as only a wealthy thegn might own, dressed one of the room's lime-washed walls. Taken with the loom and the mydercan, Ettith could see that this was the house of a successful seamstress, a woman whose work adorned the houses of the rich.

The child's crying stopped, jerking her from her thoughts. She looked about with a start. In a corner she saw a wooden crib. The babe inside it was a girl of about a year and a half. She was painfully thin, her little bones pushed against her skin. Ettith's old heart went out to her. "Oh my little love, how could he have missed seeing you?" she said. "Trust a man to do only half a thing."

She reached to pick up the child, but stopped herself on noticing that she still clutched the leather thong and its bluish purple gemstone in her hand. Panic gripped her. She had not meant to keep it. It belonged to the little girl. She must give it back. Rushing from the house, as fast as her old legs would carry her, she went after the warrior, calling out for him.

It was too late. He had gone.

．．．．．．．

CHAPTER TWO

Mercian England 633 AD

The longhouse shuddered, its timbers groaning as a tree, torn from the earth for a battering ram, smashed again into the wattle wall. Scabs of plaster broke away, revealing the coarse weave of hazel lath on oak studding beneath. Smoke rippled down through the thatched roof, smothering beam and rafter. Wynflaed watched it ooze menacingly above her. It swelled and barged, gathering bulk, before flopping down the wall and splashing towards her across the earthen floor.

"They've torched the roof!" she cried, bridled fear cracking her voice. She pressed a kerchief to her nose and tightened her grip on Buhe's hand.

Buhe's father beckoned. Like a rock in a sea storm, he stood amidst the chaos of his burning hall calmly directing his terrified household. "Come by me, you two," he said. "They'll soon be through the wall and the thatch'll go up like a marsh devil when the air gets to it."

Though he tried to appear calm, Wynflaed sensed his apprehension. She allowed herself and Buhe to be ushered away from the fiercest burning, pretending not to see the old thegn's fearful, secret glances at his smouldering roof.

"Pull that table against the wall - get under it," he said, inserting his fist into the iron boss of his lime-wood shield.

Spears punctured the wall. Cold air rushed in, feeding the hot, glutinous smoke. The under-thatch was aglow, as red as sunset. It burst into flame, sucking the breath from Wynflaed's lungs. Noise crashed in through the broken wall, dragging men with swinging swords and axes behind it. In their refuge beneath the table Wynflaed and Buhe clung grimly to each other. Between them and certain death stood Buhe's father, the old warrior, magnificent in his battle harness — though it no longer fitted. He stood his ground, exchanging blows with the raiders, mocking them as smoke and the unexpected ferocity of the heat shrivelled their thirst for blood, driving them back through the shattered wall in scrambling disarray.

The old man pressed them, prodding and slashing as they fell back. "Cowards!" he yelled. "You came to kill Uhtred. Well, I'm here. Come and fight me, you scum."

As the last frenzied raiders retreated ignominiously, Buhe scrambled from beneath the table and ran to her father. She was sobbing, but more from love and pride in him than from any sense of fear for herself. She threw her arms around him and stretched up to kiss his bearded cheek. "Father, we must get out" she said, tugging on his shield arm. "I'd rather be fleshered by an axe than fried like pig meat."

Startled, the old thegn gazed into her soot-stained face, as if trying to remember who she was. He looked around his hall at the faces of his frightened servants and then back at Buhe. In her blue eyes, so painfully scoured by smoke and tears, he saw her fear. He gathered her gently behind his shield and kissed her forehead.

"Think of Wynflaed and Luffa and the others," Buhe said. "They might not kill the servants. We have to get them out to give them a chance."

"You're right, little mother," he said. "It's better we die out there where the gods can see us." He took a short dagger from his belt and pressed its handle into her palm looking at her with tear-glossed eyes. "You'd better take this," he said. "You mightn't think yourself quite a woman yet, my sweet Buhe, but those men out there ..."

Buhe looked at the knife, then at her father. Despite her youth, she needed no further explanation. "What about Flaedy?" she asked, glancing towards her friend.

"I'm all right," Wynflaed cried, scrambling out from beneath the table. She brandished a small boning knife and forced a pugnacious smile. "They'll get some of this if they touch me."

Uhtred chuckled and held out his sword arm to encircle her as she joined them. "That's it then," he said, hugging the two. "We're ready. Let 'em do their worst."

Turning to his household, he summoned them to follow him. Flames now barred escape by the door, so he led them to the broken wall, his shield held aloft to fend off flaming gobs of thatch and pitch dripping from the burning roof. Buhe followed then Wynflaed and the other servants, jostled into line by old Luffa the senior house woman. Gasping for air in the smoke and heat, they clung to each other like a string of blind beggars at a harvest fair.

Outside in the chill night a ring of cruel, eager faces, lit as bright as lamp-drawn moths, confronted them. Uhtred rushed at the nearest man and felled him with a single blow. Astonishment still showed on the dead raider's face as Uhtred advanced over the corpse.

Coughing and choking, Wynflaed struggled out blindly. She stumbled over smouldering debris, gasping as fresh air drenched her face, stripping stinging threads of smoke and heat from her eyes and lungs. Her ankle turned on something round and hard as her bare feet probed for safe footing. It was the head of a corpse, almost severed from the neck. Trying to focus, she peered with tear veiled eyes and recognised a friend. Her legs faltered. She swayed on the brink of collapse. Instinctively she reached for Buhe's arm. "Look what they did, Buhe," she sobbed. "They killed Quiet Eadie."

Buhe caught her hand. She was sobbing, her sooty face riven with tear-washed lines. She clung to Wynflaed's hand as the pair gazed about the longhouse garth, seeing for the first time the bloodied corpses of Uhtred's ingas, his slaves, servants and tenants; friends and neighbours she had been raised with. At the far side of the enclosure, huddled in the smith's compound, the few who had so far survived, mostly women and children, cried out to their master as they saw him.

The raiders had begun wrenching open the doors of Uhtred's great barn. Others were driving his oxen, horses and mules from their stalls and harnessing them to carts, yokes and pack-harness to haul away their plunder.

Wynflaed watched them, the true worth of all that the barn contained impressing itself upon her. Years of work and planning had yielded a good harvest. The villagers had thanked the gods and feasted around a bonfire. They had sacrificed a sheep to Nerthus the Earth Mother, and placed flowers and fruit on the little shrines to Frigg in the fields and lanes, to thank her for the magic of fertile seed. In Thunner's glade virgins had danced naked around his oak, praising him for restraining his anger and granting them soft rains and fine weather. Now it was all to be lost in a single night. There would be nothing left - and nothing to replace it.

Desperately wondering what she could do Wynflaed gazed around her. She saw two raiders squaring up to the old thegn. Others milled around him like snarling dogs, eager to jump in should their comrades fail to cut him down. The hopelessness of their situation struck home even deeper, bathing her in cold sweat. Something snapped like a bowstring inside her brain. She found herself running, blind to danger. She leapt between the posturing men and threw her arms around Uhtred's neck, placing her slim body between him and his attackers.

"No - no stop! Please don't hurt him," she cried. She had not an idea in her head, except that she must stop them killing Uhtred. She would not allow it. She would not let them slaughter this kind old man, her father in all but blood. Twelve years earlier Uhtred had saved her, a helpless orphan no more than three-years-of-age. Now she would save him. It was not bravery. What she did was pure impulse, the blind reaction of one much loved and loving.

Despite being a widower, the old thegn had brought her up like his own. Whatever his daughter Buhe had, so had she. The girls had studied, eaten, slept and played together. Each had borrowed clothes and toys from the other. Never was there a hand-me-over, or make-do-and-mend that they did not both endure. Uhtred had never done a thing to make Wynflaed feel unwanted. She would not see him killed.

The lightning slash of a knife flashed from the hand of one of the raiders. Uhtred spun away, following his out-thrown shield as though borne up by a powerful gust of wind. Blood spurted from his neck, salting Wynflaed's lips. She turned on the attacker. "Stop! Stop!" she screamed, flinging herself to her knees and wrapping her arms around the startled raider's legs. The man gaped down at her, an odd look of embarrassment and confusion smoothing the murderous creases from his brow. His comrades too seemed baffled. For a moment they lowered their axes, glancing nervously at each other and laughing in bewilderment.

An officer approached and stood between his men and the wounded thegn. His eyes flicked from one to the other. In all the chaos and sickening confusion, a strange calm enveloped them. It was as though Wynflaed, by some magic in her actions, had drawn an enchanted circle around them driving out chaos and violence.

The silence spread to the horde, honouring the officer's raised hand and his steady gaze along their churning ranks. In the enjoining quiet, Uhtred's groans and curses seemed harsh above the crackle and hiss of burning and the choral murmur of quieting voices. Buhe fussed beside her father, overlooked by old Luffa, fat and wheezing tearfully. Wynflaed watched the officer, her heart pounding, stomach sick with anxiety.

He was tall and broad at the shoulder. His chest was heaving from exertion beneath silver studded armour of dark red leather. Blood bespattered his scarred, muscular forearms. He wore brecs of dark green wool and boots of soft leather, bound to the calf. Wynflaed returned his gaze, annoyed to see that he seemed to find the situation amusing. "I'm commander here," he said, his sword seeking out a silver trimmed scabbard at his belt.

"I trust you find nothing to be proud of in that."

Her boldness surprised him, though he tried not to show it. "Is he your granfer?" he asked, nodding in Uhtred's direction.

She took a step towards him. "No, your honour," she said, and pushing her red hair from her eyes went on. "He is my lord Uhtred Bergredsunnu, master here. I am his bonded seamstress."

The commander looked thoughtful for a moment, his gaze switching from her, to Buhe and her father, then to his men pressing about him. "I know the rebel's name," he said dismissively. "I meant to know who you are."

"Wynflaed," she said, adding as an afterthought, "Alfwalddohtor." She cursed herself inwardly for trembling as the full realisation of what she had done began draining her strength. "May I know your name?" she asked, summoning boldness from somewhere.

The officer smiled and cast a jocular look at his men.

Despite everything Wynflaed could not help noticing his smile. The faint hope that he might not be the cruel killer he had seemed flashed through her mind.

"You're a strange one," he said, with a chuckle. "You say you are bondswif here, a seamstress, yet you demand my name and look me in the eye like any freeman of rank ..."

"I am of family," she said. "I told you ..."

"Yes — yes. Alfwalddohtor," he said, mocking her, and grinning at his men. "I'm sure we all heard you. Yet here you are in this nest of traitors."

With anger surpassing her fear, she watched him remove his battle helmet and push a hand through his mop of light brown hair. His face was pleasant, if rather roughly hewn, when not squashed between the silver cheek plates of his helmet. He was younger than she had expected, perhaps not more than twenty, yet he bore the scars of many battles. One, a faint blue line running from his right eye to his ear, intrigued her. It tugged at his eyelid, lending his eye a mischievous glint. His nose, which had clearly been broken more than once, showed him capable of much more than simple mischief. Still, she told herself, as her hope rekindled, it was not the face of a brutal man.

"Well, daughter of Alfwald," he said smiling, his clear blue eyes mocking her, "as you demand it, I shall tell you." He saluted her with an extravagance intended to amuse his men. "I am Wulfric Aelricsunnu of the Cenwulfingas. I come to this rebel's house for supplies. I serve Lord Cenwulf. He marches to join King Penda. I don't suppose your rebel master cares that our lord Penda and the Wealh king, Cadwallon Gwynedd, march to face the Northumbrians. He's obviously content to hide here in this house of women while loyal men fight and die."

Resisting the urge to rise to his mocking, Wynflaed pulled back her shoulders and looked him in the eye. "Your men have already stolen all they can carry," she said. "Killing us will neither swell their packs, nor help them carry what they have." She eyed him haughtily as she went on. "Or do you simply want an old man's blood on your swords for sport?"

Wulfric bristled, but made no reply. He crammed his helmet on, tied its straps beneath his chin and turned to his men. "Put the rebel and his whelp in the smith's yard with the others. Let's get out of this traitor's midden."

An officer at his shoulder relayed the order. Buhe and her injured father were led away. Luffa and the other servants followed. Wynflaed alone remained, held there by Wulfric's gaze. His anger was clear, yet he seemed torn by indecision. She glared at him, wondering what sort of man he could be. How could he do what he did? She felt confused and angry. Part of her wished she was a man, wished she could strike him for his violence. He should suffer for what he'd done. Yet he raised feelings inside her such as she had never experienced.

Wulfric turned and strode away towards the main body of his men. Wynflaed remained, a small, solitary figure in the bright, hot space before the burning hall. She watched him go, wanting to hate him but unable to take her eyes off him. Just before he vanished into his crowding warriors he turned and looked back at her. She knew there was something about that glance that she would never forget, but harder to accept was that she feared she would never want to.

All around her raiders rushed about loading carts and mules, gathering up all the copper and bronze, and stripping precious iron from plough and hearth. She scanned their faces expecting to see evil, but saw only ordinary men, working and sweating like field hands, their swords and axes encumbrances now, slung across their shoulders.

Wynflaed wandered about the burning village as if searching its ruins for the hatred and anger she expected. What she saw was certainly distressing, but she was denied the hatred she wanted to feel.

Later, as the fires died and the noise and chaos subsided, a grimy faced youth approached leading a skittish white mule. Skinny and dressed in torn tunic and cow-skin brecs he kept his eyes lowered in the manner of a slave. His unkempt hair blew across his face. As he neared her, he stopped and waited, as if for permission to speak.

Wynflaed was puzzled. "Do you want me?"

The young muler nodded and looked up through his tangled hair. Now he saw clearly the young woman he had seen only from a distance, boldly standing up to his master. She was every bit as beautiful as he had thought. She had long, coppery hair that fell about her face and neck in the deep, glossy remnant of linen-bound braids. Her large, green eyes were bright and haughty. They shone at him like lamps from beneath thick, coppery eyebrows and dark lashes. Even through the soot and grime of her ordeal he could see her skin was clear and smooth. She wore a shift of wool held at the waist with a belt of plaited, holly-green leather. Her small, maiden's breasts pushed gently at the faded green. A plain circlet of gold at her wrist reflected the light of the fires around them. Otherwise, her soot-marked arms were bare to the shoulder. She was about his age, he guessed, certainly no more than sixteen, though her manner lent her maturity beyond her years. No wonder his master wanted her.

"What is it?" Wynflaed resented his searching gaze.

"My master commands me to say ..." He stopped and gulped for breath. "And I'm to say exactly these words, my lady ..."

"You needn't address me so," she interrupted. "I'm a bond-servant like you."

"Lord Wulfric was precise, my lady," the youth insisted. "I am to say that you are free to travel where you wish. But my master wants you to know that *his* wish is that you will travel with him. Me and my mule are to ..."

"Travel with him?" she cried. "Huh! In what capacity I wonder?"

The muler dropped his gaze and took a step back. "I — err — I'm to say that you'll be well cared for ..."

"Huh! I don't doubt it," she said. "I expect your master is well used to caring for such — travellers." Her clenched fists beat slowly on her thighs as she tried to contain her mounting fury. "Tell your master — tell him, that if he were the last man on middle earth, I would rather prick out my eyes than ..."

***

When Wynflaed reached the blacksmith's yard, Buhe greeted her with tearful relief. "Oh thank Thunner you're safe," she cried. "We thought — well — we didn't know what to think. You are all right aren't you? I mean they didn't ..." Buhe's facial acrobatics told a fearful story.

"I'm fine," Wynflaed said. "How's father?"

"Oh, they say he'll be all right." She threaded her arm in Wynflaed's. "That commander sent us his healer. He's in there now." She nodded towards the smith's cottage. "Where were you? Gods, Flaedy!" she said. "You saved our lives. We'd all be dead but for you. You were so brave. I don't know how you could do it — just stand up to him like that."

"Neither do I, but maybe I didn't save us at all - just postponed our deaths. We'll likely starve over winter," she said, her eyes sweeping the destruction around them. "They're taking everything, even the bell from its pole."

"But we're alive," said Buhe. "And you did it. At least we've a chance. And if father's not too badly hurt, he'll soon think of something."

Setting Wynflaed walking, Buhe snuggled close and squeezed her arm. She was half a year younger than Wynflaed, and although they shared the same clothes, somehow on Buhe they seemed always to be in delightful disarray. Wynflaed was groomed and shining by comparison, and where she was calm and deliberate, Buhe was giddy and excitable. Buhe giggled a lot, often for no apparent reason, though she had the most infectious laughter. When Wynflaed laughed however, men noticed her, much less her laughing. The two were best friends, seldom seen apart. Accomplished in many skills from farming to music, they both worked hard. Buhe was a fine needlewoman, though she could not match the artistry of Wynflaed's work. She lacked patience, Wynflaed often told her. She could seldom sit for more than half an hour at anything. If her work went badly she would fling it down and become unbearably bossy. Throughout these outbursts, Wynflaed would remain serene, something Buhe found exasperating.

"Of course, father's been expecting this for a long time," Buhe said, her eyebrows shooting up in a gesture of bored inevitability. He always said they'd come for him one day." Then, frowning, she whispered, "Let's face it, he's said some pretty harsh things about King Penda."

"Is that the healer?" Wynflaed interrupted, on seeing a dark, solemn faced man emerge from the smith's hut.

Buhe nodded, eyeing the figure in flowing black cloak and large floppy hat. "I heard them call him Crowman," she whispered, with an elaborate shudder. "Gods! He looks like old Grim his-self, doesn't he?"

"I've got to speak to him," said Wynflaed, rushing off, leaving Buhe bemused.

The healer saw her running towards him and paused. He was tall and thin. His black clothes flapped about him like great black wings. His long, sad face wore a distant, weary look. At first Wynflaed thought his expression reflected Uhtred's condition and she wondered if his injuries were worse than Buhe had told her.

"What is it? Is he dying?" she asked.

The Crowman studied her for a moment. "We are all dying child, but your master no sooner than most of us."

"So he's all right" she asked, flustered by his answer.

The Crowman nodded.

"Oh, thank the gods," she said, and then checking herself smiled gratefully.

He nodded and started to move off, but she grasped his arm. "Don't worry," he said, patting her hand. "He'll recover. In a week or so he'll be fine." He peered into her face, wondering at her reluctance to release him. "Is there something else, daughter?"

She nodded with a grateful urgency. "I — I wanted to ask ..."

Crowman frowned impatiently. "Well Child?"

"I want to know about — your master."

"My master?" he queried. "I serve only Wyrd. Only by the whim of Wyrd may we serve even the gods. We are the dolls of Wyrd to be danced and toyed with."

"No, I mean Lord Wulfric," she said.

Crowman shrugged. "You know his name. What more would you know that cannot be seen in his eyes?"

"I wondered - what sort of man he is."

Crowman prized her fingers from his arm and squared up to her. She fell back a step, bracing herself. He was gazing deep into her eyes. She felt as if her soul was being laid bare before him. "In time, child, you will know everything," he told her. "You have a long journey ahead; far beyond a place of streams and lime trees. I see your chains broken by sunlight where there is no sky."

"Journey? What journey? What chains? I'm not going anywhere."

He turned away and set off towards the woods beyond Uhtred's smouldering fields. "Your journey starts soon, daughter of Alfwald," he called back.

"No. No, you're wrong. I'm not going anywhere. This is my home. I'm staying here. I'll never leave."

Buhe joined her, slipping an arm about her. "What's wrong? You crying. Is it father? What did he say?"

"No, it's not that," Wynflaed sobbed. "He's wrong, Buhe. I'm not going on a journey. I'm staying here. I don't want to leave."

"Of course you're staying. We all are," Buhe said. "What are you getting so upset about?"

"He said I'm going on a journey, and something about sunlight where there is no sky breaking my chains. What chains? I have no chains. I'm free and I love Uhtredstun and you and your father."

"Sunlight   without   sky?" queried   Buhe.   "That's silly!"

. . . .

CHAPTER THREE

Fourteen new graves scarred the margins beside Uhtred's fields. Exhausted, Wynflaed sat down and wiped earth from her hands on the grass. She lay back under the dark green boughs of an ancient yew tree, the living totem of their burial ground, and fought back tears. Fourteen good friends now lay beneath the earth, their pathetic belongings with them. In their dead hands she had placed a pinch of flour and salt. All that could be scraped off the floor of the empty barn. It would have to serve for the bread and ale they should have taken to their graves.

"They got the best of it," she said, cleaning her fingernails with a twig.

Buhe tossed aside her wooden spade and flopped down beside her. "They're dead, we're not. How can you say they got the best of it?"

"They're out of it. They don't have to get through winter with no food. They've got the only flour there was. We've nothing, not even the spillings. And until father's on his feet, it'll be up to you and me to feed the village."

"We can do it," Buhe said.

Wynflaed shot her a withering look. "How?"

Buhe looked bewildered. Her lip began to quiver. Her fingers withdrew from Wynflaed's arm to wind themselves around each other like frantic worms. She hated having to confront the reality of anything unpleasant. Whether it was a dog vomiting in the hall, or imminent starvation, she was equally hopeless at dealing with it. "I don't know," she said, pouting. "You're the one who — who knows everything. You must think of something."

Wynflaed sighed. "Gods, how I envy you, Buhe. You just smile sweetly and wait for somebody else to make it all better. Why can't you ever face facts?"

Buhe's trembling lip curled downward. She stuck out her chin, aware that Wynflaed was about to deliver one of her pointed reproofs.

"We've got no food," Wynflaed said, as if dealing with a spoilt infant. "Nothing! No animals, fuel, axes, plough. And if we did have a plough, we don't have oxen to pull it, and there's no seed to sow anyway. And, if we did have seed and the strength to pull the bloody plough ourselves, we still wouldn't have wheat to grind for a whole season. All we've got, Buhe, are the nuts on the trees and the vetches on the forest floor."

Buhe blinked and looked relieved. "Well then, that's better than nothing, isn't it?" she said, more in gratitude to Wynflaed for thinking of nuts and vetches just when she had thought there was nothing whatsoever.

"But, my dear sister, if we don't plant a crop we'll have to eat weeds for the rest of our wretched lives, which, thank Mother Frigg, won't be for very long because we'll starve to death."

"I'm not your sister," Buhe cried, huge tears clinging to the sweeping curl of her thick, brazen lashes. "You just want me to be miserable. You always want to spoil things for me. You're jealous. You hate it because you're not real family. I'm glad you've got no family."

Wynflaed shrugged, and cast her a pitying look. As usual, when lost for answers, Buhe reacted with cruelty and spite. She would hit out at anything and everyone, but usually those she loved. Moments later she would beg forgiveness, and offer everything she owned in exchange for it. "Poor Buhe," she said, putting her arm around her shoulder. "This is one problem you can't ignore until it goes away. We have to do something. Huh, if we don't there'll be more graves before Yule and two of them will be ours."

"What are we going to do, Flaedy?"

Wynflaed gave her a motherly hug. "Hunt for nuts and pray there's still some melde about."

"I'm sorry, Flaedy. I didn't mean it," Buhe said.

"Mean what?"

"You *are* family. We are sisters. I didn't mean ..."

Wynflaed laughed, "I know, I know. Come on now, let's go back. Father will be trying to get out of bed. He'll open up his wound again."

***

Six days later, in the smith's house where many of the villagers were still lodging, Thegn Uhtred demanded his boots, insisting that he was well enough to get out of bed. Nothing Buhe or Wynflaed could say would stop him. Helpless, they watched him totter to the open door, knowing that the sight of his hall and farm in ruins would deal him yet another vicious blow.

The old man leaned on the doorpost and looked out. He did not speak. The girls and the village folk around them watched him, his bulky frame filling the doorway, darkening the crowded room. When at last he spoke, his voice was artificially bright. "Well, there's plenty to do."

Buhe kissed his cheek. "We can do it," she said, floating an apologetic glance in Wynflaed's direction.

Unable to answer for fear of releasing his tears, the old man nodded and grinned. He reached for his daughter's hand and Wynflaed's too, and led them out into the dull, autumn morning. In silence, they walked the ruined homestead.

The main hall had once been the pride of the district. For longer than anyone could remember it had stood proudly in its goose-cropped garth, surrounded by apple trees, sheep, and pig pens. A deep porch, roofed with thatch, had leaned against its southern wall, sheltering a heavy oak door.

Beyond the garth had been the village; wide green spaces, velvet-cropped by wandering sheep, milk cows and geese. Single roomed wooden houses, grey with age and sprinkled with coppery coloured lichens, had dotted the green. A deep pond, fed by a narrow channel from the nearby stream, had been noisy with ducks and splashing children. Flag iris and willows hemmed in the dark green waters, alive with frogs and fish. A row of washing stones, beaten smooth by wear and water, waited for their daily pounding.

To the north plough-land rose gently towards the forest. The Goddess Eostre had always favoured the spot, blessing it with early fertility. The rich brown earth never clung long to frost or snow. Pigs and cows thrived in the forest, though wild beasts were sometimes a problem. To raise a pig was to court wolves, and only a fool would leave his stock unwatched for an instant.

Now, all was ruin. The fields were cinder black. Most of the houses and beast hovels were ashes. A few crude tents and shanties, hastily fashioned from the debris, had sprouted up. A subdued group of survivors huddled over a fire. When they saw their master on his feet, they crowded round him. But, as they weighed the impact on him of all that he saw their spirits slumped back.

"Look at 'em," Uhtred said, leaning on the girls' arms. "What do they think I can do? How can I feed 'em? I've less than they have now."

"You can do it, father," Buhe said. "You did it in the three-year famine. Old Luffa told me all about it. She said there were bodies unburied in some villages, but not here.

You kept everyone alive. You even saved folk on other farms — like you did Flaedy when her mother ..."

"I was twelve years younger," he said, interrupting her. "You were just bairns. You don't know what it was like. This is different." He kicked a blackened spar as he picked his way through the bones of his house. Near what had been his high table he sat on a fallen beam. His eyes glazed in reflective mood. He smiled and chuckled softly. "When I found you," he told Wynflaed, "you were howling like a kicked pup. I don't know how you'd stayed alive, you were so thin." He gazed off into distant memories. "Your father was a brave man, a great fighter. He was one of the last to be killed you know. The enemy was beaten. But he died before the day was over. I promised him I'd look out for your mother and you. He would have done the same for me. I went looking for your mother, to tell her what had happened and to take her some food. She was a fine woman, a real fighter too, but it was the famine, she had nothing. Somehow, she'd managed to keep you alive. I swear she died the very moment I lifted you from her arms. There was nothing holding her here but her love for you." He gazed around dismally. "Huh, we could do with her sort now."

"I am her sort," Wynflaed told him. "But I'm even more than that, because you took me in and made me into your sort too. That's why I know we can rebuild. We have to believe in ourselves. That way we'll do it."

He smiled at her with moist, loving eyes. "You've certainly got the guts for it. I expect you'll make us survive whether we want to or not. I don't know which is going to be worse," he quipped, "starving to death, or having you keepng us alive."

***

A week later, Uhtred pronounced himself fit enough to visit his brother in the north. He would ask him for supplies and tools. He stomped across his ruined hall, blowing his nose fiercely on a rag of linen. He and his brother had barely spoken in five years. It would be a humiliation, but he had no choice. The girls followed him at a distance, deciding it would be better not to intrude too closely. As they reached the edge of the enclosure and turned a corner by the scorched walls of the old smokehouse, a white mule could be seen grazing the tired autumn grasses by the stream. On the far bank, Wulfric's young muler sat by a fire.

"Who's that? Uhtred asked, showing an indignant flash of his old self.

Buhe glanced at Wynflaed. "He wants Flaedy. He's been here over a week," she told her father.

"Wants her? Who, a filthy muler? Grim's cods! I'll rip his guts ..."

"No, not him - the raiders' commander. He — err— he asked her to go with him," Buhe explained.

Uhtred turned to Wynflaed. "What in Grim's name is she blathering about, Flaedy?"

Wynflaed avoided his gaze. "Wulfric, the officer," she said, "asked me to go with him. That's the muler he sent to carry me."

"Carry you? Carry you where, for Frigg's sake?"

"Off with him somewhere - wherever he's gone. I don't know where."

"Blasted nerve. I'll soon see the little sod off. You go back to the smithy."

Despite their protests, Uhtred strode towards the muler's camp, his shoulders hunched indignantly.

Wynflaed and Buhe did not move. Helpless to stop him, they waited, watching fearfully. Though he might think himself recovered, they both knew that he was far from strong. If it came to blows, even the weedy muler could be a match for him in his present state of health.

From the muler's perspective however, Uhtred appeared every bit as threatening as he had on the night of the raid. Quickly considering his options, he decided that there was no sense in getting killed and depriving his master of an excellent muler. So as Uhtred reached the far bank of the stream, the muler blundered backwards through his camp in hasty retreat. He did not even wait to consider Uhtred's yells of derision. He simply grabbed his mule's bridle and hauled the beast away as fast as he could.

Uhtred jinked along the bank hurling river stones and abuse. His exertion brought him up sharply and pain throbbed in the wound on his neck. Gingerly putting a hand to the dressing, he eyed the fleeing muler. "It's a damn good job you didn't stay to fight, lad," he whispered with irony. "You might have bloody killed me."

Buhe ran to her father, squealing excitedly at his victory. Wynflaed remained still and thoughtful. She watched the muler disappear into the forest and thought of the Crowman's strange prediction. The muler's presence had somehow made the likelihood of a long journey seem all the more possible, even though she had no intention of going with him.

A long journey beyond a place of streams and lime trees, he had said. What could it mean? And what had he meant by her chains being broken? She was free. If she wanted to leave Uhtredstun, she could. Uhtred would not make her stay, although with love as strong as any real father's she expected he might try.

How can my chains be broken, when I have none? She asked herself. What had he said, "Broken by sunlight in a place where there is no sky."

"Huh, it makes no sense."

***

It took Eadwin the muler two weeks to reach and find his master in the thick of Mercia's massing armies. Wulfric's small cohort had by then joined up with the rest of Lord Cenwulf's Peakland legion. Eadwin's arrival passed without ceremony. Most of the men there were his neighbours and friends, and all were too busy singing and drinking and enjoying that special comradeship which only the eve of battle breeds.

Eventually he found Wulfric in his tent, and nervously delivered his report. He was surprised when his master took it all so calmly. He simply thanked him, and offered him food from a board covered with cooked meats, cheeses and bread. But the following morning, Wulfric, grim-faced and secretive, sought him out amongst the other pack drivers and carters. Wulfric led him back to his camp where he directed him to sit at his fire. Eadwin saw his master was edgy; he kept looking about as if fearful of being watched or overheard.

In silence, Wulfric poured a cup of ale and handed it to him. When at last he spoke his voice was a whisper. "Is she well, Eadwin? Tell me again how she looked."

"She is well, your honour," Eadwin replied, not daring to add how beautiful she was, or how he had thought of no-one but her since leaving Uhtredstun.

"Eadwin, you did well," Wulfric said. "But I need another service. It'll be even riskier. Are you willing?"

Common sense told him he should run away quickly, but he liked Wulfric. He had known him all his life, and enjoyed the scrapes they got into together. He nodded his head and grinned.

"Good lad," Wulfric said with relief. "I want you to go to my father's house. Tell him you want three of his strongest pack ponies and your own mule to be loaded with flour, salt-meat, ale, tools and seed."

Puzzled, Eadwin glanced at the carts full of food and supplies parked around the camp. "But there are mountains of supplies, my lord."

"It's not for us. It's for old Uhtred and his people."

Eadwin gaped not sure he'd heard correctly.

"Take it to them. Make sure they don't see you. They can't know where it comes from. Put it somewhere they'll quickly find it before animals get it."

Eadwin was puzzled. Why raid a village, steal its food, then replace it with your own? Which of them was the bigger fool, Wulfric for suggesting it, or himself for agreeing to do it?

"Tell no-one but my father where you take the food," said Wulfric. "You know our Lord Penda thinks of old Uhtred as a traitor? So what I'm asking you to do — well — in a way it makes traitors of us both. It will stain my father too if anyone finds out. It's very risky. If our lord Penda finds out, our cods will smoke in a row."

Eadwin's hand moved protectively to his testicles. He nodded, misery carving deeply into his young face.

"Penda hasn't mentioned it," Wulfric went on gloomily, "but I'm sure he thinks I killed old Uhtred and his family. You know how he wants every friend and hearthmen of old King Cearl dead. He won't feel his crown is safely on his head until they've all gone. I'll be skinned alive if he finds out I let Uhtred live." He studied the young muler's worried expression. "Are you sure you want to do this? You can say no if you want. I'll understand." He sighed and sagged onto his war chest which was serving as his seat beside the campfire, and gazed into the flames. "You've seen her, Eadwin," he went on softly. "I can't let her starve, can I?"

Eadwin shrugged, hopelessly lost in agreement.

"Anyway, old Uhtred's no traitor. He's just a bit outspoken. He never plotted against Penda. He just refuses to pay his taxes. Frankly, it would do Penda no harm to have a few more like him on his benches; men unafraid to speak out. Apart from Immin and Cenwulf the rest of 'em would swear piss was pie if Penda said so."

"What if your father won't give me the supplies?" Eadwin asked, hoping he had found a flaw in his master's plan that would save his neck.

"Don't worry about that. He'll do it for me, even when you tell him the whole story. You will have to be careful of my brother though. You must say nothing to Rendil. I don't mean that he would betray us, but my dear brother Rendil hates giving anything away. He'd whine and complain and make life difficult for my father."

Someone rash and stupid was now speaking, using Eadwin's voice and mouth. "Don't worry, you can depend on me," he heard himself say.

"Thank you, Eadwin. I won't forget this." Wulfric grasped the muler's hand and shook it heartily. "Tell my father I'm well. Give him all the news." He bent close and whispered, "Tell Rendil nothing."

***

Blotmonath, the eleventh month of the year, is the season for slaughtering beasts for sacrifice to the gods, in thanksgiving. Aware that the gods are all-knowing, Wynflaed had often pondered why it had never occurred to them that Blotmonath was also the best time of year to kill and salt those animals one could not afford to over-winter. It was also a good time for cleaning and curing hides, there being less stink and fewer flies around than in the heat of summer. Furthermore, as daylight hours were few, it was useful to have the extra lamplight hours inside the hall for fleshering and salting meat. By the end of the month the rafters in most halls would be dressed with a variety of meats drying in the fire smoke where flies and birds are loathe to go. Not like summer when the hearth slumbers and thousands of pests gorge in the rafters.

There was nothing to salt and hang at Uhtredstun that year. The only animals were a couple of sickly milk cows and a few pigs, grudgingly donated by Uhtred's brother, together with a skin of flour and some cheeses. The flour had weevil and the cheese would blunt an axe.

Uhtred travelled ceaselessly about the region, bartering what few valuables he had left, calling in favours and testing old friendships to find food for his people.

Mercifully, the raiders had spared the great barn in their haste to empty it. Uhtred quickly adapted it to living quarters for himself, his household and any homeless who did not have family to help them. He ordered that all the temporary shanties and tents be torn down, and forbade rebuilding until the ploughing and sowing were done. The great barn was soon warm and cosy, though full of stink and noise. Once inside, at the end of a day of toil and uncertainty, things did not seem quite so bad, especially when the night wind howled and the lurking spirits of the dead that roam abroad in Blotmonath capered in dark lanes and shadowy corners.

On the last day of Blotmonath, on an icy, sparkling dawn, Wynflaed went to the river for water. Seeing the remains of the muler's camp she was reminded of Wulfric. Where was he now? Was the battle over? Was he dead or injured? Did he think of her as she did of him? Why could she not get him out of her mind? She hated him – didn't she? He was a brutal thief, a killer. Why could she not drive him from her thoughts?

***

From cover, Eadwin watched the villagers. He had four horses and his mule, each loaded with mixed supplies. Wulfric's father had added the extra horse with sweetmeats for the children and mead for the adults. Eadwin unloaded near a well-trodden path and lit a smoky fire to attract attention before he quickly made his escape.

Moments later, a small boy found the fire and the supplies. Puzzled, he followed the sounds of departing horses, just in time to glimpse a familiar white mule amongst the retreating train.

. . . .

CHAPTER FOUR

Chill winds from the north and driving rains scoured all vestige of summer. Autumn began like furious winter, filling the rivers and uprooting trees. Roads disappeared beneath floods and impassable mud.

At Holmesfelt, on the eastern edge of the Peaklands, Wulfric's elder brother Rendil stomped about the yards and barns in a foul mood. His habitual autumn checks of the settlement's hordeons to ensure that winter stores would be safe from pests, mould, and rot, had revealed significant deficiencies.

He had marshalled his father's house-reeve and servants to take down all the bags, barrels, and boxes in the main hordeon and count everything again. Flour, several cheeses, a sack of dried peas, at least two sides of pig meat and a barrel of salted sheep-meat were missing. The reeve and his labourers were sullen and evasive, causing Rendil to suspect even greater discrepancies yet uncovered. Only after he had raged and beaten them with his walking stick did they produce the tally-rods showing the record of what was supposed to be in each store. Even then, the reeve insisted that the notches carved on them were not "up to date".

"Some items withdrawn have yet to be properly recorded, your honour."

Rendil was not convinced. "Thieves are at work here," he said. "They're helping themselves. And if it's not you lot stealing it, it's your incompetence that allows it."

"Your honour, I assure you, nothing is gone that was not approved by Lord Aelric," said the reeve, wiping a trickle of blood from his temple.

"My father? Blast your eyes, man! Do you dare to accuse my father?"

"Rendil, leave him alone. What gives here?" This was Aelric speaking from the barn's wicket door, his tall, stooping figure silhouetted against brilliant daylight.

Leaning on a stout ash-wood staff, he shuffled deeper into the barn. "I take what I want from my own hordeons without accounting to you," he said, glancing about at his labourers' faces. "I see you've been free with your stick. Did any admit guilt? Of course not. They're not thieves. They're my trusted men – my friends. They don't steal from me. They can't. What's mine's theirs. They all know that." He stepped up to his reeve. "Finish up in here," he said quietly. "Make all secure again, then look for me in the hall." He gave the man's shoulder a friendly squeeze.

***

Penda, king of the Mercians, joined forces with the Wealish king, Cadwallon of Gwynedd, to challenge the might of King Edwin of Northumbria. In driving rain, their shield walls were stretched out for battle on a heath at Hatfield near Doncaster.

Wulfric and his small cohort jostled to stay together in the steaming crush of warriors. They followed their lord, Ealdorman Cenwulf and his legion of Peaklanders. As usual, Cenwulf thrust himself into the middle of the shield wall, his boldest warriors beside him. He would be amongst the first to fall if the shield wall broke. The men in the flanks would have some small chance to flee and regroup, but at the middle of the shield wall only death, or glory waited.

Sweating and sick with apprehension, Wulfric swallowed his fear and took his place, carefully locking his shield into the line. He was fourth man to the left of

Lord Cenwulf, an honoured position, earned by courage. Behind him, his cohort stood in rank, ready to protect him, or to step into the wall if he fell.

He looked across the boggy heath to where the enemy's shields stretched out as solid as a rock face. Their awesome splendour was a thrilling, but chastening sight. The Northumbrians were well armed. Most wore iron helmets and carried spears. Many brandished deadly Francisca battle axes. Most of the men behind Wulfric were bare headed and armed with little more than a pitchfork or kindling axe.

As the two ranks faced each other, sporadic squalls of cheering and catcalls erupted from either side. The shield walls bulged and rippled like a giant serpent as young hotheads leapt out from behind it to make feint charges at the enemy, taunting, gesturing and hurling insults and abuse. They capered recklessly along the swaying lines, baring their backsides at the enemy, or spitting and pissing at them. Then strutting and clowning, they would disappear into anonymity in their ranks. In the general crush at the rear, fearful men searched for courage in ale skins. They bolstered flagging spirits by cursing the enemy and singing songs and chants about their leaders and heroes. Others silently trembled amid the drunken bravado, stomachs churning, bladders spilling, and vomit staining their tunics where soon their blood might spill. Despite their fears, every man knew that if he died that day the waelcyrge would carry him in honour to Wealheal, the hall of the dead, there to spend eternity feasting with Woden and the heroes. Wulfric knew this too, and though he feared death, as all men do, he feared dishonouring his lord and his men more. To die in the shield wall was the most honourable death a man could have. Nothing could confer greater honour upon his name and family.

For almost twenty years the Northumbrians had crushed all enemies. They were the most formidable army in Britain. Edwin reigned supreme of all British kings, whether English or Wealish. He feared no one, certain that the new Christian God he had embraced would grant him victories, especially over a heathen such as Penda of Mercia, and his Wealh ally, Cadwallon.

The battle on Hatfield Heath was short and bloody. The Mercians had firmer ground underfoot. Even so, men struggled to stand in the churning mud. For the Northumbrians it was worse. Their shields dipped and fell as men lost their footing and scrambled to stand. The Mercians' battle dogs, trained to disable men's ankles under the shield walls, found easy prey as men stumbled and fell. Many were savaged and fell to be trampled in the mud by their own men. Mercian and Wealh spears soon pricked through the enemy's faltering defences. Axes swung gouting blood onto the wielders' chests and faces. It ran down their arms and legs into the mud. The Northumbrians collapsed in chaos. Screaming men scrambled on all fours, frenziedly trying to escape the slaughter. Hacking and chopping into the Northumbrians' undefended spines, necks and shoulders, the Mercians and Wealish pursued them, stepping on the corpses and fallen shields that paved the bloody slime.

The River Idle flowed red with Northumbrian blood. Edwin and his son Osfrid were killed, another son, Eadfrid, was captured and taken to the house of King Penda's queen. Soon, he too would be dead, poisoned by an unknown hand.

Cadwallon and his triumphant Wealhs went on to rampage throughout Northumbria, raping, killing and looting. Penda too, loosed his English army to sate their appetites. Northumbria would be in flames for months.

But there were those in Penda's army with no stomach for such cowardly slaughter. The sight of Cadwallon's Wealhs murdering defenceless English farmers, even though they were Northumbrians, repulsed them. So it was with Wulfric. He turned his back on war and headed for his father's house on the edge of the Peaklands.

Wulfric's father Aelric was stiffly formal, even with his own two sons. With womenfolk, he was at times indifferent, or patronising. Few men found him easy. The pain of old wounds and arthritis had long since deprived him of his sense of humour. Nevertheless, Wulfric loved him. They shared a secret understanding; a sort of warrior bond, which excluded even Wulfric's older brother Rendil, who had never known the sickening terror and insane elation of the shield wall.

Wulfric expected his homecoming to be polite, and restrained. His father would have his ingas lined up to cheer him. Rendil's daughters would present themselves in crisp, clean smocks and polished faces. His father would observe all due form, but the proceedings would be as sterile as a boiled bone.

**

Word of Penda's victory reached Uhtredstun on a day when frost was thick in the fields. Several months had passed since the battle. Stories of the savagery of Cadwallon's army rampaging through Northumbria seeped down slowly from the north, like a bloody stain.

Wynflaed and Buhe were working in the fields, coaxing the winter wheat they had struggled to plant, hopefully not too late in the season. They were weary and hungry. Seeing Uhtred's impassive reaction to the news, Wynflaed watched him and wondered what he might be thinking. "I can't tell how he's taking it," she told Buhe.

Buhe straightened up painfully from her work and looked across the sparse scatter of bent backs in the frosty field. She saw her father picking his way through the ruins of his settlement. Wynflaed reached for her hand. "Come on, let's go and cheer him up. Anyway, my back is killing me. I've got aches everywhere. And look," she stuck out her palm for inspection, "blisters on my blisters."

Uhtred straightened up and forced a broad grin onto his face as he saw the girls approaching him. "Have you seen who's turned up again?" he asked them.

"Who?" queried Buhe.

"That muler. I saw him skulking about earlier. He took off when he saw me."

Wynflaed almost swooned. She thought her legs would give way, but somehow she managed to stay upright and conceal her swirling emotions.

"I hope he brought food, did he?" Buhe asked.

Uhtred shook his head. "If he did, he didn't stay long enough to hand it over."

"I'm going to look for him," Buhe told Wynflaed. "Are you coming?"

Wynflaed gaped at Buhe's extended hand. "Look for him, why?"

"Food, of course. For a change I'd like something in my bowl that doesn't look like leaf mould." She set off at a trot, hauling Wynflaed with her.

Carrying their shoes, they crossed the icy stream and passed by the muler's old campsite, its blackened hearth now pierced by the first greening of spring. Beyond the village the forest, already decked in damp green buds, closed around them. Bird-song echoed in the emerald air. Weak sunlight sparkled on melting frost. Celandine glowed between emerging grasses and ferns. Everywhere the lush promise of Eostre glistened in its coat of gems.

Buhe stopped abruptly and looked around in wonder. "Look, Flaedy. I hadn't noticed until just now," she said, her voice hushed in reverence. "Eostre! She's here and we've been too busy to notice. It's spring isn't it? It's Eostre's time."

Wynflaed too was taken by surprise. She gazed in awe at the wonders the goddess had performed. "We've survived," she whispered reverently. "Winter is ending and we're still alive."

A sound from behind a holly bush broke the moment. Wynflaed picked up a hefty stone, expecting danger, perhaps a wolf or wild pig.

Eadwin the muler stepped out from his prickly hiding place. He looked at the two apprehensively and yanked on the reins of his white mule and a stocky pony, urging them forward, as if for moral support. "I - I've got flour and salted meat," he said. "I've been sent with word for the master."

Wynflaed blushed from head to toe, her skin tingling so much that she felt sure it would make a sound. She glanced guiltily at Buhe, who mercifully appeared not to be hearing it; her attention already seized by the promising packs on Eadwin's animals. Wynflaed watched her go forward eagerly and tug at the muler's sleeve. "Come on then. We'd better take you to him at once."

Eadwin hung back, warily. "Is he — err — alright?"

"Strong as a bull," Buhe replied, careless of the damage such news would do to Eadwin's fraying confidence. "He told us you were here. He saw you."

"Both of us?" he queried.

"Both?"

He wiped hair from his eyes, looking flustered. "Well I mean me and – err – Snowflake. The mule. I call her Snowflake. Oh, and the pony."

"That's three. You said both," Wynflaed said, her misgivings growing.

"Don't worry, father won't eat you," Buhe said.

Wynflaed hung back beside Eadwin. "How is — err — your master?" she asked.

Eadwin looked about nervously, arousing in Wynflaed the expectation of some remarkable revelation. "He's fine," he said at last, from the side of his mouth.

She scowled. "Did he say anything?"

He looked at her blankly. "About what?"

"About me, you fool!"

Eadwin wound the horses' reins around his hand, studying them as if they contained the entire record of Wulfric's utterances. His face was colouring hotly. "I don't know," he said, helplessly aware that this was not what she wanted to hear. Then, as if struck by a particularly apposite afterthought, he tossed in with relief. "He fell off his horse though. That's why he's – I mean – he wants ..."

Tossing her head angrily Wynflaed sniffed and stomped away.

"No luck, eh?" Buhe said, as Wynflaed bustled past her, fording the stream in splashing strides.

On the opposite bank Uhtred waited, impassive as a rock. Around him had gathered a few excited villagers. They cheered as Eadwin nervously waded into the ford, leading his weary animals. "Come ahead, lad," Uhtred said. "Don't be frit."

"He has salt-meat and flour," Buhe announced.

"Well that's good, but a traveller is welcome here with nowt but sore feet," Uhtred said regally and reached to help the muler up the bank, adding, "Providing he comes with no daft notions in his head."

"Notions?" queried Eadwin from beneath his tangled fringe.

"Yes, notions like taking my girls away from me; them sort of notions."

Eadwin gulped, looking as if he was about to be sick.

"Does he still want Flaedy?" asked Buhe without a hint of tact. Her mind was only partially on her question as she tried to loose the lashings on the food packs.

Wynflaed's stomach flipped with embarrassment. The muler's uncomfortable reaction was making her deeply suspicious. He was gaping around forlornly, evidently on the brink of panic.

"Blessed Mother Frigg!" Buhe cried, holding up a clay pot of honey. "Look what I found." The villagers joined her celebration and pressed around the mules, eagerly picking at the pack's lashings. Children joined in, their smaller fingers quickly unravelling straps and ties. Squealing with delight they discovered smoked pig-meat, white beans and peas, salt, onion sets and cleaned flour.

Uhtred, Wynflaed and the muler seemed apart from the excitement. They stood motionless, trapped in each other's gaze like frogs in ice. The question of the muler's true purpose at Uhtredstun hung between them, unanswered. At last Uhtred spoke. "Put it all back," he ordered grimly. "Tell your master no-one here is for sale. He can send a hundred horses loaded with the sweetmeats of a king's table, the answer is the same."

"But, your honour," Eadwin pleaded. "It's not like you think."

"I know exactly what it's like, lad," the old thegn said, raising a disdainful hand. "Oh, don't worry, I'm not blaming you. You're just doing as you've been told. But, now that you know my will, you can take my words back to your master. And tell him this too: if he sends you again, he'll be sending you to a sword's edge."

"And if he wished it, I'd gladly come," Eadwin replied, surprising himself with his sudden boldness. "You just don't listen, do you? My master is an honourable man. He would not do what you're thinking. And lowly as I am, I insist you hear his words from me so that you will not keep such a low opinion of him."

Uhtred looked surprised. His hand plunged into his white hair and scratched around as he studied his boots thoughtfully. "That's quite a mouthful for a muler," he said. "You must think a lot of your master." His foraging hand withdrew from his mane and came to rest gently on the muler's shoulder. "Come on then, lad. I'll hear you, but first we'll drink and take bread and cheese. Any man who faces me as boldly as that deserves what little my table can offer."

"Forgive me, your honour, but I have something I must show you first. I am here to ask you to receive my lord Wulfric. He sends you his sword as a gesture of trust and friendship." Eadwin pulled a sword from under the pony's pack.

Uhtred glanced at the sword, and then ran his eye along the trees adjoining the settlement clearing. "He's here now?"

"Yes, your honour. He was thrown from a horse a few days ago and still carries the injury. He wants to come in under a truce to talk to you."

"I won't stop him," said Uhtred, cuffing the proffered sword aside. "He knows where I am." He turned and headed to the barn which now served as his dwelling.

Wynflaed also searched the tree line, but could see no sign of Wulfric. Eadwin handed the pack ponies' reins to Uhtred's horsener and jogged back across the river towards the woods. Wynflaed watched him go and tried to calm her bubbling emotions. Was she about to see again the man she could not forget?

At her father's side, Buhe was putting everything together in her head and coming up with answers she did not want. "It's that Wulfric isn't it? He's here, isn't he? He's come for Flaedy. You're not going to let him take her are you?"

"I won't stop her doing whatever she wants. She's old enough to make up her own mind."

Buhe gaped at him, horrified. "But you must. We've planned everything. She's to come with me as my companion when I marry. It's what we've wanted for years."

Uhtred took his daughter's hand and kissed it. "Bairns' talk, Buhe. Nothing but the games of two little bairns. Our Flaedy is a woman now, and by summer so will you be. You'll see things differently then."

"But what if he hurts her? What if …"

"Don't worry. I'll hear what he has to say. And she will have her say too. I promise you, I won't let her go unless I'm convinced he's a good man. He will have to satisfy me on that. He must swear to treat her well, give her a fine home and a morgengifu, just as if she were truly my own daughter." He hugged her, and kissed her forehead. "But we must be ready to face the facts, Buhe. Our little Flaedy is probably leaving us. She's starting that long journey she's been talking about."

…….

CHAPTER FIVE

It was mid summer before Wynflaed could leave Uhtredstun. Old Uhtred wanted the best for her, and negotiating at a distance with messengers passing back and forth between him and Wulfric's father Aelric, was a slow process. Agreement in principle was eventually achieved; the final details to be settled when the two old warriors met face to face at the wedding.

Buhe took the time to come to terms with the situation. She even managed to grant Wulfric an occasional smile. Wynflaed realised things were improving when Buhe stopped referring to him as, "that man". Uhtred and Wulfric were polite and businesslike with each other. A fond friendship however, was never likely. The villagers largely ignored what went on in the hall, though some were openly hostile towards Wulfric. They could not forgive him. His various attempts to help them were sourly rejected. He got round this by paying the families of each man killed their full wergild, as decreed by law. This was sullenly accepted, though of course it could never dim the memory of the raid. Even so, for Wynflaed's sake, many villagers hid their feelings and stayed out of Wulfric's way.

When all seemed well, Wynflaed confounded everybody by insisting on seeing Wulfric's home and meeting his family before her wedding day. After heated discussion and much against his better wishes, Uhtred finally agreed to let her make the journey a week or so before him and Buhe. It was due as much to his confidence in Wulfric as it was to his weariness in argument with Wynflaed.

When the day for their departure finally arrived, Buhe's tears flowed as though Wynflaed's leaving was no less absolute than death itself. Wulfric however, was elated. His heart pounded in his chest at the thought of at last being alone with his love, and free from the villagers' hostile glares. His joy soon evaporated on seeing two grim faced old women, mounted on stocky ponies. They were being led out to join him by Horse-Ebell, Uhtred's head groom. Without a flicker of expression on his grizzled face, the old horsener led them up to Wulfric and pushed them into the train of ponies. Seeing Wulfric's distraught expression, Horse-Ebell chuckled behind his hand..

Wulfric glared at Wynflaed. "Pillow watchers!" he said indignantly. "Does Uhtred have such a low opinion of me, or is this your idea? Do you think I'll ravage you before the wedding?"

Wynflaed eyed him coyly. "Well, I hope you'll at least try, my lord."

***

The journey took four days. Wulfric's horse fell sick with the early summer grass and had to be left at a farm on the way. He was obliged to ride one of Eadwin's jaggers, a foul tempered beast which missed no opportunity to bite or unseat him.

The first night out, they stayed with a woodsman and his family in a little house deep in the Shire-wood. The huswif took Wynflaed to her own bed. She slept with a felling axe beside her. Wulfric, the woodsman and his four mud-stained children crammed themselves into the only other bed. Wulfric refused to make any demands for the pillow watchers' comfort, so they had to sleep on the floor. Later he told Wynflaed, he had not managed to sleep a wink. He complained that by the time he had grown used to the strangely feral smell of the woodsman's children it was morning and he was rolled out of bed.

On the second night they stayed with a wealthy freeman; a man who kept his farm as neat a gentlewoman's garden. Its lane was pristine, the fences straight and sturdy, ruts and potholes levelled with river stones and grit. The white-washed house stood in a cobbled yard which the children of the family: shy twin girls of twelve and two boys, one fifteen, the other an imperious eight-year-old, solemnly swept every day. A range of stabling, hordeons and barns, their walls bright with lime-wash, stood around the yard. The whole place was so scrubbed and tidy that Wynflaed could not help noticing a luxuriant dandelion growing beside the paddock gate. How on earth had it managed to seed and prosper in such a place? she wondered.

The huswif was a cold body who controlled her household, including her husband, with a rod of iron. She took her duty to provide hospitality to travellers precisely as far as she had to and no further. After a simple meal of plough meat pottage at a scrubbed table, palliasses and blankets, smelling of wood-smoke, were pulled out of a void in the roof space and laid along the floor in a neat row. Wynflaed was conducted sedately to one end of the line, Wulfric to the other. The lamps were extinguished, except for a single rush flame. As if upon some coded signal, the family undressed in silence and milled about naked, pecking each other on the cheeks with all the warmth of a snap frost. Nakedness was no shock to the visitors, indeed it was quite normal, like making love with others sleeping about you. What struck Wynflaed was that without at least one bawdy remark, or jocular reference to the genitals, it seemed positively indecent.

As they prepared to leave the following morning, Wynflaed caught hold of Wulfric's sleeve, alarmed by the sight of a young girl approaching them across the pristine yard. She was a short, pale child not more than thirteen-years-of-age. At first glance, she had appeared to be carrying a crudely fashioned milk pail in her arms, but as she drew nearer Wynflaed saw it was a heavy timber block with a chain running through it. The chain hung down heavily and connected to an iron band around her ankle. Another chain ran from that and appeared to be fastened around her body beneath her short, shapeless dress.

Even without her chains the child's suffering would have been obvious. Her hair was roughly cropped, showing patches of scalp. Her face, arms and legs were covered in scars and bruises. At the edges of her tattered dress, the angry red weals of a lash showed on her shoulders and thighs. Wynflaed had never seen such a wretched child.

"We have to do something," she told Wulfric.

They were standing near the door of their host's house, waiting to take their leave. Wulfric glanced back into the house looking embarrassed. "What can we do? She's their slave. They can do as they want with her."

The slave girl was shuffling closer, staring at them, her eyes full of hatred and defiance. "But look at her! They're treating her worse than a dog."

"We don't know that for certain," he said. "I mean, I can see she's had a beating, but she looks well enough apart from that. She's obviously being fed. Maybe she keeps running off. That'll be why they've chained her up - for punishment." He dropped his arm about Wynflaed's shoulder and started to move her on as the slave girl stopped in front of them, glaring. "They'll not keep her chained up like that all the time," he went on. "She can't work like that."

Wynflaed refused to move. She stared up at him, appalled by his acquiescence. "Is that all you're going to say? Don't you feel anything to see her like this?"

He faced her and put his hands on her shoulders. "Look, I don't like it any more than you, but that's life. Some are bonded, some are free. That's how the world is. It's always been so."

"If you care, you can change things," she said, shrugging his hands from her.

He sniffed with frustration, taking a moment to gather his thoughts. "Very well, I'll see if I can buy her." His shoulders sagged in capitulation. "But I think you're mad. Just look at her. She looks as wild as a wolf. No wonder they chained her up. She'll probably murder us in our beds."

"Then buy her and free her."

"Huh, she'd be back in chains before you could say thief," he said. "She's too wild. You can't help folk like her. Freedom is wasted on her sort. She'd have to steal to stay alive. She'd probably murder some poor old widow for a cup of milk."

Wynflaed was silent. She glared at him, feeling chilled by her disappointment in him. Why did he not see what must be done?

Wulfric was glowering at the miserable wretch before him. The girl glared back with murderous defiance. Then turning to Wynflaed, he gave her an ironical smile and said, "You're right aren't you? You're right again, damn it!"

A spark of hope burned briefly in the slave child's eyes, but she made no move or sound. Wulfric turned to her and shrugged with disdain. "Look at the surly bitch," he growled. "She'd slit your throat for a crust." He sighed and shook his head. "Nevertheless, you'll have your way."

He went back into the house to find the master, leaving Wynflaed facing the slave girl. They were two young girls, one fifteen and on the threshold of marriage to a rich man she loved, the other around twelve and about to start a new life that in all probability would be no better than the old one. Barely three feet of cobbled yard separated them, yet the gulf between them was more like an ocean. Neither could have the slightest idea what the other's life might be like.

"What's your name, girl?" Wynflaed asked, as behind her Wulfric emerged from the house with its owner. The girl looked alarmed as she saw them and began backing away.

"It's done," Wulfric said grandly. "The lass is now freed. They've agreed to send her on her way with a bag of food and a hoe. Apparently she's told them she's got kinfolk in the west somewhere. That could be true. It might explain why she's been so keen to run away."

Wynflaed drew Wulfric to her and away from their hosts. "Are you sure you can trust them?" she whispered. "What if he just takes your payment and keeps her, or sells her to somebody else?"

"He won't do that. It's a matter of honour," Wulfric said.

Wynflaed eyed him doubtfully. "You wouldn't do it, but would he?"

"Of course not," he assured her grandly. "Don't you understand? There's a code of honour and decency that exists between men - and anyway I'm leaving Eadwin behind to make sure the snooty bastards don't cheat us."

Wynflaed laughed and threw a friendly punch at him. Even the eavesdropping slave girl allowed a hint of a smile to flicker briefly on her lips.

***

Two days later, as the last rays of the sun faded from the sky, they saw the lights of Wulfric's home flickering in the distance. Holmesfelt sits on the eastern edge of the wild Peakland, on the border between Mercia and Elmet. The gently rising land is good and fertile above shallow runs of peat bog. Sheep, cattle and pigs prosper there, and the rich plough-land is sheltered from the winds by the Peakland's thick forest.

Lord Aelric was in his bed, "Where all right minded folk should be." As usual he had retired three hours before midnight. Wulfric, who well knew his father's habits, told Wynflaed, with some relief, that there would be no reception for her this night. She looked thankful and worn out. He surmised that all she wanted was to collapse into a soft bed and sleep for a week.

Wynflaed gazed around at her new surroundings, anxiously wondering where she would be sleeping and when.

"Are you having second thoughts?" he asked, noticing her apprehension.

"Oh no - I - err - was just looking ..."

"Don't worry. I'll show you everything in the morning," he said. "We'll break our fast with father and Rendil. Then I'll take you round and show you off to everybody." He paused, peering at her closely. "You do still love me? What's wrong? It's not that slave girl is it?"

She laughed. "Of course I love you. No, I'm just tired."

"You had a strange look ..."

"I want to be married. I don't want to leave you." She glanced back at the pair of pillow watchers. They were yawning and leaning wearily against a fence. "I wish we didn't have them around us every moment."

"Me too. I want you now — right now."

"When will we be married?"

"Soon - a week or two at the most. Word is being sent round the shire. The deeds are being written for your morgengifu ..."

"I need no morgengifu. I'll marry you now, right this moment."

"And me too, Flaedy, but you want time for Uhtred and Buhe to arrive. And father has kin and old comrades all over the shire. He'll want them all here to witness the deeds, and to show you off. And, whether we like it or not, Uhtred and my father will make it as much their big day as ours."

"Oh, I know," she said. "Holy Mother, are you always going to be so proper?"

Wulfric pushed his bulging crotch against her and hugged her tight. "How proper do you think that is? If I don't get this thing into you soon it will burst."

"Is that what it is?" Wynflaed asked, in mock, wide eyed astonishment. "What sort of girl do you think I am? Would you press that wicked thing upon a pure virgin before her wedding?"

"Onward and inward," said Wulfric. "Come on, let's find a corner and get this marriage started, before the bower and the salt."

"And when we step through the bower, would you still take me, the tainted, fallen woman you would have made of me?"

"Aye, so long as I do the tainting, and I do it right now," he said. He grabbed her hand and pulled it to his penis. "See, feel what you've wrought here. I must have you now. I can't be seen in my father's house with my brecs sticking out like a gibbet."

She glanced at the pillow watchers. Weariness had at last overcome them. They were sitting against the fence, heads lolling, eyes closed, snoring peacefully. "Very well then," she whispered. "Where can we go to lower your gibbet?"

She led him by the hand to a screening stand of hazels and pushed him gently to the ground. He rose to kiss her pulling her down to him. She moved up to him eagerly, pushing him firmly with her mouth until he was on his back. She quickly unlaced his woollen tunic to bare his chest, and moving over his body, kissed and nibbled his skin, brushing it with her hair. Her fingers found the cord at his waist and loosed the top of his brecs so that she could slide her hand beneath them.

She had seen men naked, swimming in the river, or washing, or sleeping in the hall at Uhtredstun. She had seen them aroused, their cocks sticking out like broom handles when they coupled with their wives. She had watched at the spring feste, when the young men chased the lasses and danced around the great pole, but she had never touched a penis, never felt its warmth and life. Its hardness surprised her. With a finger tip she traced its vine-like network of blood filled veins pumping life into it, making it strain at its enfolding skin. She kissed it, letting her hair fall around it. Smiling secretly, she remembered the bawdy riddle that older women often sprang upon blossoming girls at Modrenacht, *What boneless object increases in size under the skilful handling of the proud bride?* The answer of course is bread dough, but invariably the poor adolescent would collapse in embarrassment thinking of some other boneless object soon to come within her domain.

Wulfric was groaning ecstatically. Cupping his balls in her hand she kissed them gently, rubbing her cheek against the root of his penis. Turning her head she squinted up at him wondering if he liked what she was doing. She had seen one of the skivvies do it to her man at Uhtredstun.

When it was finished and he whimpered and stretched like a drowsy cat, she loved him all the more. She loved his vulnerability in that moment of purest pleasure. She loved his confusion and embarrassment as ecstasy faded and the real world flooded back into his mind. She loved his tearful gratitude and his hard enfolding arms. She loved his unspoken promise to always love her.

By the time they emerged from the hazel thicket the village fires had died. Apart from a couple of old drunks, and the pair of ineffective pillow watchers, everyone had gone to their beds. Wulfric led Wynflaed to a substantial cottage standing a little way off beyond the common ground in front of his father's hall. A four branched lamp burned at its door, shedding light on the slender fingers of a middle aged woman sitting in the doorway, sewing.

"This is her, widow Guthrum, safe and sound," said Wulfric, as he neared the house.

"Huh, she might be safe, but how sound is she?" the woman challenged bluntly. "I saw you go into that hazel stand. There'll be no more of that, young Wulf. Once she steps over this threshold I shall take my responsibilities very seriously, not like that pair of dozy dormice you brought with you."

Widow Guthrum took Wynflaed's hand from Wulfric's and pushed him back a step. "Your father bid me lodge the lass to keep her safe from you. I'll do so with a stout wand and a bucket of cold water if you come a-sniffing at the door jamb. So be told. You mun take yourself in hand if the urge seizes you. You've had plenty of practice, I'm sure." She eyed Wynflaed, mocking tragedy, and led her off into the house. At the last moment she turned back to Wulfric. "Go on then. Take yourself away, and don't come a-sniffing again."

Wulfric backed off miserably. "I'll see you in the morning," he told Wynflaed.

"You will not!" snapped widow Guthrum. "You'll see her on the day and not before, lest you're up a tree and she's in a cart full of mothers and bairns."

Wynflaed was pulled into the house. She watched dumbly as Widow Guthrum fetched in her lamp and shut the door on Wulfric's gawping misery.

"That'll cool the throbbing in his robin," she quipped, beaming warmly at Wynflaed. "Oh, don't worry, lass, you'll see him plenty. I just meant to set the pot steady on its trivet before he gets carried away with himself. Men are fools when their cocks are leading them." She eyed the door between herself and Wulfric sardonically. "Mind you, they're none too bright at any other time either." Moving to the central hearth, she busied herself with a wyrtdrenc of milk with honey and herbs. "Me and you will be great friends, you'll see." She handed Wynflaed a steaming cup and indicated to a chair by a table near the hearth. "Call me Gutty, they all do. My right name is Hilda, but I've not heard it for years. I don't dislike it, but I've been Gutty's widow too long to bother."

They sat and sipped their spicy milk: Gutty content in reflective mood, Wynflaed warm in her welcoming glow.

"I've had two men," Gutty told her, "and I loved 'em both as hard as any woman might. I've five sons, all as big as carts and just as brainless. They're all married and gone now, thank Frigg. I've grand bairns all over the place. Though there's nary a lass amongst 'em for me to primp and pamper. I reckon Holy Mother Frigg is punishing me for enjoying a fuck better than she does." She laughed wickedly and patted Wynflaed's hand. "But now I've got thee for a week or so. And whether you want it or not lass, I'm going to brush your hair and polish and posy you, like you were my own dear daughter."

"I know I'm going to like it here, Gutty," Wynflaed said sincerely. "And you can brush and primp as much you want, but I'd like to do your hair too. It's a lovely colour. You should bind it looser. It would let the gold shine out more."

"Aye lass, tis only weak lamplight puts gold in it. You're seeing it at its best. The sunshine shows it up for what it really is, old straw laced with iron."

***

The smell of bread baking under clay pots woke Wynflaed that first morning at Holmesfelt. Gutty was rushing about on tip toes, her face dusty with flour and pink with effort.

"Is it late?" Wynflaed mumbled as she collected her wits and took in the details of Gutty's neat, well furnished house.

"Not for the lady of a thegn's son," Gutty replied, with a motherly smile. "You stay abed and rest. You've had a long journey and you need to look your best today."

"Why?"

"Why!" Gutty cried. "You've got to meet the master and that dreadful son of his."

"Wulfric?"

Gutty clasped her hands to her bosom. "Frigg's tits! Where's your mind, lass," she howled. "Not Wulfric! Rendil, your soon-to- be brother-in-law. He's the dreadful son. Your Wulfric is a lovely boy, though whether even he is worth marrying with a brother-in-law like Rendil thrown in, I very much doubt. Gods! Your Wulfric must be hung like a horse to make such kinship worthwhile."

The remark brought the memory of what she had seen of Wulfric the night before flitting briefly through Wynflaed's mind. She blushed and smiled coyly.

"Great Grim's cods he is." declared Gutty ecstatically. "I can see it on your face."

Wynflaed stared at her astonished. "I don't know anything about Wulfric that's not decent for a girl to know. I'm a maid and I'll be a maid when he beds me. There'll be no taint on my morgengifu."

"Oh hush up." Gutty said.

Wynflaed eyed her coyly and bit her lip.

"My word, but you're a wily one. You might yet be a match for that snake Rendil." She wagged a warning finger at her. "Now he really is a little prick in every way of thinking. No more use in bed than a boy, so I've heard. Three bairns, all girls, a wife with a face like a wet day off and all of 'em as sour as vinegar." She plumped up her heavy round breasts and lifted her nose in distaste.

"You've a mighty poor opinion of him."

"He's a bad lot, young Wyn. If you can stay away from him you should. The trouble is, he has his nose into everything, like a new dog in old shit."

"I'm supposed to be breaking fast with him and Wulfric and his father."

"No you're not. The master has told me what I must do with you. You will see them at noon. Lord Aelric has business this morning. It's dues day — they'll be coming in from all around. In the meanwhile we'll have a good time together."

Breakfast was fresh bread and butter with soft cheese and blackberries preserved in honey. Wynflaed ate her food and washed it down with what Gutty called her sweet minted water. It was very good and Wynflaed had several cups. Afterwards there was some mending to do on Gutty's bed-curtains. The morning passed quickly with barely a pause for Gutty to take a breath. At noon Wulfric arrived to take her to his father.

"I'll watch you go," said Gutty. "There'll be no sneaking to them hazels."

"Don't walk so fast, Wulf," Wynflaed appealed, as they set off over the wide, goose cropped green to the great hall. "I feel a bit ..."

"Drunk," Wulfric said, with an amused chuckle. He smiled at her. "Oh don't worry. Everybody gets drunk when Gutty entertains. Did you have any mint water? It's diluted mead with mint. It's not very strong, but as she does all the talking you never get the chance to rest your cup." He eyed her studiously. "You don't look drunk. The extra colour suits your cheeks."

"Oh no! Do I look red? I do, don't I?"

"I just said you don't."

"But my cheeks are flushed. You just said so."

He looked at her again, appearing to study her more closely. "No, no they're not. I was wrong," he said. "You look as pale as a querner's ghost."

Wynflaed blew a sigh of relief and hiccupped. "Thanks be to blessed Mother Frigg. I don't want to be drunk for my first meeting with your father and that little prick, Rendil," she said seriously.

....

CHAPTER SIX

Some of the timbers of Aelric's hall at Holmesfelt glowed
with the honey warmth of newly cut oak. Parts of the
building were barely five years old, though its core
covered the bones of an old Wealh hall seized in battle
before Aelric had married. Rendil and Wulfric were born
there. Three more infants lived less than a year. Their
young mother soon followed them to an orchard grave.
Aelric beautified and extended the hall as if to honour her.

Aelric's hall was smaller than the old hall at
Uhtredstun had been, but more richly decorated. The
carved head of some great mythical beast looked down
from the peak of its west gable. Two small window slits,
their shutters thrown open to let light in and smoke out,
pierced the wall either side of it. Two more windows, one
quite large, looked out from the south wall. Wynflaed
guessed that the household's loom would be near by, to
catch the best of the light. A substantial stone built porch
shaded the threshold. Before it, a pavement of river stones
was scattered with meadowsweet and straw, to clean the
feet of all who passed across it with their petitions, duties
and rents.

Haughty geese stalked beneath trees in a stone-
walled orchard, cropping the grass and chasing away
stalking cats and playful pups. A long table with benches
drawn up to it was set in the shade. Close by, a rope
hanging in a cherry tree had a short wooden spar spinning
gently at its end. Wynflaed smiled, remembering that not
all that long ago she and Buhe had played on such a rope
swing at Uhtredstun.

"Who's the child?" she whispered to Wulfric as they
approached the porch.

"Oh, it's for one of the spinwifs' brats," he said. "She won't work unless she can see her child nearby. My father put it there for her."

"That was nice of him."

He laughed. "Nice? He only did it to get more yarn out of her."

"Well, I still think it was nice," she said, as they entered the hall.

Inside was dark after the bright sunlight. For a moment she could see very little and blinked, almost sensing the household objects around her rather than seeing them. As expected there was a standing loom beside the largest window. The spinwifs working there smiled shyly. Two long tables in lower hall faced each other across an earthen floor. Three great dogs stretched out in a shaft of sunlight leaning in from the smoke-hole high in the roof. One of them bothered to glance sleepily at the newcomers before snorting and discounting them.

In upper hall an oak planked floor, to raise those of rank above lesser men, glowed dully through a litter of meadowsweet and bracken. A large polished table, supported on four trestles, carved to look like bears, stood beyond the slumbering hearth. Around the walls stood several wooden chests, some ornately carved; a few had cushions on them for seating. Vividly coloured wall hangings brightened the windowless north wall. Weapons and shields hung about functionally from the four main roof supports, each carved and painted with endless spirals and patterns.

Several chairs were drawn up to the top table, some decorated with stylised carvings of serpents and animals. A scrubbed, neat man of around fifty-five-years of age sat in the middle one. He had a short, silver beard and luxuriant moustache. He jumped to his feet as he saw

Wynflaed enter and ran around his table with short, stiff steps, to greet her.

"Welcome, welcome, welcome," he cried enthusiastically. Long silver hair brushed his shoulders as he moved, snagging gently in the pattern of golden threads that edged his dark red, knee-length tunic. He stopped in front of her, gazing with what appeared to be genuine astonishment. "By the gods, you're lovely — a real beauty. By holy Thunner, a real ..." He stopped in mid sentence and turned to his son with a look of mock apprehension. "She is the one, I trust? I hope there is not some cross-eyed spinster outside waiting to come in. Don't tell me this is only her pillow watcher."

Wulfric laughed. "No father. This is Wynflaed. Wynflaed Alfwalddohtor, ward of Uhtred Bergredsunnu of the great shire-wood."

Aelric took Wynflaed's hands in his. "Welcome child, welcome. I'm sorry, but I don't think I knew your father, Alfwald," he told her apologetically, pausing only to kiss her hands. "I'm sure we never met. Still, no matter, I doubt he would've remembered me either. But, I think I do recall old Bergred and his son Uhtred. I'm not sure. It was a very long time ago during Raedwald's wars. If Uhtred's the man I'm thinking of then he's a fine man indeed. And a brave fighter. Err – a few years younger than me I think? What, about six or seven years would you say? About fifty he'd be?"

Wynflaed nodded.

"Yes, as I recall it he had an excellent horsener, a man called Ebell?"

"Yes, your honour," replied Wynflaed, astonished that he should remember Horse Ebell better than he did Uhtred.

"Yes that's him," said Aelric reflectively. "Cured my Slaen, he did. A beautiful mare Slaen was. I had her twenty years or more. She got spear struck the following year and died, bless her old heart." He gazed reflectively for a moment at the window slits in the far gable before going on. "Yes, young Ebell, I remember him very well, no one better with horses. He even …" A commotion in lower hall interrupted the old man, and all turned to the cause of it.

Though she had never met the man she saw entering the hall, Wynflaed knew instinctively that he was Wulfric's brother, Rendil. She stiffened, her smile slipping from her face. As Rendil approached she reminded herself that Wulfric loved his brother; she must learn to do the same.

Like his father, Rendil too was a neat, clean man, whose clothes seemed to fit him without a crease or tuck, but there the similarity ended. Rendil had a polished, gloomy face, showing weary disapproval no matter where he looked. He walked with long, slow strides, and though he carried a walking stick, put little weight upon it. He had a strangely rolling gait being unable to completely straighten his left leg. When standing his limbs seemed oddly held, as though drawing back from some unpleasant discovery at his feet. She found herself looking at the floor in front of him to see what it might be.

"So, here's the maid we've heard about endlessly all these weeks. Perhaps, now she's finally amongst us, my brother may find some other topic." Placing his walking stick on the table with a dramatic sweep, he came close to Wynflaed, reached for her hand and held it in his. "Welcome, I hope you will be – err - content."

Wynflaed curtsied. Content, she was thinking. The word struck her as odd in the circumstances. He had not said happy or merry, but "content," as if anything more than the minimum of blessings would be a waste. "Thank you, your honour. I'm pleased to be ..."

"Well father, what news?" Rendil said, interrupting her loudly, as though Aelric was deaf. "When is the great day to be?" He turned to Wynflaed before his father could reply. "I expect you will want to wed as soon as possible? Can't let a rich catch like my brother slip the net."

"As my lord Wulfric pleases," she replied stiffly.

Rendil moved to a chair and sat down swinging his good leg over the chair arm. Even lounging in such a relaxed position he still managed to look impeccable. Aelric took his seat and signalled for ale to be served.

" 'As my lord Wulfric pleases,' indeed. Is that so?" Rendil said, smirking, and turning to Wulfric. "Let's hope she continues to keep such good counsel, eh brother?"

Wulfric conducted Wynflaed to a cushioned bench opposite his father and slid in beside her, holding her hand. "Shut up, Ren. You've scared her enough," he said good-naturedly. "We intend to wed as soon as it can be arranged. Don't we, Flaedy? The sooner the better, I say. So you needn't bother trying to scare her any more."

Rendil looked at his father and smiled mockingly. For the briefest moment Wynflaed thought she saw something of Wulfric in his glance, but it faded the instant he spoke. "Ahhh! Isn't that nice, father? True-love. The boy's smitten."

"I am," Wulfric said. "And I don't give spit who knows it."

"Well I'm pleased for you," Rendil cried, raising the cup a servant had placed before him. "I wish you contentment."

There was that word again, Wynflaed fumed internally.

"If a man can find a woman he loves amongst his own kind, he's blessed indeed," said Aelric. He turned to Wynflaed. "I was blessed with their mother. She was a beauty too. She had the wit and ways to charm even the ealfen-kind. I think you're such a woman. It gladdens my heart more than I can say. It'll be a blessed day when you become my daughter."

Rendil watched his father, noting his joy and calculating how it might affect him. He had not seen the old man quite so happy in a long time. It struck him as a situation not without its perils.

"I drink to you, Wulfric, and your woman," said Aelric, brandishing his cup again. "May Wyrd treat you kindly and the gods bless you with their bounty." He turned again to Wynflaed. "Whatever you want of mine is yours. All I ask is that you give me grandsons. Oh - and lie to them about me, so they'll think their grandfather was a great man."

"Thank you, your honour," Wynflaed said, bowing her head. "I too, pray that Holy Mother Frigg will bless me with many sons. However, I'm sure lies will not be needed. I'll simply tell them the truth of your greatness."

Aelric laughed heartily and jumped to his feet. "Ho ho! A fine answer," he said. "Bring wine and a flask of mead, the best in the hordeon. Let the meadow's wraiths rob us of our senses. Tomorrow is soon enough for talk of marriage and morgengifu."

Rendil waited on his father's joy, studying him thoughtfully. He saw that Wynflaed had undoubtedly captured the old man's heart and he wondered grimly what the outcome might be. The reference to his mother was particularly worrying. He seldom mentioned her, preferring to lose himself in his work and the affairs of his estate. Now, with a woman in his heart, albeit a new daughter-in-law, there was no knowing how he might behave; especially if she bears sons, something Goda, his own wife, had so far failed to do.

When Aelric sat down and sipped his cup, Rendil spoke up, "I agree, father, but the wedding settlement must not be spoiled for the sake of a hangover. Apart from anything else we have to summon the writerer and the guests. A date should be set now, today."

"Nonsense. What's the rush?"

Rendil frowned. "You know why," he said. "It's the busiest season, what with shearing and the hay to finish. Harvest will be upon us before we know it. Men must plan their journeys and see to it that their folk don't waste daylight in their absence. It all takes time and planning."

"I agree, father," said Wulfric eagerly, thinking only of how soon he could get Wynflaed to himself. "If we leave it longer it grows too near harvest."

"Gods! Did I say it would be that long off? What itches you two?" Aelric looked from one son to the other. "Surely we can have a drink and let the maid take her ease and get to know us?"

That was the last thing Rendil wanted. "Let's settle it," he said. "Give us the *what and wherefore*, and save our worrying?"

Aelric looked at his sons and creased his brow in a frown. "I'll not be rushed," he said. "Enough of this, honour me and bide upon my word."

Wulfric and Wynflaed too felt disappointment, but by no means as much as Rendil, and certainly not for the same reasons.

***

Thegn Aelric had sent to Ealdorman Cenwulf's hall for the services of his lordship's writerer. As was the custom, he would proclaim his deeds and gifts before witnesses, and have his wishes relayed by criers to all corners of the king's realm and even beyond. But Aelric also wanted to observe the new ways and have his deeds written with ink scratched upon lambskin. Though he was not convinced of the merit such new fangled ideas, it was a growing trend amongst the great families, and he regarded his own as no less grand.

When the clerk arrived, the witnesses, all freemen of good standing, were called to formally observe the proceedings. It was an occasion for feasting and music. Folk came from miles around. Pedlars and hawkers set up stalls. Journeymen came looking for work. A man who juggled fire amazed everyone, until Aelric chased him off for getting too close to the thatch of his hall. Apart from Wynflaed, by far the biggest attraction was the young writerer with his un-dyed robe, bare feet and diet of bread and water. It was whispered that he was a Christian, and had begun teaching the Ealdorman's sister the ways of the new Roman god. Aelric would be sure to avoid the topic, well aware of the new Christian-kind's annoying zeal.

Amid the general festivities, Aelric settled Wynflaed's morgengifu. The witnesses and criers, who would commit every syllable to memory, watched and listened as the writerer scratched Aelric's words onto lambskin.

When it was done Aelric stood and raised his hands, calling for silence. "Let it be known," he shouted, above the laughter and chatter in his hall, and peered round, his gaze demanding attention. "Let it be known. Are you hearing this?" The witnesses nodded, straightening their shoulders as their moment of importance arrived. "Let it be known, that the lead rights, granted to me by the old king, for the lead-mine known as Bell Delfan, at the place called By-Streams, together with all the timber thereabouts, and in the forest known as the Bretton's Wood, are hereby granted to Wynflaed, daughter of Alfwald, and ward of Uhtred, as her morgengifu. Also, that the Home Farm at By-Streams, and the two other farms tenanted by Llellan ap Uchtryd and Rhodri ap Owain, which adjoin the lands of my son Wulfric, and all rents and dues there from, are granted to her, to be held at her pleasure without let or hindrance upon the consummation of her marriage to my son, Wulfric. In accordance with the laws of morgengifu, let no man impede, usurp, lay claim to, or do whatsoever harm to this grant. This is my deed. This is my wish and my word. Let it be cried abroad in the markets throughout the realm of our lord and king Penda.

By-Streams was an ancient settlement, long abandoned by its original Wealh owners. Most of it lay derelict. Lead had not been mined in generations, though traders from the old empire were keen to buy lead ingots to trade for Gaullish wine.

Rendil was furious. He astonished his father by professing a keen interest in lead mining. A passion he had failed to mention until that moment. The family had owned the lead rights for years. Rendil could have exploited them at any time, if he had wanted to. On occasion, Aelric had even tried to persuade him to do so. The old empire still had a healthy demand for lead. It was precisely because of Rendil's lack of interest that Aelric had decided to give the mine to Wynflaed. He was sure it could be turned into a valuable source of income, and hoped she might be the one to do it.

Rendil's objections were forcefully made, and with little thought to Wynflaed's feelings. Aelric however, had heard enough of his oldest son's bitter carping. He stood up from his chair and raised his hand to silence him.

"Before you say more," he boomed. "May I remind you that you have told me many times how worthless the lead rights are. In fact, you went further, you said all our land in the High Peak was worthless - stony, bleak and unfit for goats - I think were your actual words." He eyed his son fiercely. "By these deeds, done here before these witnesses, it all now belongs to Wulfric, and on her gifu-dawn it will all pass to Wynflaed. No man, not you, nor I, not even her husband will have the right to claim, or lean on those lands or the rights they include. Let all here hear my words and take them abroad. Let everyone know that Wynflaed, wife of Wulfric son of Aelric, is the mistress of the lead and the lands at By-Streams."

He looked around at the assembled witnesses, his chin jutting. "These are my wishes. You have all heard them. The deed is done. If there is any man here who questions it, let him speak now." He looked around, meeting each man's gaze as they gave their solemn approval. Even Rendil, the last to fall under his father's stern gaze, reluctantly agreed.

"Very well then, it is good. Matthew here is setting it all down with ink on lambskin. There is nothing more to be said on the matter."

....

CHAPTER SEVEN

A wedding in a rich man's family draws pedlars, musicians and journeymen like wasps to mead. How they learn of such forthcoming events mystifies the uninitiated. They pop out like daisies, their tents, banners and stalls enlivening village greens overnight. With no more than waxed cloth and a few sticks of hazel they create their colourful displays, lending them an air of vibrant permanence. Once assembled, such a fair will typically stay several days, creating and exploiting the spreading fame of its wonders, art and bargains. Lord and lady, lout and labourer, are soon drawn to it in search of trade, or to meet old friends, or simply to see and be seen. Then, as suddenly as they had appeared, the tents, stalls, and booths vanish, leaving behind only rubbish and their pallid, wilting imprints on the grass.

Holmesfelt quickly became crowded. Wedding guests, pedlars, jugglers and players good-naturedly jostled in Aelric's hall, and traipsed around his orchard and paddock. Harassed servants rushed about, fetching and carrying, whilst beyond the gaiety and noise the serious business of the marriage was arranged.

Thegn Uhtred and Buhe arrived with their servants and spearmen. Horse Ebell led their train of eight packhorses, loaded with gifts for their host and the blissful couple, together with supplies for their stay, mainly bedding and clothes.

Of course, Wynflaed was delighted to see them, and well understood how hard it must have been for Uhtred to raise such an array of gifts and supplies. She took Buhe to lodge with her at Gutty's house, where, like excited children, they spent the days primping and chattering.

Uhtred and Aelric used their time to get to know each other. They soon discovered many old comrades and friends in common. Even Rendil seemed to enjoy himself, though a cynic might say his mood owed more to his chance re-acquaintance with a girlish, plump woman, recently widowed. Only Wulfric seemed put out by the merriment around him. He lingered at the edge of events, looking superfluous, until a group of his comrades arrived and set him to the task of drinking everything in sight.

Among the guests that Aelric introduced to Uhtred was Colnoth, a tall, scrawny young man with black hair and a pale complexion. Aelric explained that Colnoth's father was new to the area. He'd been granted lands in the north of the shire-wood, about a day's trek from Uhtred's own. Wynflaed was surprised to see how taken Buhe was with the awkward, lanky figure, despite his being anything but handsome and far from amusing.

"I saw you flirting with Colnoth, Buhe," she said, gently teasing her.

"I was not. He's going to be our neighbour. I was just being polite. Anyway he's too old for me and much too tall."

Wynflaed laughed. "That's not how it looked to me. You were gazing up at him like a puppy dog. I just wonder how close a neighbour he might become."

Buhe tossed her head and stuck her nose in the air. "At least when I do marry I'll know my own mind and not need to be told what I think, like you did."

Wynflaed laughed, allowing the point. "Well, I hope when it happens you'll feel just as happy as I do."

"And why wouldn't I? At least I won't choose a raider and a thief."

"What? Why do you have to say such things?"

Buhe coloured hotly and turned her face away. As much as she loved Wynflaed she could not help resenting her happiness. Why couldn't she be content to stay with her at Uhtredstun? Why did she have to leave and change everything?

Wynflaed watched her descend into one of her pouting sulks. All her life Buhe had been quick to jealous and often spiteful outbursts, which she always later regretted. She knew that any moment she would tearfully fuss and fawn, eager to apologise and make up.

"Oh Gods, I'm sorry, Flaedy. I didn't mean it. It's just that I really miss you. I know you love him, but I can't help blaming him for taking you away from me. Please say you forgive me. You know that I want you to be happy. I really do."

"I know, and I miss you too, but soon you'll be off with some handsome young man."

***

Wynflaed spent the last few days before her wedding with Buhe, Gutty and Rendil's wife Goda. The four were often seen huddled in animated discussion, or rushing about greeting guests, exasperating servants, and primping flower arrangements and boards of sweetmeats.

Goda was a pleasant surprise: bright, attractive and energetic. Wynflaed quickly grew to like her. She was a perceptive mimic, with a wickedly dry sense of humour which, when put to impersonating Rendil, left them all sore with laughter. Why such a woman would marry a man like Rendil was beyond Wynflaed's understanding, and more than once she had to stop herself from asking her. Whatever her reasons, it was obvious that it was not love, but Goda's robust sense of humour, and her three lovely daughters that sustained her marriage.

On the day of the ceremony Wynflaed put on the half-sleeved linen dress she had made specially. It was as green as sunlit birch leaves. Its square neck and wide cuffs were trimmed with green and blue patterned tape, competitively woven by Goda's daughters. A belt of the same was fastened about her waist. On her head, a circlet of daisies held in place a short veil of cream linen. Beneath it, her hair was loosely bound in a lye-bleached linen snood. Once alone with her new husband, she would pull this binding away, freeing her hair to tumble about her face and shoulders, a move Gutty had made her rehearse repeatedly, declaring its effects upon men as nothing less than devastating.

In the great hall, Wulfric waited for Wynflaed. He wore his sword, belted over a thigh-length tunic of sandy coloured wool cloth. Solemn faced, he stood before his father and Uhtred on the raised floor of upper hall. Resplendent in dyed tunics over linen shirts and woollen brecs, their necks and chests glittering with silver and bronze, the two older men were now entirely at ease with each other, as if they had been friends for years. They chatted amiably amid the excited babble of the milling guests.

Aelric had ordered that the hearth should be cold and the shutters thrown open, to let in sunlight and avoid smoke. Chains of flowers hung from rafters and beams. Lamps and candles shone from walls and tables. The hall at Holmesfelt had never been so bright. Beneath the gable, before which he and Uhtred stood, a quartet of musicians trilled and plucked, readying their instruments. All tables had been cleared and scrubbed, ready for the guests. Cobwebs had been swept away from the rafters and wall hangings. A fresh litter of meadowsweet and bracken lay over the floor, even in lower hall. Outside in the open air, cooks laboured over fires, roasting meats, baking bread and the special Handfast seed-cakes which would be eaten to mark the marriage. Roasting meats sizzled over the fire pits, pots bubbled and steamed. Barrels and jars of ale, wine and mead stood in readiness, their seals broken and sniffed by the cooks and the house reeve. Aelric had spared no expense. He was determined that this would be the grandest feast the shire had seen.

The hum of voices rose, signalling Wynflaed's arrival. Wulfric craned to see her. His father clipped him on the head to make him face front. Uhtred stepped down from the raised floor and went to meet his ward and escort her to her husband.

As Wynflaed and her friends entered, the crowd cleared a way through for her. Uhtred embraced her and kissed her on the cheek. Aelric was frowning, his eyes darting about as if counting midges. He was evidently annoyed by the din his guests continued to make as they stretched and peered to see the bride. Raising a hand to call for silence, he grumpily opened the proceedings. A respectful hush fell upon the crowded hall.

"I, Aelric of the Cenwulfingas, thegn of our lord Penda, welcome you. I stand before all men to witness the marriage of my son Wulfric, to his chosen woman, Wynflaed, daughter of Alfwald and ward of my good friend Uhtred son of Bergred." Aelric paused waiting for Uhtred to speak. When he did not, he elbowed him sharply and whispered. "Go on, it's you now."

Uhtred cleared his throat and drew up his shoulders. "I, Uhtred Bergredsunnu, stand here to witness before all men the marriage of my ward Wynflaed, daughter of my dead comrade Alfwald, who saved my life many times in the shield wall, and would have been proud and honoured to see this day." The crowd greeted this with noisy approval. As Aelric waited for silence, he shook hands with Uhtred, acknowledging his thoughtful sentiment.

When it was quiet again, Aelric nodded at Wulfric, encouraging him into action. Wulfric turned to Wynflaed and slowly drew his sword, that most potent totem of family honour. Carefully, he placed a gold ring on its hilt and extended it towards Wynflaed. "I take you as my wife and promise to protect and honour you."

Wynflaed accepted the ring and placed it on her finger. "I take you as my husband and promise to honour and obey you."

Aelric spoke up again. "The deed of the morgengifu has been told abroad and set down on lambskin. In the morning the gift will be made if – err – I mean - as tradition dictates ..."

With great solemnity, Uhtred took Wynflaed's and Wulfric's hands and brought them together. The pair then held up their clasped hands for everyone to see. They further reinforced their agreement by embracing and kissing. The onlookers cheered and congratulated them. Little girls held up an arch of wild flowers and cast salt and magical wyrts before them, as they led them to the high table for their wedding feast. Throughout the meal, to emphasise the pledges they had made, they fed each other Handfast seed-cakes and drank from the same cup.

After the meal they went out into the sunlight, where more well-wishers waited to shower them with flowers and sacred charms. The crowd cheered and sang bawdy songs. The couple responded by showing off their clasped hands and kissing for all to see. Wynflaed blushed at the rude jokes she heard as she moved through the crush. She thought about what would happen later, dreading the moment when she and Wulfric would be led to their bed in the hall. There, in full view, they would

undress and climb beneath the covers together. Their
guests would wait and watch, joking and cheering when
they saw the rhythmic rise and fall of the bed covers
which signalled the consummation of the marriage. As
much as she wanted Wulfric, she was not looking forward
to her first time. Now she wished she had stayed longer in
the hazel copse.

***

Three days after the wedding, the feasting began to slow
down a little. Rendil was nowhere to be found, and Goda's
none too energetic enquiries revealed only that his
favourite horse was missing too. Gutty drew Wynflaed
aside and mentioned the coincidental absence of a certain
young widow. Wynflaed decided that Goda was probably
better off not knowing, especially as she seemed to enjoy
his absences so much.

Uhtred and Buhe, with their escort of spearmen, left
for Uhtredstun on the fifth day. As Wynflaed had
predicted, it was a tearful parting. Buhe was inconsolable.
Even her new friend Colnoth, who had decided to
accompany them most of the way, could not cheer her up.
She was led away, gouting tears over her pony's neck.

The following morning, Wynflaed walked beside
Wulfric. They followed Eadwin and his white mule at the
head of a train of pack horses loaded with food, household
goods, tools and equipment. They were bound for By-
Streams in the heart of the Peakland. Her new life with
her new husband had begun in earnest.

Wulfric beamed at her. "I'm the luckiest man alive,"
he told her, slipping his arm around her waist. "I promise
you my very best, Flaedy. I'll work and build for you. I'll
give you everything a man can. You'll see." She snuggled
closer and hugged him, inhaling his warm body smell.

The track ahead entered the Peakland forest. One by one, Holmesfelt's hall, houses, barns and fields slid from view. The feeling of separation intensified, and she felt that nothing would ever be the same again. Even the people she had known were changed in some way. Her new status had seen to that. Everything was new. Now there was only the future.

"Tell me about By-Streams."

Wulfric shrugged ruefully. "I wish I could, but as I've said, I don't really know it. I couldn't even find it without Eadwin to guide me."

"Hum, just as well he's with us then."

Wulfric smiled. "He wouldn't miss it. He was born there. In fact, he's just about the only thing I remember about By-Streams."

"Eadwin? I thought he'd lived with you all his life."

"Well he has, almost. My father brought him from By-Streams. We went there once - years ago. It was deserted except for Eadwin and his brother. All I remember is empty houses and overgrown fields. I expect it'll look even worse now."

"His brother? What happened to him?"

"I'm not sure. I was only about twelve at the time. I'm afraid I wasn't taking much notice. I'm ashamed to admit it now, but I can barely remember anything about it." He scratched his chin and stared ahead to where Eadwin led the train. "Eadwin was only about four or five then. His brother was older than me – almost a man."

"Surely you remember something about him? His name, what was his name?"

"Eofar? He was serious and quiet. I remember he looked scary - tall and broad." He laughed, remembering more. "Poor little Eadwin, he was scared stiff when he saw father and me with our spearmen. I doubt he'd ever seen many folk before that, and certainly not men with spears and helmets. It must have been quite a shock. He just screamed and threw stones at us. One hit my father on the shin. I thought he'd be angry, but he wasn't. He just picked Eadwin up and sat him on Snowflake, that white mule of his. It was father's back then. Eadwin and that damned creature have been together ever since."

"So he came to live with you?"

"Yes. His brother asked us to take him in. He said he couldn't look after him. Their parents were dead and there was nothing at By-Streams for them. Eofar felt it would be a good chance for his little brother to have a proper home. My father invited Eofar too, but he had other plans."

Wynflaed looked at Eadwin and Snowflake at the head of the column. As she did, Eadwin stepped out to one side to let the leading horses pass by him. He was grinning sheepishly as Wynflaed caught up to him. She wondered if he knew they'd been talking about him.

"It's an easy slope for the next few miles, and then it gets harder for a bit," Eadwin said. "In fine weather like this we should make good time." Sweeping his hair from his eyes he turned shyly to Wynflaed.

"I'm going to cut your hair one of these days," she joked. "You look like a shepherd's dog."

He laughed, lowering his gaze. "Sorry mistress. It just grows that way."

"What's wrong, Edda?" asked Wulfric, evidently seeing something in his manner that Wynflaed had missed.

"I need to speak with her ladyship. I've something to give ..."

Wynflaed assumed it would be a wedding gift. "Oh Eadwin, you're very kind." she cried, reaching out to take a small, tentatively offered object from his hands. It was a smooth, blue and purple pebble, through which a leather thong was threaded.

Sweat popped out on Eadwin's brow as he struggled with embarrassment. "No it's — it's not from me," he said, wishing with all his heart that it was. "It's from that slave girl. This is the first chance I've had to ..."

"Slave girl?"

Eadwin had retrieved the polished blue pebble from Wynflaed's hand and was making much of straightening its leather thong across his palm. "Yes, the girl you freed on the road. She wanted you to have it, my lady," he said. "She gave it to me when they set her free with her sack of food and tools."

Wulfric took it from Eadwin's hand and held it up in the sunlight. The richness of its colours shone out as if it were lit from inside. "I bet she stole it. Probably belongs to her master or his icicle arsed wife." He tossed it to Wynflaed. "Serves 'em right for treating her so bad."

Concern for the stone as it flew through the air made Eadwin mirror Wynflaed's catch, but she took it safely. "No, your honour, she didn't steal it," Eadwin said firmly "She's had it all her life. She told me. It was given to her by her old grandmother."

"Nonsense!" said Wulfric. "Her sort don't have grandmothers, nor even mothers, least ways not ones with possessions. Thief born and bred. Any fool can see it."

"No Wulfric, forgive me, but you're wrong," said Eadwin. "When she was leaving she showed me where they made her sleep. It was a filthy hovel with not even a proper roof. She'd kept that stone buried under her bed place. I watched her dig it up as she told me about it. She'd hidden it to stop them stealing it, and I believe her."

Wulfric pulled a face, scorning Eadwin's faith in the girl, but his expression changed when he saw tears in Wynflaed's eyes. "Oh Flaedy, what's wrong?" he cried. "Grims teeth. Look what you've done, Eadwin. Take the damned stone and ..."

"No! I want it," sobbed Wynflaed. "Don't you see? She had nothing in the world except this stone. Whether she stole it or not doesn't matter. It was all she had." She wiped her eyes on her dress. Too late, Wulfric fished out a rag from his tunic and lamely held it out to her. Ignoring it, she went on, "When I asked her name, she wouldn't say. Now she gives me this. Something she must value more than anything."

"Perhaps. At least until she pinches another," said Wulfric.

***

The Peakland is a wild region, where limestone and millstone grit shoulder each other into rugged hills. The peat bogs, birch scrub hills and oak-filled valleys of the millstone grit bulk up against the dense ash and beech forests of the limestone areas. Mountains of shifting shale slump into the landscape like the shoulders of dead beasts. Deep dales cleave the land, squeezing cataracts of white water into crystal streams, or plunging them underground to carve the limestone into secret chains of sepulchral chambers and cathedral caverns.

Poised between Northumbria and Mercia fewer than a thousand families inhabit this wilderness. The impenetrable forest of the great Shire-wood guards its eastern flank. The prickly Wealish hordes gnaw at its western marches. Even so, the Peakland sits comfortably in its place, for the land is too harsh for greedy men to covet. Many of its treasures are in the eyes of poets and dreamers, but as a buffer between uneasy neighbours, it is beyond price. That is why Mercia claims it and Northumbria eyes it warily.

Life at By-Streams during that first autumn and winter was even harder than Wynflaed could have expected. There were no habitable buildings. The fields were overgrown; some had trees growing in them to twice the height of a man. Eadwin and his pack-horses trekked back and forth bringing in supplies, but still the prospect of creating any sort of living there seemed remote. Even so, Wynflaed was happier than at any time in her life.

As autumn deepened into winter, her joy was crowned by the discovery that she was pregnant. She felt her life could not be better, even if she lived in a king's golden hall.

By Modrenacht, an important family feast marking midwinter, Wynflaed was about four months pregnant. Wulfric announced that they would celebrate the Yule season at his father's house. He said it would be the last time she could safely travel before the baby came in the summer. Wynflaed was delighted She looked forward to seeing Gutty and Goda and telling them all her news.

Wulfric sent word to his father by Eadwin on his next trip, certain that the news would delight the old man. Wynflaed too expected Aelric to make Modrenacht a doubly lavish celebration, once he knew he was about to have a new grandchild.

In all matters concerning Wynflaed, Wulfric found his father's reactions utterly baffling. "You've changed the old boy beyond belief," he told her. "He has a new lease on life these days. I don't know what spell you've used, but it works very well."

"It's the shock that you found a woman willing to have you," she joked. "I think he thought you would never marry."

Wulfric retaliated by advancing upon her, growling threateningly. Wynflaed presented her swelling stomach to drive him back.

"You use that lump unfairly, huswif," he said.

"This is your son in here. You should not call him "Lump", or he may turn out to be one — just like you."

***

At Modrenacht, children are suffered at table with their elders. Gifts are exchanged, and sweetmeats are served. Wynflaed watched Goda's daughters and the village children enjoying the seasonal games and songs, and thought of her unborn child who would one day be part of this ancient tradition.

Because children and womenfolk sit at the tables at Modrenacht, the men set aside their proudly won honour-places. Even the lord of the hall might find himself at a lowly table with bench-mates he seldom spoke to, let alone raised a cup with. Wynflaed found herself trapped between her husband and his brother.

"Your girls look lovely, Rendil." This was her effort to break his sullen silence.

"I'm blessed," he replied, without enthusiasm.

"And Goda too looks radiant."

"As do you," Rendil said. "Pregnancy suits you."

"I feel well enough," she said. "Though there's a good few months to go yet."

He eyed her critically. "Indeed, there's much that can befall even the strongest woman."

"Well thank you very much, Rendil. I needed to be reminded of that."

"I'm sorry. I didn't mean it to sound like that, but it's true nevertheless." He leaned back to study her expression. "I suppose my father has shown his gratitude?

He seems quite unable to keep the lid on his strongbox where you're concerned."

Outrage flushed her cheeks. She looked to Wulfric for support, but he was chatting with a herdsman seated beside him and had not heard the remark. "You've no cause to say that, Rendil," Wynflaed said. "Your father has indeed been generous. He's given us tools, rope, nails, and iron to help us build our homestead, just as I believe he did for you and Goda. I don't know what I ever did, or said, to give you such a poor opinion of me."

"You'd better make sure it's a boy," Rendil said. "Father already has more granddaughters than he can spare affection for. If you want to keep his favour you'll need his grandson on your tit."

Anger tightened Wynflaed's throat. Certain she would lose her temper if she spoke again, she moved to find another seat, pausing only to give Wulfric a hefty thump on his shoulder as she squeezed past him.

Rendil leaned towards Wulfric. "And you needn't think I'll spare you my men to plough all that clearance you've made. I've my own farms. I need the labour myself."

Wulfric gaped, wondering why he was being hit by his wife and chided by his brother. Looking back to Wynflaed, he found her glaring at him as she slid in beside Gutty at the opposite end of the table. Life, he thought, was much simpler on the battlefield.

As Wulfric's confusion grew and his spirits sagged, Wynflaed was finding Gutty's sparkling irreverence a much-needed tonic. She could even watch Rendil, sourly picking at his food, and pity him his inability to enjoy himself. He was so unlike her husband. How could two such different men be brothers? She gazed at Wulfric's bemused expression, no longer able to feel angry with him. And when the child inside her kicked, she even forgot her anger at Rendil too. She ran to Wulfric, climbed in beside him on the bench and placed his hand on her stomach. When he too felt their unborn child push tremulously against his palm, his face lit with delight.

Rendil scowled at them, and a small, black and white dog seized the moment to sneak a meaty morsel from Rendil's table space. It almost paid with its life. Amid howls of laughter from onlookers Rendil smashed his walking stick down, but missed the animal by a hair's breadth.

....

CHAPTER EIGHT

Damp air clawed at the rush-light flame, enfeebling it to guttering blue. Wynflaed looked back to the distant, glimmer of daylight at the mouth of the cave, and with a determined shrug, resumed her steady descent into the ancient mine workings. The passage snaked over rocks, polished smooth by generations of miners' feet. The faint peck and ring of pick hammers echoed from the blackness. After a few more yards the passage floor levelled, but its roof dipped sharply, forcing her to stoop. She knew she would be able to straighten up again about ten paces further on where the passage crossed a natural fault in the limestone. There the mine exhaled a damp breath, threatening to extinguish her light. Anxiously shielding it, she waited for the flame to settle.

Wynflaed both loved and feared Bell Delfan. She loved its mystery and brooding stillness, but feared its sublime indifference. In its glistening galleries she found solitude and a powerful sense of her being. She was never at ease there, yet somehow felt more alive within its constant, invisible evolution than anywhere else.

Distant and musical, the sounds of the miners' voices rippled over the wet walls. The passage opened out into a great bell shaped cavern; a place the miners feared as holy and magical. They called it, Belle Earegasp, the whispering bell. From high in its roof, a lark's song and the bleating of sheep could be heard; the sounds cascaded to the rising tufa, as if seeking eternity in the stone. Above the cave, in the sunlight, daisies, marjoram, and wild strawberries covered a steep hillside. At its peak, three spikes of rock, each taller than a man, were rammed into a narrow shaft in the ground, like an upturned tripod. The locals called the stones the Ealfan Pipes. Many believed that prayers whispered between the stones would reach the ears of Nerthus, the earth goddess, deep in Belle Earegasp below.

No-one knew if the hand of man, perhaps to stop sheep falling down into the cave, had plugged the shaft with the Ealfan Pipes, or whether Nerthus herself had put them there to hide her dark temple from the Sky-Father.

Wynflaed looked around the limestone walls in wonder. Wulfric had brought her to the cave on their first morning at By-Streams. As she had gazed at its shining walls, he had slipped away and hidden, leaving her alone with its deathless magic. Moments later, his voice had seemed to be all around her, reminding her that Bell Delfan lead mine was hers, her morgengifu. He told her it was a magical place, and that if she whispered three wishes into its walls they would surely be granted. She had pressed her cheek to the time scoured wall and wished that he would love her always. Second she had wished for a fine son, and lastly, that Wulfric would kill his sword and go to war no more. That night, after they had eaten, Wulfric had taken his sword and smashed it over the hearthstones. He had laid the pieces in her lap and sworn upon them to love her always. Then he had carried her to their bed, saying, "Now let us see, my lady, what can be done about a son."

That was six years ago, and now they had a fine son, five years old. His name was Eadric, which means wealthy leader. A second son had lived only a few days, but two years later, on a night of gales, Wynflaed had borne a daughter. Wulfric had named her Wyngifu, meaning gift of joy. "Joy brought upon the winds."

Warm within her memories, Wynflaed crossed the cavern floor to a broad, sloping passage. It led down to the rake where her miners were working. She visited the rake almost everyday to see how the work was going.

Eadwin's brother Eofar was her mine reeve. He was a big man, hunched, as if ill at ease with his size. Austere, thorough, and scrupulously fair, he drove the miners hard. Although they were brothers, he bore little resemblance to Eadwin. Where Eadwin was wiry and lithe, Eofar was muscular and ponderous. And though he looked much older, Wynflaed knew he was only the same age as her husband. When she'd first arrived at By-Streams, she had immediately sought him out, because everyone said there was no one who knew more about the old mine and the natural caves that led to it than Eofar the carpenter. She offered him the reeve-ship of her mine. At first he refused, but she persisted until, against his better judgment, he accepted her offer of a twelfth share and took the job.

From the very start he took her seriously. Other men sniggered and joked when she asked questions, but he took the time to explain properly. Over time she learned how to spot the fluorspar leaders which would join a pipe or rake of lead ore. Now she could identify the ore and grade its worth better than most miners.

Wynflaed smiled as she saw Eofar coming over the bouse towards her. The light from his lamp cast weird shadows over his face and up on to the wooden helmet he always wore underground. It gave him a fearsome look. "My lady, good health to you. How's it go up top? Any sign of rain?"

"No, it's clear yet," she replied, understanding his concern. Rain could flood the old Roman workings in moments. A weather eye was essential.

She swept the rock face with an expert eye and drew her foot through the day's bouse. It was high grade and the men had done a fair morning's work. She saw no need to comment. Moving to the edge of a glittering dark pool, she peered down into its crystal depths. "Still no luck with the swallow?"

"Not yet, but I'll find it," Eofar said. "This level fills up fast when it rains, yet takes days to drain afterwards. But, as you can see, it never falls below this level. There's a swallow somewhere. I think it must arch down and then back up again, like a sickle blade."

"But it could be anywhere, even miles from here."

He nodded agreement. "Or just the other side of that rock. There's no way of telling."

"What about staining the water to see where it goes?"

"That only shows where it comes out, not how it gets there."

"You're sure you've found every passage? I mean, these caves go on for miles."

"We've searched every cranny," he said, a hint of impatience in his tone. "I'm convinced only diving down will do it. We've got to keep trying."

"Have you been down this morning?" She looked at a weighted rope coiled at the pool's edge. It was still wet. "I told you not to dive when you're alone."

"There were others here," he said quickly, resenting her reproachful tone.

She knew he was lying. The amount of ore extracted that day proved that no time had been spent on anything but picks and shovels. It worried her that he took such risks. "I don't want you diving unless there are two strong men on the rope."

"I know, I know," he said. "But if I can open it up it'll drain away fast. We'll be able to work on through the rain without fear."

"Just as long as we don't fish you out dead one day," she said. "I don't want corpses. I want lead. And I don't want to lose you." Eofar made no response. "How's Eadwin?" she asked. "I haven't seen him for a week or so."

Eofar squinted at her as if she had asked a difficult question. "He's all right, I suppose. I know we share the same house, but we don't have much to say to each other. Brothers don't have to be the same, do they?"

Wynflaed thought of Rendil and Wulfric, and chuckled at the irony. "Tell him I asked about him. And tell him Wulfric misses him too, now they're not on the road together. I think he'd like it if he came to the house more, you know, a visit. They were great friends once."

Eofar nodded doubtfully and then ambled off into the gloom. She watched him go for a moment before starting back to the surface.

***

Bell Delfan mine at By-Streams was in the northern Peakland, near the edge of the White Peak. Wulfric's farms were nearby. The land shelters snugly on a wooded slope beneath an escarpment of the type local folk call an "edge". Tumbling waters had carved a deep valley in the limestone, which time and tranquillity filled with great ash trees, limes and beeches.

The fields around its scatter of turf roofed huts were little more than a brave scratch of plough-land. Even in a good year, Mother Earth yielded not quite enough beans and barley to feed By-Streams few folk, but in valley clearings flax thrived. The finished linen, woven on the villagers' looms, was traded for salt, iron, wheat and all that the stony fields failed to provide. Peakland honey and beeswax were highly prized crops. They earned top prices at the king's court, and Wynflaed increased the number of bee-skeps she tended each season to make the most of it.

As well as lead, there was silver too in By-Streams' lead mine, but only a few precious ounces, occasionally obtained from a smelt of lead on Bole Hill. In good years it seldom amounted to more than a few fist sized cobs.

Silver did not enrich By-Streams or its miners. A long dead king of Mercia had made sure of that many years before. He had granted the original charter mindful of a strange local legend he'd heard about a wealthy Roman who was said to have buried a large treasure of gold coins in By-Streams' caves. Apparently, the Roman forgot his hiding place and went mad trying to find it. His weeping ghost was said to walk the caves, searching for it.

Of course, few believed the three-hundred-years-old story, but the old Mercian king took no chances. The charter declared that the mine owner could profit from the lead he found in Bell Delfan, but not from any other metals they might turn up. These were to be sent to the royal coffers. Consequently, Wynflaed's only interest in silver was in keeping a record of what they produced so that she could give the king's gafol-reeve an accurate reckoning. The last thing she, or her husband, wanted was trouble with the tax collector.

As mistress of Bell Delfan and By-Streams, Wynflaed was never idle. Wulfric was often away on business for the Shire reeve, or the Ealdorman. At such times the management of the family's farms and tenants became her responsibility, as well as running her mine. Also, she always had to be ready to entertain the king's officers and reeves, a duty and privilege which did great honour to her husband and his family. She did this well, earning praise from the Shire Reeve and his officials. If only, she wished, she could do as much with Rendil, for despite her best efforts, their relationship foundered at every turn.

It was widely known that Rendil would, one day, inherit his father's considerable estates. Wynflaed often felt that he acted as though this somehow conferred rights upon him to interfere in her's and Wulfric's business. It certainly annoyed Wulfric. The brothers had exchanged harsh words when Rendil attempted to quiz him about his farms, or little Eadric's education, or Wynflaed's lead mine. In particular, Rendil seemed incapable of ignoring the latter. On his visits to By-Streams, he would bicker and raise spurious concerns about the lead. It infuriated Wynflaed, not simply that he felt entitled to concern himself in her affairs, but that he chose to do so, not with her, the mine's sole owner, but with her husband. Fired with indignation, she would demand to know by what right Wulfric had entertained his brother's questions? Wulfric would sigh, shake his head and make some excuse to get out of her way.

***

In the spring of Wynflaed's seventh year at By-Streams, Eadwin and his train of pack horses returned from a trip which had included a diversion to Uhtredstun. He brought iron ore, animal furs, leather and a little pot of the chalk paste Wynflaed liked for cleaning her teeth. He also brought word that Buhe was at last to marry Colnoth and wanted Wynflaed to come to her wedding. At the time, little Wyngifu was sick with the coughing fever and Wynflaed would not leave her side for anything. Most of By-Streams' younger children were laid low by the disease. More than half their number died, despite potions of Thyme wyrtdrenc and the juice of Son-Before-Father, or Colts-foot, as some call it.

Wynflaed sent Eadwin back with news of the situation and her regretful apologies. She saw to it that Snowflake returned loaded with wedding gifts, including a magnificently embroidered bed cover, made two years earlier when Buhe had then seemed about to marry Colnoth. Better late than never, she thought, as she packed it with sprigs of lavender into a leather bag.

Eadwin was back a few weeks later with Buhe's reply, together with lots of advice on the best leech-wyrts and treatment for the coughing fever. Buhe said she, of course, understood perfectly why Wynflaed could not leave her daughter, and that she would visit By-Streams herself, soon after the harvest. Little Wyngifu meanwhile, had taken one of Wulfric's dogs into her sick bed and dressed its big, slobbery head with ribbons and flowers.

***

The first day of harvest at By-Streams began, as in all villages, with songs, dancing and offerings to the gods, asking them to grant fair weather and a good harvest. It was a perfect day of clear air and bright sunshine. A fresh breeze off the southern uplands rocked the heads of the great lime trees.

Head house servant, Maud, found Wynflaed in the barn checking preparations for the storage of the new harvest. "Old Cedd's youngest is here," she said without formality. "His dad sent him to tell you that he's seen the Old Master's yellow cloak coming over White Edge."

Cedd was Wulfric's head shepherd. He worked high on the hills above the village. His keen eyesight was legendary.

"Oh gods no. Not today," Wynflaed said. "What does he ..?" She stopped, realising that all eyes were upon her, and set off towards the hall. Maud trotted beside her. "Where's your master?" Wynflaed asked.

Maud brushed a hand through her spiky hair. "Down at middle farm. They're reaping the bottom stony field."

"Send him word, Maud - and be quick. I don't want the old master here before his son. Tell Bryoni and Betla to find me."

"Yes, my lady," Maud said, all trace of familiarity expunged by the urgency in Wynflaed's tone. She bobbed a quick curtsy and ran off into lower hall. Moments later, Bryoni, a wealh woman who looked after Eadric and Wyngifu, ran breathlessly into upper hall. Her sister Betla, twenty years her junior, trailed behind her. The pair gaped, wondering what crisis had befallen them.

"Bryoni, the old master's coming," Wynflaed said. "Cedd's seen his yellow cloak on White Edge. Make sure Eadric is clean. Put Gifi in her green smock. Is it clean?"

"Aye, fresh washed, my lady."

"Mind Betla washes Eadric's face and hands – oh, and empties his poke," she added, remembering her son's love of pocketing worms and bits of dead animals wrested from the household's cats.

Betla, as usual, cowered behind her older sister. She was a simpleton and seemed to live her life in constant dread. If addressed directly by anyone, save her sister, she would burst into tears. Even little Eadric had learned of the hours of fun that could be had by simply saying hello to her.

"Is Betla hearing me?" Wynflaed asked, shooting a look around Bryoni's ample frontage. "Will she come out and listen while I talk to her big sister?"

Betla's bowed head appeared round her sister's monolithic shoulder. She pressed her face to Bryoni's upper arm and fought back her tears as Wynflaed addressed her indirectly.

"Tell Maese to make fresh bread and some of those bilberry-honey cakes the old master likes. Tell him we'll still have the pig-meat and white beans tonight."

Betla hovered, panic slicking her face with sweat. She sensed that her mistress had not yet done with her and already she was forgetting whether it was pig-meat or bilberries. She whispered something to her sister.

"What's she say?" asked Wynflaed.

"She wonders if you'll try the new brew, my lady?"

"What? There's none of the old brew left? Surely there is?" Lighting a taper at the hearth, Wynflaed dismissed the pair, and headed for her storeroom,. "I'll see to the ale. Now go quickly. Do your best please, Bryoni."

Inside her strong room, Wynflaed bolted the iron-studded door behind her and lit a mutton fat lamp with the taper. Around the walls were stacked various boxes and barrels; shelves held blocks of beeswax for trade, and jars of ale, wine and mead. Selecting a key from the bunch hanging at her waist, she unlocked her great cyste and lifted its heavy lid. Inside it were two small ingots of silver awaiting delivery to the king's gafol reeve, small jars of oils and spices from the empire, her teag containing her jewellery, and a kidskin poke with a few gold and silver coins. Across the top of all this lay a linen table runner, neatly folded with basil and lavender to keep moths away. Having only recently finished its embroidery, she decided to give it its first airing in honour of Lord Aelric's visit. About as long as a man's height, she would place it in the middle of the table for decoration, and remove it just before the food is served.

A hum of satisfaction escaped her as she lifted the linen from the cyste and buried her face in its creamy whiteness. It smelled of lavender and newness. The "Old

Master" would pretend not to notice it on his son's table, but she knew he would see it. He never missed a thing.

After relocking the cyste, she checked the ale. Betla had been right, it was almost drained. She would need to serve the latest brew. But for the night-meat she selected a jar of Frankish wine.

As she returned to the main hall, Wulfric, naked to the waist and dripping wet from having ducked his head in the yard cistern, had just entered. Maud tossed him a towel, a prurient twinkle in her eyes as she watched him rub his head vigorously, splashing all who stood within a spear's length. "You've heard?" he yelled.

Wynflaed did not answer immediately. The glint she saw in Maud's eye had keened her own interest in her husband, and she felt aroused. Trust him to get me all hot and bothered when his father's about to arrive.

"It's not long since he was here," Wulfric went on mystified.

Wynflaed waited for his face to appear above all the rubbing and splashing. "What does he want?" she asked. "Gods, I hate it when he suddenly turns up like this. Surely he could send somebody to warn us."

Wulfric tossed the towel to a servant and accepted a mug of ale in exchange. "Simple, he comes for a decent meal and a clean bed."

"If he'd bother to say as much occasionally, I'd feel more welcoming," she said. "But no, all he does is moan about having to eat pig meat."

Wulfric grabbed her and pulled her to him. "When he's moaning, he's happy," he said, and planted a kiss on her scowling brow. "You make him happy. I've told you before, he likes you. Gods! He's always telling Ren' that if his wife were half as good, she'd be twice the better."

"Poor Goda. It's bad enough she's married to Rendil without having your father hold me up as an example."

"I expect she's not too pleased about it either …" He paused on hearing voices and the scuffle of feet in the cobbled porch.

Lord Aelric bounded in, grinning like a mischievous child. On seeing his son and daughter-in-law embracing, he threw up his hands in mock despair. "Now, now, behave yourselves. Grim cods! You've been married too long for kitchen coupling."

Wynflaed eyed him suspiciously. He seemed positively aglow. His handsome face, reddened by the upland breezes, beamed at her like a beacon. He and Wulfric, though much alike in build, and mannerisms, were quite unlike in looks. Aelric was by far the more handsome man, but his fine, even features, dark blue eyes and flawless complexion served only to make him seem severe and aloof. His shining silver hair, caught in a loose bunch, like a mare's tail, brushed his shoulders as he looked around. When he smiled, his face took on new life, much more like his son. Yet still he lacked Wulfric's roguish mouth and that certain twinkle in the eye which, Buhe had once said, "Betrayed more than was decent for a virgin to know."

"Well, don't I get a kiss, daughter-in-law?"

She smiled and reached up to peck his cheek. He lifted her off her feet and spun her round, noisily kissing both her cheeks.

"By Old Grim, she's a dazzler, Wulf," he yelled. "No wonder you stay at home getting as soft as a brach's belly. I'd do the same if I had a woman like this by my hearth." He pulled at the linen tablecloth folded over her arm. "What's this girl?"

Wynflaed frowned as he let one end of it trail in the dusty floor litter, but his reaction both puzzled and calmed her. "My word this is fine work, Flaedy. No wonder your needle is so famous."

"Get it off the floor, Father," Wulfric said. "Have a care."

Aelric shot his son an astonished glance. "Hark at him! He sounds more like a huswif every day. I can see I'm not a moment too soon with my news, otherwise he'd be lost to the king's benches for good."

"What news?" Wynflaed asked.

"When we're at night-meat," he said mysteriously. "I'll tell you then." He sniffed the air for a whiff of whatever was cooking at the lower hall fire. "I hope it's not pig, is it?"

Wynflaed stuck out her chin and told him firmly that it was. He groaned, pretending disappointment, but then laughed and put his arm around her, propelling her to the cold, central hearth in upper hall where chairs awaited them.

At the noon-break, Wynflaed served a broth of fowl, with onions and barley. To follow there was Maese's bilberry-honey cakes. Afterwards they sat, chatting until the old man fell asleep. Wynflaed took advantage of the moment to rush up Bole Hill. She had to do a lead smelt tally with Eofar and her smelterer. When it was done, she hurried back to ready her household for the night-meat, hoping all the while that her guest would still be snoring. She was relieved to find the effects of the food and ale had not yet worn off, both father and son were buzzing peacefully in their chairs.

Night-meat was a success. Wynflaed enjoyed her father-in-law's company and good humour, though the news he'd brought remained a mystery. As they drained the jar of Frankish wine, Wulfric's patience finally expired. "For Grim's sake, father, are you going to keep us waiting any longer? What's the news you bring?"

"News. What news? Ah yes - Penda is calling for his spearmen."

"A spear gathering? Why?" Wulfric asked.

Wynflaed's heart sank. No wonder Aelric had been so chirpy. He had opposed Wulfric's long absence from Ealdorman Cenwulf's army. The fact that she had convinced his son to give up the sword had been a blow to his pride for which, though he understood it, he had never quite forgiven her.

"King Oswald's Northumbrians are marching against us. Penda's fyrd is already moving to face them," Aelric said, eyeing Wynflaed warily. "Cenwulf is raising his Peaklanders. You can't refuse him this time, Wulfric."

"I gave my word ..."

"To a woman, damn it!" Aelric said. "Penda is our king. Ealdorman Cenwulf is your lord. Everything we are and have comes from them. I was a landless foot soldier when I joined Cenwulf's father. I'd nothing when you were born. What do you think your mother died of? Too much rich food such as we've eaten tonight - too much Frankish wine? No, by the gods, she did not - quite the opposite."

He turned on Wynflaed jabbing his finger. "She died because we'd nothing. She was trying to feed him, a three-year-old bairn, and his brother not much older. She all but starved while I tramped from hall to hall trying to find someone to give me a place on his benches."

"Father, I ..."

"No! Silence! She must hear this." He pushed his hand across the table towards Wynflaed's, his palm down, fingers trembling. "Gods, Flaedy, you know by now that I love you, lass," he said. "Of all men, I'd be the last to upset you. But at times, you're too strong headed for your own good. You must learn what goes on in the world before you can change it."

"I just want my husband safe with his children. That's all I've ever wanted," said Wynflaed, her voice faltering on the edge of tears. "I'm not changing any rules. I'm not fighting Wyrd. I just want to make the best of it."

Aelric had turned away. He was staring into the cold ashes, the tears of times remembered smearing his eyes. Wynflaed knew he had not heard her.

"I lost everything because of Northumbria," he said. "Lands we'd held for generations. I fought alongside Lord Cenwulf's father to put bread back on our table. Now Cenwulf is my lord. He gave me a bench place, just as his father had before him. He's raised me up, and made me rich. Now your husband can rise too, even above me."

Wulfric stood up sharply, upsetting his chair. His eyes blazed angrily at his father. "No! It's not Flaedy's fault," he yelled. "I've always been ready to fight for Cenwulf - when necessary. But you must let *me* talk to her. These things are not for you to say. And above all, father, my wife does not need you, nor any man, to tell her where her duty lies."

Aelric looked at his son questioningly. "You've got to go," he said softly. "Your brother can't, not with his crooked leg. You and me can never know what he suffers, denied a warrior's place. Someone has to go from this family. I'm too old and useless. It must be you."

He turned and held out a hand to Wynflaed. "I'm tired, daughter. Show me where I can sleep."

Wynflaed, though seething with frustration, reached for the old man's hand, not sure how to deal with him. She led him to a corner under the gable, where, behind a willow screen, Maud had set up a bed and a stool with a candle burning on it.

Aelric kissed her hand and held on to it. "I don't want to lose him either, lass," he told her. "If I could prevent it neither of my boys would be hurt. But Wyrd rules us. We must each play our part and trust in Wyrd." He sat on the edge of the bed and sighed. She knelt and removed his boots for him.

"I didn't want Rendil to be crippled." He looked down at her sadly. "But it happened. It was his Wyrd to suffer that way, and mine to have to look on helplessly." He was silent for a moment as though trying to marshal his thoughts. Wynflaed straightened up watching him.

"He wasn't always a cripple, you know. Oh, I know he's prickly and humourless. I know too that he could show you more consideration, but we don't know how he suffers." He wiped a hand over his face and straightened his shoulders. "Huh! What kind of gods put a savage, starving wolf in a cave where children play? That's what happened, Flaedy. He was just a bairn, a child playing with his little brother. They were not a hundred steps from the house. It was a bit of a cave, not more than a scraped out hollow under a tree. The beast was hiding, injured. Rendil tried to protect Wulfric. It mauled and crippled him. What sort of gods do such things to children?"

Wynflaed shrugged helplessly. She wanted to sympathise, to say she was sorry and that she understood, but as she shaped her reply, he suddenly smiled, his eyes brightening in the flickering candle light. "She was a lot like you, you know" he said, his voice oddly distanced by his recollection. "She would have said what you said - done just as you did." He sniffed and sighed. "I loved her so much. I still do. If I'm hard on you, lass, forgive me.

Sometimes you remind me of her so much that it hurts me even to see you - so much like her - but not her."

***

A week later, Wulfric was gone from By-Streams. He and Eadwin had loaded Snowflake with his war-chest, tent and provisions. He had mounted his best horse and ridden off at the head of a dozen spearmen from the district. Others would join him along the road to Penda's North-worthig. There he expected to receive news of Cenwulf's Peakland legion and the main army.

Wynflaed sat alone in upper hall, her fingers absently searching for the little slave girl's blue gemstone which she wore around her neck. It was not there. She had given it to Wulfric to keep him safe and bring him luck. Instead, she found the gold ring from his finger that he had given to her, saying that it was to be given to their son if he did not return. He had hoisted the child into his saddle, telling him that he was to be lord at By-Streams until he returned.

"If you return, my lord," Wynflaed sobbed, letting the ring slide along the neck cord she had threaded through it.

Autumn approached with the risk that roads and rivers would become impassable. She knew that if there was not a quick, decisive battle it would be too late for the armies to face each other until spring. She supposed that Christian Oswald and Penda the heathen, might not meet for months, perhaps not until summer when there was good fighting ground to be blooded.

"No, my darling Wolf-king, it will be a year before I see you again — if ever I do."

....

CHAPTER NINE

Rendil arrived at By-Streams within days of his brother's departure. Wynflaed could find nothing in his coming to brighten a gloomy day of cloud and chilling rain. As he hobbled around, sticking his nose into everything, it seemed to her that winter's murk fell from the very folds of his cloak.

"Your mine reeve, what's his name?"

"Eofar. Why?"

"Do you need him? Is he trustworthy?"

Taking a deep breath, she smothered her annoyance and poured herself a cup of water. Rendil had draped himself in Wulfric's chair, his good leg swinging over the chair arm, a cup of wine held loosely in his fingers. Wine, Wynflaed reminded herself, that he had demanded from her servants without invitation. "What's all this about, Rendil? Has Eofar said something — offended you in some way?"

"I don't trust the surly brute - no respect for his betters. You should get rid of him."

Wynflaed hid a smile. "What's wrong? Did he shoo you out of the mine?" She knew that would have been unnecessary. Since his childhood mauling by the wolf, Rendil had been scared of caves. Bell Delfan would be the last place he would go. She sat opposite him at the table and watched as Maud set a wooden plate of bread and pickles before her. Bryoni followed with a bowl of butter and a cold boiled ham. "Shall I carve it, my lady?" she whispered, painfully aware that Rendil was eyeing her like a market sow.

"Thank you, no," Wynflaed said, releasing her. "Tell Maud to bring a platter for his honour." She turned to Rendil. "I assume you're staying?"

"How could I refuse such a warm invitation?" He grabbed Bryoni by the wrist. "Bring me something hot. I've no stomach for cold cuts and pickles."

Bryoni glanced at her mistress, a stricken look on her grimy face. Wynflaed nodded, gave her a reassuring smile, and turned calmly to Rendil. "Perhaps you'd like some rashers or broth, or will you wait for a pie?"

Sneering, he released Bryoni's wrist and pushed her away. "Never mind, I'll try some of this." He drew the cold ham towards him.

Wynflaed noticed Bryoni's shoulders slump with relief, and felt sorry for her. She ushered her away with a wave. "Ask Maud to bring some ale, Bry ..."

"Wine!" interrupted Rendil.

"Wine," said Wynflaed, her brow furrowing.

Bryoni padded away. Rendil glowered after her. "Does it have a husband?" he asked.

"Yes," said Wynflaed. "He's a brute of a man with little brain and a foul temper."

Rendil carved a slice of meat off the bone. "You're a poor liar, sister. She lives under the eaves with her half-wit daughter. What's wrong, you surely don't think I want her in my bed. I'd rather sleep with a sow."

Pity the sow, thought Wynflaed. "Sister - Betla is her sister, not daughter," she said, keeping her eyes turned from him.

Rendil sighed and poured more wine. "You really don't like me, do you? I've known it from the first, though I don't know what I ever ..."

"You made it perfectly clear that you didn't like me."

"How? What did I do?" he asked. "You mean because I was suspicious of some unknown without a bean coming into my brother's life from who knew where?" He rose from his seat and began to pace around the hearth, his elegant hands sculpting the air as he spoke. "Tell me, sister, when your son is grown and brings home a stranger, without name or property, will you welcome her without pause to wonder what she might be up to?"

"Your father did," Wynflaed replied. "Or at least he had the good grace to pretend so. And while he troubled to learn better of me, he was kind and courteous. I hope I would do as much for my son when the time comes."

"Oh you would - charming. Well, I'm no different to my father," he said. "It just appears so to you because your mind is set against me. I mean to say, why do you think I'm here now?"

"If only I knew."

"Because we're family," he said. "It's my duty to be here, to look after you while Wulf is away. And it's not just about duty. I'm here because I *want* to help you, just as Wulf would help Goda and my girls if it were me who'd gone away." He leaned towards her and prodded the air in front of her eyes. "Tell me this, if Wulfric did the same for me, would you resent it, or would you see it as no more than family affection and concern?"

Wynflaed's feet squirmed beneath the table. She tried not to be impressed by the logic of his argument. Perhaps she was being unreasonable? Facing him demurely, she tried to look impassive.

"Besides," he went on, his tone unctuous in the extreme, "he asked me to, but even if he hadn't, I'd still do it. You're my sister. We're family."

Guilt gnawed at her conviction. She sagged back in her chair and sighed. He was probably right, she thought.

She was letting personal prejudice get in the way of sound judgment. Perhaps she was being unreasonable. Could it be true that no matter what he did, she'd find some way of making it seem wrong? "Oh gods," she said. "Look, I'm sorry, Rendil. I just — I feel ..."

"You miss him," he said, with untypical softness. "It's bound to be a strain. I understand perfectly. If you'd only stop fighting me, Wynflaed, I can help you. Accept my help. Accept it in the spirit it's offered."

He returned to his seat and leaned across the table taking her hand in his. She desperately wanted to pull away from him, but knew she must not. In the years since leaving Uhtredstun, she had never felt his touch. Aelric had often hugged her and kissed her, as a loving father-in-law. Goda embraced her warmly at their every meeting, but Rendil had always remained distant. This was a new side to him. She knew she must try to meet him halfway.

For what seemed an age she sat with her hand in his. His palm should have been cold and clammy, she told herself, but it was not. Yet with every breath, she wanted to pull free and wipe her hand on her skirt.

"Just leave things to me," he said, releasing her finally. "I'll speak to that mine reeve tomorrow. I'm sure he's up to something. If he is, I'll soon find out."

She was staring at her hand, wondering how she could move it below the table without making it obvious that she wanted to wipe away the memory of his touch.

"Do you hear me, Wynflaed?"

His question startled her. She looked up, confused. "Wh-what?" she asked, wiping her hand on her skirt.

"I said about your mine reeve," he told her, "but never mind. You must be tired. We'll talk in the morning"

"Yes I am, a little," she said, seizing the opportunity to get away. "I'll retire if you don't mind. Forgive me."

She rose from the table and fled to the privacy of the sleeping alcove she shared with Wulfric. What was she to make of him? What did he want? How did he always make her feel so guilty?

Maud bustled into the room carrying a steaming cup of milk and shot her a disapproving glance. "You caught me on the 'op," she said. "I weren't expectin' you to bed so early. What's up? Had enough of old bent beams already?"

"He drives me mad!" Wynflaed said, accepting the hot milk. "I don't know how he does it, but he always makes me feel that I'm the one in the wrong. Gods, he's so damned infuriating."

Maud clucked her tongue unsympathetically. "He'll be gone soon. At least I hope so. Until then, just thank Wyrd you're not like us."

"Who?"

"Us lot — bondswifs and skivvies."

"What are you talking about?"

"You resent him interfering and questioning, don't you?" Maud eyed her knowingly. "Well, you'll have to learn to bite your tongue, like we do. Only for us, every day is like that."

Wynflaed studied Maud's grimy face. "I don't make you feel like that, do I?"

Maud fetched a small teag from inside a large carved chest. She approached her with its lid held open. "What ever do you mean?" she asked, sarcastically. "D'yer mean like having to take orders and keep quiet when you're being messed about, or questioned like a child, or checked up on all the time, or accused of breaking sommat what you didn't break, is that what you mean? Oh no, you'd never be like that."

"But I'm not!" Wynflaed said. "Not with you, Maud. Maybe I am with Bryoni or Betla, and even with Maese sometimes. I have to be with them, but not with you."

"It's how it is for all servants, free or bonded," Maud said. "Nobody likes being questioned and suspected. You're not different, you know. If something annoys you, you can be sure the same thing annoys me, or even poor Betla. We're all folk. We all have feelings."

Wynflaed removed her necklace of silver and green glass beads and dropped it into the teag. "But I thought we were friends."

"We are. That's why I'm tellin' you." She tried to remove the gold ring on its cord from around Wynflaed's neck.

"No, I'll keep it on,"

Maud snapped the box lid shut. "If we weren't friends, I'd just ooh and aah, and shake my head, and tell you how wronged I thought you were..."

Wynflaed bit her cheek doubtfully. "So you think I should grit my teeth and say nothing. Let him walk all over me and do whatever he wants until he's had cnough?"

Maud faced her. "No I don't, but I don't think it matters enough to get all upset." She returned the teag to Wynflaed's night chest and closed its great lid. She dragged a night soil pail out from under the bed and left it expediently in the middle of the floor. "You're making mountains out of mole hills. He's just a nosy bugger. Ignore him and he'll go away." She turned her attention to primping the bedcovers. "He's using the master's absence to poke his nose in, to find out what's going on." Her voice croaked with effort as she shook the bolster and plumped the pillows. "He's just jealous, if you ask me. I think he'll soon get fed up and go home."

She turned to Wynflaed who had just stepped away from the night soil pot. "Finished?" she inquired unnecessarily, and steered her roughly towards the bed. "Come on, get in. If you're bedding early, then so can I. Huh, you should do this more often." She gave an impish chuckle. "Maybe there's a use to old Bent Beams after all. At least I can get an early night."

At mid-morning the following day, Maud reported that Rendil was interrogating a pack horse jagger. It was the man whose pack train came each month to carry the lead dishes away to her agent at Penda's North-worthig.

"Damn cheek!" Wynflaed said. "And I expect the jagger is chattering like a pot lid?"

Maud frowned, mirroring her mistress. "He's into everything. Folk don't know how to treat him. He's got 'em all so scared, they just tell him whatever he asks."

"You said he'd get fed up and go away," said Wynflaed. "I should have known better." She stomped about her bed room, glaring at Maud as she sought inspiration. "Go and tell folk that I forbid them to talk to him. They're to tell him nothing. If they're asked, they must say that I've forbidden them to answer. They must say, he must ask me."

"They can't do that. He's the old master's son. They're scared of him. He even scares me."

"Huh, you've changed your tune, haven't you? Last night you said I was making mountains out of mole hills!"

"This's different. He's bothering folk who can't defend themselves. It's not the same."

"I'm mistress here, not him. It's because of me they have grain to grind and strips to plough. They should ..." Her maid's forlorn gaze brought Wynflaed to a stop in mid-sentence. She reached out and gave Maud's arm a consoling pat. "I know — I know," she said, then added jokingly, "Did you know he's scared of caves? He got wolf bitten in one when he was little. Maybe we should all move into Belle Earegasp. He'd not follow us in there. He might bugger off and leave us alone."

The following day, Eadwin arrived with Snowflake, bringing word from Wulfric. Wynflaed sat him in the hall and ordered food for him. He told her that the enemy were camped in the Wealish marches on the far side of a great river called the Severn. Late summer rains in that region made it unlikely there would be a battle for some weeks. Men of both armies were deserting, claiming that their farms needed them more than their kings. Most promised to come back in the spring. Wynflaed was disappointed, though not surprised to hear, that Wulfric would not be deserting. He'd rejoined some old comrades. One of them, Lord Maenche, the Ealdorman's foster brother, had appointed him his second in command. It was a great honour for Wulfric and the family. When she relayed the news to Rendil he was thrilled too, and decided at once to leave to go and tell his father.

Wynflaed did not object.

With Rendil gone, she looked forward to getting back to her routine. She knew that work was the best way to take her mind off missing Wulfric, but first she wanted to hear every last word of him from Eadwin.

"I have to go up Bole Hill for the smelt tally," she told him. "Come with me, Eadwin. Your brother will be up there and you can tell me more on the way, but I want to hear about Wulfric, not the army or the enemy."

Eadwin felt his face colour and turned away to hide his blushes. He was thrilled at the chance to spend time with her, and suggested they should take the winding cart track up Bole Hill, rather than the steep, direct climb she usually took. "It's a much easier route. It'll be better for talking," he said.

As they headed up the track, side be side, he stole a glance at her. His heart skipped. She looked radiant in the autumn sunlight, so alive and happy. She laughed and smiled at everything he told her. He revelled in the music of her laughter, and thought of little thing he could about Wulfric, just to keep her laughing. Her happiness thrilled him. No man, he thought, could want more for his beloved than to see her happy and to know that he is the cause of it. And even though his stories were about another man, that leisurely climb beside her up that breezy hill was something for his own memories, not Wulfric's.

"Are you going back there, or did he say you're to stay here?" Wynflaed asked.

"I'm to stay, unless there's word from him," he said, adding nervously. "He said that I personally was to look after you — err — and the children of course." This was not true, but Eadwin assured himself that it was exactly what Wulfric would have wanted, if only he had remembered to mention it.

Wynflaed eyed him obliquely "Well then, I will certainly be safe, won't I?"

They had reached the top of the hill, and Eadwin's few moments of exclusivity were over. The strong breezes on that high place drew tears from their eyes as they parted to attend on their respective priorities. Eadwin wiped his away as he watched Wynflaed inspecting the smelting fire and the fuel beside it.

Eofar was there with the men who had hauled up the charcoal, firewood and lead ore. Seeing how fondly his younger brother looked at Wynflaed, Eofar strolled over to join him. He placed a hand on his shoulder and leaned in close to him. "There are some roads a muler must never trek, little brother," he said, his voice barely a whisper.

Eadwin glared back defiantly. "I know the roads well enough. You needn't worry on that."

"I hope so."

Wynflaed joined them. "Why is there so much wood and charcoal?" she asked Eofar. "There's enough for a dozen smeltings. I don't want men wasting time felling and hauling wood, when they could be digging lead."

Eofar looked at the ground between his boots. "I know that. I was ordered to do it."

"Ordered! Who by, Rendil?"

"I told him we'd not need it, but he insisted. He wants a second fire for the silver."

"Silver! I don't want silver. I'm not burning up half my woodland for a few scraps of silver that I make no profit on."

"I told him that."

"What did he say?"

Eofar shrugged.

Wynflaed stared at him for a moment, and then sighed, relaxing her shoulders. "Oh, I'm sorry, Eofar. It's not your fault."

***

With no word of Wulfric, time dragged for Wynflaed. Whenever she could, she would try to lose herself in her embroidery; sitting in the light by the longhouse door until the sun sank. Her work was greatly admired. Even Lady Aenflaed, the Ealdorman's sister, had visited By-Streams to commission her. In particular, her gold thread work was much sought after by wealthy households.

As her needle steadily built rich, colourful imagery over the fine linen, she would escape into secret reverie. There she would find Wulfric, and recall strolling the margins of the fields with him, or making love in shady bluebell woods, or the times they had dangled their feet in streams on hot lazy days.

She had been at her needle for more than an hour when Maud found her, red nosed and bundled up against the cold. "It's time you was inside," Maud said. "Grim's teeth, look at you, you're freezing." Glaring at the day, the housemaid rubbed her skinny arms and shivered. "Come on inside."

Wynflaed stretched her cramped shoulders and began absently to obey. "Hum, it is a bit chilly," she said. "Look, I've nearly finished." She held her work at arm's length and studied it critically. It was a blue linen runner; a gift for the Ealdorman's sister. She had embroidered a gay summer scene upon it; musicians and children dancing. Lady Aenflaed loved frivolous things and had admired a similar piece she'd seen on Wynflaed's bedside cyste.

Maud tilted her grimy face and scrutinised the work. After a moment she smiled. "It's beautiful. She'll love it."

"She better had," Wynflaed said, with a chuckle. "It's taken long enough. I just don't get time these days."

"You've only yourself to blame for that," said Maud. Glaring at her, Wynflaed parked her needle and rose stiffly from her chair. Maud glared back defiantly. "Well, you have," she said. "You poke your nose into everything. A body can't do nowt without you're there moilin' and mitherin'." Maud never withheld an opinion.

"And if I didn't keep my eyes and wits about me this place would run itself, I suppose?"

"I can manage as well as you, given half a chance. Or perhaps you think me as dull-witted as poor Betla?"

"I do not, though Holy Mother Frigg knows how often I've wished you were as quiet. And anyway, it's not you that I'm worried about. If they were all like you, Lady Bossy Brecs, I wouldn't have to watch 'em all the time."

The two moved into the house carrying the chair and sewing box between them. "Look at those apples the other week," Wynflaed went on, "You said yourself that you told them they were on the turn, but it didn't stop them storing them with the good-uns did it?"

"Oh, I just knew you'd bring that up," Maud cried. "The one time that sommat goes awry and you have to let it salt the whole damn pig."

"Awh shut up!" Wynflaed felt she was losing the case and wondered why she had even bothered to argue.

Maud went off in a huff. Wynflaed smiled and watched her go. She liked Maud and admired her spirit. Small and thin, she looked more like a scrawny fifteen-year-old than the mother of five children, three still rudely alive. As far as Wynflaed knew there was no man in Maud's life to own to her offspring. Moreover, as each one failed to resemble its siblings in looks or character, she had always thought it best not to delve too deeply.

***

When there was no work for his mules, Eadwin joined his brother to hew lead in the mine. On a dull day of listless dogs and crying sheep, a sudden thunderstorm brought tragedy to Bell Delfan. A miner was drowned and several injured when storm water flooded the mine. Eadwin was one of those hurt in the scramble for the surface. Eofar brought the news to Wynflaed.

"We've taken him home. I think he's broken a rib."

"Is he conscious?"

"On and off. He's a strong lad. He should pull through."

"Is there any bleeding from his mouth?"

"There was a speck or two at first, but not now."

"I'll come at once. I'll get my wyrtcyste." He watched her push past him and vanish into the shade of the deep porch. Rain was beating down, forming rivulets to sculpt the gravel of the sloping courtyard. People watched from their doorways. Occasionally, someone would run from one tiny house to another, a shawl or apron held over their head. Leaden clouds boiled, over the Bretton uplands. Lightning flashed and thunder shook the air, echoing down the limestone valley to the turbid torrent that only an hour before had been a chortling stream.

Wynflaed emerged with Bryoni and Maud in train. Bryoni carried Wynflaed's beech-wood box of medicinal herbs. Maud had a large bundle of bed-furs looped over one shoulder. They were wrapped in a waxed linen cover, a corner of which she pulled over her head to keep the rain off. Wynflaed checked and adjusted the cover before they set off. Eofar stepped up to meet them. Maud declined his offer to carry her bundle, so he took the wyrtcyste from Bryoni and led the little column towards his house.

The miners' cottages were at the far end of the village, on higher ground than the rest. Their smoky doorways overlooked the smithy, main barn and the hall. Beyond them, a wooded hillside rose steeply, vanishing into the sodden clouds. A stubborn scrape of plough land fell away from the path down to a tree-choked valley and Bell Delfan mine.

As she followed Eofar up the road to his house, Wynflaed looked down on the lead mine. It did not look much from up here, she thought. There was little to mark it: a few grassy hillocks of spoil, a small stack of timber, two broken baskets and a few tools hurriedly cast aside in the rain. Not much to show for all that happened there.

Even the striking floor, where the ore was graded, cleaned and washed, looked nothing more than a scar of bare limestone in the grass.

She was breathless by the time they reached the cottages. In the yard next to Eofar's house, a pair of shaggy coated ponies sulked in the rain. Occasionally the stocky beasts shook the water from their broad heads and blew clouds of steam. Beyond them, she saw Eadwin's white mule, cannily sheltering under the eaves. Seeing it brought memories flooding back, treasured images that lifted her fondness for Eadwin sharply into focus.

Eofar's was the largest of the miners' cottages. By any standard, it was a fine house, worthy of a freeman. Its single room was about eight paces long and six across, twice the size of a typical miner's house. In a corner, beyond a small central hearth, Eadwin lay on a narrow bed. Along the opposite wall, a variety of carpentry tools hung from pegs. Beneath them, a sturdy table, which also served as a workbench, stood against the wall. The remains of an oatmeal breakfast competed for space on it with wood chippings and an adze. Eofar's unmade bed had been pushed under the table to clear floor space. From the food stained top of a large elm wood cyste, an antique, three-branched bronze lamp shed light. Wynflaed guessed it would be one of the many Roman items that were turned up in the mine.

Eadwin tried to sit up as he saw Wynflaed enter. She rushed forward and eased him back onto his straw mattress. "No, no Eadwin. Lie down. You mustn't move."

"You shouldn't be here, Lady," he said, his voice hoarse with pain.

"Nonsense. You're very special to me; you and that lumpy old mule."

Eadwin laughed weakly, flinching with pain. "It all seems so long ago now."

"Maybe, but I remember it well enough. You don't know it, but I used to peek at you every day, terrified that you'd leave without me."

"I know," he said. "You'd watch from behind the holly stand."

"You knew? You never let on."

"You were regular as noon. I always ..." He winced, clutching his chest, and fainted away.

Wynflaed wasted no time. She opened his tunic to see his ribs. "Quick, Bryoni, we can bind his ribs tight while he's unconscious."

Eofar leaned forward to watch as the two women salved and bound his brother's bruised chest. They worked quickly, without words.

When they had finished, Maud unfastened her bundle. She handed Eofar a ceramic flask stopped with a wooden bung. "Broth," she told him. "Make him take it warm or cold when he wakes." Next, she took out a fur bed cover and arranged it over the bed. "Keep him warm and still," she said. "When he wakes, put this pillow under his head. It's got healing wyrts in it and the wing bones of a crow. They've been blessed by a powerful healer."

Eofar nodded with satisfaction. He knew that the wyrts would drive out the evil which caused the pain and the wing bones would carry it harmlessly away. He now felt sure his brother would soon be well again.

A speck of blood smeared the corner of Eadwin's mouth. Wynflaed wiped it away and bent to listen to his breathing. Her face was dark with worry. She turned to Eofar. "He doesn't sound good, but I don't think the bones have speared his insides."

Maud wiped Eadwin's forehead. "It could be sommat else, not just his ribs,"

"There were men in blind panic, trampling on each other to get out," said Eofar. "Anything could have happened in that mad scramble."

"I'll sit with him tonight," said Wynflaed. She turned to Eofar and touched his arm. "Go to Badecanwell. Find Lord Cenwulf's healer."

"But won't he have gone with the army?"

"Probably not. They say there'll be no fighting until summer. With any luck he'll still be at the Ealdorman's great hall. Don't worry, we won't leave Eadwin alone. When I'm not here, Maud will watch him. We'll soon get him well again."

Maud pushed Eadwin's hair back from his forehead. "He should be kept warm and rested. That's the best thing if his insides are busted," she said. She glanced out at the rain beyond the open door and frowned. "Huh! Anyway, you'll have little to do but rest for a week at least."

Her meaning was well understood. Even if the rain stopped that moment, it would be several days before the Bell Delfan drained and the miners could start work.

Eofar nodded in agreement. "We need to find that swallow," he said. "That'd drain it. Then there'd be no accidents like this either And if we can't we should dig a sough into the next cave."

Wynflaed looked up from her patient with an indignant frown. "Cut a sough in that rock? That could take months and still gain us nothing. They can't dig lead if they are cutting a sough. We need the lead ore now, not next year."

Eofar glared sullenly. Wynflaed reflected on her thoughtless words and sighed miserably, hardly able to believe what she had just said. Men's lives or lead? She should have no doubts about which came first. "I'm sorry, I didn't mean ..."

Turning back to Eadwin she stroked his brow. It was Rendil who was making her so jumpy, she told herself. His snide carping about the king's share had her so worried about output that it was constantly on her mind. She was forgetting the risk to men – even Eadwin. How would she feel if he'd died? What would the king's thirteenth dish of lead matter then?

She stayed at Eadwin's bedside all night. Eofar went the eight miles or so to the Ealdorman's hall at Badecanwell. She guessed he would arrive too late for the healer to journey back with him immediately. So was not expecting him until mid morning. There was also the chance that he might not be there. Lord Cenwulf was with his army. His healer might have gone too. If so, she hoped Eofar would not bring back some old night hag. There were plenty of those nearer to home; superstitious old women whose potions did more harm than good.

Wynflaed wanted Ealdorman Cenwulf's man, the Crowman, the one who had treated Uhtred with such skill. He had the genuine gift. She had seen that for herself. Uhtred's wound should have killed him, yet he had lived another five years. Not finally succumbing until he went in his sleep one night without a whimper. If the Crowman treated Eadwin, she was sure he would survive.

She watched all night, occasionally dozing, unable to stop her mind wandering. Eofar's words had hit home. She knew he was right about digging the sough. If she had done more about draining the mine, Eadwin would not be injured now, nor a miner killed.

When she had come to By-Streams, there were just a few squatters trenching ore near the surface where the rakes of lead outcropped. They were disorganised and often worked alone, seldom mining deeper than four or five feet. As soon as their trenches became too deep for them to lift out their baskets of spoil and ore by hand, they would move along the rake, leaving a trench behind them. This type of mining did not suit Wynflaed's purposes. She had no control over it. Neither could she tell how much ore they were digging. Unless she could control the mining and the trading of the lead, her morgengifu would be no more than a lambskin with words scratched on it in ink.

This was why Rendil had failed to see its potential. He thought the lead rights were worthless and had told his father so. He could not be bothered with it and saw no shame in passing it over. For Wynflaed, it was much more of a challenge. She was determined to make a success of it. She had to find the way.

The miners were freemen. They worked only when they wanted to. In most cases mining was no more than a spare time occupation to fatten a poor income from the farms they squatted on. These small upland farms produced very little surplus to trade with. The lead made up for this, enabling them to barter for the things their stony fields could not produce.

For Wynflaed to gain control, she had to change this haphazard system. She realised she must somehow improve their lives, whilst at the same time increasing their dependence on the mine. She convinced them that they could produce much more lead with far less work and time, if they all got together and mined the old Roman workings in the galleries running off Belle Earegasp. She explained that such an organised approach would enrich them and allow them more time for their farms and other interests. Personal enrichment was a popular idea. The miners were happy to adapt, even though it meant scrapping old customs and tying themselves to Wynflaed once and for all.

She rewarded them with legal title to their farms. This gave them improved status, peace of mind and something worthwhile to leave to their children. It also created an income from rents for herself. She granted them rights to cut timber for fuel and improving their houses. It was a good deal for all, and soon her morning-gift was a growing asset.

Eofar's voice startled her. She sat up and blinked her eyes. Dawn had crept across the threshold. The rain had stopped. Eofar moved aside at the door and admitted the Crowman.

Wynflaed jumped to her feet and ran her fingers nervously through her hair. The heahrune approached, looking at her. He seemed pleased to see her. "How is your husband?" he asked. "We've not crossed ways for some time."

"He's very well, your honour. I'm sorry he's not here to greet you. He left to join the Ealdorman's legion a few weeks ago."

"Of course, as I will soon be doing. Perhaps I shall see him then." He knelt beside Eadwin, his hands moving quickly and hovering for a moment above the dressing she and Bryoni had applied. "What poultice is this?"

"Woundwort and betony pulped with honey to cleanse and bind it. I gave him pounded willow for the pain."

"You've done well, Wulfricswif." His hand slid into a pocket in his black robe and emerged with a small wooden flask. "This is oil of poppy. It takes away pain, though it can bring bad dreams to a troubled soul. Give him a drop or two in warm milk. When it's all gone, if the pain persists, an infusion of the husk of the poppy pounded in hot water with willow, honey and wine will help him. Do you have them dried from summer?"

Wynflaed looked inquiringly to Maud, who nodded, showing her personal satisfaction. "My woman has some," said Wynflaed. She took the flask and sniffed its stopper. "I'm grateful, your honour, but what of his insides?"

"Rest is the best healer. I can feel his ribs are broken, but he's not speared inside. He must not rise, or talk, or eat hard food. Let him drink nothing but small ale and good broth. Let him piss in a flask without rising from the bed. Keep his ribs bound. In a week let him sit up. Move his bed to the door, but keep him warm. If he can see outside, he'll be less restless."

He straightened up to his full height and looked down into Wynflaed's face. "Miners are vain men. They think themselves above others. They are the same proud stuff as warriors, except that a shovel and a pick are their spear and sword."

Wynflaed grasped Crowman's arm and drew close to him as he stepped back from Eadwin's bedside. "Thank you, your honour. I'm sure now that he'll be fine."

"He would have lived anyway. He's young and he's been well treated."

Wynflaed touched Bryoni's shoulder to show that she too deserved his praise. The heahrune nodded and smiled, making Bryoni's cheeks redden.

"If you see my husband, tell him — tell him I send my love," said Wynflaed.

"You ask me to waste words, woman. He knows that already." He looked her in the eye, studying her closely. He seemed sad and distant. "Little has changed, Wynflaed Wulfricswif," he whispered. "The time comes soon. You will journey far. You will hear much and see many things before the truth reclaims you. Guard your opinions. Curb your pride, or what you carry may not fruit."

Wynflaed was alarmed and felt her heart beat faster. "But I have journeyed, Master."

"I'm sorry," he said. "It was in your mind to ask me of these things. That's what I see. I can't tell you more." He ducked his head to leave by the low door.

Wynflaed stared after him, her mind in turmoil. Surely she had journeyed? She had come to the very place he told her, *a place of lime trees and streams*. How could nothing have changed? Surely everything had changed. And what did he mean that she should guard her opinions? What will not fruit? What did he mean? How could he say nothing had changed?

***

Buhe had not changed. Wynflaed could hardly believe her eyes when she arrived like a flurry of feathers in sunlight. Her escort of spearmen and three horses, loaded with her belongings, filled the yard. They brought noise and excitement on a quiet, misty day. It was early autumn. The trees scattered gold as the two walked and chatted, lost in happy reverie.

"You're pregnant again, aren't you?" Buhe said later that evening as they sat alone. "Does Wulfric know?" She studied her critically. "You didn't tell him did you? You let him go without saying. How long is it?"

Wynflaed closed her eyes and let her head loll against her chair back. "It's not certain. It's too early — only eight or ten weeks I think." She clutched Wulfric's gold ring at her throat and kissed it. "I've only come to terms with it myself in the last day or so. I've often passed a month with no show and nothing happened, so I wasn't sure until …" Her voice trailed off.

"Until what?"

"Oh nothing," she said. "I told you we had that healer here last week?"

Buhe sniffed, refusing to let her change the subject. "Never mind about him. Who knows about the baby?"

Wynflaed sipped her ale and traced the rim of the cup thoughtfully with her finger. "I expect Maud has guessed. She knows more about childbirth and everything that goes with it than Holy Mother Frigg herself."

"You've got to be careful, Flaedy. I know what you're like. And now that Wulfric's away, and what with all this stuff you've been telling me about Rendil — well — I just hate to think."

"Oh gods, Buhe, I do hope you're not going to mother me."

"Well why not? You'll just have to come to Uhtredstun. I can look after you there."

"Uhtredstun, certainly not," she said. "Live with you and Colnoth? Gods no. I'd spend all my time worrying about you and your sex life, especially after what you've been telling me. No thank you, sister. I'll stay here with the wolves, and the murderous Wealh sheep rustlers, and the flooding, and my devious brother-in-law. It'll be much less wearing."

Buhe pouted. "Well thank you very much," she said, her bottom lip trembling. "That's the last time I'll tell you anything. Since father died, you are — no, were — the only one I could talk to. I thought you'd understand."

Wynflaed reached for Buhe's hands. "Oh, I'm sorry, Buhe. I didn't mean it. I — I was trying to be funny."

"Yes, well some of us are not as — well — earthy as you are. I only told you those things about Colnoth because I didn't know if all men expected it of their wives. I ought to have known you'd be laughing at me."

"Oh come now, don't make such a fuss. It's me who's supposed to be in need of consolation, remember?" Buhe shrugged and dropped her gaze. "So tell me everything," Wynflaed said. "Are you and Colnoth happy?"

"He's good to me. He's sober. He doesn't hit me. He gives me everything I want, and he's so proud of me, it's embarrassing to hear him tell people about me."

"So why are you so — upset?"

"He doesn't love me." She clasped her hands around Wynflaed's and squeezed it firmly. "You're so lucky. I mean, having all this –- you know, responsibility, status — the mine and everything." She shook her head sadly. "Colnoth won't let me do anything. He thinks I'm just some sort of decoration; something to be brought out on big occasions, like grandmother's wall hangings. He treats me like a child. He parades me and picks fights with any man who so much as looks at me. Yet he dresses me like a queen so that every man does."

"He's proud of you."

"He's proud of himself!" Buhe said. "I'm his prize, not his wife. Why doesn't he stay at home more? He visits his father all the time. At least that's what he tells me. Sometimes I don't see him for a week. He neglects the land. If it wasn't for Horse Ebell and his son, there would be nothing sown or ploughed."

She smiled and flashed a sparkling glance at Wynflaed. "You remember how proud father was. He worked like a beaver to rebuild after the raid. It was ten times better when he'd finished. But now that he's gone, I'm scared Colnoth will let the place go to ruin. I think he only married me to get the land and the rents. The trouble is, I love him so, and that's the really stupid part."

Wynflaed watched her sadly, her heart aching at her unhappiness. She was almost lost in her loveliness. She was still the golden child she had always been. Her skin looked smooth and glowing with health, like an infant's. Her hair was glorious amber, tumbling about her elegant neck in deep, loose curls. Her eyes, sad now beneath long dark lashes, were the deepest blue. And even now, despite their tearful sparkle, the fire that burned in them was full of a careless mischief. It was a look men could so easily misunderstand. Buhe still did not comprehend flirtation. If she were to discover what she did to men with her eyes and pouting mouth, Wynflaed imagined she would be quite shocked.

She had taken to the idea of marriage with all the enthusiasm of a child for a puppy dog. It was to be a cuddly, woolly, bouncy thing. There would be no dirt, or mess, no nasty smells or inconvenient noises. Marriage was to be bluebells without rain, barley without backache, or honey without dead bees. And despite the lack of connubial privacy in the great hall of her childhood, and the many times she had seen Horse Ebell put a stallion to a mare, sex had come as a shock to her.

As the evening drew on, she watched Buhe chattering, hardly hearing her. She was still thinking of the Crowman's words, chewing them over in her mind. What did he assume of her opinions that she must guard them? And what did he mean - may not fruit? Did he somehow know she was pregnant? Buhe had guessed it so perhaps he had too. She kissed Wulfric's gold ring. I miss you so much, she said inside her head.

....

CHAPTER TEN

Aelric flushed with pride as Rendil gave him the news of Wulfric's promotion. "They say there will be no battle until spring, or even summer."

"And what of Wynflaed, how d'you think she's coping in Wulf's absence?"

'Quite well, for a woman," Rendil said, airily. "And with me to keep an eye on her, I'm sure my brother's interests will be well served." He poured himself a second cup of ale and leaned back in the chair his father had set for him in the hall at Holmesfelt. Rendil's boots and clothes still bore the mud of the road from By-Streams. But he knew his father would regard his news of Wulfric as too important to have to wait on formality.

"Of course wagging tongues are trying to blacken her name," Rendil said, adopting a reproachful tone to subtly sow the lie in his father's mind, "but what can you expect? There is always somebody ready to smear a better name than their own."

"Aye that's true, but it's worse for a woman," said Aelric, "especially one such as Wynflaed. Her biggest crimes are her beauty and intelligence. Folk are always ready to believe the worst of a good looking woman, especially a clever one. It's envy. I'm sure there are many who'd be happier if she was rag headed and not the astute businesswoman she is."

Rendil nodded, looking thoughtful. "Most ridiculous of all is that they are trying to link her with that mine reeve of hers, a great hulking brute without the wits of an ox. It's all nonsense of course." He eased himself in his chair and let silence hang between them. Tapping his boot steadily with his walking stick, he watched his father's reaction and gauging the effect of the little worm of doubt he had placed in the old man's mind. After a long pause he spoke again. "Anyway, I'm having none of it. I'm determined to find out where these rumours begin and put a stop to them. It makes my blood boil to see my sister-in-law's name abused."

Aelric leaned towards him and patted his son's arm. "Don't take it so hard, Rendil. You're a good son and a loving brother. I doubt Wynflaed will be much concerned by stupid gossip." He checked Rendil's cup and topped it up with ale as he went on, "It certainly doesn't impress me. I know the lass. She loves her husband. She won't dishonour him. I'd stake my life on it." He smiled reassuringly at his son.

Rendil nodded, concealing his disappointment. It infuriated him to see how besotted his father was with Wynflaed. How could he show such blind faith in her? Surely he must have some doubts after what he'd just heard?

"And the mine - it goes well I hear."

"Very — yes very well," said Rendil, slightly startled by the question. "As I said father, she's a clever woman and as good a master of her miners as any man could be. She doesn't suffer idle slackers." He was almost squirming in his seat as he fought to maintain his outward calm. "Of course she gets a lot of help from her mine reeve," he added, giving a prod to the little worm he'd set to work in his father's mind. "She appears to trust him a great deal. She consults him frequently — and at all hours of the day or night."

Aelric laughed, making himself cough. He coughed easily these days. Taking a sip of ale, he smiled reflectively. "She reminds me of your mother. She had a way with slackers too."

"Indeed," Rendil said, with apparent admiration. "There's not much her servants can do better than she." He was fuming beneath his calm exterior, particularly at the reference to his mother. Was there nothing he could say to shake his father's confidence in Wynflaed?

***

After a week of gaiety and chatter, Buhe left By-Streams, seeming to take the last of the autumn sunshine with her. With her escort of spearmen, her presse-maid and a groom, she rode away, turning back to wave every few paces until the sun-gilded boughs of ash and lime trees finally screened her from view. Wynflaed watched the empty space left upon the road and thought of all that had passed between them. In some strange way, Buhe was the wisest of all, she thought. Her life was cluttered and disorganised, her ambitions simple, her fears innumerable, and yet most could be put to rights with no more than a hug, such as even Colnoth could provide. She had accepted her life. Her girlish dreams of true love had failed to fruit, but she settled for what she had. Bizarrely, her fear of almost everything in life meant that even the simplest pleasures or merest whiff of good fortune thrilled her.

"I like her, and it's done you good having her here," Maud said, at Wynflaed's shoulder. "Though I'm glad she's not my mistress."

"Why not? You'd be able to bully her much easier than you do me."

Maud sniffed and said, "She's nice but she's spoiled. I couldn't cope with her moods."

"Buhe, moods? What *do* you mean? I know she's bossy and wants her own way, but otherwise she's quite placid, just giddy ..."

"With you perhaps, but believe me, she can be ..."

"What? Silly, you mean?" Wynflaed suggested sardonically.

Maud did not join in the joke. "I don't think she means it," she said, "but she can be quite spiteful if things don't suit her."

Wynflaed knew that was true, but was surprised that Maud had discovered it after only a few days of her company. "Did something happen, Maud?" she asked.

"No, not really. It's just a sense I picked up from her maid - nothing specific. In fact, I wish I was more like her myself."

"You, like Buhe! Gods help us," Wynflaed said. "I thank Holy Mother Frigg you are not, or nothing would ever get done around here."

"No, I mean — sort of hopeful and always expecting things to get better," said Maud. "Now me, I always look at the dark side of everything. It stops me enjoying things more. But she expects everything to eventually be alright – or even better. I wish I was more like that."

"Poor old you," Wynflaed said, laughing softly. "Well, I'd still rather be you than either Buhe or me."

"Me? Gods no," she cried. "You'd have to put up with my children and my useless men. You'd have no tits, bad skin and nothing worth a spark."

"But you don't have Rendil for a brother-in-law or Colnoth for a husband."

Maud stared back at her, weighing the respective merits of their lives. "Hum, yes but I'd handle 'em different if it were me."

"Oh yes," Wynflaed said. "So you're the expert on men? So what would you do?"

"I'd bed 'em until I was bored, then I'd treat 'em to a foxglove and hemlock posy," she said, with deadly coolness.

Wynflaed shuddered, genuinely shocked. "Frigg Maud, you wouldn't!"

"Would I not?"

A frown crossed Wynflaed's face. She thought of Maud's disparate brood and their absent fathers. "Maud," she asked. "You haven't … I mean you never …"

Maud laughed. "Grim's cods no, Lady!" she cried. "I've never had a man who stayed around long enough to need poisoning. I've a knack for picking ones that run off to escape nowt more poisonous than my sour looks. I'm a poor lot, Lady. Men soon see that. They fucks me and flees, faster than mice from a burning thatch."

"Gods Maud, you had me worried."

Wynflaed left Maud and went to the mine. At the rake face Eofar greeted her as usual, with a brief report of the day's work. After the heavy rain, the water in the main gallery was still thigh deep, preventing ore extraction.

"When it's drained, I want you to have another go at clearing the swallow," she told him. "I've been thinking about what you said. You're right, we must drain it or there'll be more injuries – even deaths. Besides, I wouldn't be surprised if it's just old tailings down there. I don't think there'll be the need to cut through rock."

"Tailings?" Eofar queried doubtfully. "We don't chuck tailings down there. It all goes in the old tunnels."

"I'm not saying our men did it. I think it's tailings from the old empire miners, years ago."

"Well I know nowt of them."

"No but you said your grandfather found lots of their old tools and stuff?"

"Old Delfan Eaffa, aye, but he mined it for most of his life, until the master took it off him. If it really was once an old Wealish or Empire mine from way back in the before times, how can we know what's down there? Some folk say they were mining it for hundreds of years, then one day they just stopped, and nobody worked it until Delfan Eaffa, and he was on his own. One man working on his own doesn't make much tailings, especially as all he wanted was the silver."

Wynflaed nodded thoughtfully. "But if he was on his own, he wouldn't spend time carrying baskets of tailings very far when he could just dump them down a convenient hole. I think maybe it was Delfan Eaffa who blocked it."

"No it wasn't him," Eofar said, feeling his family's honour was at stake, "but I'll see what I can do all the same."

"Good. How's Eadwin? I'm going up to see him later. Maese has baked a pie for him. Is there anything he wants?"

"Oh he's fine now," said Eofar, a touch of comic despair in his tone.

Wynflaed mirrored his grin. "What do you mean?"

"He's got Snowflake with him now. The damn beast sleeps in the house next to his cot."

***

Gods, he eats like a pig, thought Wynflaed, as she watched Rendil at his night meat. He had arrived three days after Buhe's departure, shattering the happiness her visit had brought to By Streams.

"You've been here a week now, Rendil," Wynflaed said sharply, abandoning all pretence at hospitality. "Shouldn't you be going home? What about Goda? She's all alone. She needs you. You should be with her."

"Four days. I've been here four days. I hope your counting is more accurate when you tally the king's thirteenth dish. We can't afford mistakes there, can we?"

"We? What do you mean, 'we'? It has nothing to do with you. It's only me who needs to worry about the king's dish. It doesn't concern you or anyone else, not even my husband."

"Everything that concerns you concerns me too, my dear sister. My brother asked me to look after you and I have every intention of doing so. Penda's dish of lead is something I certainly need to concern myself with. In fact it is possibly the most important thing. The king takes his dues and gafols very seriously."

Wynflaed took a deep breath and straightened her spine. They were seated in upper hall, at the large table. She sat in the high backed chair, on which Wulfric had carved a design of crossed picks and hammers to show that she was mistress of Bell Delfan. Rendil sat on a cushion on a bench opposite her. "You know very well that I don't want your help, Rendil. It's very kind of you, but I can manage well enough on my own. In six years or more, even Wulfric never so much as enquired into my business unless I asked him for his opinion. I don't see why you should concern yourself. And as for Penda's dish, I can assure you that the royal gafol reeve is perfectly content with what he gets from me."

"Huh, I don't doubt it," he said sarcasm oiling his tone. He pretended to scrutinise his food as he went on, "Perhaps if my brother had taken a closer interest the mine would be yielding more and the king be better served."

"I resent that," she said. "Bell Delfan was in your family for years, yet you did nothing with it. Not one single dish of lead was mined. How well was the king served then?"

"I merely meant ..."

"You've no grounds for saying such things," she said, interrupting him. "Bell Delfan does very well — for this family, and for the king. He's certainly better served than before I came."

"I didn't say you were not doing your best," he replied, evidently amused by her anger. "But why, if you're so sure it can't be improved, do you fear another taking a closer look at it?"

"I don't fear it. I just don't want it," she said. "And certainly not your interference. I don't tell you how to run your farms, though from what I hear you could use advice."

"Tittle-tattle," Rendil sneered. "My affairs do well enough, lady, but even if they were in shreds," he went on piously, "I would still regard my duty to my brother as paramount."

Wynflaed did not know whether to puke or laugh. In the end she resorted to verbal abuse. "Just go, Rendil. I've had enough of your poison. You're worse than a belly ache."

Rendil glared back at her. "Very well," he said. "I shall leave for now, but I'll continue to do what your husband asked of me, lady. Depend on it."

***

The miners of Bell Delfan worked on clearing the swallow. They grumbled incessantly about losing payment as no ore was being mined, but their complaining was abruptly ended by the discovery of a thief amongst them. A man was caught stealing bing while they were busy working on the swallow. He was taking a little from each man's bing place and hiding it in his own. A barmote was called to try the case.

Wynflaed heard of it from Maud, even before Eofar had the chance to tell her. "It's Wittna, the bald man with the duck pond. They say he's guilty. They were already suspicious, so Eofar set a lad to watch him. He was caught red-handed."

"But Wittna?" Wynflaed queried. "He never struck me as a thief. Are they sure?"

"The lad saw him. They say his bing place was twice as full as any other man's, yet he'd not worked for several days because of the rain. That's what made Eofar suspicious. And anyway, he confessed. He just broke down and wailed like a bairn when they caught him."

"But he lost kin in the flood when Eadwin was hurt" said Wynflaed. "Maybe the extra lead came from his kin's bing place."

"No, it was his wife's father who drowned. The widow took all of his lead and a bit more besides. The men do that when a man dies. They whip round to give a bit extra to the widow."

"What will they do?" Wynflaed asked.

"There'll be a Barmote. They'll pin him, I expect. That's the old way. It's the lead law. It's older than these hills. You can't do nothing about it. It's the Barmote that must decide."

The following noon, Wittna was found guilty by the Barmote jurors, miners like himself. He was brought out to the common and dragged to the stocks at the edge of his own duck pond. His wife was there, a wiry young woman with two small children at her skirts and a bairn on her hip. She wailed and sobbed, begging her neighbours for mercy. Her children howled, setting other children and mothers to tears.

Wynflaed wanted to stop it, but Eofar caught her eye. He glared at her sternly and shook his head to warn her off. One of the Barmote jurors moved in beside her and leaned close to whisper to her. "This is the lead law, Lady. You can't interfere. You should not have come really. This has nothing to do with any but the miners, not even the king's magistrate."

Wittna's wife ran to Wynflaed and fell to her knees, begging her to stop the proceedings. Around her the miners gazed impassively. The Barmote master stepped forward and pulled the woman away.

"This is not a good day's work, lady," he said gravely. "But it's the law. Wittna did wrong and got caught. No matter what you or I might think about it, it's the lead law."

"I am not about to interfere with the Barmote," said Wynflaed. "Though it's regrettable a less severe punishment can't be found. From what I hear, pinning will probably cost him the use of his hand, even if he manages to tear himself free. He has three small children to provide for. You don't need me to tell you that he'd do that better with two good hands rather than only one."

"You're right, Lady Wynflaed, I don't need you to tell me. Many a man has torn himself free of the pin and worked on after it."

"Yes, Barmote Master - but not as miners. It takes two strong hands to swing a pick."

"There's always the striking floor."

"The striking floor is for old women and infants," said Wynflaed.

"It's the lead law. It's been this way since who knows when. It will not be changed because you sniff at its ways. The Barmote is our court, our way."

Wittna was held at the stocks. His left hand was tied behind his back and his right hand was pinned to the timbers with a knife hammered in all the way to the hilt.

The Barmote master then announced formally that Wittna was to be left there and that no person was to give him food or drink. If he could tear his hand free he could go, his punishment over. If he could not, he would remain there until death.

Wittna pulled himself free overnight, but his wound never healed. He died a few weeks later of lockjaw.

***

The Yuletide season comprises the last month of the old year and the first of the new. Yule looks both ways, back into the past and forward to the future. It is a time for joy and feasting, for giving and receiving gifts and for family gatherings when children join their elders at table.

In humble hovels and great halls maidens hang boughs of yew, holly, mistletoe and ivy. A great log of beech, or ash, felled before the previous Yule, is burned during the height of the festivities. A boar is sacrificed and eaten on Modrenacht, the night of mothers. This important feast is celebrated just after the winter solstice. In the calendar of the Christian kind, this is around the twenty-fifth day of the month they call December.

With the master and so many men from the village away in Ealdorman Cenwulf's legion, many at By-Streams felt that there was little to celebrate that year. Wynflaed was delighted to receive her father-in-law's invitation to spend the height of the Yule season with him. She looked forward to it, hoping it would make Wulfric's absence more bearable. She felt that being amongst others who loved him and missed him, as she did, would somehow bring him closer. It would also be a good time to talk to Aelric about Rendil, and hopefully get him to leave her alone. Eadric and Wyngifu were excited too. They enjoyed being with their grandfather. He spoiled them, allowing them everything they asked for.

Holmesfelt was a good day's march from By Stream, across hill-forest, peat-bog and windy upland scrub. She would travel with Eadwin and an armed escort of half a dozen of her miners, for protection against the bandits and rustlers that roamed the wilderness. Maud, Bryoni and of course Bryoni's sister Betla would accompany her, to look after the children and to serve her during her stay.

When the time came, despite the dangers of travelling such a distance at that time of year, she set off in high spirits. With only a sprinkling of snow on the hills, Eadwin had assured her that the track would be passable without too much difficulty. He told her that a firm frost had stiffened the ground, making river crossings and marshes easier to negotiate than might otherwise be the case. The river Derwent was the first, and the biggest, obstacle on the journey. It took half the morning to get everyone across, even though as Eadwin had forecast, firm frosts had locked up groundwater and stemmed its flow.

The whole journey was accomplished in a single day, though by the time they tramped wearily into Aelric's homestead only its dogs and geese were awake to welcome them. The commotion they caused soon brought bleary eyes to dimly lit doors all around the village. Aelric appeared, wrapped in a thick fur robe. He swept Wynflaed up into his arms and hugged her, flattering her comically. Then dumping her with good-natured abruptness, he took his granddaughter Wyngifu, from her nurse. The little girl who had been sleeping soundly, obligingly awoke in a sweet temper and stayed awake long enough to hug Aelric's head, before returning blissfully to her slumbers.

"Little Wyn," he sang into her drooping eyelids. "Look at you, you're getting so big and so pretty. I think all the boys will soon be after you."

Wynflaed watched him, tears glossing her eyes. Aelric spied his grandson looking solemn at his feet. It was not considered seemly for a boy child, even a six-year-old, to show emotion openly, and little Eadric played the role expected of him. "Where's Eadric, that big man of the household?" Aelric demanded, pretending he could not see the lad and looking the wrong way.

Eadric stood his ground and waited, his bright little face reddening with delight.

"Where's my grandson?" Aelric demanded accusingly. "Has he not come? Have you left him to fight off the robber gangs? Has he gone to war? Where is he?"

Eadric could bear the suspense no longer. He grabbed his grandfather's robe and tugged it for all he was worth. "I'm here, Granddad."

Aelric's scrubbed old face was a picture of delight. It brought laughter to all, even the weary miners in Wynflaed's escort. He bent down and picked the lad up, and made a great fuss of finding him at long last. His exertions however, brought on a coughing fit. Dismissing it, he led them all into his hall.

Inside was warm, smoky and bright with lamps. Servants were rushing about putting flames to the last few candles, others set bread and broth and ewers of ale on the long table. Wynflaed saw the great Yule log beside the hearth, ready to be rolled onto the fire at Modrenacht. Yew boughs, holly, mistletoe and ivy hung around the roof beams. In lower hall, the gutted carcass of the Yule boar was displayed on a low carving litter. Soon it would be spitted and cooked over a fire in the yard outside.

When she had finished her broth and drunk a steaming cup of buttery hot milk, Aelric showed Wynflaed to a bed chamber, partitioned off by a withy screen, in a corner of upper hall. It was furnished with a large curtained bed, an ornately carved oak presse and a small wax polished table, beneath which was an ancient mydercan. Dried wild flowers had been scattered on the wooden floor, scenting the air with honeysuckle and meadowsweet. Beside the bed, a fur rug had been placed for her to step on when she rose in the morning.

Around the walls were small hangings depicting a wedding and the life of a young warrior's family. Wynflaed took up a lamp to examine them more closely. She saw that the yarns and colours were poor, like those unwound for re-use from old clothes, but the embroidery was good work. It was stitched on to wool cloth that had been reused, not the usual expensive linen of such things. Wynflaed realised she was looking at the work of Aelric's wife. Emotion caught in her throat. A tear splashed down her cheek as she traced the fine stitching with a finger. Until now, Aelric had kept this room to himself. Apart from the woman who cleaned it every week, no-one but he had seen inside it for years.

Wynflaed felt him watching her from the curtained doorway as she took it all in. She knew that he was paying her the highest possible compliment. Kneeling, she opened the mydercan. The smell of lanolin and beeswax rose up to her nostrils. The box had removable wooden trays, divided into compartments. Each could be lifted out to reveal another beneath it. Some contained shiny whorls and spindles. There were needles for sewing and knitting, pins and yarns and shears. One tray had bobbins and loom weights. At the bottom was a length of green wool with cut edges where a piece had been made up from it. Underneath it were pieces of old clothes, unpicked for use as patches. These were the ordinary, well-used things of a poor woman. This was a woman who knew hardship and struggle, a woman who patched and mended and made do.

This had belonged to the young woman who had died before her husband made his fortune.

Wynflaed closed the mydercan lid and turned to Aelric. They embraced in silence, before he left her and went to his bed place in another part of the hall. She watched him go, realising the depth of his loneliness. They'd exchanged not a word, yet their understanding was complete. For her there was the hope that Wulfric would return. For the old man there was no such hope. The closest he could be to his love was that dry, lifeless room with its old hangings and threads.

The following morning, Aelric found her walking the margins with Goda. Bowing with exaggerated politeness, he pretended to be dazzled by their beauty.

"Oh dear, I know that approach," said Goda. "This is going to be about business. Which of us is it to be, father-in-law, me or Wyn?"

Slightly put out by Goda's directness, he faced her sternly. "I see you've already been entertained by Widow Guthrum this morning," he said. "Her minty mead has emboldened your tongue. I merely wanted to tell you that your daughters are looking for you."

Goda guessed they were not. Wynflaed thought as much too. This was his way of getting Wynflaed alone. Goda squeezed Wynflaed's hand and left her with him.

The old man took Wynflaed's arm and fell into step beside her. "I'm afraid Goda can't hold her drink, it loosens her tongue," he said. "I think I must blame you for it. Until you came on the scene she never went near the wayward widow's house. Now they thrive in each other's company like poppies in corn."

Wynflaed said nothing. She expected it would be difficult enough defending the things she had done, without worrying about those she had not. She was sure that Rendil had been stirring the entrails and Aelric was now about to pick through them.

'Rendil tells me Bell Delfan prospers under your hand."

'Rendil! He does?" she cried. If he had told her his pigs were growing webbed feet and wings, she could not have been more astonished.

Aelric looked at her oddly. "You seem surprised?"

"Well I — err — he has been … I mean he has seemed ..."

Laughing softly, he shook his head, appreciating the irony. "Oh, I see. Well don't bother to explain. I'm afraid my son has some difficult ways. I often find him impossible too. Nevertheless, I assure you he has your best interests at heart."

Much as she loved and trusted Aelric, she could not bring herself to agree with him on that, but she hid her scepticism. "I'm very grateful to him," she said, trying to sound sincere, "but as you say, his manner can be difficult." Crossing her fingers behind her back she decided to press on gently. "Though I wish he would trust me to ask him for help when I need it, and not simply turn up and insist on giving it. To be frank, father-in-law, he sometimes ventures into matters where even you or Wulfric would not."

For what seemed a very long time Aelric appeared to weigh her words. She had the impression that he was digging well below the surface. "I think it goes beyond that," he said at last. "As a hard working, competent woman, you resent the help of others, no matter how well meant. If you feel it's uncalled for, you see it as criticism, and frankly I can understand that. But there are things you may not know."

"Then I would immediately ask you, or him."

Aelric raised a staying palm and winced impatiently at her interruption. "No, I mean about the personalities involved. For example, did you know that your mine reeve is the grandson of old Delfan Eaffa, the man I bought the mine from?"

"Yes."

'So you know why his grandfather sold it?"

"Wulfric told me it was gambling or drunkenness or something. He lost his wealth and came to you for help."

Aelric nodded and leaned towards her. "That's right. I settled his debts in exchange for the mine. I saved him from disgrace or even worse. The old fool never forgave me for it."

"But you paid him a fair price."

"Ah maybe, but resentment is a blind hawk, it finds any prey, usually the wrong one. Delfan Eaffa was a fool, or at best a luckless gambler. Whichever it was he hated me for helping him and afterwards blamed me for everything that beset him."

"But that's not fair," Wynflaed said.

"I kept out of his way. I was sorry for him. He even tried to provoke me by keeping on working the mine. It was theft, of course, but I ignored it. I couldn't do anything with it myself and Rendil refused to." He laughed softly, starting a mild coughing fit. Wynflaed waited as he calmed his chest and recovered his breath. "You know he found it by accident? The story is that he was hoeing his bean strip one day when he fell through the ground into the caves. He found it full of old Roman mining tools. He thought the gods had given it to him. In fact it was never legally his. He didn't realise or care about that, and just worked it anyway. He did well off the silver, but then, after a few years, he became lazy and started drinking. He hardly ever worked, lost his wealth and came to me for help. I secured proper legal tenure of the mine from King Ceorl, before Penda. And I paid off Delfan Eaffa's debts for him."

"So actually you needn't have paid him anything?"

'I felt sorry for him. He had mined it for twenty years or more. I reckoned he deserved something. It weren't much. The old king gave it to me for nothing but a thirteenth share, and I got the land too."

"But what has this to do with me? Delfan Eaffa is long dead."

"Your mine reeve, how can you trust him? He's the old fool's grandson. For all you know, he could be nursing a bigger grudge than his grandfather ever did. Rendil thinks so too. He thinks you should get rid of him."

. . . .

CHAPTER ELEVEN

Solmonath, the month of cakes, the Christian-kind call it February. It is a busy time for the farmer with muck to spread, hay fields to mole and fence, stubble to plough in, beans and sets to sow and harrow. The gods too demand their portion: cakes of bread must be sown in the first furrows, to give thanks for the good bread of last season and to crave blessings on the next.

"I have to go to the mine, Maud" said Wynflaed. "Take Eadric and Wyngifu to Bryoni, but keep an eye on them yourself too. I worry about Bryoni's catnaps. She doesn't always keep a good watch."

"It's you who needs catnaps. You should be taking it easy," said Maud from the smoky distance of lower hall. "That child inside you needs its rest."

"Oh really, and you think I'm different to you and every other woman, I suppose? I'm a puny, pampered thing that needs to rest all the time, is that it? Whereas you and Maese's wife and the others can just drop out bairns while you're querning or scrubbing."

"Them as must quern, must quern, them as needn't, shouldn't," Maud said, adding for good measure, "They'd be fools to work if they needn't."

"Are you calling me a fool?"

Maud stood her ground, her red bony elbows sticking out like spines. "If the cap fits," she replied, defiantly. "Your man is off at war. He'll expect to find you, and his new son, as sound as a new thegn's bell when he comes home. If you're all wrung out and grey faced, it's me what'll feel the switch for letting you toil and moil when you should've been taking it easy. Do some sewing if you must be at sommat."

Wynflaed wilted slightly under the rebuke, but persisted doggedly. "This place doesn't run itself you know. I have to ..."

Maud was not ready to give in. "Think of the babe," she interrupted sternly. "Go and rest on your bed. I'll open the shutters and bring you some mending. Little Wynnie's drawers are through the arse again. You could do them, if you must."

"Who is mistress here?" said Wynflaed.

"Someone deaf to commonsense."

Bryoni, pink and huge, joined the pair, drawn by the sound of raised voices. She waded in behind Maud, her sister Betla clinging to her spine like a hump. "She's right, lady. There's no point tempting Wyrd. Maud and me can do all that's spoiling. You needn't stir."

Wynflaed thumped the table and gave in to the pair. "Oh gods," she cried. "Fetch me the mending basket - if only to silence you." She stomped off to her bedroom.

***

Wynflaed had not seen Rendil since Yule, and had assumed, with some satisfaction, that her discreet words with Aelric had paid off. Her spirits crashed when word came one morning that he was approaching By-Streams with several men at arms. Sleepless nights, backache, loneliness and Maud's constant nagging about her alleged neglect of her unborn child were enough to worry about, but the prospect of also having Rendil to deal with sent her back to her bed, leaving orders that she was not to be disturbed, even if the king himself dropped in.

Maud decided to ignore her instructions, believing it would be less stressful for her to know exactly what he was doing rather than spend her time worrying about what he may or may not be up to. So it was that Wynflaed learned that Rendil had ignored the path to the village and led his men straight up to the smelter. She was furious to hear this, and immediately climbed from her bed and started dressing. Nothing Maud could say would stop her.

"You can't go running up the bole hill," Maud cried. "You're six months gone and that path is steep and frosty. One slip and you'd break your neck. I won't let you go."

"Get my fur cloak and my boots and for Frigg's sake shut up, Maud!"

Maud obeyed her, grumbling fiercely under her breath. Wynflaed felt compelled to explain as she watched her help her on with her boots. "I'll not take the footpath. I'll take the lead-cart way; it's not so steep or slippery," she said. "Will that suit you?"

Scowling, Maud left the room. She returned moments later with her own cloak, which she swirled about her shoulders. "I'm coming with you." Wynflaed refused her flatly and set off towards the lead-cart road in the burning glare of Maud's disapproval.

The lead-cart road was the longer of the two routes up to the smelter, but was a much easier climb. Its wider, metalled track was kept smooth for the ponies and carts that carried the ore and charcoal up to the smelter. Wynflaed thought of the last time she had climbed it. Eadwin had been at her side, telling her all his news from Wulfric and the army. If Wulfric were with her now, she told herself, Rendil would not dare to behave so arrogantly.

The fire was already roaring as she approached the smelter on top of the hill. She learned that Rendil had demanded more wood from the valley, where she kept it stacked to season and dry out for burning.

"What's going on?" she asked him, astonished by his nerve. "How dare you use my timber and trespass on my land? You can't bring up more, it's still green. It's not fit for use."

Rendil ignored her and carried on issuing orders as if she were not present.

'Stop, Rendil. Stop and explain yourself, or I'll be forced to send for men to remove you."

Still he refused to acknowledge her. In the valley below, she could see that his men had harnessed ponies to her carts and were loading them with fire wood. Others were leading ponies hauling shallow tub-sleds, filled with lead ore. Rendil stood beside her and peered down at them, a smug smile on his face. He moved off to the furnace, tinkering with it as though his needless fooling was of vital importance.

"Very well, I'm fetching my miners," Wynflaed said. "They'll soon see you off."

He stood and faced her, at last acknowledging her presence. "I am here on the king's orders. I must insist that you allow me, as the king's appointed officer, to carry out my work," he said, facing her, triumph glowing in his eyes. "Don't interfere, or threaten me, or my officers."

"Officers! What, this lot?" she said. "These louts are not fit to guard a night bucket."

Rendil sighed, straightening to look at her. "I've been asked to determine why more silver cannot be extracted from the lead. The king's man himself wants to know. He's appointed me to find out." He eyed her smugly. "It seems you don't properly understand the process. At least, that's his impression." He pointed casually to a man at the fire. "He's an expert. He'll demonstrate how simple it is."

"Huh, not today he won't," Wynflaed said.

"If you attempt to prevent him, I'll be forced to exercise my rights as a duly appointed officer of the king's gafol."

"Oh, really and what does that mean?"

"It means I can do whatever I want, in the king's interests. I could even order your mine confiscated."

Wynflaed laughed. "Don't be silly, Rendil. You're losing your wits. You're so envious of my small success here, it's addled your brain."

"You will lose a lot more than your mine, Lady, if you've been cheating the king."

"Cheating! Very well Rendil, I'll stand aside. I won't try to prevent you, or your so-called expert, from doing whatever you want. Go ahead," she said, "but if he really is an expert, he will know that no amount of dry wood, charcoal, goose-fat, or even whale oil, is going to make that fire hot enough to toast cakes let alone extract silver today."

Rendil gaped, his confidence punctured. "Why? What have you done?"

"There's not enough wind, you fool. Oh, and another tiny point," she said, with a twinkle in her eye. "Did he line the furnace with new clay before lighting that fire?" Rendil shot his smelterer a stricken look, then turned back to her as she went on quietly. "One other small thing if — err — I may speak?"

Eyeing her obliquely, he nodded, a look of mounting dread on his face.

"When he does line the furnace, make sure the clay is thoroughly pugged and kneaded. There must be no air or chaff left in it. It's only a small thing," she said, "but if it is not done properly, it will explode and spray you with molten lead." She turned on her heels and strode off, leaving Rendil simmering like a rag pudding.

He glared at his smelterer. "Fool!" he raged. 'Is she right about the exploding clay thing? You could have killed us all, you stupid idiot."

In her anger, Wynflaed forgot to take the lead-cart road back down to the village. Habit led her onto the steep, rocky path down, as her indignation filled her thoughts. She was so angry that her head ached and her heart pounded. A third of the way down the steep climb she paused and tried to calm herself. She sat on a rock and moistened her fingers in the frosty grass and wiped them across her aching brow. After a moment or two she felt calmer, and realising she had taken the wrong path, considered turning back to descend by the easier road. She rejected the idea as that would involve facing Rendil again. Regretting that she had not allowed Maud to come with her she set off cautiously picking her way down the rocky path. Half way down, the climb crossed a hidden trickle of water where a willow tree clung precariously. She tried to pull off a sliver of bark to chew, to relieve her headache. Reaching to tug at it, she slipped and tumbled headlong down the hillside, coming to a thudding stop against an outcrop of limestone.

In the village below, Maud heard her screams and ran up the path. She found her moaning and barely conscious. Within moments, Rendil arrived at the scene, his face as white as a querner's corpse. Maud quickly checked her over. Her fingers were stained with blood.

"Is she bleeding," Rendil cried. "Is it the child? Dear gods don't let it be the child."

Maud looked up into his face. It was the face of a frightened man, a man who knew that his scheming has gone badly wrong and far beyond what he had wanted.

***

Aelric travelled to By-Streams as soon as he heard the news. He took gifts and food, ready to stay as long as needed. Rendil went with him, taking Goda and her midwife. They found Wynflaed confined to her bed by Maud, who took strict control of everything.

The child was stillborn. "I want her named," Wynflaed sobbed. "Aelfgifu, gift of the fairies. She's to be buried as a child, not as a ..." Maud cut her off with a staying hand. She could not speak, but nodded, weeping silently over the bloody bundle in her arms.

In Wulfric's absence, Aelric carried the child to its grave where he spoke of her with love, almost as if he had known her. Rendil watched the child's burial from a distance, furious that events were conspiring against him. Even when she loses a child, she turns it to her advantage. Was there nothing she would not do to humiliate him? Once again his father was at her heels like a doting dog. Why could he not see what sort of woman she was?

....

CHAPTER TWELVE

Weodmonath, the month of weeds, in the eighth year of Penda's rule, by the Christian kind's way of reckoning that is August 641 Anno Domini. Word of Penda's victory over the Christian king, Oswald of Northumbria reached By-Streams. The news had come quickly. Only a few days had passed since the Northumbrian king had fallen near Maserfeld, at a place some were now calling Oswald's tree. But the war was not over yet. King Penda wanted the enemy's strongholds looted and razed to rubble. He led his legions north into Northumbria. The king ordered Wulfric and his Peakland cohort to sprint ahead of the fleeing Northumbrians to stop them reaching Bebba's Fort, their impregnable stronghold on the coast overlooking the Frisian Sea. Penda well knew that even just a handful of Northumbrians could hold such a strong citadel indefinitely. He wanted to occupy Bebba's Fort before they could.

Penda intended to choose the next Northumbrian king himself; a puppet who would do his bidding and pay him handsome tribute for the privilege. If he could prevent the fleeing Northumbrian army from reaching Bebba's fort, he could pull their teeth and cut their claws. Otherwise they would regroup inside their stronghold, and elect a king of their own choosing. He did not want that. They would be sure to choose some prickly upstart, bent on revenge, and the war would go on for ever.

**

For two weeks Wynflaed waited, expecting Wulfric every day. She went about the Peakland following word of those who had returned. Each time the news was the same. "Yes, my lady," they would say, "I saw His Honour alive after the battle. He went north with Penda and Cenwulf to hound the Northerners." But still she hoped they might be wrong, or that he might soon catch the fleeing Northumbrians and return home. Perhaps he was already on his way.

After four weeks, confirmation of his whereabouts finally came from King Penda's court, carried to her by the king's own runner. He arrived with an armed escort, at the head of a string of ponies loaded with booty. It was Wulfric's share from the victory at Maserfeld. One of the items, a gold ring with emeralds set in the shape of a Christian cross, was said to have been taken from the finger of King Oswald himself. She gave it barely a glance. It was Wulfric she wanted. She would gladly exchange a thousand jewels for his face on the pillow beside her.

Wynflaed entertained the runner and his guards to the best her table could offer. She asked each man for his account of Wulfric's doings. She learned that he had fought in the front of the field and bravely distinguished himself. This was not what she wanted to hear. She would have been happier to learn that he had cowered at the back and kept safely out of trouble, but she knew that was not her husband's way.

***

Ealdorman Cenwulf's gafol reeve came to By-Stream soon after the harvest. It was only the second time he had visited the village in the six years since Wulfric and she had moved there. He was a thin, wiry man with a jolly face and a quietly humorous manner. He assessed the village for dues with a beaming smile and a most jocular courtesy, as though everyone should be glad of his attentions. Accompanied by his clerk and with several men at arms to protect him, he entered every house, measured every strip of plough land and counted every bee skep. Maud commented sourly that it would not have surprised her if had lined up all the bees and counted them too.

Like most, Wynflaed resented his intrusion, but was courteous and cooperative. Whenever his presence annoyed her, she would tell herself that the Ealdorman and the King had every right to their share of the country's wealth. She would remind herself that almost everything she and Wulfric possessed had come from them in one way or another.

Throughout his stay, the gafol reeve and his men lodged in the hall. Wynflaed obliged him to tell her stories of the ladies of the King's court. On the third day, the assessor was ready to leave, but said there were a few points he wished to raise about the lead mine.

"Would you like to visit the mine?" she asked him, knowing he had every intention of doing so with or without her invitation. "We have a magical cave, shaped like a great bell. Perhaps you have heard of it."

"Aah yes, The Whispering Bell. I have heard about it. It's said that only the Peak's Arse is bigger."

"Bigger yes, but lacking magic and beauty," she said, adding playfully, "as is the way of arses."

The reeve giggled, spluttering mead down his chin. "I look forward to seeing Belle Earegasp," he said trying to compose himself. "When I came here six or seven years ago, the miners delved at outcrops. Surely that's a much easier way of getting the ore?"

Wynflaed thought his question seemed suspiciously rehearsed, but answered confidently. "Certainly much easier," she agreed, "but riddled with practices far too restrictive for proper taxation and control. As Your

Honour knows, ancient custom can be a stiff clay to work with. It is often better to begin again from scratch."

She saw that the assessor understood. He shifted topic and asked her another question. "I have heard that ore from an outcrop often contains more silver. Is that true?"

Wynflaed sensed Rendil's interference behind his questioning. It explained why the gafol reeve had decided to visit By-Streams, after so long without concern. "If there is silver in the lead," she answered, choosing her words carefully, "it can be richer in an outcrop of ore than in ore deeper down."

"Is it not wasteful then to reject it?"

"I firmly believe that our lord Penda is better served by his thirteenth dish of lead," she told the gafol reeve. "If we mined only for the silver, he would see only a paltry poke from us compared with what he currently gets in his lead dish alone."

The reeve appeared confused, "But lead contains silver, does it not?"

"Barely any," she said. "Not more than three ounces to a ton of our lead."

"But even so my lady, does it not follow that if you have a ton of lead, you must therefore have three ounces of silver? I'm sure you can see my point."

"The silver is brought forth only when the hearth is extremely hot, much hotter than needed for simply extracting the lead. The process demands that much more timber is cut and charcoal made. More clay must be dug and cleaned and pugged for the furnace. All this extra work requires so many men that they would have little time for mining the ore. So you see it's much better for the king that we dig lead and not waste our time felling trees, making charcoal, and digging clay, just to win an ounce or two of silver."

"This alchemy is a puzzle to me, but I understand your reasoning." He leaned back in his chair and nodded thoughtfully. "Yet you do send the king some silver? Why is that?"

"Sometimes we get silver if the fire is naturally very hot, for example when the wind is particularly strong and favourable."

"Aarhh I see. Very well, I'm satisfied, but tell me one more thing, Wynflaed Wulfricswif, what would you do if the charter allowed you to benefit from the silver and not the king solely? Wouldn't you extract it then?"

"I would not," she said.

"Why not?"

"It's very simple, your honour. If I did, you'd be here constantly, complaining that the king's thirteenth share was such a paltry purse and not the fat juicy one it is today."

The reeve put his fingers ends together and stared at them thoughtfully. A smile grew slowly on his face and he began to chuckle.

Wynflaed filled his cup with mead and pushed a plate of soft biscuits towards him. He sipped from his cup. "I don't think I'll bother to see the mine tomorrow," he said.

***

Autumn mouldered into winter. The Peakland locked its brilliance in ice and hoary mists, as if to preserve it for another season. Stags moved down into the forested valleys from the hills above By-Streams, their roaring voices silent now after the rut. In steaming groups they scratched the mast and leaf mould to expose rare shoots of green.

Each day, a few warriors limped home from the north. They brought captured weapons, tools and iron, even sheep, cattle and slaves. Most looked thin and weary. Many a man carried useless booty, little more than junk to be shown off briefly and then lost in a barn or dumped on the midden. They all brought word of a failed attack on Bebba's fort, and of good friends and neighbours killed there.

Wynflaed visited their homes seeking news of Wulfric. She heard the same story many times. Wulfric, they told her, had led his men to the foot of the citadel's massive wooden walls. The fort stands perched up high on a rocky peak overlooking the sea. After weeks of pointless siege and numerous failed attempts to scale the walls, Wulfric tried to burn a breach in them. He built a great fire of the timbers and thatch from the houses of a nearby village. The flames roared up the walls and it seemed his plan would succeed. But then, when the fire was at its greatest, the wind changed. The flames blew back on to the attackers. Many were burned to death. Barely a handful escaped, running with their hair and clothes alight. No-one could tell her with certainty that they had seen Wulfric alive afterwards. They said he had been at the very front, where the heat and flames were the most intense. Many around him were killed. None she spoke to believed that he could have survived.

For weeks the news of Wulfric's death hung on the chilling air like a shroud of elmwood smoke. It permeated every action, governed every course. By-Streams and the old master's hall at Holmesfelt were weighed down by grief. Wynflaed buried her feelings beneath a frantic bustle of work. Every waking moment she busied herself. Every night she went to her bed exhausted.

Maud saw only disaster ahead. She tried to persuade her mistress to ease up on herself, but to no avail. Wynflaed was locked away inside herself, her thoughts trapped in a mire of grieving from which nothing could raise her. Then, just when it seemed most hopeless, Maud noticed a change. Wynflaed began telling her children stories of their father at bedtimes. As winter wore on, she devoted more time to them and entrusted more of the business of Bell Delfan and the farms to her reeves and to Maud. Life at By-Streams began slowly, returning to normal.

***

His son's death was a bitter blow from which Aelric was never to recover. He blamed himself for pushing Wulfric to follow Lord Cenwulf's army. His sense of guilt was so deep that he could hardly face Wynflaed or her children. His house servants told her that he spent his days locked away in the room he had shared with his wife. He stopped walking with his dogs along the margins of his fields, and as spring approached, it was clear his health was in serious decline.

With that strange and saddening resignation that often catches folk in old age he began to give away his prized possessions. To little Eadric he gave his battle helm and armoured leather coat. A heavy gold torc, taken in battle from a Wealh chief, he passed to Wyngifu. On a blustery day in the third month of the year, Aelric sent Wynflaed the Mydercan his dead wife had treasured. It arrived strapped to Snowflake's back, with word that Wynflaed was not to open it until she was alone in her bed chamber. Eadwin and Maese carried it into her bedroom. She followed them and watched as they carefully placed it on her night chest. Thanking them she pulled the curtain over the door and stood alone, remembering how Aelric had shown her his wife's room and the mydercan.

She ran her fingers over the mydercan's polished surface. It felt cool and as smooth as silk. Raising its lid she inhaled the smell of wool, lanolin and beeswax. Inside, she found not only the spinning, weaving and sewing instruments she had seen before, but a teag of boxwood inlaid with carved walrus ivory. It was packed to its lid with jewellery. She ran to her bedroom door and called for Maud, then returned to sit on the bed, staring at the box as if it had spoken to her. As Maud bustled into the room, her look of weary concern was banished by her astonishment as she saw the open box.

"Look Maud," Wynflaed whispered. "Close the door." She began laying out the contents on her bed. There were necklaces of amber, and of green and blue glass. There was a heavy bracelet of Peakland blue gems, set in silver. In a kidskin bag, Maud found a pair of slippers with silk and garnet butterflies embroidered on them. There were earrings, jewelled buckles and cloak pins of bronze and chased silver.

The two women looked at each other astonished. Neither had seen such fabulous things, but the most striking and heart-wrenching fact about them was that not a single item had ever been worn. Most were wrapped in linen or kid-skin pokes that bore no mark of wear or soiling.

Wynflaed realised that for years the old man had been buying gifts for his dead wife. It was as if he was sharing his good fortune with her in a secret world of his own. She realised that the teag contained much more than riches; it held a statement of love and of death. Aelric was not just saying goodbye. He was begging for her forgiveness, for what he knew was unforgivable. It was his fault that Wulfric was dead; his fault that she would be alone, just as he had been alone. He knew that he had condemned her to a life filled with the same emptiness as his own. Nothing, not all the jewels in the world, could change that.

She felt so desperately sorry for him, and though she had wanted to blame him for Wulfric's death, she knew her husband and his sense of duty. He had not gone to war because of his father. He had followed his own advice.

"It's so awful," she told Maud, "to have outlived his wife and now his son too."

Maud sighed, agreeing. "But he's still got you and the bairns," she said, adding without conviction, "and there's Rendil."

Wynflaed well knew Maud's opinions of Rendil, but she also knew that Aelric loved him as much as he had loved Wulfric. Also, she reminded herself that he carried a deep-rooted guilt for Rendil's injuries and saw him as a man cheated of his rightful life.

Maud began wrapping each piece and replacing it carefully in the teag. She did not expect to see any one of them adorning her mistress. She knew they would be locked away and held until Wyngifu and Goda's daughters came of age. Then, untarnished by painful memories, guilt and grief, they would glitter on slim young necks and wrists.

"He must think he's dying, Maud," Wynflaed said. "He knows it's ending. That's why he's sent this now. Quick Maud, send for Eadwin and some men. We must go to Holmesfelt. See that my wyrtcyste is loaded. Bryoni will come too. Send a man to find the Crowman. I want him to meet us there. I think we could have need of him."

***

As Wynflaed started out for Holmesfelt, the last snows of winter still covered the high Peaklands, its misty greyness dulling the edges of earth and sky. Eadwin led Snowflake down the steep track to join the valley road. Wynflaed followed with the others.

Ice encrusted emerald green mosses around the mouth of Linen Spring, sharpening the water's voice as it tumbled beside the path into the frost clamped valley. Wynflaed looked beyond it to the wide, low entrance to Bell Delfan in the distance. Deep underground, in the mine's dark constancy, she knew the miners laboured unaffected by winter's icy breath.

After crossing the fast flowing river, they began a two-mile climb towards the high, craggy edges of millstone-grit overlooking the valley. Once at the top, Wynflaed paused to catch her breath. She brushed snow from a time-scoured rock and sat down. A bitter wind rushed up the cliff face, pressing tears from her eyes, splintering her vision. Below her, black and brimming, the River Derwent flowed, hidden, save for occasional glimpses, by the crowding skeletons of the oak trees that gave it its name. Beyond it, in the seeping greyness, the bulk of By-Streams edge piled up to the horizon like a giant dead ox. Its snow covered shoulders pressed against a leaden sky. She could see no sign of By Streams, hidden beneath dull patches of leafless forest, save for a trace of wood smoke.

She told her escort of four miners to wait a while, so that Eadric and young Betla, who was carrying Wyngifu on her back, could rest. Ahead the scrubby upland lay smothered by snow, drawing mists and frost about itself like a beggar garners rags. Here and there, ghostly crowds of skeletal oaks and birches gathered around massive toadstones, as if waiting for them to move once more by whatever magical means had brought them there.

Eadwin's voice burst in on her thoughts. "If we had waited for tomorrow, we'd never have got this far," he said. He was watching the gathering clouds with concern.

"What?" she asked absently.

The muler nodded towards the clouds. "That's snow in them clouds," he said. "I was just saying, that if we'd set off tomorrow, we'd probably be snowed in. As it is we'll have to move a-pace to get there before the weather does. It's coming this way."

Wynflaed sighed and eased her aching back. "Hum, I expect you're right," she said. "What did you hear of the old master on your last visit?"

"Beg your pardon, my lady?"

"Oh nothing, I was just wondering how the Old Master is — really."

The young man shrugged nervously. "He seems much older these days — in spirit, I mean. I think he expects to die soon."

"Die? Why do you say that?"

"It's the way he talks, you know, as if everything is in the past. Nothing is in the future. And he's giving his things away. He gave me this the last time I was there." From inside his fleece lined jerkin he pulled out a silver and ivory handled seax. It was almost as long as his forearm. "He gave me five silver coins too." He hung his head and kicked at the snow at his feet.

Wynflaed thought of the jewellery box. "The winter gets to old folk. It brings them low."

"No, I think it's because of Wulfric," said Eadwin. "His death has hit him very hard. No man should die after his children.

Wynflaed silently choked back her feelings. She agreed with him completely, but dare not speak for fear of weeping.

Eadwin sniffed and quickly wiped a hand over his eyes. "He's been like a father to me."

"Yes, of course. He fostered you."

"My mother died when I was about two; my father a few years after. Eofar says I was about six. I'm afraid my old dad he weren't much use, though we loved him of course. Well, you do don't you? But he weren't like the old master. You can look up to him. He's always been good to me."

Wynflaed touched Eadwin's forearm. "I'd forgotten how close you are. Forgive me. I wasn't thinking."

"No, it's alright," the muler said.   "I know he's getting old now. I try to be ready for whatever Wyrd throws at us."

They were silent for a while, and then Wynflaed said, "Perhaps your father had much sadness in his life."

"Him? No, lady. Eofar has told me things about him. I'm afraid he was a drunk. He hated his own father for losing the mine. You ask my brother. All he ever did was moan about old Delfan Eaffa for making him into a poor man's son." He stopped abruptly, blushing with embarrassment. "Sorry, my lady, I didn't think."

"You mean about the lead rights?" queried Wynflaed. "Yes, I suppose your father might've been — well ..." She stopped and smiled. "So, I suppose when he lost your mother that was the last straw?"

"Well, maybe. I've not thought about it much. You get what Wyrd gives you, don't you? It's up to each of us to make the best of it. Being rich can't make some folk happy can it? Look at Rendil?" Too late he realised that he had stuck his foot in his mouth again. It was not for him to criticise his betters, and he was now frantically wondering how to extricate himself when he saw that Wynflaed was laughing.

"Mother Frigg yes. You're right about that. What a sorry sight he is. I don't think he could smile at fools' day feast."

Relieved and emboldened by his success at conversation with his betters, Eadwin stood up and adjusted his cloak to show that he felt it was time they resumed their trek. He turned to his fellows and roused them with a lordly wave.

At the journey's half-way mark, Bar Brook, usually a musical trickle, raged across their path. Even so, seeing it cheered Wynflaed. She always felt that the worst of the trek was over when she reached Bar Brook.

Accepting Eadwin's helping hand over the brook's icy stepping stones, she started to ask him a question. "Do you ever feel that ...?" she stopped herself and looked away from him.

Once on firm ground Eadwin faced her, seeing her concerned expression. "Do I feel what, lady? What is it?"

"Oh nothing, it's stupid. Forget I said anything."

"Tell me, lady, please. You look upset. What is it?"

She sighed and gathered herself. "Do you believe Wulfric is dead?"

Eadwin's shoulders slumped and he dropped his gaze to the snow covered ground. "I know what you mean. I feel the same way sometimes, but the facts are hard to ignore."

"But nobody saw him die."

"Yes, I know, and I think those same thoughts too, but ..."

"But you don't think he survived?"

He shook his head. "No, lady. I'm afraid I don't. I want him to be alive, just like you do, but common sense ... Sometimes I have to stop myself. I take my time and think it all through rationally. That's when I realise he cannot possibly be alive."

"Then convince me, Eadwin."

"Nobody saw him survive. I asked lots of men who were there. They all told me the same story. He was at the front, closest to the fire when the wind turned. None of the men at the front escaped. But that's not the biggest proof."

"Tell me what is."

"If he had survived — we'd know it because of his ransom. Forgive me, lady, but as a rich man's son his value in ransom would be huge. The Northumbrians would never miss such a chance for riches."

Wynflaed looked back at him carefully weighing his words.

"But that's not all," he said. "There's one more thing that really proves it. Nothing could stop him coming back to you if he had survived."

Leaning into the snow flurries, Wynflaed turned from him and walked on in silence. The weather was worsening. The little column plodded onward, every man and woman snuggling deeper into their cloaks and jerkins. Heavy snowfall beneath the darkening sky robbed the landscape of its features. Despite this, Eadwin led them as surely as if he were drawn to his destination on a cord. Soon, they spotted the lights of Aelric's settlement. A flurry of chatter marked the relief felt by everyone. A friendly snowball tossed at Eadwin carried its thrower's unspoken gratitude for their safe delivery.

Aelric, Wynflaed learned, had taken to his bed three days before. The house reeve told her that apart from the odd flicker of an eyelid, he'd barely moved since. Wynflaed noted the house reeve's concern in his red-rimmed eyes. "Will you take me to him and then see to my people. They're cold and hungry."

"Of course, Lady. Follow me." The old man led her into Aelric's hall and through to the door of a separate room in upper hall. Wynflaed nodded gratefully and thanked him with a pat on his forearm. She leaned on the door but found it barred. Gently, she tapped on it and waited. It was opened by a scruffy hag whom she recognised as the village's so-called healer. Inexplicably, Aelric trusted the woman. Wynflaed did not. She despised her dubious ways.

"Oh it's you," the sour old woman said. "I suppose you're going to tell me I should have him up and dancing by now."

Wynflaed brushed her aside and entered the room. Aelric was lying on his carved oak coffer bed in the dimly lit room. His breathing was shallow, and occasionally caught on the fluid in his chest, making him cough painfully.

"He's dying!" said the woman, not caring that Aelric might hear her. "Not long now."

Wynflaed ignored her and moved to the bedside to assess his condition for herself. Aelric's face was grey and sweating. Looking around the room she saw that the old woman had been lazing comfortably in a chair with her back to the bed. On a small table she had a cup, a flask of wine and a board with a generous serving of cheese, cold goose and bread.

"He's so thin," Wynflaed said.

"Yes, I know. I've been struggling to feed him." Her eyes flicked guiltily to the food beside her chair.

"Not as successfully as you've been feeding yourself. Has his breathing been like this long?"

The woman cast her sour look. "That's the end you can hear," she said. "It's the death rattle. His lungs are full of death. They always sound like that before they go."

Some movement at Aelric's throat caught Wynflaed's eye. It was perhaps a trickle of sweat, or lamp light reflecting on a pulse or muscle spasm. It drew her to inspect the woollen cloth wound around his throat. Something moved beneath it. She bent closer to see it better. Leaf mould, stuffed between layers of the wet woollen fabric, seethed with shining grey beads. She picked at a loose fold and gingerly pinched it back. Revolted she revealed a slimy mess of wood lice and earthworms, wriggling in a mouldy morass. "Gods! What's this?" she cried. "Holy Mother Frigg! Get it off him. Take it off now."

"No. You need 'em to eat the poison. They stop it rising to his head," said the old woman, pushing between Wynflaed and the bed. "You'll kill him quicker if you take it off."

Wynflaed turned on the old hag and slapped her hard. "Get that foul thing off him!" she said, and running to the door she heaved it open, her face red with fury. "Eadwin," she called into the dimly lit hall. "Edda, come quick."

"How long have you had him like this, you night-hag?" she asked, turning back into the room. "Gods look! The bedding's alive with them."

Eadwin came panting into the room. "I was bedding down the animals."

"Find Gutty, then come back and help me."

When Eadwin returned with Widow Guthrum, Wynflaed had them lift Aelric from the bed and lay him on a clean mattress of straw and furs. The old mattress was taken out and burned. She and Gutty bathed him and combed his hair and put him in a clean shift. They sat with him and kept his brow cool with a cloth soaked in brine, lavender and willow shoots. Watching his face and flickering eyelids, she saw how much the troubles of the last months had drained him. He looked old and fragile, and so very close to death.

Gutty bent forward and kissed him on the cheek. "You old fool," she said, sobbing softly. "I would have come if you'd only have let me. I tried, but they turned me away three times. That old witch always did have him in her thrall." She looked up at Wynflaed. "When I was a girl, I used to look at him and wish he was mine. I would have done owt for him, but he never thought of anybody but her. I never knew a man who loved a woman as much. He wouldn't look at me, even when his heart was broke with grief and there was nobody to share it with."

Later that evening, Aelric opened his eyes briefly and focussed on Wynflaed. He smiled, his face seeming briefly to shed the years. "I knew you'd come," he whispered.

"Why didn't you send for me before, Father?" she asked gently. "I didn't know. No word came to By-Streams."

He slipped into sleep again, looking peaceful and at ease. Slinking in the background, the old woman eyed Wynflaed malevolently and nursed her injured pride. After an hour she found the confidence to ease towards the sick-bed. Gutty glared at her, but seeing that Wynflaed did not send the old hag away, she relented slightly. The old woman drew closer and offered to take over mopping Aelric's brow.

"Did you know he'd asked for me?" Wynflaed asked her.

"He never asked for nobody but me."

Wynflaed sensed she was lying. "Have you been here all the time?"

"Yes, I came when he took ill three days ago. I've not shifted, save to piss."

"Did he say anything?"

The crone dabbed Aelric's brow. "I'd 'ave said so if he 'ad,"

"Mind your tongue," said Gutty.

Wynflaed sat on the edge of the coffer bed. "Tell me exactly what he did say."

"He's not spoke a word. He's had three days with nowt but dying on his mind. He'll 'ave gone by morning — you'll see."

Aelric's eyelids flickered. He moved his head, trying to focus on Wynflaed, but the effort was too much and he sagged back onto his pillow.

"Look, I've got something," Wynflaed told the old woman, and delved her hand down into a pocket in her dress lining. She brought out a little leather pouch and dangled it before the old woman's face. "It's a potion, a tonic. It'll give him strength."

"It'll do no good to give it him now. It's too late."

"Shut up and mind what the lady says," said Gutty.

"But he's all but dead. Only the gods can say if he's going to come back now."

"No. I want to give him some of this," said Wynflaed. "I know it will help. It's a powder ground from wild vine and adreminte. It will help his head and clear his chest. It might be too late to cure him, but at least he'll be more comfortable. Fetch me some honey and clean boiled water, quickly."

"I'll keep an eye on her," said Gutty.

"I don't think you should give it him," the old witch said defiantly." I've been tending sick folk long enough to know when it's all over. What he needs is leaving to die in peace."

Boiling water and honey were stirred together under Gutty's watchful eye. The potion was added and then put to cool beside the sick bed.

"It'll do no good," insisted the old woman.

Since Wynflaed's arrival, several of Aelric's house servants had slipped quietly into the room to watch the proceedings. The old woman, who had excluded them until then, now turned to them seeking their support. "He's done for," she told them. "I've seen it all before. He'll be gone by morning, mark my words."

Wynflaed's patience snapped. She turned angrily and pushed her to the door. "Get out! You've done enough damage with your stupid ideas. Don't come back."

"I'll tell Rendil," she said. "He'll have something to say about this. It wasn't you he called for, it was me. I birthed him and Wulfric too. I was the one he always called for, not you, and not that dirty whore neither."

Gutty slipped an arm about Wynflaed's shoulders and smiled. "See, my fame is spreading."

Breaking gently from the embrace, Wynflaed dabbed her eyes and returned to Aelric's bedside. Maud stepped up behind her and laid a comforting hand on her shoulder. Wynflaed touched it thankfully. "Oh gods, Maud, what a mess. Did you see it? Now she says she's going to find Rendil."

"Huh! They'll make a lovely couple."

Wynflaed and Gutty looked at each other across the sick-bed and allowed themselves a moment of silent laugher. "Oh thank you, Maud. I needed that. I don't know what I'd do without you two. Come on now, give us a hand with the bed. I think he's just peed."

Moments later, Rendil burst into the hall. The old woman was hovering at this shoulder. He watched as Wynflaed, Gutty and Maud finished making his father comfortable. He had been furious as he stormed through the hall but quickly calmed down as he saw his father. "Wynflaed," he said, his voice choked off to a whisper. "He ... How is he?"

She moved towards him and reached out her hand. Rendil took it absently, not really seeing her, only his father's pale face on the pillow. "It's not good, Rendil," she told him softly. "He's very poorly."

"Old Mother Ilam says he'll be dead in the morning."

"She might be right," Wynflaed said, "but at least he's clean and comfortable now. He needed to be washed and his bed changed."

Rendil sat on the edge of the bed. "Changed? Huh, just like a bairn," he said. A tear welled in his eye and rolled down his face. He glanced up at her, but quickly dropped his gaze to his hands folded in his lap. "I'm – I'm glad you're here."

Old Mother Ilam slipped away.

Rendil sat with Wynflaed at his father's bedside for most of the night. They spoke little. Even there, the tension between them prevented it.

Aelric was to live another two weeks. Twice he was able to lean on Rendil's shoulder and walk about his farm a little, seeing his old friends before finally his long life's thread was snapped during his sleep.

Wynflaed found him cold and peaceful. She sent word to Rendil. An hour or so later, a tentative knock at Aelric's door drew her eyes from the winding sheet covering the corpse. Numbly she turned to Maud, who had helped her so much during the old man's last days. "That'll be Rendil. You'd better let him in."

Three men, one an older man whom she recognised as Manwine, Aelric's farm reeve, entered quietly. With slow measured steps they walked towards her, the older one preceding. "I heard he'd gone?"

"In his sleep," she said.

"We've washed him and got him ready," Maud said.

Wynflaed saw the old man's eyes flick to the thegn's shield where it hung on the wall. It was the look of one remembering things long past. She recalled Wulfric telling her that Manwine had served his father since long before he had won his lands and wealth. After a moment Manwine blinked and straightened his old shoulders. He blew a decisive sigh. "These are my sons," he said. "That's Manred. This is Alfwine. They'll do your bidding; whatever is needed. I'll see to the farm and the labourers. You needn't worry about anything. We'll see to it all."

"Shouldn't you be saying this to Rendil? He's master here now."

"Aye, but I've not seen him, lady. We don't know where he is."

"I've sent word to him," Wynflaed said. "He'll be here soon. It will be a hard blow for him, even though he knew it was coming."

"I know, but life goes on," said Manwine. "A hall needs a master, especially now. Aelric's friends and tenants will expect to see Rendil here. They'll all be arriving soon for the funeral. Word will travel fast. He was a great man. There'll be plenty wanting to pay their respects."

"But we must wait for Rendil," Wynflaed insisted. "I'm sure he won't be long. You can post a man in the porch to help callers, and another outside this door to keep all but the family out until Rendil's back. That's fitting, I think."

Manwine looked relieved. "Yes, I think so too. Thank you, lady. Meanwhile, I'll see to a grave." Turning to leave, he shooed his great lumbering sons out before him like a brace of geese.

....

CHAPTER THIRTEEN

Eadric's seventh birthday, Wynflaed decided, would be the most splendid occasion she could possibly make it. There had been enough misery and mourning at By-Streams. This would be a chance to brighten the place up and try to put back some of its sparkle. She would invite folk from all over the shire.

Since Wulfric's death, many of their old friends had been rather coy about visiting her. They had paid their respects formally, as custom dictated. Unfortunately, their good manners and reluctance to intrude was depriving her of their company. She felt that her children, and indeed the whole of By-Streams, needed a celebration, something gay and frivolous to breach the wall of correctness that constrained it.

For the children's sake she knew she had to break out of her own cell of grief. Little Eadric may not have a father to groom and guide him, but his father had been respected and admired. His old friends and comrades would remember that, especially if she prompted them with the sight of the little boy standing beside her in his father's stead. Then, she hoped, they would rally to help him for the sake of his dead father, their old friend and comrade from the shield wall.

Lord Maenche ap Ebell was a Wealish man. He was also Ealdorman Cenwulf's foster brother. Wulfric had served as his second in command. It was Maenche who had brought Wynflaed official news of Wulfric's death. In the months that had passed since then, Wynflaed had lived that terrible moment time and time again. It was her waking nightmare. She knew that if she was going to change the mood at By-Streams, she would have to start by changing herself. She must face Lord Maenche again. He was the most senior and powerful of Wulfric's old friends. He should be the one to take little Eadric under his wing.

Maud burst in on her thoughts. "Are you all right? You look - err - different."

"I feel different, Maud," Wynflaed said, shaping her shoulders decisively. "I've decided we'll have a great feast for Eadric's birthday anniversary. I shall invite everybody."

Maud greeted the news with mixed feelings. She was pleased to see her mistress in better spirits, but the thought of all the extra work that putting on a feast for "everybody" would entail did not thrill her.

Wynflaed noted her doubtful frown. "Oh, don't worry, it'll not be that bad. There will be plenty of help from our neighbours and guests, and I'll help you myself."

Maud's frown deepened. "You'll help. That's what I'm worried about. I'd rather do it all on my own than have you peering over my shoulder at every tuck and turn."

"Very well then," Wynflaed said. "So you will. I shall stand back. You'll be in complete charge." She winked at Maud's gaping face. "Satisfied? Good. Now I'm off to see if Lord Maenche is at Badecanwell. You'd better get cracking."

"Lord Maenche? Why on earth ...?"

"I'm going to invite him," she told her. "If the master had been alive, he would've asked him. A boy's seventh year anniversary is a big thing, especially for the son of a great warrior. It's time he met the leaders of his clan and took his place amongst them. His father would have wanted it. With Maenche here, the whole shire will come. Eadric's star will shine like the sun, just as it should do for the heir of Wulfric Aelricsunnu of the Cenwulfingas."

"What about — you know who?" asked Maud, with a grimace that could have turned milk.

"If you mean Rendil, he'll be invited too. He's Eadric's uncle and head of the family. Anyway, Eadric likes him — for some strange reason."

"Which only goes to show how much the lad's got to learn," said Maud.

Wynflaed busied herself to leave. "Right," she said, "now that we all know your opinion, can we get on with the things that really matter."

"Huh! Don't worry. I know my opinions count for nothing around this place."

***

On the eve of the feast, Rendil was the first to arrive. Maud and the rest of the household kept well away from him, an option unavailable to Wynflaed. For some time Maud watched apprehensively as her mistress and Rendil engaged in, what looked to her, a deeply mystifying, whispered conversation. Gradually, as their control slipped and their voices grew louder, Maud strained to hear.

"What in the name of Holy Mother Frigg are you talking about, Rendil?" Wynflaed cried, her tone poised uncertainly between exuberance and despair. "I mean to say, usually you're about as subtle as a blizzard. Now you've got me baffled."

"I merely said you should keep in mind the purpose of this feast."

Wynflaed shot him a doubting frown. "No, that's not what you're saying. Beneath all your warping and wefting, I think you're accusing me of arranging this celebration for some secret and quite unworthy reasons of my own."

The two stared at each other for several moments in tense silence. It was Wynflaed who spoke first. "I know what you think," she said, her eyes alight with fury. "I know what's going on in your head."

Rendil sniffed and peered around the hall as if counting cobwebs. "I don't know what you're talking about."

"You think that I've arranged all this so that I can get a man. You're scared I might be looking for a husband. Admit it. You are, aren't you?"

Rendil shuffled in his seat. "Some folk might see it that way."

"Some! Who but you, Rendil?" she cried. "Only you, brother-in-law, could see it that way. Nobody else but you has such a low opinion of me."

"You're my brother's widow," he said. "My father and brother have left you a very rich woman. Men are bound to come here with ..."

"With what? You mean devious plans to seduce me and strip me of my fortune?" She laughed at the irony. "And you think I'm so stupid, or blind, or cock happy, that I'm going to tumble into their beds at the flash of an eye. I think you've lost your wits, Rendil."

"Well, what else am I to think?" he said. "Wulfric is dead barely six months and you've invited half the shire, even the Ealdorman's brother."

"Might it not be because I want everybody to see Wulfric's son, the child who has inherited his father's mead bench place? It falls to me – a woman – to have him accepted into the circles his father and grandfather would have introduced him into, had they been alive."

"I suppose by that you're saying that I could not do the same for him. I'm the boy's uncle, aren't I? Couldn't you have talked to me first? Or do you think that because I was never in the shield wall I have no influence?" He stomped around glaring angrily and banging his walking stick on the wooden floor of upper hall. Pausing, he turned on her accusingly and wagged his stick at her. "You think because of this leg that I've no place on the warrior's benches. Well that may be true, but my name still counts for something. And you needn't think Lord Maenche will take the lad under his wing. He's far too busy to be bothered with him, without — without ..."

"Without what?" she asked. "A little bit of fun on the side with the boy's mother?"

"I was going to say ..." He paused, as if struck by second thoughts. "Well yes, as a matter of fact. But I expect it will be you, and not him, who'll lead the way to the bedroom. After all, that's how you got Wulfric isn't it? Why change successful tactics now?"

Wynflaed sat back in her seat, demurely smoothing her skirt on her thighs. She lifted her gaze to Rendil's face and fixed him coldly. "I'm glad you're here for the boy's sake, Rendil," she told him calmly. "But when this is over and they all go back to their farms, I never want to see you again. We have nothing more to say to each other. Out of respect for Aelric and my husband, I'll send Eadric to visit you from time to time, but I never want to see you again."

"Oh yes, you will. You'll be seeing much more of me, whether you like it or not. You hold too much of my family's fortune in your greedy claws. I'll not neglect my duty. Wulfric and my father didn't leave you so well provided for just so you could squander it on some curly-headed flute player. It's meant for Eadric. I intend to see he gets it." He stalked to the door, his head rising and falling stiffly to the beat of his walking stick. Turning, he faced her. "One way or another, I'll stop you, woman. Mark me well. I'll stop you no matter what it takes."

"Flute player? What are you babbling about?"

**

For three days and nights, By-Streams echoed to music and the antics of plegerers, poets and old friends. The village common was covered with their tents. Pedlars arrived with their carts and ponies loaded with everything from kindling axes to Asian rose oil. In the lanes children played in giggling gangs, or crowded on the meadow to watch their fathers and brothers racing their horses, or competing with bow, boulder throwing and hurling the javelin.

Wynflaed had given a bonus to her miners and servants equal to all they would earn in a good quarter, though she was careful to exclude wheat and dried beans from the payment, otherwise some might not work at all until their pantries were again bare. Instead, she gave them lengths of good wool cloth, goose feathers, honey, beeswax and mead. She made room for them at the tables, so that they could eat like lords and enjoy the music and mummers.

Each night the feast was laid out on her tables. Flesherers, brewers, bakers, cooks and skivvies laboured endlessly. Cooking fires were lit in the yard and servers dodged back and forth bringing every manner of meat and drink to the tables. The forty or so grand folk seated in upper hall accounted for about two hundred more, with their servants and grooms, in the yard and common green outside. All had to be fed from Wynflaed's coffers.

Eadric's birthday was undoubtedly the event of the year. Wynflaed achieved exactly what she had set out to do. Nervously dismissing the cost of it all, she spoke inside her heart to Wulfric, begging him to look proudly upon his son, as he was honoured by the best in the shire. "Have I done as you would do, my Wolf-King?" she prayed secretly, tears silvering her eyelashes.

There was no doubt that she had. In the eyes of every man there, the presence of Lord Maenche, the Ealdorman's foster brother, marked Eadric as a lad with a golden future. Many a little girl's parents made secret, wishful plans for their tiny offspring, and ambitious mothers eased their daughters into Eadric's path, whether he was shyly moving about shaking hands and bearing the questioning of his guests, or playing on the ground with the dogs.

The only black cloud on events was Rendil's obsessive scrutiny. He seemed to spend the entire time spying and trying to eavesdrop on Wynflaed. He followed her about, hovered at the edge of her conversations and even quizzed some guests about what they had said to her.

On the second day, Wynflaed chose to sit amongst her miners after first serving them with ale and food. She was puzzled to see that Eofar was missing. "Where's my mine reeve?" she asked. "He should be here too."

"Old Eff? He'll be fiddling at his work bench," one miner speculated.

"Yeah, I heard he's making a bigger bed so's he can get his bloody great feet in it," another quipped.

"Aye, or fit somebody alongside of him," another said with a bawdy laugh.

"Somebody?" queried Wynflaed. "Has he a sweetheart then? I hadn't heard that."

"How would we know, lady?" the man said. "Maybe you'd know better than us, you being in touch with him so much." The man smirked and looked aside. "I mean, like at the smelt and the tally and everywhere else."

Wynflaed was shocked, sensing the innuendo woven into the remark. She stared at the speaker, feeling her face colour with indignation. The man dropped his gaze. "Well, you know Eofar," she said, trying to appear unconcerned. "He betrays less to me than to anyone." She stood tensely and smoothed her skirts. "Well, eat and enjoy," she told them. "Have you everything you want?"

"Thank you, lady," they chorused. "And blessings on the little master."

She could not get away fast enough. What was wrong with her? How could she let such a stupid remark upset her? Her mind buzzed with questions as, forcing laughter and smiles, she passed through her crowding guests. Was it guilt? Did she really harbour such feelings for Eofar? No, that was ridiculous. So, why then? Was it what Rendil had said? Had his words struck deeper than she knew?

She headed for her sleeping room in the hope that she could have a moment's quiet to review her thoughts. She found herself confronted by Rendil. He brazenly barred her way, a supercilious scowl on his face. "Do you imagine folk don't know what you're up to?"

"For Holy Frigg's sake, Rendil, drop this nonsense. Go and drink more wine and try to enjoy yourself?"

"I'm enjoying every moment. I couldn't be happier. This all goes well for me, lady. I can promise you, when this is over, you won't be making a fool of me and my family for much longer."

. . . .

CHAPTER FOURTEEN

As summer moved on, Wynflaed tried to forget about Rendil. She concentrated on the harvest. It had been a dry year. The fields looked thirsty. Worse yet, a sudden summer downpour flattened the barley, making reaping even more difficult. But it was not all bad; the bees were doing well, and despite the dry conditions, Wynflaed expected there would be plenty of honey. And on the windy, high ground, where even when it didn't rain, moist clouds dampened the heather, her flocks had prospered.

Perhaps, Wynflaed dared to hope, things were as well as they could be in a life without her beloved husband.

***

Eofar smothered his torch and blinked in the daylight. He saw Maud waiting for him, silhouetted in the bright wedge of light at the mouth of Bell Delfan, and dismissed the lad she had sent to fetch him from the rake. At a distance he saw Bryoni and Betla hanging back nervously. All three women were sobbing.

"What's up?" he asked, apprehension stiffening his hunched shoulders.

"They've taken her away, Eff," Maud cried. "They just came and took her."

"Who? What are you babbling about?"

"Some men came and took the mistress."

Eofar's lips were dry beneath a coating of stone dust. He ran his tongue over them and spat at the ground. "Who were they? Where've they taken her?"

"I don't know. I got there too late. I just saw 'em riding away, about eight armed men. One had a rich coat. They'd put her on a horse. Bryoni says they just walked straight in and took her. She said she never even struggled with them."

"Well if she didn't put up a fight or argue it must be all right," said Eofar. He walked past her and confronted Bryoni, his great bulk towering over her. "Tell me exactly what happened? Did she say anything?"

Bryoni whimpered with confusion. "I didn't see 'em come. Me and Betla was doing some skinning with Maese. We heard her shouting. We didn't do nothing at first. We just thought it must be old Bent Beams had come again. You know how they shout at each other. But then we heard the voices and we knew it weren't him, so we stopped skinning and went to look. They just took her away."

"But you say she didn't resist?"

"No, she was just arguing, you know, angry but not loud. You could see she was upset. She handed little Gifi to me and told me to look for master Eadric to keep him close until it was all sorted out. Then they took her away, but she was calm and cold, though you could see she was angry."

"But nobody manhandled her?"

"No, they weren't rough with her. She said I was to tell you to go to Lord Maenche. She said you'd know what to do about the children."

"I'd know?" Eofar said. "Frigg, what do I know?"

Maud stepped between Eofar and Bryoni and faced him. "She said you've to go and tell Lord Maenche. You must do that first. Don't worry about the children, I'll take care of them."

"I can't go to Lord Maenche, you silly mare. What can I say? It don't even sound as though anything bad's happened. They weren't violent, you say - and she just went along with them. It sounds like nothing to worry about."

"It don't matter what you think it sounds like," said Maud. "She wants you to go to Lord Maenche. We heard her tell Bryoni - didn't we?"

Bryoni nodded. "And she were real serious about it too – you know – worked up like."

Maud squared up to Eofar, her chin jutting. "So, you thick head, you'd better do it. And then maybe we can find out where they've taken her, and who they are. And somebody'll have to tell old Bent Beams, an' all."

Eadwin joined them, having followed Eofar up from the rake. "It could be the Shire Reeve's men."

Eofar shot him an annoyed glance. "Shire Reeve. Don't be stupid. What makes you say that? It could be anybody — some business she's doing – something we can't go sticking our noses into."

Eadwin was shocked by his brother's reaction. "It's obvious," he said. "She went without a struggle. You know what she's like. If they'd been strangers with no right to take her, she would have put up a hell of a fight."

Eofar scratched his chin and walked the few paces out of the cavern's shady mouth into the sunlight. "Well if it is, we'd better keep out of it. The Shire Reeve's men won't do nothing that isn't called for and proper."

Trembling with fury, Maud was glaring at Eofar. "They went east, towards the river," she said, trying to hold her temper. "Shire Reeve's men would've taken her west, towards Badecanwell. So it can't be them." She looked about anxious and frustrated. "She wants you to go to Lord Maenche. She told Bryoni - plain as day. You must do it, Eofar."

Eofar stretched his shoulders and shrugged, blowing a weary sigh. "It's not our business. And anyway, it don't look like it's anything to worry about," he said. "She went with 'em without a struggle. Whatever it is, we should wait and see."

Eadwin shot his brother a stricken look. "You can't mean that."

"You heard me! I'm done with it," Eofar said angrily, spitting the words out, his face reddening. "We're miners. We dig lead. It's not our concern. I don't see us getting any thanks for sticking our noses into things that don't concern us. I say we wait and see. If we've heard no word after a time, we'll think about what to do then. Meanwhile, there's work to do." He stormed away leaving them all staring after him, shocked and bewildered.

Eadwin shrugged apologetically. "Don't worry," he told the women. "I'll speak to him. There must be something - he knows – some reason behind it. I mean – err - maybe it's something he can't tell us. Maybe she told him some secret. You know how she confides in him."

Maud eyed him unconvinced. "She said she wanted him to go to Maenche. Why would she say that if she didn't mean it? You'd better tell your brother that if he doesn't go I bloody well will. I'm not letting it pass."

Eadwin set off back into Bell Delfan, determined to confront his brother. In his haste he did not select and light a torch, but chased after the faint glimmer of Eofar's light, still visible up ahead. He knew the caves well, and was not unduly concerned. Ducking to avoid the low roof of the soot black passage into Belle Earegasp, he followed the path his senses laid out for him. His fingers glided along the wet walls steering him through the blackness. At the end of the passage he paused sensing the great cave opening out around him. He was surprised not to see Eofar's light, and held his breath to listen for sounds of movement. The unique acoustics played back the usual voice of the mine, but there was also a strange rustling sound. He stiffened, trying to hear it more clearly. Pain struck his head and he crumpled unconscious to the floor.

When he came to, Eofar's was the first face he saw amongst a ring of faces bending over him. "What happened? We've been looking for you."

Eadwin sat up rubbing his head. "I banged my head — I think."

"On what?" Eofar asked doubtfully, lifting his light to let him see the clear headroom and great height of the cave roof above him."

Eadwin shook his head and tried to stand. Hands reached to assist him. "I'd just got to the end of the low passage," he said, "and whack!"

"That's way back there, twenty paces or more. How did you get here?" asked one puzzled miner. "There's nowt to hit your head on."

"It could be a rock fall, or tailings somebody was chucking about," suggested Eofar.

There was a murmur of doubting discussion. "Yeah, I suppose that might explain it. Who was working up here?" asked Eadwin.

Nobody admitted guilt. Eadwin smiled ruefully. "Well it was a bloody good throw in the dark. Whoever tossed it got me right on the crust."

"It's late, near enough work's end," said Eofar. "Let's call it a day."

"Late? I must have been out for hours," said Eadwin. "It wasn't noon when I got here."

Noisy banter washed over the mystery, rubbing it out like rain on footprints. Eadwin stumbled into line and shuffled towards the surface with the others. Though he kept quiet, he was not ready to forget what had happened. If he had been struck down by accident, as they all seemed ready to accept, why had he not seen a miner's light? If somebody really had been clearing rocks away from the workings, they wouldn't be doing it in the dark. The more he thought about it, the more convinced he became that somebody had deliberately lain in wait for him, or maybe for Eofar. Either way somebody meant harm to one of them.

The following dawn, Eadwin's sleep was disturbed by the sounds of Eofar packing his carpentry tools and belongings. He had rolled his few clothes into a bundle and was now emptying the tool racks on the cottage walls.

"What are you doing?"

"Leaving! We both are. Get ready."

"Why? Where are we going?"

Eofar wrapped his bundle of clothing inside a ragged tunic and tied it with the sleeves. "We've got to get away. I can't go into it now, but this place is finished."

"Finished, what do you mean? What's going on?" He got out of bed and began dressing. "Is this about yesterday? You know sommat about the mistress, don't you?"

"Look," Eofar snapped. "I know nothing. I just think we'll be better off away from here."

"Where would we go?"

"Cousin Sebbi's," he answered, shouldering his bundle. "I can work for him again. He's always asking me to come back. And you've got Snowflake. There'll be plenty of work for us both. We'll be all right. It was good enough before. I should never have left him to come back here. I'm a carpenter, not a bloody miner. I was happy enough working with Sebbi, and you've never liked the mine."

Eadwin ignored his arguments. "Tell me what's happened to the mistress?" he asked. "You know something, don't you? I thought it was no surprise to you yesterday. You were expecting it. You knew all about it."

Eofar looked back at him, shamefaced. "She's had it coming," he said. "There weren't nothing I could do."

"What?"

"She's been cheating on the king's silver."

"Her, cheating? No, I don't believe it."

"Well it's true, brother. While we've been sweating our bollocks off to make the king's share enough to keep him quiet, she's been holding on to his silver for herself. Our innocent mistress is a conniving thief. Worse than that, she's a bloody fool too. She cheated the one man who was bound to find out. She'll not be coming back here. Never!"

Eadwin stared in disbelief. "It was you that clobbered me, wasn't it?" he said, gingerly rubbing his bruised scalp.

"Get ready. We've got to go. There's nothing for us here now. Not just yet."

"It doesn't make sense," Eadwin said. "I can't believe she'd steal. She wouldn't do it. She's no fool and shc's ccrtainly not a thief."

"You see, there you go. This is why I had to stop you. You'd believe piss is pie if she told you, but Rendil's got the proof."

"Rendil? How do you know what Rendil's got? Have you talked to him?"

"Me, talk to him?" he said. "You've got a lot to learn, little brother. We don't talk to the likes of Rendil about such things. They tell us. We just listen and keep our mouths shut."

"So, they really were magistrate's men who took her yesterday?"

"Yes. They've taken her to the old master's hall. She's to be tried there."

"Why there? Eadwin asked. "Why not take her to the magistrate's hall at Badecanwell? That's where a trial should be." He scratched his head, bemused. "In fact, if it involves the king, why isn't the trial being held at the Ealdorman's? Something stinks about this"

"I don't know. It's not our business."

"You could have said something. You know she wouldn't steal. You could have stopped all this nonsense."

"How? What could I do? She's guilty. They found silver buried in the floor under her bed. Maud didn't tell you that did she?"

"Well of course it was hidden. Silver has to be hidden somewhere safe, doesn't it?" said Eadwin. "That doesn't prove she was stealing it. She was keeping it safe until she sent it to the king."

"She has a strong box for the king's silver; iron bound with a special locking clasp-thing on it and a key. It's not hidden under her bed like a bloody thief's robbings. She's guilty, little brother. It's as plain as day. And even if they don't get her for that, Rendil has a whole list of other charges against her."

"What charges?"

"How about adultery? How about poisoning?" said Eofar. "Rendil has got it all, and plenty of witnesses to prove it."

Eadwin stamped a foot into his boot and sat on his bed to pull on the other. "Adultery? Poisoning? This is madness." He glared at his brother, his thoughts racing, and then jumped to his feet. "I'm going to that trial. It's all a pack of lies. She's being set up – somebody has planted the silver. It's not even very original. I bet Rendil did it.

And as for adultery, you know that's rubbish too. I'm going to speak up for her."

"You can't. If they see you, they'll arrest you," said Eofar. He turned his back on Eadwin and continued packing his tools. "That's why we're leaving. There's a witness who will testify that she spent the night here — with you."

"Well, she did. When I was sick!" howled Eadwin. "Everybody knows that. She nursed me while you went for the healer."

"I know that," said Eofar, "but when Rendil and his witnesses have finished, it will sound a whole lot different." He turned to his brother and paused, gathering his thoughts. "Look, he's promised me that he won't name you if we both move away and don't interfere. I agreed. That's why we're going."

"So that's the so-called adultery is it? And who's the witness? Some halfwit we've never heard of?"

"Wittna's widow."

"Oh her, I might have known it. She hates Wynflaed. She blames her for Wittna's death. She was always raving on that she could have stopped them pinning Wittna's hand. You know that's nonsense. Nobody could have stopped that, it's the lead law. That poor, mad woman will say anything." He slumped forward, his head in his hands. "What else has Rendil cooked up?"

"They can say anything. There are plenty besides Wittna's widow who'll sing Rendil's tune for a few silver coins. And he can easily afford to pay 'em. No matter how you protest, he'll have the last word. Our only chance is to get away and lie low until it all cools down."

"Lie low. No, we should be standing up for her. There are plenty who would stand witness with us. It only needs you to give them a lead. We could find that healer, the Crowman. He'll tell them what really happened that night. They'll believe him. He's a friend of the Ealdorman. And there's Lord Maenche. He'll help us if we ask him." Eadwin stopped, his face as white as ashes. "Gods!" he gasped. "That's why the trial's not at Badecanwell, isn't it? They don't want Maenche to hear about it until it's too late. That's why she wanted you to go and tell him."

Eofar scowled. "Not necessarily. Trials are held all over the shire. It doesn't mean anything."

"You can believe what you want to, but I'm going to that trial," said Eadwin. "You must go to Lord Maenche, like she asked you to do. This is not over yet, brother. With Maenche's help, we can stop it. It's not too late."

Eofar grabbed his brother and pushed him back onto his bed. "No!" he yelled. "It is too late. We are not doing anything."

Eadwin stared at him, bewildered. "Why not?"

Eofar was purple with rage. "It's not our business, you fool! Stay out of it, or I'll stop you myself. If we put one foot wrong, they'll blacken you along with her."

"What with, some bloody fairy story? I don't care if they do."

"How about treason? Do you care about treason?"

Eadwin gaped at his brother. "Treason?" he echoed weakly, his mind flashing back to the time with Wulfric at Hatfield Heath, before the battle. At Wulfric's bidding he had carried supplies to Uhtredstun. Wulfric had warned him that Penda might see it as an act of treason. But that was years ago and Wulfric had given his life for Penda since then, surely Rendil could not hope to make a charge like that stick.

"If we don't keep out of it," warned Eofar, "you'll spoil everything." He reached onto the work bench behind him and grabbed the first thing that came to hand, a short handled adze. He brandished it slowly making clear that he was ready to use it, even on his brother. "Rendil has promised to give us back the mine," he told him. "All we have to do is disappear for a while. Then, when it's over, he'll make it ours again."

"Give it back? It never was yours."

"It should be mine." shouted Eofar, tears coming to his eyes. "I've every right to it. It was our grandfather's. And without me, it wouldn't be anything now. I showed her what to do. I found the men. I cleared the swallow. What did she do?"

"She owns it," Eadwin yelled. "It's her bloody mine; her morgengifu. It's not yours, Eofar. It never was. You can't do this to her."

"I want the mine back," Eofar said, choking with fury. "It's ours. We were cheated. Aelric cheated us. It should belong to me — to us — me and you."

Eadwin stepped towards his brother, his arms hanging loosely by his side. "I'm going to the trial, brother," he said, his voice almost a whisper. "You've got the adze. You're going to have to use it to stop me. I won't raise a finger against you."

***

It was late that same day when Maud came to the brothers' cottage. Eofar met her at the door, closing it firmly behind him as he came out towards her. "Look, don't start, Maud."

"I came to tell you that Rendil has sent a couple to look after the children. A man and his wife. Bryoni and Betla have been told to find other work."

"Well, that's not a bad thing. Betla's too soft to get out of the rain and Bryoni is too old to cope with Eadric. He's getting a real handful for her these days."

"Where are you going?"

"Look, I know what you're going to say, but you can save your breath," he told her. "I'm going to Badecanwell. I'll try to see Lord Maenche, like she said, but I'm not coming back."

"You're running away? After everything she's done for you, you're running out on her."

"Think what you like, Maud, but I'm still leaving."

"She trusted you. She asked you to go to see Lord Maenche for her …"

"I just told you, I will do. I'll do what I can, but I'm not coming back." He hoisted a basket of tools in his arms and carried it towards the rail where Eadwin's mule was tethered.

Maud barred his way stubbornly. "Where's Eadwin?"

"He's gone already."

"What, without Snowflake?"

"He left her here for me and my stuff."

"Where will you go?"

"It's better if you don't know. We'll be on the move for a while."

***

The following day Eadwin approached Holmesfelt like a hunter stalking a deer. Not only was he unsure of his reception, but he still had no idea what he was going to do. He stole into the cover of a clump of hazels, relieved to have got so close unseen.

A cold breeze played in the trees, teasing his senses, making him flinch and look about in dread with every rustle and leaf-twitch. It had rained all day. He was cold and soaked to the skin. Shivering and rubbing his arms to get warm, he peered out at the village. Sky of dark, unbroken cloud hung over its huddle of dripping houses. At the far side of the village the great boughs of gently rocking oaks sagged beneath their burden of rain. Holmesfelt seemed to slump into the landscape like a sodden rag. Apart from a tall woman wrapped in a shawl, the fields and lanes were deserted. He watched her wandering across the common, apparently uncaring of the rain. Every few paces she stopped and bent to pick up something and place it carefully in her apron, clutched up to her waist to make a pouch.

Probably gathering mushrooms, Eadwin surmised, and shifted his attention to the hall. Wynflaed would be inside there, he told himself, and probably Rendil and the magistrate too, though there was no sign of activity.

"Eadwin! Hey, is that you?"

The voice came from behind him. He spun round, his heart racing. It was the mushroom picker. Eadwin recognised her immediately. "Widow Guthrum! Gods woman, you startled me."

"You'd make a poor hunter," Gutty said flatly. "I saw you from my house - prancing about like a spring hare. I think everybody must know you're here by now apart from old Sethrum."

"Sethrum?" he queried.

"Yeah, he died last year."

"You should have a care, woman," he said, "creeping up like that."

Gutty eyed him despairingly. "What do you think you're doing? From what I hear, you and your brother have sold her out. She didn't stand a chance."

Eadwin gaped. "Is it over already?"

"What did you expect with nobody to speak up for her? They accused her of everything from adultery to murder."

"Murder?"

"Yeah. They said she poisoned the old master. That old night hag Mother Ilam testified against her. She said she poisoned him with powders and potions. Luckily the magistrate tossed that out, and old hag too, but by then the harm was done. There's always a fool to coddle rubbish."

"But you were there. We both saw what happened."

Gutty sighed. "Yes and I told 'em. Even Rendil said it was rubbish, but with everything else they've accused her of it didn't make any difference. They even said she put a spell on the wells at By-Streams and dried 'em up."

"That happened when we opened up the swallow. A couple of wells did dry up, but there were others that flowed even faster. Everybody understood why."

"Well, some surly farmer testified that she did it by magic to get even with him."

"Then what happened?"

They said she'd lain with her miners. They had a woman who swore her husband was one of them that had slept with her."

"Wittna's widow?"

"Yes, she named several men who ... "

"Yes, and I bet I could name them all – every one of the men who served on the Barmote court that punished her husband." Eadwin sighed and thumped his fist into his palm. "So I'm too late. What happens now?"

"They've confiscated her property. The children are made Rendil's wards and she's been driven out of the shire. Anyone who helps her or gives her food, water or shelter can be strung up. If she's caught inside the shire bounds, she'll be taken for a slave or even killed. She's outside the law; no more safe than a prowling wolf."

"But it's all lies. How could they believe it?"

"I don't think they did. I was watching the magistrate. He looked as scared as a cat in a dog pen. I'm sure he was part of it; bought and paid for by Rendil. So were all the witnesses. They were all liars. But Rendil had flung so much mud with all those trumped up charges that it didn't make any difference. Some of it was bound to stick."

"But she didn't do anything."

"Well she did do something," said Gutty. "And she admitted it too."

"What?"

"She pleaded guilty to a charge of treason."

"Treason! That's ridiculous."

"They said she stole supplies from Aelric for her stepfather at Uhtredstun. She admitted it. She condemned herself. She's lucky they didn't hang her."

Eadwin shook his head. "She only said that to protect her husband's name. She didn't even know anything about those supplies. It was Wulfric who arranged it all. I know that for a fact. It was me who carried them to Uhtredstun. They weren't stolen. Aelric gave them freely. We all knew it was wrong at the time, all except Wynflaed. She knew nothing about it. She has deliberately sacrificed herself to keep Wulfric's name clean. It's for the sake of her children."

"Huh, Rendil certainly knew what he was doing. He's an evil, crafty bastard," said Gutty. "He worked it all out to the last detail. He must have guessed she'd protect her children." She leaned back against a tree and blew a bitter sigh. "He's always been an evil sod. Now he's got everything, even her children."

"I've got to stop him," said Eadwin.

"Don't talk daft. What can you do against him?" she said. "I'm sorry, love, but you're just a muler. He's a rich man. He bribed the magistrate. Anything you could do would be squashed like a flea. Rendil has won. If you try to stop him, he'll squash you too. He can buy all the witnesses he needs to see you hung."

He shrugged his shoulders, feeling helpless. "What about you? Rendil won't thank you for standing up for her. He could make life hard for you."

"I don't care. He doesn't scare me. You're the one who should be careful. He's got everybody scared of their own farts. You can't trust anybody. None of her true friends are safe now." She stood up and peered out of their tree cover, towards the village. "You'd better stay hidden. I'll find old Manwine. He'll know what to do."

"Manwine, the old farm reeve?" queried Eadwin.

"Don't worry. He's a good man and certainly no friend of Rendil's. Stay out of sight until he comes for you." Eadwin sighed miserably and watched her go. He shivered, feeling stiff with cold. A debilitating sense of dread and hopelessness bore down on him.

It was dark when Gutty returned with Manwine. The old man eyed Eadwin doubtfully. "I was hoping you were the other one, that big lad," he told him, with unconcealed disappointment.

"Just thank your Wyrd I'm not," Eadwin replied.

"Hum! But this is going to be a job for a tough bloke. You're a skinny little bugger, hardly more than a youth."

"Stop quibbling," snapped Gutty. "It's him and he's all we've got."

Manwine turned to her, appearing not to have heard. "Give him the food and go back to your house, woman. They'll be keeping a close eye on you now."

Gutty handed Eadwin a heavy poke. "Food," she said, her voice thick with emotion. "It's for Wynflaed, not you. And give her this." She unwound the shawl from around her hips. "Don't get it mucky."

As Eadwin watched Gutty slip back towards the village, Manwine was inspecting him closely. "Why are you so concerned about her?" he asked.

Eadwin felt his face redden and wondered if Gutty had misjudged the old farm reeve. "I want to help her. She's always been good to me, and her husband was the best friend I ever had. Besides, I know the roads. I can take her somewhere safe, or wherever she wants to go."

"The best thing you could do is forget about her. Take my advice, lad. She's as good as dead, and so is any fool what helps her."

Eadwin was furious. He grabbed the old man by the front of his tunic and raised his fist in front of his face. "I came here to help her and I will. She's still the mistress at By-Streams, no matter what. If you don't want to help, you'd better scram and keep your mouth shut."

Manwine smiled. "I'm impressed," he said. "Maybe you're tough enough after all." He extricated himself from Eadwin's grip and patted him on the shoulder. "I had to be sure, lad. Wynflaed needs real friends now, not them as just want to line their nests."

"I might have killed you, you daft old bat," said Eadwin.

"Oh, I don't think so," Manwine said. "What do you say, boys?" Manwine's two hulking sons emerged from cover, each armed with a club.

Eadwin gaped at them, towering over him. "You'd better hold me back before I kill 'em," he quipped, swallowing hard.

Manwine chuckled and sent his sons away with a nod. "She was whipped and taken to Crows Crossing. It's north, just past the boundary stone," he told him. "The widow stole a word with her before they set off. There's a herdsman's hut – a quarter of a mile past the cross roads. She told her to hide there until we can get help to her."

"Help? And that's me, is it?" asked Eadwin. "What is this place? Is it far?"

"Crows Crossing? It's not far, half a day's trek. As long as she stays on the north side of the crossroads she'll be safe, but Rendil's sure to have people watching."

"Why? He's got what he wanted, hasn't he?"

"Maybe," said Manwine. "But I don't think he'll be content until she's out of the way, permanently."

"You mean dead?"

"She's a danger to him, alive. He'll always worry that one day she'll convince somebody that she's innocent. Rendil went to a lot of trouble and expense to get this far. Killing her now would be a small thing. And he can do it legally if she stray's inside the shire boundary."

"Do you know what's happened to the children?"

"They belong to him now. He's got them."

"How do I contact you?"

"The widow walks the north field margins every day before the sun sets. It's sommat she's done for years, so it won't look suspicious. There's a large stone, shaped like a frog, near the edge of the road. If you want me, just put two pebbles on top of it. I'll find you somehow. If you want to talk to the widow, you can do that from the cover of the woods without showing yourself. Stay off the road. Use deer tracks."

. . . .

CHAPTER FIFTEEN

Three huge trees, gallows elms, stood at Crows Cross. They marked the border between Northumbrian Elmet and Mercian Peakland. Their boughs, bent low from weighing the corpses of thieves and murderers, bore the refuse of death. With pounding heart, Eadwin ran past them, looking neither left nor right. Whether imagined or real, the cloying smell of death caught in his throat. He felt the dead gaze of empty eye sockets burning into the back of his neck, spurring him on through milling crowds of crows and red kites too gorged to fly off. They flapped lazily out of his way, eyeing him balefully.

Half a mile past Crows Cross, he spotted a cowherd's shelter. It looked barely big enough for a single bed space and sagged into its scrubby clearing like a fallen cloak. From its turf walls and drooping roof of twigs and bracken, smoke clung to a weary wind.

Inside the hut, Wynflaed had heard his approach. Terrified that Rendil's men may have found her hiding place, she peered through a chink in the roughly built wall. As soon as she recognised Eadwin, her grip loosened on the handle of the small knife Gutty had smuggled to her. She returned to the smoky fire in a corner of the floor and carefully added a few twigs, preparing for his arrival. A flutter of relief glossed her eyes. With the toe of her shoe, she selected a cobble from the makeshift hearth and rolled it into the fire to heat it up for a boiling stone.

Eadwin called out as he came close. When she answered, he knelt and came ahead on all fours, pushing aside the cow skin curtain door at the low entrance. "My lady," he gasped, beaming nervously.

Both kneeling under the low roof, Wynflaed threw her arms around his neck and hugged him tearfully. She clung onto him, gripping him tightly. For a long time her silent, desperate sobs shook her trembling body. Her tears wet his neck. "Edda, oh Edda," she cried. "Thank the gods you came. I hoped it would be you. Thank you — thank you." She fell silent a moment. Great sobs shook her body as she tried to compose herself. "Giffi and Eadric, are they all right? Where have the taken them? Do they know what's happened to me? What will they think?"

Eadwin was too overcome to answer. He stroked her back as she clung on to him, but she flinched painfully and he saw her blood staining his hands. She was wearing a simple shift of undyed wool, belted with a grubby strip of cloth at the waist. Her head was roughly shorn, her scalp scratched and scarred. Bruises marked her right cheek and temple. Dried blood outlined her nostrils. The sight of her wretchedness overwhelmed him. The magnitude of her problems swamped even his most optimistic thoughts.

Why was he here? Panic churned his stomach. He had no ideas to offer her, no comforting solutions. He had nothing except his ridiculous, dog-like devotion. He was useless to her - a false hope. She would probably have to save him.

She drew back from him, wiping her face with her hands. He noticed the red welts of the lash on her arms. "I never expected to see you," she said. "I thought I would never see anybody again. I was ..." She stopped in mid-sentence and smiled, trying to raise her spirits. "Gutty told me to wait here. I don't know what I'd have done without her. Throughout that so-called trial, she sat there, beaming at me. I could feel her trying to cheer me up. When she spoke up for me, they ignored her. I daren't think what trouble she's brought on herself" She noticed him looking miserably around the tiny hovel. "Do you like it?' She waved at the walls. 'Snug isn't it?" She laughed, a tight, desperate laugh, tottering on the edge of tears.

Unable to speak, Eadric grinned back at her.

"Frigg! Do I look that bad?" she asked, responding to his shocked expression. "It's the black-eye, I expect. It doesn't hurt, and look, they didn't get this." She unrolled the rag tied at her waist and fiddled to uncover a gold ring, hidden there. "It's Wulfric's. He gave it to me for Eadric. When this is over I'll ..."

Eadwin barely glanced at it. "You look awful. I mean, you look — it looks painful. And — and your lovely hair ..."

"It's customary. You know how Rendil enjoys old customs." She slipped the gold ring back into its hiding place. "You get whipped across the border. He wasn't there, of course, just his paid bullies."

Eadwin watched her select two short sticks and use them to pick a hot cobble from the fire. She dropped it gently into cold water in a small leather pitcher and watched as the liquid began to sizzle and steam. She added a pinch of shredded herbs from a little pile she had on a dock leaf. Holding her face in the rising steam, she sniffed deeply. Her tears welled up again and she spoke, her voice choked off to a feeble croaking sound. "What will happen to my children?"

"I don't know, but don't worry – I think Maud ..." He bitterly regretted that he'd not thought to do something about them before he left By-Streams. "I just came here as soon as I heard. I'm sorry. I never thought. I didn't know what was happening."

"Maud will have it in hand. She's so good," she said.

"She went to see Lord Maenche," Eadwin said. He watched her, his sense of helplessness swelling inside him. "Manwine told me where to find you. And - Gutty sends her love. Oh, and this." He pushed forward the sack Widow Guthrum had given to him. "I know I'm useless, Lady. I'm sorry. I just wanted to help – somehow?"

"Thank the gods you came. I can't tell you what it means to know there's a few out there who still ..." She sniffed and shook her head as if to clear it. "You're taking a big risk though. You might not be able to go back."

"I don't care."

She smiled at him, making him blush. He lowered his gaze and bathed in her approval for a moment, before his sense of uselessness washed back over him.

"I have to see Eadric and Gifi. If you can help me to do that, I'd love you forever. I won't speak to them, of course. And they must never see me like this. But I must know how they are."

"I'll find a way. We'll find out where they are."

"Are you hungry?" she asked. "Let's see what Gutty sent us. Poor Gutty, she looked devastated at the trial."

"Why didn't you tell them the truth?" This was blurted out, startling her. "You didn't know anything about the supplies for Uhtredstun."

"I know," she said, taking hold of his hand. "But you weren't there. You didn't see their faces. Believe me, Eadwin, they all believed I was a liar and a thief and a whore who slept with every man in By-Streams. It wouldn't have made any difference. I couldn't let them blacken Wulfric's name too. It would ruin Eadric and Gifi's future. Wittna's widow told them her lies, and I could see people changing their minds about me. I watched their disappointment grow as they started to believe what they heard. Some looked shocked - went as pale as sops." She sagged back against the turf wall. "It was too late for the truth. Rendil did too good a job. For Eadric's sake, I said nothing. His father's good name is all I can give him."

"But you're innocent."

She shrugged. "Let's eat."

"No thanks," said Eadwin, feeling angry.

A whiff of herbs from the sweet infusion in the leather pitcher wafted across his face. He raised his eyes, eased his shoulders a little and glanced at her shyly. Although she was trying to smile, her eyes glistened with tears. She offered him the steaming pitcher. His fingers brushed against hers as he took it. Her touch lingered in his mind.

"What will you do?" he asked her softly.

"I know what I want to do, but gods - how to do it."

"Tell me."

"I want my children. I want Wulfric back alive." She clenched her hands into knots of bruised knuckles as her fury burst through the tattered veil of calm she had drawn about herself. "I want that swine off my land and out of my life. Gods Edda! I've never wanted a man dead, but I swear I'd kill Rendil with my bare hands …"

Eadwin reached out for her, smashing down barriers. Blindly she fell into his arms. He drew her close feeling her slim body shake like a crying child's. If there had ever been the slightest doubt in his mind that he would do anything she asked of him, it was driven out forever in that moment.

Eventually her sobs eased and she tried to compose herself. She wiped her face with her hands and combed her fingers through the tufts of her chopped, blood stained hair. "I'm sorry," she said, forcing a smile.

For a while they were silent, locked in desperate thoughts. "You know what, I don't even know how Wulfric died," she said finally. "Sometimes I can't believe he's dead. I feel him alive, inside, just as he always was." She knelt up, bumping her head on the low roof. "First I want to see the children. Then I want my linen runner."

"Linen what?"

"A linen runner. I made it for Lady Aenflaed the Ealdorman's sister. It's in my big cyste. If I could send it to her with a message, she might agree to see me. If she heard my side of the story she might help me. She's a good woman. And she's tough - not the sort to be constrained by rules and formalities."

"But she can't see you. Nobody can. It's forbidden to even talk to you."

"It didn't stop you."

"But if you cross into the shire they can kill you, or enslave you. Even if you did get to see her, she can't speak to you. It's against the law."

"I only met her a few times, but she struck me as a woman who wouldn't give in to anything she was set against. She's the only one I know who could influence the Shire Reeve, or better still, her brother. That magistrate is a crook. I have to go over his head to get a fair hearing. She could do that for me."

Eadwin saw it was pointless to argue. "We need to hide you somewhere safe." He tapped his knuckles against his forehead trying to think where. "There's my cousin's place. I do a lot of work for him. He'd help me.

"What's his name?"

"Sebbi. He's the one Eofar used to work for."

"Sebbi the carpenter?"

"Yes." Eadwin brightened as he thought more about his idea. "He lives at Badecanwell. That would be the perfect place. You can see the Shire Reeve's hall from Sebbi's house. It's so close nobody would dream you'd ever hide there."

She laughed and gave Eadwin's hand a little squeeze. "You mean nobody would dream I'd be so stupid."

"No really, it's perfect. There's a little house on Sebbi's land, in the woods at the back, nobody goes there. It was his first house, before he got married. You'd be safe there. You could grow your hair back a bit. You'll have to wear skivvies' rags, just in case you're seen." His face brightened as he warmed to his idea. "I could fetch that — err — linen runner-thing for you. Aenflaed's hall is close by. We could find a way to get it to her without being seen."

"Oh Edda, do you think so? Oh gods yes, let's do it. Let's try."

"But — there's a problem," Eadwin said.

"Only one?" she joked. "Thank Frigg for that. I thought there were dozens."

"Eofar," said Eadwin, dropping his gaze. "He's made a deal with Rendil."

"I know," she said. "Rendil enjoyed telling me all about it. I don't care. It's you I trust."

"But you don't understand. He'll be at Sebbi's."

"Don't tell him. You can say you couldn't find me. I can't stay here. I have to make a move. I promise I'll keep out of sight while you fetch my linen runner. It might only be for a couple of days. Eofar needn't know."

Eadwin looked doubtful. "I'm scared. I wasn't thinking straight. It won't work. Eofar always knows what I'm thinking. I'm no good at lying. He always finds out. He's betrayed you once. He'll do it again." He took a swallow from the leather pitcher, and pulled a face. It tasted bitter and slightly soapy.

"I'm sorry," she said, seeing his grimace. "I found some Betony and Bergamot - it needs honey to sweeten it."

"I think he's gone mad," Eadwin went on, putting the drink aside. "All he wants is that damned mine. He'll do anything for it."

"He'll never get it."

"He's already got it. Well, at least Rendil's promise."

"I don't care what he's promised. Rendil won't keep his word. I know my brother-in-law. He'll say anything to get what he wants, and do anything to keep what he's got." She stared at him, letting her words sink in. "I think you'll find your brother will soon be a bitter and disappointed man."

Eadwin looked doubtful. "I hope so. I don't understand people. I prefer mules. They're a lot less complicated, and much more honest."

"I'm so glad you came," she whispered, and kissed his cheek.

Eadwin shied away, trying to be dismissive. "It'll be dangerous. We can't travel in daylight. There's not much moon, so it won't be easy. First, you must stay here while I find out where they've got Master Eadric and little Gif. We must work out how you can see them. Manwine'll help. I think Rendil's men have gone to fetch them."

"He doesn't waste time."

"There's nothing to be done until then. Once you've seen them we'll go to Badecanwell. It'll be hard going. They're watching all the roads."

"I'm sure of it, and that won't be all he's doing. Rendil wants me dead." She was peering into Gutty's sack. "Look, she thinks I'm a shepherd," she said, grinning and pulling out a pair of man's woollen brecs and a sheepskin jerkin."

***

"How long will this take, Modbert? Can't you hurry the king along?"

Rendil and the magistrate were alone in the small room that had once been Aelric's private chamber at Holmesfelt. On a table between them lay an assortment of lambskin documents and a deed box. In his final years, Aelric had taken enthusiastically to the modern way of having deeds written on lambskin, although he had still observed the old tradition of having them proclaimed before witnesses. Even his will had been set down several months before his death. Much to Rendil's annoyance this had limited his scope for preferred interpretations.

The magistrate stretched opulently in his chair and sipped the wine Rendil had poured for him. He was idly leafing through the deeds, sorting them into two piles, one close to Rendil, the other at his own elbow. Some of the documents applied to Rendil's own lands and farms, but most had come from Wynflaed's hordeon at By-Streams. They were the deeds and titles to her now confiscated rights and properties.

"Rendil, you've won your case. You must not be impatient," said Modbert. "Her estates are as good as yours already, except, of course, for the king's third. I have prepared a document naming you reeve of all the estate's affairs until everything is settled. It will be a fine juicy roast for you to grow fat on until it's all settled – then it will all come to you."

Rendil licked his lips. "When will you see the king?"

"Don't worry about that. You'd be better employed finding Wynflaed, preferably within the scir's bounds.

When you do, arrest her – and make sure your men don't kill her. That's not part of our bargain. I won't stand for it. It would draw the wrong sort of attention to us. It's better she's caught alive, and put beyond all help as a slave. We'll never hear her name again. We can forget her."

"I understand perfectly, Modbert. Don't worry. I know where she is. I've got men watching her this very moment." Sitting back he rubbed his hands together. "You're sure the king will accept what you tell him."

"Of course, he always does. Believe me, he'll barely notice. These days he's got so much Northumbrian booty to play with he sees little else. Nothing excites him."

"Except horses and fat women," quipped Rendil.

Modbert chuckled. "But only women who look like horses."

Rendil laughed, smothering his unease. He squirmed in his chair. "But when can I be sure it's mine, a month, a year, how long?"

"Oh, I don't know, a few months, no longer. The law won't be rushed. And we mustn't look impatient. Don't worry. I'll do my best, Rendil. After all, I want my share too, don't forget." He studied Rendil's face, demanding confirmation. When it was grudgingly provided he went on grandly, "Which brings me to the point we discussed a week ago. I — err — hate to have to remind you, but ..."

"Don't worry, Modbert," Rendil interrupted sourly. "I have your silver here, but for Frigg's sake be careful what you do with it. That gafol reeve of yours wasn't impressed by this trial. I was watching him. He didn't like some of what he heard. If he sees you've suddenly acquired a pile of silver, he might ask some awkward questions."

The magistrate scowled. "I can manage my own servants well enough, Rendil. Just hand it over."

***

When old Mother Ilam spotted Eadwin coming from the direction of Crows Cross, her suspicions were confirmed. His part in her humiliation when the old master had lain dying still rankled. Both he and Gutty's widow had a reckoning due to them for that. Now that Rendil was master, she felt it was only a matter of time before she would have her revenge. Keeping out of sight, she followed him.

Eadwin stopped near the edge of the village and hid in the cover of trees. Old Mother Ilam chose a comfortable vantage. The sun had almost buried itself behind the Peakland's distant, violet hills. She assumed that Eadwin would wait for darkness before he risked making contact with anybody in the village. Pulling her shawl around her bony shoulders, she settled down to wait.

Eadwin crawled beneath a holly tree. It was a good hiding place. Women working in the fields came close, but none saw him in his prickly den. As the sun finally sank behind the forested uplands, the field-hands headed home. Oxen bellowed at the gloaming, no doubt pleased to be out of harness. Frowning Eadwin looked up at the sky. Its mid summer glow was still too light for secrecy. Settling back, he resigned himself to a long wait for covering darkness

Silence fell on the homestead. As if to take advantage of it, a pair of blackbirds sparred in song, their music echoing from the tree tops. Gradually darkness stole over the houses, smoothing out nooks and crannies. The bird's singing finally ended, and one by one lights burned from opened shutters. Eadwin sniffed the smells of stock pots on the stirring air.

He convinced himself that it was now dark enough to move about unseen. Crouching low, he crossed the fields and ran to the back of Widow Gutty's house. Mother Ilam watched and willed her old bones to follow. She reached the edge of the fields in time to see him creeping on all fours up to Gutty's door. She saw it opened briefly, admitting him into darkness. Her spirits soared triumphantly. She hobbled to the house and pressed into the shadows of its eaves, where she cocked ear to the open window shutter and listened.

Eadwin accepted Gutty's offer of bread and ale and drained the first cup at one go. "She wants to see the children," he said, watching his cup being refilled. "She's in good spirits, except for missing them, and she's already talking about fighting back. She's even got a plan."

Gutty placed cheese and apples before him. "How can she see the children? That's impossible. They've got them in Rendil's old house - with Goda. Apparently Goda has moved out of the hall. They had a hell of a row, and she's refused to live with him. He's on his own. His daughters live with their mother. I expect he'll leave Wynflaed's children with her too now." Gutty reached inside her dress and scratched her armpit. "Maybe I could get Goda to take them for a walk near the hazels?"

"Yes, that would work. We could hide there and watch as they walked past. She says she only wants to see them. She won't speak to them, or let them see her. She says it'd upset them. She's right, too. She looks awful with a black eye and everything."

"It won't be easy," Gutty said. "I'll talk to Manwine. He'll help. You wait here. Help yourself to more food."

It was an hour before Gutty returned. She found Eadwin sleeping on her large curtained bed having eaten his fill. Gutty smiled wantonly and began to pull his boots off. Eadwin barely stirred, even as she climbed onto the bed and threw her leg across his body to sit astride him. "Hey, wake up muler. You've got work to do."

Eadwin opened his eyes in time to see Gutty's naked breasts appear as she pulled her dress off over her head.

"Come on, wake up. There's nothing we can do until morning, so get cracking."

He gaped at Gutty's large, pendulous breasts, hung on her skinny ribs like a pair of bag puddings. He took hold of them, somewhat dutifully at first, but soon revelled in their malleable warmth.

By no means did Eadwin think of Gutty as his preferred type. In fact she had few of the qualities *he* found attractive in women. Until then he had never entertained a carnal thought about her, yet as he was to discover to his lasting delight, no quality in a woman is more desirable or rewarding than enthusiasm.

Over the next few hours, Eadwin learned a great deal about life, women and pleasure. Before dawn, feeling far from rested, he set off back to Crows Cross. Bending low he ran along the leafy edges of the road to avoid being seen. He thought of Wynflaed and the uncomfortable night she must have spent in that draughty hovel. He felt thoroughly ashamed of himself. How could he have been so …?

"How did it go?" Wynflaed asked when he poked his head through the door flap.

"Better than expected," he said, ambiguously.

"Well, what happened?"

"Manwine will see that the children are brought to the north field tomorrow morning. We'll have to hide there tonight when it's dark. It will mean having to stay hidden all day before we set off to Badecanwell. He'll bring them close to where you'll be hiding. You'll see them clearly."

"Are you sure they won't see me?"

"Yes, Manwine will be told. He'll understand."

"Are you in pain?" she asked him. "You seem a bit stiff?"

Eadwin smiled ironically. "No, not any more."

***

Mother Ilam had followed Eadwin all the way back to the cowherd's hut. She had heard enough to know that Wynflaed would soon be within the shire. All she had to do now was tell Rendil. In one strike she would have her revenge on Wynflaed, widow Guthrum and the muler. All three would fall together.

....

CHAPTER SIXTEEN

Modbert, magistrate of the Peak Scir, hid his amused satisfaction. He was checking his train of three ponies and issuing final instructions to his jaggers and spearmen before starting his journey home to Badecanwell. He expected Rendil would be watching from some dark window, no doubt regretting his loss of the silver and the lands Modbert had negotiated for himself. It had been a most profitable week. Rendil, as fraudsters so often did, had flattered and fawned and entertained him lavishly, so long he believed he was getting his way. Wynflaed's trial had gone well, and although the witnesses Rendil had produced were clearly all liars, it had made for a simple, open and shut case. The packs on his horses contained the deeds to two farms at By-Streams and five ingots of silver. But this was merely a down-payment. Modbert could expect much more from Rendil in the coming months.

Witnesses had sworn that Wynflaed had buried the silver in the earth floor beneath her bed. He smiled, recalling how, somewhat dramatically, he had called it, "A blatant, criminal and treasonous act." Displaying outrage he had written in the court records that three ingots had been recovered from the thief. The other two would quietly find their way into his personal coffers, and with any luck, a grateful monarch would share the remaining three with him, as a reward for his honesty.

The king would have much to be grateful for. On his death, Wulfric's considerable estate had passed to Wynflaed. In time, she would have passed most of it to her son. Now that she had forfeited everything, the property would be held in trust for Eadric, but first the king would get a third of it. As it would take time to ratify these matters, it had been agreed that Rendil would supervise the holdings, and, for his trouble, enjoy any benefits. He would probably go on doing so until Eadric reached manhood. And, of course, much could befall a vulnerable young boy before then.

***

Rendil's preoccupation with the magistrate placed him far out of Mother Ilam's reach. She had run about the village, her secrets burning inside her, quite unable to pass them on. There was no one else she could turn to. She knew most of her neighbours were sympathetic to Wynflaed. They would probably turn on her if they learned what she was up to. There was nothing she could do. She fumed bitterly as Wynflaed watched her children from hiding as Goda paraded them before her. Goda, played her part perfectly, playfully chasing them about the field, making them dance and skip. When finally Wynflaed and Eadwin slipped away, Mother Ilam was powerless to stop them. Her hope of vengeance faded and vanished

***

Travelling only at night, Wynflaed's trek to Badecanwell took most of a cold and rainy week. The track wound over grit-stone rocks, through trackless peat bogs and thick forest. It crossed a harsh, upland landscape, where strong winds carved great boulders, some bigger than a king's hall. They sat like sculptures of giant frogs, ravens and ships among the waves of scrub and silver birch. It would have been an impossible journey without Eadwin's help. Each dawn Eadwin found safe shelter to hide and rest during the daylight hours. At night he tramped ahead of her, warning her of obstacles as though seeing them in sunlight.

Near Badecanwell, he led her to an abandoned shack on a bosky hillside. Wynflaed thought they had arrived at their sanctuary and liked it as soon as she saw it. It nestled in trees high above the village with its fast, sparkling river. Entering gratefully she flopped onto a rickety bench and pulled off her wet boots, relieved to be off her feet at last.

"We daren't stay long, woodsmen sometimes use this place, but we can rest a little while."

"It's a palace compared to that herder's hut," she told him.

Eadwin looked around doubtfully. "I've got to scout the road," he told her, adding the warning, "No smoke and no light. It'll be seen." He glanced at her as if assessing whether he dare leave her or not.

"Don't worry, I'll be fine — *master*," she said, teasing him lightly.

He blushed and hid his face. "Please stay hidden. You'll be able to watch the road unseen. I'll check out Sebbi's old house. When I'm sure it's safe, I'll take you down there. You'll be safe there while I go for your linen runner."

"Stop worrying about me. I'll be fine." She looked down into the valley from the shack's slit of window. Eadwin seized the moment to look at her. He had enjoyed their journey together and despite the circumstances regretted it was over. He treasured every word she had spoken along the way; every occasion she had sought his hand to help her over a brook, or down a bank. Above all, he would remember the hours they had rested side by side, so close that he had only to reach out and touch her as she slept. He had lain awake watching her, listening to her breathing and the soft whimpers of her dreaming. Once he had brushed her close cropped hair with his finger and bent his face to hers intending to steal a kiss, but she had stirred in her sleep. He had pulled back and not dared to try again.

With a lingering look back at her, he set off into the valley. What about his romp with Gutty? he asked himself. How did that sit with his heart? In many ways it was memorable too, but shameful, and he should stop trying to find excuses for it. What was the point? The fact was he had enjoyed it and knew he would do it again if he got the chance. What sort of person did that make him? Weak? Stupid? Immoral?

"Probably."

Later he led Wynflaed down into the valley. She was excited and nervous. She kept looking about with jerky, fearful glances that set him on edge.

"Isn't that Sebbi's place beneath the hill?" she asked, sounding tense and breathless. Below them, misty moonlight flattered an untidy sprawl of buildings, hemmed in by piles of seasoning timber. "It looks weird at night," she went on, gripping his arm with both her hands as she picked her way beside him.

"That's it," he said, thinking how he would probably never again be alone with her.

She bent her head to look up at him. The spark of gaiety their safe arrival had ignited dimmed momentarily. She became thoughtful, as if reading his thoughts. Reaching up to his face she kissed him gently on the cheek, her lips lingering, brushing softly on his skin. "You'll always be special, Eadwin."

"Let's go," he said. "You might be seen. There are still folk abroad, even at this late hour."

They walked on, keeping to the edge of the track nearest to the trees. After a while, he led her off the road into a small clearing with a dilapidated house at its centre.

"This is it. It's not much, but it should be dry and safe. "Nobody comes here." He pushed open the door on its time-seized hinges and led her inside. "Don't light a fire."

'I know, don't worry. I'm getting used to being a fugitive."

Eadwin stood in the doorway in a pool of moonlight. "It'll be all right," he said. "I promise." He stepped outside and paused to look back at her. He was smiling. "I'll get us some food and drink from Sebbi's. I'll be gone some time."

"What if Eofar's there? Will you tell him I'm here?"

"No, only Sebbi's wife. Nobody else must know."

Wynflaed had found an old stool. She stood it upright and began pulling away grasses and vines that had overgrown it. "Don't be long, Edda. Please."

A couple of hours later Eadwin returned, contrition written large on his face. "I'm sorry it took so long. I don't know what you'll say," he said. "I don't even know how to tell you. I can't believe I'm asking you ..."

"What's wrong? What have you done?"

"It's too stupid. You can't risk it. I can't ask ..."

"Eadwin, what arc you talking about?" She grabbed his upper arms to stop him pacing about. "Start slowly, say the words."

He looked at her distraught. "It's my brother. He wants to talk to you."

"Does he know where I am?"

"No, but it won't take him long to work it out." He sagged onto an old bench. "I can't, after all that ..."

"What did he say?"

"Well, he said he's sorry. He certainly looked as if he meant it. He was as sullen as a slapped bairn. But I just can't trust him. It's not long since he clobbered me with an adze handle."

"I don't think I could face him," she said. "I know I should try, but I just ..."

"You don't have to. We'll be gone by noon tomorrow. I'll get Wilma to make sure he stays put until then."

"Wilma?" she queried.

"Sebbi's wife. She's wonderful. She'll make sure he doesn't ..." He paused, straightened an old table, dusted it off and placed a woollen bag on it. "Food," he said. "There's meat, bread and a jar of broth. I got some milk and ..." He began looking around puzzled. "Oh no, I left the milk. I'll be back in a blink. I remember, I put it down while I tied the cover on the broth." He rushed off suddenly.

Wynflaed opened the bag and began unpacking the food. The moon slid behind a cloud plunging the little house into darkness, but she carried on, fumbling to set the things out on the table. She laughed as she heard a footfall on the threshold. "I know you said no lamps, but this is silly, Eadwin."

When there was no reply. She peered at the dim silhouette in the doorway and saw immediately that it was not Eadwin. It was a man though — a much taller, broader man.

"Eofar?"

"I had to see you," said Eofar. "I knew he'd bring you here."

Wynflaed's heart raced. Tense and breathless, she backed away from the hulking figure in the doorway. Anger and revulsion swelled inside her. Then she was breathing again, controlled, trembling breaths that made no sound. Where was Eadwin? What had happened to him? What was Eofar doing here? After what he had done - he had no right.

"What do you want? Where's Eadwin?"

"I followed him and waited," he said. "I suppose he's told you everything?"

"You mean how you betrayed me when you knew my husband was dead?" Fumbling in the darkness, she grabbed a cloth wrapped parcel from the table and hurled it at him. "I already knew. I found out when I was dragged from my home – when my children were taken from me. I found out standing before the magistrate when I was stripped of everything I own." She grabbed at something else from the table and threw it at him. It was the pot of broth. It struck him on the chest and bounced off to shatter unseen in the darkness.

Passing clouds unveiled the half moon. Its ghostly light filtered around them, finding gaps in walls and ancient thatch. Eofar peered into the shadows where she stood. He dropped his gaze immediately when his eyes found hers. "Believe me I — I didn't know it'd be like this. I thought they'd just take the mine. I didn't ..."

"Liar! Don't make it worse. At least have the guts to admit you're a thief and a betrayer. You didn't consider your brother, or Maud, or any of us." She stepped forward, making him back off. "Big as you are, Eofar," she said, "you're a puny little man really; a greedy, selfish little man. You don't deserve Bell Delfan. You haven't the guts to make anything of it. You'll probably lose it too, like your grandfather did."

"I don't have it to lose!" he said angrily. "That bastard cheated me. He promised but ..."

"Oh dear, what a shame," Wynflaed said mocking him. "Tell me Eofar, what does it feel like to trust somebody then have them betray you? Does it feel anything like losing your children and your home - and your friends, and your freedom, and all your hopes for the future? Is it anything like that?"

"I swear I didn't know it would mean all that. I just thought ..."

Eadwin came running into the hut and shoulder charged Eofar aside. He stood defiantly between them and faced his brother. "I didn't know," he told her over his shoulder. "He must have followed me."

"It doesn't matter," she said. "I don't see anyone here but you and me."

"They want me to fetch you."

"Fetch me! I can't go down there," she cried. "I'd put them all at risk. I mustn't go anywhere near them."

"I told 'em you'd say that, but they won't hear of it. Wilma says she'll come for you herself if you don't come down."

"What about him?"

"He'll keep quiet. He can't say anything," said Eadwin. "Me and Sebbi and Wilma are all he's got. He needs us. If he betrayed you again, he'd be condemning himself as well as all of us. He doesn't matter now. He's not dangerous anymore – just pathetic."

"The greedy are always dangerous, especially when they're also fools."

Eofar looked at her and shrugged. "I heard Edda say about a linen runner," he said. "Let me fetch it? I know I can't ever make it up to you, but at least let me do something."

"I'll go!" snapped Eadwin. "I already told her I would. We don't want nothing from you."

"Eadwin's going," Wynflaed said flatly. "I can trust him."

"Give me a chance. Let me do this one thing. It could be dangerous. Rendil's men are everywhere. They won't bother with me, but Eadwin might be caught. Let me do it."

That at least was true, thought Wynflaed. It would be dangerous for Eadwin. Why put him at risk when Eofar could do it? All he had to do was fetch the linen runner.

"Very well then, you can fetch it," she told him coldly. "It's blue linen with lots of gold thread work and coloured stitching. I keep it in a linen bag in the great cyste in the hordeon. If you can't find it, ask Maud, she might have hidden it. She knows what it means to me."

***

The following morning ice lidded the water trough in Sebbi's yard. His numerous children, encouraged by their mother, celebrated the fact by dropping lumps of it down their dozing father's tunic, filling the house with his bellowing and their squeals of laughter.

Wynflaed had accepted Wilma's generous invitation and spent the night in their house. It was a large, noisy, warm, smelly place, full of children, dogs, cats, hens and cantankerous Wealh servants. The children, about six of them, slept on a great palliasse beneath a ladder up to a loft where Sebbi and Wilma normally slept. The servants laid out their own beds in snug corners or under the table. The dogs slept in the warmest places near the central hearth. Cats slept on dogs or children. Guests had to find a spot for themselves. On this occasion however, Wilma had obliged Sebbi to give Wynflaed his usual place, against her large and shapely body. In consequence he had spent a fitful night beneath a table. His cousin Eadwin had curled up with the dogs, dreaming and whimpering like one of them. Only Eofar had slept alone. He had taken himself off to a barn. Wynflaed was not sure whether it was she or Eadwin he was trying to avoid. It turned out to be Wilma. She had given him a tongue lashing for his treachery, and threatened him with a visit from her brothers, three well known giants with unimpeachable credentials for bone breaking.

Eofar was again absent as the family gathered for breakfast. One of the children said they had seen him striding down the path towards By-Streams. "He might be going for the linen thing," suggested Sebbi. "He was talking about it last night."

After her meal Wynflaed walked in the yard, turning anxiously every few moments to the road Eofar had taken. Wilma joined her. "I know he's my husband's cousin - and I shouldn't say it, but if I were you, lady, I wouldn't trust him."

Wilma was a large, pink-faced woman of about thirty-five. Her poker straight spine carried wide square shoulders. Everything about her seemed bigger than it should be. Beneath thick brown eyebrows she had large, black eyes and a broad nose. Her red-lipped mouth smiled constantly, flashing untidy rows of big white teeth. When she spoke, her voice was louder than it needed to be. And when she moved, on what Wynflaed could only guess were massive legs, she took great steps that made her huge breasts jiggle like piglets under a sheet.

Wilma put her muscular arm around Wynflaed. "Truth to tell, I wouldn't trust the selfish arsehole at all." She squeezed Wynflaed's shoulders to the edge of dislocation. "Watch him, my lady. He's a man in the pains of disappointment. And it's not new to him neither. He's been like it all his life. He used to work here with my Sebbi. There was always jealousy. He seemed to think my Sebbi got where he is by no more than Wyrd's favour." Wilma's encircling arm steered Wynflaed back to the house. "Best you keep out of sight," she said. "You never know who might be up in them woods."

Sebbi was still eating at the table. Wilma snatched his bowl from under his nose and tried hoisting him up from his seat. "Time you were working, my lad" Sebbi smiled wryly and left for his workshop, saluting her grandly.

"You bairns are done too," Wilma told her snotty litter, lingering at the table. "You've all got work. Get on with it. I'll be round to see you in a bit. The lady and me want some peace."

She seated Wynflaed and slid in on the bench beside her. Grabbing a bowl that one of her children had been using, she cleaned the inside of it by rotating it on her breast. "I know I shouldn't say so because they're family," she whispered, reaching for a jug of milk and filling the bowl. "But you must be very watchful of both of 'em."

"Who? Not Eadwin." Wynflaed said in disbelief.

"No, Mother Frigg bless us," Wilma cried, giggling at such a preposterous idea. "Eadwin's lovely. No Eofar and my Sebbi; them two. My Sebbi's honest, but he's careless. He says too much without thinking." She broke a piece of bread from a flat loaf and dipped it in her bowl. "I have to keep an eye on him, or everybody would know our business." She sighed and ran her hands over the wide expanse of her hips. "If you must trust a man at all, make it one like our Eadwin. He ain't got much brain, poor love, but there's not a bad bone in him. And if he did get awkward, and believe me they all do sometimes, he's little enough to be wrested back into line."

Wynflaed laughed, feeling completely at ease with Wilma. They spent the morning chatting as Wynflaed patched, darned and sewed a pile of little girls' shifts, and boys' tunics. Shortly after noon the children ran into the house squealing and laughing. They had seen Eofar coming up the lane.

Wynflaed felt sick. If he had found the linen runner she might soon be talking to Lady Aenflaed, the Ealdorman's sister.

Eadwin rushed inside and stood behind her, his hand on her shoulder as everyone watched the door and waited for Eofar. Sebbi appeared looking fearful, his cropped hair peppered with sawdust. He paused at the door and ushered Eofar in. Eofar looked round at every face, starting and finishing with Wynflaed. "I didn't get it," he said. "I found ..."

"You bastard!" yelled Eadwin, leaping at his brother in fury. He wrestled him to the ground frantically punching him in a mad rage. Sebbi, Wynflaed and Wilma dragged him off. Wynflaed calmed and reassured him as Eofar recovered his feet and brushed himself down. He moved defensively behind a table.

"I had trouble getting into the hall at first, but Maud helped me," he said. "The magistrate has men guarding it. It's all barred and locked. I had to break in through the thatch at the back. I found the cyste, just where you said, but it was burst open. The linen was slashed to ribbons. It was beyond saving or I'd 'ave ..."

"Thank you," said Wynflaed impassively.

"You don't believe him, do you?" Eadwin cried, struggling to break free of Wilma's grip.

Eofar looked at Wynflaed. "I'm really sorry."

Later, at the night meal, even the animals in Sebbi's house seemed to sense the tension. Wilma sighed repeatedly, desperate to help, but at a loss for an idea. Finally she spoke. "Why can't you just go to her without it? Lady Aenflaed's a good woman. I talked to her when my Sebbi made her some tables and a bed. I'm sure she'd help if she knew the truth." She patted Wynflaed's hand. "I'll come with you."

"You can't do that! You mustn't be seen with me. Nobody must. Besides, I'll only get one chance to talk to her," Wynflaed explained. "I wanted her to have the linen runner first. I know she likes such things. She'd have understood what it means – and what it says about me. I wanted her to hold it and wonder about it, to look at it in the light of several mornings before I went to her. I thought it might make her curiosity about me. I suppose I thought it might make her more sympathetic." She looked fondly at Wilma and squeezed her hand. "Thank you, but you can't risk more for me."

"Can't you make another?" Eadwin asked naively.

"Gods! There's almost half a year's work in it!" Wynflaed told him sharply. "Some of it was gold thread too, and silk yarns. Where would I get them now? Even if I had something to trade for gold thread, you can't get it without attracting attention. And anyway, it might be months before a merchant with any to offer comes by."

Eadwin scowled, feeling stupid, but did not give up. After the night-meal he invited Wynflaed to take the evening air with him. She smiled coyly, "Why yes, how kind," she said.

Outside in the privacy of darkness, he spoke softly. "I'm sorry, but I didn't want Eofar to hear me. I've had an idea. What about your friend — your sister? She'd help you. I could take you there. And she could get silks and gold thread for you too. Nobody would think it was strange of her if she did."

Wynflaed smiled. The idea had crossed her mind too, but she had not wanted to put Buhe and her husband at risk. "Buhe? Yes, thought of that, but she's a married woman now and ..."

"If she was in trouble, wouldn't you help her?"

"Of course I would, in an instant."

"Then why deny her the same pleasure?"

Pausing she looked at him thoughtfully. "Buhe would certainly help me, but I'd be putting her in danger."

"No, not really. Not in the Shire-wood. It's well off the main ways," he said. "Nobody goes there much. Wulfric told me that was why old Uhtred settled there in the first place."

"Perhaps you're right, but I'd have to tell her everything. Anyway, look at my hair and my face. She'll have to know." She frowned and bit her cheek. "And I don't know the road, and Uhtredstun is such a long way,"

"I'll take you," Eadwin said, his heart soaring. "But we can't even tell Wilma where we're going."

***

The following evening, it was already dark when Wynflaed bid Wilma farewell and kissed each of her moist, feral children. She was sad to be leaving, but relieved to be removing the family from the danger her presence had placed them in.

Eadwin, now reunited with Snowflake, led off up the steep track out of the valley. From the brow of the hill, she looked back and waved one last time, not even sure if they could still see her. Up ahead, Snowflake, loaded with supplies, nodded patiently as she trailed Eadwin into the uncertain gloom.

…….

CHAPTER SEVENTEEN

"This here is a real good spot," Horse Ebell told Eadwin proudly. "I slept here for years until I was made up to head horsener. Then they made me have a cottage and a wife to go with it." He shook his wrinkled bald head ruefully.

Eadwin looked around the low-roofed stable with satisfaction. He knelt in the sweet hay and plumped it up to make himself a bed. "This is fine. I'll be as warm as a pup's flea."

"You'll do all right, lad," said the old horsener. "Will you want owt else?"

"No thanks. The cook fed me in lower hall and I'll be off at first light. I'll just get my head down now."

"Huh, you needn't think you'll be up afore me," Ebell said. "Nobody's ever up afore me. I'm always first up. It's me what wakes the sun."

"I just meant that I don't want nothing else."

"The birds wait for me of a morning. They'd not wake up, if they didn't see me around bright-n-early."

Eadwin hoped a theatrical yawn might remind the old man of his weariness and take him away to leave him in peace.

Blind to the hint, Horse Ebell went off on a new line. "Married life's not what it should be, mind," he said gravely. "Truth to tell, she's a lazy old bitch and about as warm as a frog's tit. It's amazing how they change. It were a joy to cover her afore we was wed, but she soon took to wifely ways once I was harnessed. I blame her mother. Terrible woman, eyes like an adder and a mouth like a dull axe."

Eadwin's brow knitted in fake sympathy. "Aye, you can never tell," he said, launching another expansive yawn. "Well, I thank you for letting me stretch out here. I'll get my head down now then." He arranged his blanket with a flourish, hoping Ebell would finally take the hint and leave.

Ebell jumped to his feet suddenly, a grave look on his old face. "Ayup! I've got to get along. I can't stay here chomping the bit with thee all night. You young uns don't seem to value time at all. I've work to do, daylight or not."

Eadwin laughed quietly at the irony and pulled his blanket up around his shoulders. He felt warm and comfortable. Above all he was pleased with himself for having delivered Wynflaed safely. Uhtredstun was such a nice place, he thought. And certainly the best place for Wynflaed right now. She could be happy here and in time, with friends to help her, she could restore her good name.

Beyond the stable, Uhtredstun's new hall, lime-washed and pristine beneath its fresh yellow thatch, stood on the spot where Uhtred's old hall had been. Its internal support timbers rose from the ground like an avenue of trees. Some were already decorated with intricate carved patterns and spirals, picked out in bright colours. Old Uhtred had built in many refinements before his death, including wooden planks over half the floor area and willow screens under the west gable to hide the sleeping quarters and storage heordens. Above them, he'd built a loft for keeping dry stuffs such as yarns, leather, fleeces, salt and flour. This too was screened off, to prevent smoke and soot from the central hearth spoiling the stores. The eastern gable, or lower hall, where animals were kept in the worst of the weather, housed a workshop, dairy and farrowing pens. For convenience it had a stone-edged well not forty feet from its door, and a lean-to where the cooks worked.

In upper hall, Buhe and Wynflaed talked late into the night. Buhe wept and gasped, and cuddled Wynflaed as she listened. At times she shook her small fists and banged them on the table, cursing Rendil.

When she could, Wynflaed shifted the conversation from herself, hoping that Buhe would calm down and stop weeping. She tried complimenting her on the waxed shine on her table, the feather-stuffed cushions they were sat on, the ale they drank and the horn beakers they drank it from. She asked her about her life and marriage, and eventually managed to get her to relax and cheer up a little.

Buhe was still childless, though she pretended not to care. Wynflaed could not help thinking that she still seemed too young and giddy to even consider sex, let alone motherhood. It was obvious she worked hard to be the wife her husband wanted. Despite everything however, it was clear that she was not, and she knew it. She was as out of place as the grand lady of the hall, as she would be on a battlefield. Her servants bullied, or mothered her, or just ignored her. Beneath her thin veneer of adulthood the Buhe of Wynflaed's childhood, of tree swings, rag dolls and tearful tantrums, was still apparent.

"I wanted a son," Buhe said, folding her hands beneath her chin as if in prayer. "Gods, Flaedy! I did everything that old night-hag, Morash, told me, but it didn't do any good." Her shoulders collapsed in a gloomy sigh. "You're so lucky to have a son," she said, then remembering Wynflaed's precarious situation, wailed and clutched apologetically at her hands. "I'm sorry, I mean — when you get him back and …"

Wynflaed smiled forgivingly. "I know what you mean."

"Oh, you will get him back, Flaedy. We'll see to it," she said, sitting up stiffly and wagging a finger. "You should have stayed here. You would have had a lovely time with me. You could have had your own things, even that ugly loom of yours with the wolf head stodlans. I've still got it. It's in a barn somewhere. You'd have had your own servants and everything. You would never have had any of this trouble. I knew it was a mistake to go off with that ..."

"Buhe, don't be silly. I have my children. I've had seven marvellous years with Wulfric. He was wonderfully exciting, and a most loving husband. I loved him. I still love him."

Indignation flashed in Buhe's eyes. "Well, Colnoth is wonderful too."

"Of course he is. I didn't say he wasn't. I just meant I wouldn't have missed those years with Wulfric for anything. Surely you can see that, especially as you and Colnoth are so happy."

"We *are* happy," she said. "He's marvellous. He'll come straight back tomorrow. He had to be away. His father sent word. He always stays overnight when he visits his father. It's a long journey and he's a very thoughtful son."

"I'm sure he's a fine man," Wynflaed said.

"Yes, well — you keep your hands off him," said Buhe. "Now come on, let's get you settled in. I'm going to make you so comfortable that you will forget all about your troubles and stay here forever - just like we always planned."

Taking Wynflaed's hand she led her to the screened-off sleeping area and pulled aside a woollen curtain. Beyond it Wynflaed found a small room, sparsely furnished. It smelled of lamp smoke and new timbers. A bench seat stood against one wall. Furs covered a narrow bed in the middle of the room. Beside it smoked a mutton fat lamp on a stool.

"I'll have a cyste and some other things brought in tomorrow. For now you can use that seat. There are pegs on the wall to hang things on. Colnoth and I sleep next door. Ours is the corner room. It was father's." Tears glossed her eyes and she reached to embrace Wynflaed. "I do miss him, Flaedy."

***

Uhtredstun lay south of a small river, on loamy slopes near Meden Dale. Around it, for seemingly endless miles, stretched the great wilderness of the shire-wood. The settlement had prospered in the years since the raid. And as if to thumb his nose at Penda and the new Mercia, Uhtred had rebuilt his hall bigger and finer than the old one. More land had been cleared to provide the timber for it, and he had raised a stout palisade around it. Uhtred had offered it to incomers to encourage them to settle.

The little stream where Eadwin had camped with his mule all those years ago had been dammed and stocked with fish. Now, just as the old man had intended, dozens of waterfowl nested there providing, along with fish traps, a valuable hedge against famine.

Buhe had married after Uhtred's death. Colnoth, whose father held lands to the north of Uhtredstun, had immediately moved into the big new house. At first he had worked hard, but unlike Uhtred was not keen to get his hands dirty. He preferred to spend his days hunting and fishing with his friends. He bought slaves and bonded labourers to do the work, leaving their supervision to a trio of surly overseers.

On first acquaintance Wynflaed had thought of Colnoth as a softly spoken, rather studious young man. She soon found that he studied little but his own whims and wishes. He was tall and slim. His long face sank gloomily into a shaggy, brown beard full of holes and ginger streaks. His eyesight was poor, and when he needed to see something clearly he tilted his head to one side like a bemused dog. He had the whitest, most perfect teeth. What a pity, Wynflaed thought, that he smiled so rarely.

After Eadwin left to return to his new and somewhat uncertain life at Badecanwell, Wynflaed's days at Uhtredstun began to assume a pattern. She felt safe enough to start thinking about the future, in terms of more than just the next morning or afternoon. Buhe regarded her presence as an endless treat, made entirely for her amusement. She loved her life now that Wynflaed was back in it. Each day she planned all sorts of things for them to do together, and would stamp petulantly if Wynflaed said she had other plans. By her third month at Uhtredstun Wynflaed had begun work on a new linen runner, inspired by the colours and the winter light of her old woodland home.

"Do you like fishing?" Colnoth inquired, surprising her one morning as she walked by what Buhe now called Father's Pool. "I can make you a rod and line if you want."

It was the first time she had found herself alone with him since her arrival. She felt oddly uncomfortable about it. He had caught her daydreaming about her children.

"I'm sorry, did I make you jump?" he said, placing his hand on her shoulder and sliding it down to gently grip her upper arm.

She eased away from him. "No, I was just thinking," she said, taking time to frame a suitably innocuous reply. "Buhe and I used to fish somewhere, but I've forgotten where it was. There was a beech tree and a clay bank. We used to wet the bank so that we could slide bits of wood down it and pretend they were otters."

"Aah, that's Mers Brook. I know that pool. Buhe told me about it. You'd be surprised how much I know about you already," he said. "She was always talking about you. Frankly, I expected you to be wrought of solid gold instead of flesh and blood. I'm so pleased she exaggerated everything but your beauty." He faced her, his eyes lingering over her breasts and throat. "You really are exceptional, you know."

Wynflaed blushed, wanting to tell him to remember his wife, but she was flustered and annoyed. All she could manage was a nervous laugh. His attentions disgusted her. She hated such obvious flattery at the best of times, but coming from him it was sickening.

"I'd better get back" she told him. "I've got my work ..."

"Ah yes, your embroidery," Colnoth said. "I've watched you working. You're very skilled. I admire your dedication. I've never seen such beautiful work."

"I'm grateful to you and Buhe for giving me the silks and the linen. You can have no idea how much it means to me."

"It's our pleasure. I'm sure we look forward to seeing the results."

"I hope to use it to get my children back."

"Well I'm glad I'm able to help you."

"I'd better go now, Colnoth, or I'll get no work done today."

"You're quite a woman, you know," he said, moving to bar her way. He took firm hold of her hands. "Few women could have run a lead mine and farms as you did. That shows courage and wit. I admire that. And even now, you're still fighting. Your needle is your sword."

She nodded politely and tried to pull away without being too obvious about it, but Colnoth held on to her. "It can't have been easy for you — all alone," he said, moving his face closer to hers. "I mean without a man to help you, to console you, to remind you how beautiful you are."

She pulled her hands away sharply. "Look Colnoth," she cried. "I need no consoling or reminding ..." She paused, calming herself before going on quietly. "I'm content, despite my problems, because as long I am here, I can see an end to them. You and Buhe are very kind to me." She looked up at him, sensing that she must quickly say something to soften the tension between them. She smiled and touched the back of his hand. "I know you're only trying to be kind," she said, "trying to make me feel wanted and attractive again — despite my chopped hair. But I really am alright. You needn't worry. I could not imagine two nicer people for friends."

"We could meet here again — tomorrow," he said, "just to talk and ..."

"I don't think we should, Colnoth. What would Buhe think?"

His expression hardened. "I'll be here tomorrow. I know you'll not let me down. I hate disappointment."

Nausea drained the strength from her limbs and set them trembling. "But what will Buhe think. She loves you. It would hurt her if she ..."

"Then you'd better make sure she doesn't get the wrong idea," he said. "You obviously care more than I do about what she thinks. So make sure she has no reason to wonder ..." He turned away to leave. "I'll see you here tomorrow — same time."

***

At Badecanwell, Eadwin soon found work for his mule, and despite Eofar's presence, lodged at Sebbi's house while he looked for other accommodation. With new settlers arriving and plenty of loads for pack horses to shift, he expected he would soon have his own house and a strip of land.

Penda's treaty with the western Wealhs and his continued success in battles with his English and Saxon neighbours brought growing prosperity to Mercia and the Peakland. Every week new settlers arrived, many with land grants and war booty earned in Penda's service. They cleared land and built houses, fuelling trade and prosperity in the south of the region. Even in the wilder northern Peak, craftsmen and traders were doing well, and Eadwin soon had work for a couple of extra ponies.

His relations with Eofar however, were at best indifferent. They went to great lengths to avoid each other whether inside or outside the house. Wilma employed careful domestic scheduling to keep them apart. Wynflaed was never mentioned, and any accidental reference to her or By-Streams or Bell Delfan was quickly passed over.

Increasingly isolated, Eofar kept out of the way. When he was not working, he walked in the hills, brooding on Bell Delfan and trying to devise ways to punish Rendil for not keeping his word, though he never did anything about it.

***

Colnoth was laid low with the winter fever. He took to his bed and stayed there for two weeks, coughing and wheezing, his eyes streaming, his nose blocked. Buhe was distraught. She fussed over him endlessly. Wynflaed secretly thanked whichever ealf had shot him with its mischief for keeping him away from her.

As Yuletide came and went, Buhe's selfless ministrations seemed to have diverted Colnoth's attention, not only from his designs on Wynflaed, but from

whatever, or whoever, had drawn him to visit his father so
often. He stayed around the house, courting and sporting
with Buhe as if he had rediscovered her. Wynflaed often
came upon them in corners, store rooms and stables, with
Buhe in giggling disarray and Colnoth rampant.

Apart from minor embarrassment, it made
Wynflaed's life a great deal easier. She could spend her
free time working on her linen gift piece for Lady
Aenflaed. Her confidence that one day soon it would bring
her to the great lady's attention grew with every stitch. Her
work reflected the cold pastels of winter, silver instead of
gold, and iron grey with pale blues and soft misty whites.
Soon it would be spring and the greens, yellows and
fluttering creams and pinks of Eostre would be stitched
into place.

She day-dreamed as she sewed, thinking of how,
when it was finished, she would take it to Aenflaed, and
how the great lady would make it possible for her to go
home to By-Streams with Eadric and little Wyngifu. The
nightmare would be over, and then what colours she
would stitch into her life.

***

Uplifted as always by her early morning walk around
Uhtred's pool, Wynflaed turned back towards the
farmstead, her head full of the colours she would use that
day. She giggled self-consciously, rebuking herself for the
juvenile glee with which she found herself anticipating
breakfast. Appetite, like so many other good feelings, had
returned in the peaceful weeks with Buhe. Her hair was
growing, and though she kept her head covered she could
now brush it into something other than a spiky fuzz.

It was a bright morning, chilly with silver sunlight
and wisps of frosty mist. Eostre had taken her first
tentative steps in the woodlands, scattering the first

primroses. Frosted catkins hung on polished boughs where blue-tits courted in noisy flurries of sapphire and mustard. In the smithy yard, swirls of randy sparrows trilled and scuffled with each other, worrying the horses and distracting the bellows boy.

There are many woodland things a man might bring to a woman without declaring particular intent: blackberries, mushrooms, a bundle of fire wood, a honeycomb, or a bunch of herbs picked in their moon, but not primroses on the first spring day. When Colnoth held out a bunch to Wynflaed, she drew back from them as though they were a sneer of vipers.

"They're lovely, Buhe will love them," she said, praying her meaning would not escape him.

"They're not for her. They're for you."

"No! They're for Buhe, surely?"

"Don't you like them? I can throw them away."

"No, don't do that. I'll give them to Buhe. I'll tell her you sent them."

"I want you to have them," he said, loading the innocent sentence with blatant innuendo. He squinted his poor eyes, straining to see her reaction. "I thought only of you as I picked them. If you give them to Buhe, she'll probably put them beside our bed and I will see them and think of you as I ride her tonight."

At breakfast Buhe, bright and giddy as ever, chattered inconsequentially. Colnoth sat brooding across the table, gloomily fiddling with his food, his head tilted to one side, watching Wynflaed's every move.

Buhe had accepted her posy of primroses and given it without comment to a house maid. The girl ran to put them in water, getting more pleasure from them than any who saw her.

"I think the mattresses could go out for an airing today, don't you Flaedy?" Buhe queried regally. "It's high time they breathed something but smoke and soot."

Slightly startled, Wynflaed volunteered suddenly. "I'll give you a hand."

"Grim's blood no. Let them do it," Buhe said, casting a disdainful glance at the servants around the hall. "Let's you and I go for a walk." She rose from the table inviting Wynflaed with a tilt of her head.

Colnoth watched sourly as the pair went outside into the sunshine, leaving him to finish his meal, food for which he had little appetite.

***

For Eadwin, life at Badecanwell soon lost its attraction. For the first time in his life, he found tramping the roads to remote farms and settlements, hauling loads here and there, dull and boring. "I'm leaving," he told Wilma, one evening.

"I thought you might. What will you do?"

"I hear Penda's planning to go against the East Anglians. He'll need men to handle his pack animals. One of the new settlers said I could make my fortune in a few weeks for doing nothing more than my normal trade."

"Speak to Eofar before you leave. Brothers should not part in hatred."

"I can't, but I don't hate him. I just can't forgive him."

***

At Uhtredstun, Colnoth's unwanted attention to Wynflaed grew worse each day. He followed her around, blatantly obvious and not caring who saw him. Finally, he cornered her in her bedroom. "I didn't want Buhe to be upset by us, but if you won't be sensible, she will have to be," he said.

"All I want is a bit of fun. You know what I want. Stop acting like a virgin. I won't wait much longer."

"I don't want to. It's not right. Buhe is my friend, my sister," she said. "Now go! This is my room. You must leave. If you won't, I must." She moved to the door, but he stopped her. His strong hands gripped her tightly, hard fingers digging in.

"For Grim's sake, Colnoth, Buhe is only just outside. Please don't do this to her."

Colnoth pulled her to him. His lips brushed her short hair. "When I fuck her, I think of you. I close my eyes and imagine you beneath me."

Wynflaed pulled free. "No no, I won't hear this."

"Since you came here, I fuck her more than ever. That's because of you, Flaedy. I want you. I can't think of anything else."

Wynflaed squirmed free and ran into the hall. She saw Buhe busy with the servants, but thankfully she had not noticed anything. The hall was often full of people going about their business, working, chatting to each other, coming and going, one more was hardly cause for its mistress to notice.

Colnoth had not entered her room before. There was no door or lock to keep him out, only a woollen curtain. What was she to do? She felt sick. He was bound to try again and next time, she feared, he might come to her when she was in bed, or washing, or undressing. If Buhe even suspected such a thing she would be heartbroken. Besides, she had a jealous streak. Wynflaed had often seen it when they were young girls. When she was the one being generous and giving, Buhe was fine, but if she thought someone had more than her, she could quickly become jealous and spiteful.

For most of that day Wynflaed stayed away from the house. She walked in the woods, pondering her situation. She had been with Buhe about six months and had made good progress with Aenflaed's linen gift piece. But Colnoth's pestering put everything at risk. If Buhe found out, her reaction was sure to be ill-considered and might even be extreme. She could react like a spoilt child. Wynflaed worried that she might deliberately damage the linen gift piece, knowing that it meant so much. She felt sick with worry. She even considered hiding it to protect it from Buhe's temper, should trouble flare up between them.

Colnoth had been drinking all day. By the evening meal he was barely able to stagger to his chair. Buhe pretended he was not drunk and tried to have a conversation with him. He swore and raged, but made no sense. Across the table Wynflaed watched him, terrified he might blurt out something about her. When he tried to eat he was sick behind his chair. Buhe finally had to acknowledge his condition, and with the help of servants took him to his bed.

In the darkness of her own room, Wynflaed lay wide awake. She could hear Buhe crying and wanted to go to her and comfort her, but Colnoth's presence prevented that.

***

The steady rhythm of the weeks was broken a few days later by the arrival of a small train of merchant pedlars. The enclosed yard filled with people, laughter and excitement. For the folk of Uhtredstun, the arrival of pedlars was a significant event, an excuse for a bit of fun and relaxation. They came out of their houses, workshops and fields to peer into the boxes and trays the pedlars set out on the ground to display their wares. It was, of course, the master and his lady whom the pedlars wanted to attract, but anybody with something to trade was welcome.

The village women, even the lowest slaves, were swept up on the spirit of feste which blossomed around the pedlars' pitches. Unreservedly, they offered Buhe their opinions as she looked at cloth lengths and woven coloured tape.

"Choose the blue, lady. It'll go lovely with your short cape," one begrimed skivvy from the smokehouse told her mistress.

"Rubbish!" another interrupted," the green's much better with her hair."

"I think the blue suits you best, lady, and when you're fed up with it I'll take it off your hands," quipped another cheekily, raising a laugh.

The traders also brought news and gossip. These were the first of the year, and as welcome as snowdrops for being conclusive proof that the isolation and uncertainty of winter was ending. Buhe was kept in a constant flurry of coming and going. She traded beeswax, honey and furs for a Kentish glass wine jug and a short end bolt of Eastern silk. For four deer hides, the antlers, and a length of undyed wool cloth, she got a dress length of the finest gentian blue linen. An old string of reddish beads that she had never liked fetched a pot of sweet-smelling balm to soften her skin. The pedlar assured her it would keep her skin young and "glowing like a virgin's".

From cast-offs Buhe had given her, Wynflaed gave up a multi-coloured woollen shawl and an embroidered kid-skin purse in exchange for a fine bronze needle. The pedlar, a fat, cheery man, agreed to throw in a turned beech-wood needle box, if only she would mend the seat of his brecs. It was a transaction she entered into with alacrity, despite the bawdy accompaniment of the villagers watching the proceedings.

That night the merchants invited everyone to join them around a huge fire in the garth for singing and dancing. As usual, some told tall tales as the evening wore on. Pedlars, being worldly men, can voice a turn of phrase to heat even a portcwene's painted cheeks. Wynflaed, who considered herself a seasoned audience, having heard much the same from her miners, was soon blushing at their bawdy stories. Colnoth, on the other hand, loved it. He rolled about helpless with laughter and, as usual, drank too much. That night, despite the snoring pedlars stretched out on the hall floor and tables, Wynflaed slept soundly, certain that Colnoth would be quite unable to rise to any ideas his head might have.

In the morning, as she worked at her embroidery in the sunlight by the hall porch, the fat pedlar, whose brecs she had repaired, paid her a parting visit. He announced himself as Blackbird Dawe, and proudly told her he was a simpleton, a sluggard and a liar.

"I've come to take my leave of the prettiest woman who ever saw my backside. A fine job, seamstress …" He stopped abruptly, his jaw dropped, cutting him off in mid sentence as his eye fell upon the embroidery in her frame. He leaned forward, gazing upon it with a trader's practised eye. "Grim's teeth, but that's the finest I've seen," he said. "I tell you, lady, I've been in every king's hall you could name, but I've never seen better. I even saw old king Edwin himself once, got up like an emperor in purple and gold. Even he had nothing so beautifully stitched."

Wynflaed allowed him to draw the frame from her fingers to admire her work. "I'm pleased you like it," she said, watching him lean to the light, his piggy little eyes following every line and swirl of the mythical beasts and serpents that wound around the edges of the gift-piece.

"Trade it with me when it's finished. I'd give you a gold brooch, or some silver combs and a disc of bronze, polished so fine that you can see your face in it as others see you."

"I can't, Master Dawe. It's a gift-piece for Lady Aenflaed — err — in the Peaklands."

He scratched his chin. "Aenflaed? You mean Ealdorman Cenwulf's sister? Aye, aye I know her, a grand lady right enough, but you'll get little from her for it compared to what I'd offer. Did she bespeak it?"

"It's to be a gift. She doesn't know of it yet."

"And why would you make such a splendid gift? You must owe her a great deal, or …" His eyes took on a crafty glint. "Or perhaps you seek a very great favour in return?"

"I have my reasons."

"And would they have anything to do with that gold ring you are trying to hide about your neck?"

She was shocked by his question and grabbed at Wulfric's gold ring which she had thought was well hidden on its leather thong under her dress. "Your beak is long, Blackbird."

"That's the way of pedlars' noses, my little lady seamstress. A big nose to a pedlar is like a needle and thread to a seamstress, without them nothing is made."

"Well, it won't serve you here," Wynflaed said, laughing as she recovered her frame and gave his nose a friendly tweak.

He laughed and stepped back, blushing slightly. "But I only mean that I can get you the best deal in trade of any man. Still, if you're to make a gift of it, then that's a dog of a different bark. No trade is equal to a gift. So, I turn up my hands and they're empty. Oh no, look, they're not." A small hank of green silk thread had mysteriously appeared in his palm. He dropped it onto her lap. "For you, a little gift."

Wynflaed smiled and scooped up the silk. "Thank you, Blackbird Dawe. I'll use it next. It's just what I need."

"Well, if you won't trade, that's that, but it's a terrible waste to give away such work. I just hope she'll appreciate it." He reached for his leading pack pony's reins and turned the animals towards the same road that his fellows had taken. "I wish all the blessings of Holy Mother Frigg upon you, my little lady seamstress. I must hurry now and catch up with the others, or I'll make easy meat alone for the wolves this forest breeds, two-legged and four-legged."

Wynflaed waved him goodbye as he turned again to face her, beaming cheekily. "If you change your mind, save it for me: just put the word out for Blackbird Dawe, the most cheating, lazy liar of a pedlar this side of the Frisian Sea. They all know Blackbird Dawe."

Missing him instantly, Wynflaed watched him go. He had reminded her of the crafty old jagger who used to collect the lead dishes from her at By-Streams. She laughed, thinking how they were a breed, these mulers and pedlars: free men no master could tie down and certainly no respecters of place or position. To them, pricking pride was meat and drink. Only trade was sacred, and the gossip that nurtured it.

Later, Colnoth entered the hall and stood behind Wynflaed where she worked by lamp light. He watched her silently. His closeness made her flesh creep. Without a word, he dropped a small ivory case into her lap and walked away before she could speak. She stared at the case and then at him. He disappeared into upper hall without looking back.

For a moment she let the case lay under her palms. Its carved ivory faces felt warm to her touch, like a living thing. Yellowed and smooth with age, it was flat and slightly smaller than her hand. Its lid was covered with fine carvings of men, naked to the waist. Some had the heads of birds and dog-like creatures on their shoulders. Carved silver lion paws hinged the lid to the base. Around the sides marched a procession of godlike beings: kings, priests, surgeons, warriors, reapers and winnowers. She had never seen anything so rich and exquisite.

She opened it. Inside were several sewing needles, some fine bone pins, and a tiny nacre handled knife for cutting thread. She recalled Buhe had chattered on about one of the pedlars displaying something just like it. She had not really been listening at the time, but now she realised this was probably the very same thing Buhe had seen and wanted. She had begged Colnoth to get it for her. He'd said it was too costly. Now it was on *her* lap, a beautiful, desirable object, but one she could not enjoy for a moment.

For two days Colnoth avoided her, making it impossible for her to return the gift. Several times she thought she had got rid of it by slipping it into his room, only to find he had returned it, secreting it amongst her personal possessions where she might accidentally reveal it in Buhe's presence. It was a ridiculous situation, which he treated as a huge joke. To Wynflaed, it was far from funny. If Buhe were to see her with the needle box she had been refused, it could plunge her into a jealous fury. Colnoth simply stood by, enjoying every moment of Wynflaed's discomfort. He seemed to enjoy her torment more than he might any sexual liaison he could force upon her.

Wynflaed decided to fight back by using his own tactics. She would give the needle case to Buhe at their meal that evening, springing it on her as if it were a delightful surprise arranged by Colnoth. If she timed it properly, she could trap him in his own silly deceit and force him to go along with her. His insidious game and the threat it posed would be over. She joined him and Buhe at the table that evening, feeling uplifted and charged with excitement.

Unfortunately, Colnoth seemed to have anticipated her. He began taunting her as she took her seat. "Strange how quiet it is without those pedlars," he said loftily. "I really enjoyed having them here. Of course they are all rogues, all pedlars are." He held his cup out to the side and waited impatiently as a servant refilled it with ale. "Did Buhe tell you about the beautiful ivory needle box she saw? She loved it, didn't you, my sweet? She really wanted it, but when I tried to get it for her, the damned pedlar refused my offer. She was heartbroken. Such a gift would be a sure sign of true love"

Buhe giggled and leaned to kiss his cheek. "He wanted far too much for it." she said innocently. "We couldn't afford it, but it was such a lovely thing. Did you see it, Flaedy?"

"I wonder what happened to it?" Colnoth asked. "Did you see it, Wynflaed?"

"Never mind," Buhe said to Colnoth, pouting and stroking his cheek. "I know you wanted it for me and I love you for it."

"I did, my sweet. A man would only give such treasure to the woman he truly worships."

Wynflaed sat, dumbly smiling at Buhe, who simpered and giggled, bathing in Colnoth's attention. Wynflaed felt the ivory case, hidden in the folds of her dress, its weight seeming to bear down heavily.

For most of that night she lay awake in her room, afraid to sleep for fear that Colnoth might come in to her. She was now certain that things could only get worse. For some reason, he seemed determined to destroy her friendship with Buhe, as well as his marriage. It was obvious he didn't love Buhe. Wynflaed had thought so from her first meeting with him. And to her, his frequent trips to see his father were an obvious smoke-screen for some illicit affair.

Colnoth and Buhe had met and become friends at Wynflaed's wedding. According to Buhe, there followed an intense love affair, leading up to their marriage. Wynflaed had her doubts about that. From what Buhe had said, it did not seem that Colnoth had been in any great hurry to be a married man. It had taken him five years to pop the question, and only then because Old Uhtred's life had seemed to be drawing to a close. Colnoth had gained a wife with a dying father and the expectation of a considerable estate.

Wynflaed lay on her bed, wondering if driving Buhe away would finally give Colnoth what he had really wanted all along, Uhtred's land and wealth without encumbrance.

She decided that she had to leave as soon as possible. The gift piece was almost finished; a few days more and it would be. She would secretly ask Horse Ebell to help her get away.

It rained heavily the next day. Rainwater flowed in around the lime washed walls. Furniture and stores had to be lifted off the ground, disrupting life in the hall.

Colnoth's neglect had caused the trouble, though he stomped around angrily blaming everybody else. Eventually, he put field hands to work cleaning out ditches that he had allowed to choke with leaves, weeds and old thatch. Wynflaed helped Buhe to save her bed linen and dry stores.

The next day was fine, a bright day of soft breezes and clean colours. Birdsong filled the trees as if the birds were determined not to waste a moment of the watery sunlight, after the downpour. Wynflaed sat by the porch working at her needle. She was embroidering a scene of a little fat blackbird having a green patch sewn onto its rump. Her concentration and the detached reverie it permitted were broken by Buhe declaring that she was bored.

Wynflaed shuffled to one side of her chair to make room for her to sit. "How can you be bored? It's Eostre's time and there's lots to be done."

"Work, work, work! I don't want to work. I want to do something nice. I want to have some fun. Come with me. Let's go down to Mers Brook like we …"

"No. I'm doing this. It's nearly finished. Why don't you get the dry store sorted out? Some of the grain we moved smelled musty, and there are mice everywhere. I don't know what use your cats are."

"I don't want to."

"Do some sewing then," Wynflaed said, annoyed by her pointless interruption. "You used to like it."

"I hate it," said Buhe, too self-involved to notice Wynflaed's mood. "Anyway, I said I was bored, not suicidal. I'm sure to stitch my finger and bleed over everything. I usually do — remember?"

They sat silently for a while, Wynflaed plying her needle, Buhe watching her, pouting like a spoilt child.

"There's only one thing that spoils you," Buhe said finally.

"What?"

"Why can't you be nice to Colnoth? It upsets me to see the way you avoid him. You never talk to him or laugh at his jokes. Don't you think he's funny?"

Wynflaed shrugged. "Well I …"

"I know what!" Buhe cried with sudden excitement. "Why don't you take him his noon meal, instead of me? It's a lovely sunny day. The walk will do you good. He's down in the bottom field beyond Father's Pool."

Wynflaed smiled, trying to hide her true feelings. "That's for a man's wife to do, or his lowliest house boy, and I am neither."

By noon, swan clouds glided through a bright blue sky. Sunshine gilded cart ruts in the lane and fences steamed. Imperious hens stalked the yard, peering into puddles and gobbling up rain-summoned worms.

"This is a pleasant surprise," Colnoth said as Wynflaed approached him. "Decided you're ready to talk, eh? Well, it's about time."

She handed him the cloth-wrapped food Buhe had prepared for him. "I am here because Buhe insisted."

"You're here and that's all that matters," he said, rummaging in the bundle and pulling out a strip of cold mutton. "Listen, I've got a cottage a mile or so down the road. We can meet there. The old woman who keeps it for me knows the ropes."

"I'm not meeting you anywhere, and certainly not in some secret whore's den. Talk is all I came for. I'm doing this for Buhe. She asked me to bring you your food. I was tempted to put something nasty in it."

"Oh, dear me, that's not very friendly. And after I've been so generous."

"I can't keep the needle case. You should never have given it to me. If Buhe sees it, it will break her heart. You must give it to her."

"I suppose I should, really," he said, mocking her. "She might be upset if she found you had it. Where is it now, by the way?"

"It's hidden where Buhe will never see it."

"You mean here?" He pulled it from inside his tunic and waved it at her.

"You've been snooping through my things again," she cried, clutching at Wulfric's gold ring on its cord, briefly wondering if he had taken that too.

He laughed and slipped the case inside his tunic. "You can hide nothing from me. The servants are mine, remember. I can make this turn up anywhere I want. Do you don't want Buhe to find it somewhere embarrassing?"

"Why are you doing this?"

"Simple," he snarled. "I want you willing and eager, and not in some back of the barn scramble. You'll come to the cottage, ready to be very friendly. If not, Buhe will find this in your sleeve." He studied her coldly. "I wouldn't give much for your chances of staying here then, would you?"

"I don't care about me. I care about Buhe. Doesn't it bother you that you'll hurt her so?"

"Why should it? Even Buhe's not completely stupid. She knows I see other women. That's why she's so pleased that I've been staying home a bit more these days. She's fooling herself. If she finds the needle case, she'll know it was you that I stayed here for. So, whether you come to me or not, it will still be you that breaks her heart."

He laughed and draped himself back against a fence spar, a confident leer on his face. "Take the east road for about a mile," he told her. "There's only one cottage. Wait for me there in the mid-afternoon. If you're not there, Buhe will find this somewhere that will mark you as her enemy for the rest of your life." He laughed and stroked his bulging crotch. "See, I'm ready now. Don't disappoint me."

. . . .

CHAPTER EIGHTEEN

Eostre's feste was at its height when Eadwin arrived at King Penda's Tame-worthig, the royal enclosure on the banks of the river Tame. He found its lanes crowded and noisy. Carriers and runners, shouting the importance of their errands, shouldered their way through the throng, the self-important runners beating off with sticks any who would impede them. Merchants' tents and stalls covered every green space. The town's hard-pressed elders had to crack skulls all day long to keep the king's meadow clear for the intended dancing and games in honour of the goddess of spring. Eadwin felt nervous and excited. Not since the battle at Hatfield Heath had he seen so many folk gathered together.

***

For Wynflaed, a grim cloud hung over Uhtredstun's Eostre festivities. It came with the arrival of the king's theow-reeve, a chilling reminder of her illegal status. Wite-theow, criminals condemned to a life of slavery, were widely thought unsuitable for all but the meanest of hard labour. Dogs and lepers enjoyed higher status. With little prospect of ever achieving freedom in their joyless lives, they were troublesome, surly and dangerous. Their lives were hard and short.

Colnoth, often kept a few wite-theow for the heaviest work. His overseers would work them brutally hard until they either died or escaped, but they were cheap and easily replaced. All he had to do was put out word that he wanted more, and within a couple of weeks some typically thuggish theow-reeve and his team of bully-boys would arrive with a string of the poor wretches for his inspection.

Officially Wite-theow belonged to the king. The chief magistrate would send them about the shire, digging and hauling on the kings business. Unofficially theow-reeves, the overseers hired to guard, discipline and transport them about, made a small fortune for themselves by hiring them out along the road, or selling them to unscrupulous buyers and claiming they had died in captivity. Colnoth knew perfectly well that the practise was illegal, but as it meant that the prices were much lower than for a legal slave, he was happy to go along with it.

Watching from hiding, Wynflaed shuddered on seeing how defeated and hopeless the slaves looked, roped together in a huddle. She and Wulfric had always avoided buying slaves, especially convicts. They were poor workers, and much too troublesome and dangerous.

After close inspection, Colnoth chose three men. The reeve pulled them out of the line and stood them to one side, where they waited sullenly. After haggling fiercely over the price they were eventually handed over to Colnoth, whose overseer put them straight to work. The theow-reeve counted and thoroughly inspected every one of the old empire coins Colnoth had paid him before sharing them with his men.

Colnoth looked pleased with himself. He had beaten the price down so low that even if one of the men died within the month he would still have a bargain. Wynflaed felt sorry for the wretches, but she hoped that working them would keep Colnoth busy and away from her. She had not kept any of the assignations he had tried to force on her, and felt constantly on edge, fearing what he might do next. Every day she worried that this might be the one when he carried out his threats, and every night she lay awake, tortured by fears of what might happen if he did.

Tricking Buhe into believing his lies would be easy. Buhe was often quick to leap to the wrong conclusions, especially where her pride or possessions were concerned. Jealousy could seize her in a flash, and she'd become vindictive and irrational. Afterwards, when she calmed down, she would be deeply penitent and go to extremes of generosity to make up for any damage she had done, but usually too late.

Throughout the week of Eostre's feste, Colnoth left Wynflaed alone, but as Uhtredstun returned to normal, so did he. After dodging him several times, she was eventually cornered on a narrow path between a barn and a thorn hedge. "I've waited long enough," he said. "Meet me this afternoon, or say goodbye to your life here."

"Colnoth, please, you can't mean it. You'll destroy Buhe."

"You have the power to prevent it. She need never know. Go to the cottage. Meet me there. Buhe will never know."

Wynflaed squeezed past him and ran away through sheep pens, scattering lambs and ewes. Again she had left him without the answer he wanted. She felt his baleful glare on her back. It was chilling and signalled clearly that her time at Uhtredstun was fast running out. There was nothing left to do but leave. She must go quickly and in secret. Not even Buhe must know.

At the night meal, Wynflaed and Colnoth sat in icy silence. Buhe chattered, seeming unaware of the tension at her table. Wynflaed had no appetite. She felt sick and merely picked at her food. Claiming a headache, she went to bed, slumped on top of it and silently wept.

Later, she heard Buhe and Colnoth through the thin screen wall, preparing for bed. They did not speak to each other and soon all sounds of their activity stopped.

Wynflaed stared up into the darkness, sobbing and listening to the faint hiss and crack of the hall fire dying in the hearth. Her mind raced over her problems, looking for a way out, sifting through the wreckage of rejected, unworkable solutions. In the blackness, something disturbed her, a sound, or some change of ambience in the room — a presence. She sat up sharply, realising she had dozed off leaving her lamp burning. In its dim light, she saw Colnoth. He was naked.

"Keep quiet, and maybe she won't hear us."

Wynflaed scrambled out of bed and backed away until her shoulder blades pressed against the wall. "For the gods' sakes, Colnoth," she whispered, "please no. You can't ..."

Lunging he grabbed her wrists. "I can do whatever I want in my own house," he said, clearly unconcerned that Buhe would hear. Wynflaed struggled to break free, still trying to keep quiet. He forced her onto the bed and pressed down on top of her. Desperation fuelled her struggle. She abandoned trying to be silent and fought him with all her strength, but he was the stronger. He drove his bony knees painfully between hers, forcing her legs apart. His clawing hands ripped the fabric of her woollen dress, tearing it to her waist.

Buhe called out from her room. Wynflaed could hear the rising panic in her voice as she must have realised what was happening. Colnoth laughed, seeming to enjoy his wife's misery. Buhe hammered on the wall, screaming.

"You see how she is? She wants to know what we're doing. This is all your fault. You could have saved her this." Wynflaed was rigid with fear. She felt him thrust into her, pressing down brutally and ramming hard. Panting and groaning like something wild and monstrous.

As if seeking strength, Wynflaed's fingers scrabbled to grab hold of Wulfric's gold ring on its cord around her neck. She clutched it tightly and, clamping her eyes shut, disconnected from what was happening to her. She sagged, emptying her muscles, unlocking her joints, unwinding fists and clawing fingers. Like a rag doll, she let her limbs flop down from pushing and fighting.

As if from somewhere far off, she heard Buhe's pitiful wails. She knew, in that sickening moment that all the secrets, joys and innocence of their lives together were being fouled. Everything they had been to each other was being soiled and marred. It decayed and dissolved into slop, like rotting fruit.

Colnoth climaxed and rolled off her, smearing her thighs as he pulled away. Wynflaed pushed and kicked him off. She grabbed the bed cover and pulled it up to the tears on her face.

Not attempting to cover himself, Colnoth left without a word. She heard him go into his bedroom. Buhe fell silent at once, except for the occasional shuddering sob.

Wynflaed heard his voice, harsh and cold. "You had to find out some day," he told her. "I don't love her. It's just sex – physical pleasure with no meaning. She means nothing. She has wanted me to do it since she arrived. I'm just a normal man. You must take it or leave it. It means nothing. She wanted it and I gave it to her."

Wrapping herself in the bed cover Wynflaed ran into Buhe's room. She was trembling and felt weak and sick. "Buhe, you must listen to me," she pleaded. "It wasn't like that. I never wanted …"

"It was just for fun, Buhe. Forget it. Look, I've got something for you." He reached into a small chest beside the bed. "I bought it for you. I've been saving it to surprise you." He brought out the ivory needle case and handed it to her.

Sobbing and confused Buhe took it from him. Her red-rimmed eyes moved between his face and the beautiful object in her hands. She pressed the ivory case to her breast, her face a mask of misery.

Colnoth turned to Wynflaed and shrugged. "I think you'd better cut yourself a walking staff, you filthy whore. We don't want you here anymore."

She wanted to hurt Colnoth, to punish him, but she knew it was too late for that. The future, as with honey spilled in sand, was irrecoverably spoiled. She reached out to Buhe, but she pulled away from her as if from a viper's jaws. Everything had changed. Things would never be the same again.

In her room Wynflaed washed herself, rinsing deep inside to cleanse the filth that she felt Colnoth had put there. When finished, she lay on her bed clutching Wulfric's gold ring and staring at the floor timbers of the loft above her.

She would not sleep; she could not with all her thoughts and fears barging around inside her head. She knew she had to leave, but where could she go? She feared that Buhe would not let her take the linen gift piece. It was all but finished, and now more than ever it seemed her only hope. She had to have it, but Buhe had been deeply hurt. There was no knowing what she might do. She had provided the silks and the linen, just as she had given her the clothes she wore and the food she had eaten. She knew that if she wanted, Buhe could stop her taking anything.

Perhaps if she were to hide, Wynflaed thought, and stay out of Buhe's way for a few days, until she had the chance to think about everything. She desperately wanted the gift piece, but if she could somehow give Buhe the time to see things calmly, they might even be able to salvage something of their friendship too.

The harsh scrape of the hall's heavy door on the threshold cobbles gave her a sudden start. She realised she had been dozing; morning had come. Thin slivers of sunlight speared through gaps between the loft's floorboards above her. She was still wearing her torn dress. She pulled a shawl about her waist to cover her nakedness. Peering warily around the curtain in the doorway of her bedroom she saw Buhe coming in from outside. She looked pale and stony faced. Grimy tear marks streaked her cheeks. The theow-reeve and his men followed her in. They all stopped as they saw Wynflaed. Buhe glared at her, her eyes filled with loathing. Slowly she raised a trembling hand and pointed her finger. "That's her. That's the runaway."

....

CHAPTER NINETEEN

Crab-hand Connah spat into his campfire at the door of his tent and strained to break wind. Pleased with the results, he grinned into the complaining faces of the three others sharing the tent with him. "It's a good arse that speaks its mind," he said, mocking them.

A bony man with crossed eyes and teeth like a muck rake grumbled inaudibly. Connah glared at him. "If you don't like it, fuck off outside!"

"If it wasn't pissing down, I would," said the bony man, and drawing his cloak tighter around his shoulders, leaned to peer out through a rip in the sopping wet tent. "Will it never stop? We'll be lucky if half of 'em are still alive by morning."

"So what? We gets paid for the bunch, not the 'eads," said Connah, helping himself to an onion and a piece of grey bread from his food sack. He shuffled gleefully on his buttocks and sucked on the onion. "I think I'll have that little fat un again tonight," he said, rolling back onto his bedroll with an excited shudder. "She's a really good shag, she is."

The bony man licked his lips. "What about her we got this morning?"

Crab-hand Connah shrugged. "Naah, piss off! That prissy piece is too icicle arsed for me. I don't fancy it much. And, you're not having it neither. It's too classy for a turd like you."

"A dead sheep is too classy for him," interjected a sallow skinned youth, the third of the four men crammed into the tent. The fourth was sleeping his head hidden under a bearskin.

The bony man appeared to think it over for a moment then shook his head. "Naah, I don't fancy it anyway."

"Scared of it, more like." the youth said.

"Scared? I'm not scared of no woman, especially not slaves."

"It's a pity her hair's not a bit longer," said Connah. "You can get a good trade for a hank of hair that colour."

A few steps away from the tent, rain beat down on a shivering huddle of folk hunched around a smoky fire. There were seven men and four women, fastened together at the neck and feet by an assortment of restraints. Some by iron slave-collars, euphemistically called the king's necklace, others by ropes or stout twists of leather thong. Wynflaed was the last on the chain, her fine woollen shift with its embroidered neck setting her apart from her ragged companions, even ripped as it was.

She looked round the group huddled over the fire. They did not look like violent criminals. She guessed that some might be debtors, or just unlucky folk whom Wyrd had tripped up, making them fall foul of neighbours, master, or landlord. She had already learned that two were petty thieves. They kept celebrating their luck at being there, having avoided mutilation or death, the more usual sentence for theft. Whatever their crimes or misfortunes, they all now belonged to the king. He could put them to work building his ramparts, roads and ditches, or sell them on to new masters. The only certainty was that they all faced a life of slavery unless they could buy or win manumission from a generous master — an idle dream.

The moonless night promised no respite from the rain. A chill breeze rattled in the trees beside the old Roman road where the magistrate's slavers had pitched their tent. Chained to Wynflaed was a sullen young woman, a tough, ice-cold cynic with not a good word for anything or anyone. She wanted nothing less than a horrible death for all who crossed her, especially her captors. Yet beneath the grime and bloody bruises of her captivity, Wynflaed saw that she had a pretty face with smooth skin and large blue eyes. She still had her hair too, long coppery blonde tresses that wound around her neck in soft curls. Wynflaed watched her sleeping, thinking how beautiful she looked, almost childlike. Yet once awake, she could have felt safer chained to a wolf.

The next woman on the chain was small and fat. She wept continually. Red spots and blotches covered her skin. Her button nose, which she never wiped, oozed offensively. Her name was Brinna. She said she had been a kitchen skivvy. Her master had accused her of eating more food than he and his family did. "I swear I never sat down for a meal in all the years I worked for him." Considering her size, Wynflaed could not help thinking that her guilt seemed somewhat self-evident, but said nothing, beyond asking her to wipe her nose.

"I'll not let them corpse me," Brinna said, between snorting and pinching off snot with her fingers and wiping it away in the wet grass. "And neither should you," she told Wynflaed. "If they want you to go with 'em, don't argue, do it! And make sure you give 'em a good time. At least you'll get to sleep in the dry, and maybe even have a bite to eat besides. Otherwise, you'll spend your nights like this — in the bloody rain." She eyed Wynflaed pityingly. "You're not used to it, are you, love? I can see that. A feather bed is more your style. Much more o' this and it will get on your chest. You're the sort what don't last long, I'm afraid. Anyway, think about what I said. When you're dead, what good will it do to know that you kept your knees together? The worms will still be up your kirtle as fast as the rest of us. Take my advice, pick one of 'em out and make him like you. Suck his cock. They love that. And tell him you think he's smarter than the others. You might soon be in the dry with some decent food in your belly."

Wynflaed eyed her doubtfully. The magistrate's men seemed barely human. Submitting to any one of them was a repulsive thought. They were coarse, filthy and stinking. Their leader, Crab-hand Connah, was a huge Irishman with red hair and an absence of front teeth. He had a square, red face, slashed open by a large, flabby mouth. His right hand was missing all but a thumb and first finger. It was the sort of injury common to old soldiers.

His second in command was the small, cross-eyed man with whom he bickered constantly. The third was a large, slow man who never spoke. The others had various names for him including Wineslop, Liverface and Brunbasso. His right cheek and throat bore a deep purple stain which accounted for the epithets. The junior amongst them was a blonde, pale-skinned youth whom they called Whitey. In many ways, Wynflaed feared him most. His pink-rimmed eyes seemed dead. He enjoyed hurting people. Beatings and abuse were usually his handy work. His fists would fly if a slave so much as looked his way, or hesitated for an instant before obeying an order. Generally, the others seemed bored with brutality; though they would watch Whitey beat a prisoner senseless, with an almost detached curiosity.

As the days dragged by, Connah occasionally sold a slave or picked up another. They trekked on unfamiliar roads. None of the slaves knew where they were, or where they were being taken. Brinna said that wite-theow were usually taken to Penda's South-Worthig on the river Tame. She hoped a farmer would buy her before they got there. She did not want to spend her life digging latrines and ditches for the king's army, which, according to her, was what awaited them.

Wynflaed too hoped that she would be sold to a good family, perhaps as a seamstress. There might then be the chance to earn her freedom, or if not, escape. She expressed this hope to the others, joining in with their useless frequent speculation about their futures.

Her neighbour was not optimistic. "Looking like you do, you'll be whored to death, sweet bird," she said. These were almost her only words so far despite being chained to each other. "Face it," she went on, "nobody looks for a seamstress on a magistrate's chain."

"My word, you must be special," said Brinna. "The miserable cow has never spoke a word to me, nor anyone else before."

Wynflaed turned to Brinna, but was shocked to see her eyeing her strangely. She realised she had been distracted by the sight of Wulfric's gold ring on its leather thong around her neck. It had slipped from hiding under the embroidered trim at the neck of her torn dress and was now in full view.

"What's that?" Brinna hissed with sudden alarm. Before she could answer, Brinna had grabbed it and ripped it from her neck. Wynflaed tried to snatch it back, but despite her size, Brinna was fast. She dodged aside then lunged at Wynflaed. The pair rolled about on the ground wrestling frantically, tangling their chains and bindings and dragging the others with them.

"Shove it up your cunni, or you'll lose it," Brinna whispered into Wynflaed's ear, as she clung on to her neck and rolled on top of her. "Hide it. Hide it now. If they see it, they'll steal it. Shove it up there quick. It's your only chance."

Wynflaed glimpsed her face, as Brinna pushed the ring secretly into her hand, shielding it from view with her fat body. Wynflaed took her advice, though it hurt, and Brinna was not pulling her punches in the brawling distraction she had created. The guards watched, laughing. Eventually, Whitey broke it up and set to beating them with his stick. Wynflaed curled up into a defensive ball, taking the opportunity to finish the job Brinna had suggested. Whitey turned on Brinna, who despite his blows flashed Wynflaed a quick smile. It was a small moment of triumph, a spark of success they could share.

When Whitey tired of beating them, the group settled down around the fire. "Any more of that and I'll stick both you," warned their sour neighbour. Brinna ignored her and began inspecting her bruises. Wynflaed smiled apologetically, feeling the strange pressure inside her vagina. She felt aroused and thought of Wulfric.

Brinna glanced up from her bruises to where Whitey had now joined his comrades. "He's a sick bastard that one. All he wants to do is hurt you. I don't think he's got a cock. I tried to get hold of it once, but he just punched me away."

"Is it right what she said?" asked Wynflaed. "Will they make me a whore for the army?"

"I'm afraid so," said Brinna. "You're too pretty to waste on digging latrines." She shook her head and patted Wynflaed on the forearm. "Look, if you don't get lucky and are bought before then, you need to make yourself as ugly and filthy as possible. Like I do."

"Why?"

"So you don't get picked by the whore masters. The best thing is to look filthy and a bit touched. You know, slobber and smile like this." She rolled her eyes and smiled vacantly, whilst blowing snot bubbles. "That puts 'em off."

"Really? I wonder why?" cried Wynflaed laughing. "How do you know all this?"

"It's just what they say. I've heard 'em talking. Anyway, it's obvious."

Wynflaed's sour neighbour was not amused. She swung a punch at Brinna, just missing her jaw. "Shut up you stupid cows. I'm trying to sleep."

………

CHAPTER TWENTY

The lanes and yards of the king's south-worthig on the banks of the River Tame teemed with people. Wynflaed's mouth watered at the smells of food cooking on fires by the roadside. She had not eaten more than the odd piece of stale bread in five days. The sight and smells of so much food and so many people stuffing their mouths with it made her drool.

Crab-hand Connah led them through the crowds to a stockade built against a sturdier, more permanent looking palisade. Somebody whispered that King Penda's golden vill lay beyond it. This met with various grumbles from the group, mostly that Penda could stick his golden vill somewhere impossibly uncomfortable. Inside the stockade Connah detached the ropes and chains from their iron collars. Wynflaed joined the others to peer through gaps in the timber wall, hoping to see the famous golden hall for herself.

Without chains she felt as light as a bird, and walked about quickly, reacquainting her limbs with freedom. It felt wonderful. Tilting her head back she looked up at the sky and thought how little Eadric and Wyngifu might be looking at the same hazy sunshine.

"Sit down here," said Brinna. "What's up? You look sad."

Wynflaed quickly wiped tears from her eyes and sat on the ground beside her. "Nothing," she said leaning back against the rough timber wall. "I suppose I'm just relieved to have made it this far."

Brinna grunted. "Made it? Huh, you're not nowhere yet, lovie."

"A golden hall?" Wynflaed mused absently, closing her eyes.

"I can't see it," said Brinna, peering through a gap between timbers. "They say it's solid gold from floor to thatch."

"Thatch?"

"Yes, it's made of spun gold."

"Sounds a cold place for a sparrow to nest."

The stockade gate shook and then emitted a tortured howl as it swung open. Brunbasso and the cross-eyed man followed a pair of burly, armed guards. They carried two leather buckets of water and a basket of loaves. Squinty-man upended the basket, shooting a dozen stale loaves into the mud. His comrade placed the buckets next to them and slouched away. As the gate closed behind them the slaves attacked the pile of bread.

"Dinner is served, my lady," cooed Brinna. "Shall you eat here or in upper hall tonight?"

Wynflaed chuckled. "Right here, girl. It's so lovely in the orchard just now."

A fist fight started around the loaves. The guards stood back to watch, laughing as blows flew. The stronger men dragged out the women, tossing them aside like dolls, until the brawl stopped abruptly. The heap of writhing bodies parted and backed away like splash rings on water. Brinna quickly surveyed the scene, grabbing Wynflaed's arm. "Come on, let's go see."

At the centre of the expanding circle of faces crouched the sour young woman to whom Wynflaed had been chained. She held a jagged, sliver of metal, partly concealed in the folds of her ragged dress. At her feet were the loaves of bread and a man, writhing in pain, clutching a bloody gash on his arm.

She sorted through the loaves, picked the cleanest, and strode away, her defiant glare challenging anyone to dare to stop her. After a moment's silence, the slaves dived back onto the pile of bread, fighting as before. Brinna and Wynflaed fought too, punching and kicking until they each emerged with a chunk of bread. Wynflaed's piece was coated in mud. She wiped it clean on her dress and bit into it. It was food. She was hungry.

She ate thanking Wyrd that she was not the poor man left bleeding. He was now crawling about picking up the few crumbs left to him. In this new world in which she now found herself, she knew she'd have to fight to survive. If she didn't, it would be her picking over the leavings and nursing her injuries.

As night approached, the noisy arrival of several men at the gate jerked her from her thoughts. Through gaps in the timbers, she saw that some carried steaming pots. The appetising smell of meat stew carried to her nostrils, making her mouth water. A couple of the men had bales of blankets and lengths of waxed cloth and ox-hide tenting. A cart full of straw drew up beside the wall and the carter began pitching his load over the stockade. The gate opened and the unexpected luxuries were rapidly distributed.

Brinna grabbed Wynflaed's arm and pulled her towards a man dishing out hot stew. He grinned at Wynflaed as she held out her hands for a wooden bowl full. "Don't worry, there's plenty. You're being fattened up for the army."

"The army? Aren't we going to be sold?"

"Not this year. Our lord Penda is on the move again." He laughed, blasting her with rancid breath. "He needs skivvies and whores, and you beauties fit the bill nicely . But first, we've got to feed you up and cut your hair."

More slaves arrived each day. For over a week, Wynflaed and the others ate well and slept on straw in narrow tents of waxed cloth and leather. Speculation was wild and endless. New arrivals were pumped for news. The gaolers were cajoled, but nobody discovered what was to happen to them. Curiosity and impatience flared. The Tame-Worthig's charged atmosphere reached in over the palisade, touching everyone, shortening tempers and raising fears. Every day, Wynflaed peered through the timbers, trying to see what was going on outside. She saw skittish horses stamping and snorting at tethering rails. Pack ponies and traders passing this way and that. Folk were dashing about on last-minute errands, and Mercia's swaggering warriors grew ever more boisterous.

Two weeks after her arrival at the Tame-Worthig, Crab-hand Connah entered the compound dragging a bunch of chains. "Come on my lovelies, the boys will want you tonight. Let's get you all prettied up in your necklaces."

As she felt the weight of the chain on her collar again, Wynflaed struggled to be next to Brinna. She grabbed her hand and clung on. "She's next your honour — please." Connah grinned indulgently, and began feeding the chain towards Brinna's collar, but Brinna's hand was wrenched away and another forced in to replace it. It belonged to the same malevolent woman Wynflaed had been chained to before. "I'm next to her," she shouted at Connah, her eyes blazing fiercely. Connah shrugged, not caring.

Wynflaed eyed her curiously. The young woman glared back. "What are you gawping at?"

"I don't know. You won't tell me your name."

"Just leave me alone, see. I don't want no friends."

"So why did you want to be next to me then?"

"Not just you, both of you," she snarled. "You're both strong. You keep the chain up. It doesn't pull so much."

Wynflaed shrugged, wondering about her cold logic.

"Oh dear, I've hurt your feelings, have I?" Her lip curled in a sneer and she pushed her face threateningly into Wynflaed's. "Look, you mean nothing to me. Get in my way and you'll regret it. Same goes for your puss-faced friend."

Wynflaed backed off, raising her hands defensively. "All right, all right, don't be such a sour apple."

***

The following day they were marched alongside a train of oxcarts and jaggers. If a cart became stuck in the mire, they had to lift and push and haul it out. After only a couple of miles, Wynflaed was exhausted and covered in mud and bruises.

The king, with his glittering warriors, rode at the front of the column. Wynflaed, Brinna, Sour-Apple and hundreds of other slaves and servants, together with the warriors' wives and families, had no evidence for this, apart from fresh horse dung on the churned-up mud of the road. Wynflaed soon discovered it was easier on her sore feet if she walked in the horse manure at every opportunity. She chuckled to herself, wondering what Eadwin would think of her seeking it out with such enthusiasm.

The march took them through the southern edges of the great Shire-wood and beyond it towards the mysterious fenlands, said to be home to all manner of water spirits and marsh devils. Soldiers who knew the place told of men eaten by multi-headed snakes and billowing mists that swallowed up whole armies. Wynflaed shuddered and tried to dismiss the tales as fanciful nonsense. The trouble was she had heard of even stranger things in her own Peaklands.

One day, word filtered down from the front of the column that the men of the Gewissa and East Wixna were to join them where the Spalding marshes wash out into the Frisian Sea. Wynflaed knew nothing of these lands, or their clans. She could not say if they were near or far from her beloved Peaklands. She just tramped along with the others, struggling to keep upright in the sucking mire created by so many tramping feet, carts and horses.

Each day snatches of news arrived. As usual, it was garbled and mystifying. The latest rumour was that they were to turn north into the lands of the Lindissi. Penda evidently wanted to extract tribute from the Lindissi and remind them where their loyalties should lie, before he turned south to invade the East Anglians. The man who brought the news said it would be a long, hard march. He predicted they would not see one place for more than a few days at a time for over a year.

***

On that same day, a lone pedlar led three pack ponies into Uhtredstun. Buhe watched his arrival, remembering the last time she had seen him. It was Blackbird Dawes, the same fat pedlar whose brecs Wynflaed had repaired. A tear swelled on Buhe's eyelashes and spilled down her cheek. Wiping it away, she went to greet the man.

"Good day, Mistress," Dawes cried, bestowing his well practiced smile upon her. After tying his horses to a rail, he splashed his face at the yard water trough. "Is your mother at home, pretty miss? Oh forgive me, my lady, it is you, isn't it? By the gods you look no older than a maid."

Buhe ignored his flattery, well knowing that all pedlars were accomplished liars. Dawes apologised saying that he was short of time. "I left the main train," he said, "I must be brief. A merchant man is not safe alone."

The merchants' train, about fifty men and their pack horses, was now on the southern stretch of its annual, endless journey around the country. Blackbird Dawes had left the safety of its numbers to make another attempt to trade with Wynflaed for the linen runner. If he didn't get it this time it would be a whole year before he would have another chance. By then one of his competitors could have snaffled it up.

"Is your pretty little seamstress about?" When he saw Buhe's expression harden, he realised at once that something was wrong.

Buhe tossed her head. "She's gone. If you have business, it must be with me."

"Gone? Gone where?"

Bristling with unease Buhe eyed him coldly. "Her business is not for you to know. What do you want?"

"Trade, my lady," Dawes said lightly, unaffected by her hostility. "Honest trade, as ever: no more, no less. Here, look, I have a rare spice all the way from the magical east. They say it will make a young bull out of a dead ox. Some say it is the cure for all that ails men, but I make no such claim for it. See, it is a root. Some call it the man-root because look — it's shaped like a man. He held out a gnarled root for her inspection. Buhe was surprised by its blatantly masculine appearance.

"It's a powerful thing, my lady. Some say that even a pinch in a drop of wine will tie a young husband to an old wife for his lifetime."

"We've no need of such things here."

"Holy Mother Frigg save us. I can see that, bless your heart," he cried. "I meant to give it to you. A gift, a little joke for you to play with your husband, that's all."

Buhe's expression softened. Her head wobbled indulgently on her slim neck.

"It's a pity the seamstress isn't here," said the pedlar, scratching his chin. "She promised to trade me a fine gold thread piece," he said. "Still, it can't be helped."

The presence of the linen runner in her house troubled Buhe. At first, she had wanted to get rid of it along with every other trace of Wynflaed. She had even thrown it out once, only to fetch it back later. It was such beautiful work. She could not bear to look at it. Her feelings about Wynflaed were as different from one moment to another as clouds riding the wind. Mostly she missed her and bitterly regretted what she'd done. And even hidden away, the linen gift piece haunted her house like a wandering ghost.

"I know the piece you mean. She was making it for my aunt, but she doesn't want it now. What would you have given her for it?" Buhe inquired, attempting indifference.

"Well, if it's finished, I could give you a good trade, maybe even a few pieces of silver or some eastern unguents. I have a very nice length of silk."

"Well, she did leave some things behind." Buhe looked about avoiding his gaze. "She told me to dispose of them. If you wait, I'll look to see if it's amongst them." She started to leave, but paused and turned back to him. "Go round to lower hall and tell them to feed you."

Dawes tried to look wearily unconcerned, though his heart was soaring. Whatever had occurred between Buhe and Wynflaed was mysterious and possibly even fascinating, but it was not his affair. The linen runner, on the other hand, definitely was - and now it was almost his. He must play his cards very carefully indeed. He must not lose it now. He bowed and trotted off to the cooks' fire.

Later that day, as he led his horses away from Uhtredstun, he fingered the linen gift piece thoughtfully. Apart from a fish at one corner, it was finished. The colours glowed; its superb detail drew the eye ever deeper. He wondered about Wynflaed. There had been something very odd about the way Buhe had thrust the linen runner at him. She had not seemed remotely interested in what she could have got for it, yet she had haggled like a querner's brat over some dyestuff she needed. Any fool could see that the embroidery was a work of art. If he had left his horses and half his stock as trade for it, he would still have been the winner.

He remembered that Wynflaed had said she was making it as a gift for Lady Aenflaed of Badecanwell and not, as Buhe had said, for some aunt who no longer wanted it. It was obviously special. He was old enough and cynical enough to know that nobody, not even a charming, open-faced beauty like Wynflaed, gave away such treasure without good reason. "Such a fine gift," he told his animals. "It must be for something very important." That, he surmised, might make it worth even more if he played with care and cunning.

**

At the Tame-worthig, Eadwin had secured regular work on the staff of Penda's house reeve. At the time, he had been delighted to win such favour and could barely believe his luck. He thought it remarkable that within a couple of weeks of leaving Badecanwell, he was not only in steady employment but was also, with all the talk of war and booty, facing the prospect of gaining actual riches. It mystified him why the other jaggers and mulers had not trampled over him to get the appointment. It was not until later that the mystery explained itself. His job with Penda's house reeve meant he would not be going with the army. His dreams of a fortune in captured booty, evaporated. Adventure and wealth it seemed, had eluded him yet again. For him there were only the mundane tasks of a muler: fetching and carrying, lifting and hauling. And, as the army marched eastward, his first task was to guide a group of envoys to Northumbria. They had gifts and letters from Penda, intended to calm and reassure the Northumbrian king, to keep him out of Penda's war with East Anglia. It was hardly a mission for heroes. He even fancied that Snowflake looked ashamed.

***

More than a week had passed since Wynflaed and the other slaves had had their hair shorn. Her scalp still felt cold and uncomfortable. Following Brinna's advice, Wynflaed kept her face and arms smothered with mud and ashes, and as Brinna had predicted, she stopped being the object of quite so many lustful stares. Being filthy with roughly cropped hair and bald patches had its compensations after all. She stiffened her protection against rape and abuse even more by letting Brinna teach her the insane smile she used in moments of threat. Finally, to complete her armour, she kept well away from places where men gathered in idleness.

Sour-Apple somehow managed to escape the slave master's shears. Her thick, loose curls marked her out from the other women, though even this did not sweeten her. She remained waspish and unpleasant. And although she directed her venom at humankind in general, she seemed to harbour a particular dislike for Wynflaed. She constantly picked on her and caused trouble for her. She accused her of stealing food and even of trying to poison the water skins. Unimpressed by Wynflaed's insane smile and dribbling mouth, Connah moved her away from the others and kept her for the filthiest jobs. Denied Brinna's company, Wynflaed felt miserable and alone. Even so, Sour-Apple did not seem satisfied. Wynflaed noticed she was always watching her. It seemed that every time she lifted her head there she would be, spying on her. Wynflaed struggled not to give her the satisfaction of seeing her brought low.

Two weeks into the march, Connah told her that one of the whore masters had purchased Brinna. It was depressing news. Wynflaed liked Brinna and had hoped to rejoin her at some stage. It was now unlikely she would see her again. A few days later Sour-Apple too vanished from Connah's camp. Her departure however, was cloaked in tantalising mystery. One rumour was that she had found a handsome young warrior who had fallen desperately in love with her. Wynflaed thought it unlikely, given the circumstances, but clearly some man liked her enough to buy her for his own pleasure. That seemed far better than the horrors of life in the whore tents.

Wynflaed thanked the woman who had brought the news, and pretended to share her curiosity and enthusiasm for more of the same. Since Connah had removed her from the others, occasional bits of gossip were important to her, and she did not want to put off any useful sources.

Strangely, in the days that followed she found herself missing Sour-Apple almost as much as she did Brinna. Her toughness and surly independence had been reassuring. According the the gossips, Sour-Apple had been a slave most of her life. If that were true, it proved that the human spirit really could triumph over the injustice and cruelty of enslavement; something she often thought about as King Penda pushed his legions eastward.

The march followed an old Roman road, frequently blocked with fallen trees and mud. As they went deeper into the wetlands conditions worsened. Connah recalled her to join the others, pushing, lifting and hauling carts and horses stuck in the mud. Where the road was not washed away or deep in mud, pot holes or fallen trees blocked it. Wynflaed and her group spent most of their time filling potholes or hauling aside branches hacked off by woodsmen with great axes. Progress was extremely slow; the work back-breaking. Tempers were short; there were fights and complaints from all quarters.

In an effort to lift his army's morale, Penda declared a week of sports, with hunting and feasting. Foragers went out to bring back whatever the country had to offer. Tents were set up and a clearing made in the scrubland for horse races and games. Plegerers and musicians were brought up from the back of the column to put on shows. It was an effective incentive for the warriors, but for Wynflaed and others it simply meant more work.

To make things worse, a hundred men from East Wixna and Spalda joined the army, bringing with them their dependants and horses. Penda's cooks had even more mouths to feed, more grain to quern, water to carry and wood to cut and haul. Servants and slaves were kept running from dawn to well after sunset. Horseners struggled to find feed, and bedding for so many animals.

Heavy rains spoiled the king's plans. Instead of games, the great army shivered for four days in dripping tents. Footpaths vanished beneath mud, roads became rivers and lakes. Tempers flared again as the cooking fires spluttered and died. Grumbling warriors greased their rusting weapons with mutton fat and vented their frustrations on slaves and servants. Once again fights broke out, and with so many weapons around their outcomes were seldom trivial.

On the fifth day the rain stopped, and as if by some magician's hand the sun shone. Above the knees it was summer; warm, dappled shade and flitting butterflies. The buzz of bees filled the air. But underfoot, oozing mire tripped and toppled the great and the lowly alike. A journey of as few as ten paces required considerable effort and concentration. Wynflaed supposed it would be several days, if not weeks, before Penda's invincible warriors could move more than a few paces. Worse yet, the Spalda Fenland and the broad, meandering rivers that drained it into the Wash still lay up ahead. Men who knew the country warned it might be weeks before the waters receded enough to allow the progress of beasts and carts. Many stayed in their tents, firm in the opinion that the promised riches of the Lindissi might just as well be on the moon.

***

"Rabbian, now he's the worst of the lot. He's raided right up to Penda's front porch before now, but we can never catch him." These were the words of a warrior, chatting idly with his fellows as they watched Wynflaed and a group of slaves clearing a flooded latrine. She had heard the name Rabbian before, and cocked an ear to their conversation. It seemed that whenever people mentioned it, they awarded it a certain, grudging respect. She guessed that Rabbian was a nickname, as it meant literally, rage of the devil. Perhaps it was no wonder that people had respect for a name like that. But what intrigued her most was, who would have such a name, and why?

"They're talking about Rabbian again, who is he?" she whispered to the woman beside her. "I've heard the name before – I keep hearing it."

"Holy Mother Frigg bless us," the woman wailed. "He's a terrible, wicked monster. They say he eats bairns and the unborn."

"Really, boiled or fried?" asked Wynflaed with a disdainful sniff.

"It's true!" protested the woman. "I heard it from Connah."

"But who is he? Is he a king? Has he got an army, or what?"

"I don't know. I just know I don't want to meet him."

"I've met him," a skeletal man put in. "He can run on water and vanish like steam. I've seen it with my own eyes."

Wynflaed eyed the man doubtfully. "You've seen him?"

"Yes, I've seen him alright. It were a terrible thing an' all."

"Terrible? Why?"

The man coloured pink, and lost his enthusiasm for story-telling. "Well, I sort of saw him at a distance, not exactly face-to-face, but it were him right enough."

"When?"

"A few years back. We was chasing him, see. I can't rightly say what he looked like from the front. But he ran on the water and vanished into thin air."

"How do you know it was him then?" asked a younger man.

"Oh, I know all right. He's the most vicious killer in these parts. Even the great lord Penda keeps out of Rabbian's way. You'll see if I'm right."

A derisive laugh summed up the doubts of his ragged audience. Turning back to the excrement floating around their knees, they took up their spades and went back to work. Wynflaed, however, was not quite so ready to dismiss the old man's story. She waded over to him and whispered. "Is he a robber or what?

"Aye, a robber. Though in these parts he rules everything; he's as good as a king," said the old man. "And even in the forest an' all. He's got men and weapons. I don't know how many, but believe me, he rules these parts, whether Penda likes it or not." He glared fiercely at the others around him. "They can laugh if they like, but if he didn't allow us on this road, he'd soon have us off it. We'd all wake up with two smiles."

The aggressive younger man butted in again, his face twisted in derision. "Don't talk shit, granddad! Penda's got thousands of warriors. Rabbian's just some local robber. He's no king."

"Aah, but he's one of the ealfen-kind. He can turn himself into a tree or a rock or anything. You'll never see him unless he wants you to. Then when you're not looking, he pops out and slits your gizzard."

"How come you got away then?"

"I *see* things," the old man said. "I see what other folk can't see."

"Oh yeah," sneered the youth. He picked up a floating turd and pushed it into the old man's face. "You didn't see that coming, did you? You silly old sod!"

The old man howled and spluttered, wiping the filth from his face. "You'll see," he cried. "You'll see."

Wynflaed did not laugh with the others. She helped the old man to clean his face. His story hadn't convinced her, but when added to what she had heard about Rabbian, it deserved some respect. She was sure he could not simply be a superstitious invention. Too many people were worried about him for that. She'd heard that even Penda's war-chiefs were unhappy to be bogged down where they were. Surely, they would not be so worried by a simple ruffian.

Rabbian was an outlaw, people said. So what? If she escaped, she would immediately become an outlaw too. In that respect she was exactly like him. It seemed to her that Rabbian must be clever and cunning. It appeared that he fought for what he wanted and then melted away without trace.

Maybe that was what she should do. Her doubts that she would get her children back by legal means grew with every day that she struggled to stay alive. The idea of trying to escape and steal them back often teased her mind. Dare she take the law into her own hands? Was this what Rabbian had done? Perhaps, like her, the law had let him down too. In her experience the law's officers were corrupt. How could they allow her back into society? They dare not. To do so would expose their corruption. They were far more likely to want to prevent her from clearing her name. Perhaps Rabbian, if he really existed, was also a victim of a similar self-sustaining dilemma. Perhaps she should be looking to men like him for help and not pinning her hopes on winning the approval and support of distant and inaccessible figures such as Lady Aenflaed.

....

CHAPTER TWENTY-ONE

The Wealish lord, Maenche ap Ebell, Ealdorman Cenwulf's adopted brother, could not easily forget Wulfric's widow. Rumours of the conduct of her trial had shocked him. Even now, almost two years later, he could not get the matter out of his mind, and not merely because of the repugnance of the charges and evidence brought against her. His confidence in his own judgment had been seriously undermined, showing him to be both vulnerable and gullible where his emotions were concerned.

Wulfric had been his friend and comrade. They had shared much on the long marches and struggles of Penda's Northumbrian campaign. He had met Wynflaed only a few times, but felt he knew her well enough to form an accurate impression of her. In addition, Wulfric had often spoken of her, especially during the tedious days and nights of the siege of Bebba's fort. The hardships of the battlefield often breed close friendships between comrades. So much so that at times they will entrust even their most intimate thoughts to each other, especially when the mead flows. Maenche had enjoyed hearing Wulfric talk about his wife and children. His tender words of them were a privileged glimpse through Wulfric's eyes. This was why it had been such a bitter shock to learn of her adultery, treason and crooked dealings. In an instant it had frozen his mind and heart against her.

As time slipped by, dulling the edges of his outrage, he found his feelings becoming increasingly confused. After all, adulterer or not, Wynflaed was still the widow of his dear friend. Moreover, in the way of warriors, he owed Wulfric a duty to protect his widow and children. Clearly he had failed, though in Wynflaed's case he did not feel greatly at fault. No man could excuse such appalling betrayal. But what of her children - did not they deserve his protection? He knew, of course, that they did, and so resolved to take a closer interest in their guardianship.

Rendil, their legal guardian, was well known to him. He had no reason to suppose that he would not take his duties seriously. Nevertheless, he decided to pay him a visit. If he found the children well and properly treated, he would keep his distance. His interest would be seen as nothing less than the respect due to a good friend's memory. On the other hand, if they faired badly, he would have much to say about it.

***

By the time Penda's army finally extricated itself from the northern fenlands and marched north into the flat, windswept lands of the Lindissi, the idea of escape was constantly in Wynflaed's mind. She dreamed of finding the help and comfort she needed with others whom the law had failed, so-called outlaws. But then, in a cooler mind, she would tell herself it was no solution. Such a course would deny her children their rightful places in society. Little Eadric would come of age to nothing more than the shadows and bolt holes of an outlaw's domain. His sister would be denied marriage to a son of one of the shire's great families. The best she could expect would be a landless lad with a quick smile and a thief for a father. Wulfric's name would again be sullied. Escape, would never work. For her children's' sake she had to find a better way.

Brinna's bright voice burst into her day dreaming. "Did you hear about Emma?" she cried, crunching over the fire sticks Wynflaed was scooping together ready to bundle and carry to the cook fires.

Startled, Wynflaed clutched her heart and spun round to face her. "Holy Frigg! You make a body jump, Brinna. Who's Emma?"

"Vinegar puss - the sour apple; her right name is Emma. She's been bought by this rich man. He's old and as ugly as Old Grim, but as rich as a king."

"I'd heard he was a young man and handsome."

Brinna looked distraught. "Oh shit, I hope not!" She chewed her cheek for a moment then cheered up again. "No no, I'm sure he's not. He's ancient and horrible, but he is rich."

"You seem to know a lot about it, or are you just making it up?"

Brinna waved in the general direction of what she clearly regarded as her clientele. "Well there's no pleasure in being fucked by these worthless fools all night, except for the gossip they bring." She eyed Wynflaed sombrely. "That's what makes it all bearable."

Wynflaed spotted the crack in her tough veneer. It was easy to overlook that beneath her large, brassy boldness, Brinna was a frightened young woman, clinging to survival with all that her limited options gave her. Her powerful arms and shoulders, her huge breasts and pink, chubby features belied her vulnerability.

"Is it bad?"

Brinna pursed her lips. "It's better than this," she said, casting a critical eye over the pile of fire-wood Wynflaed had gathered and tied in faggots. "I get good food. I eat what they eat. There's ale to drink instead of river water that gives you the shits." She grimaced comically. "Most of the time I'm too pissed to know whether I'm being fucked or flogged." Her smile faded quickly. "Not that there's that much difference with some of 'em."

"What do you mean?"

"Oh you know, sometimes you get one who's a bit rough."

"Rough? You mean — you get hurt?"

"Not often, thank Frigg. But some of 'em like to knock you about a bit. They can't get it up in the normal way, so they slap you around instead."

"Oh Brinna. Can't you do something?"

Brinna looked at her pityingly. "What, like complain to Penda that his men are being nasty to me? Who cares what happens to the likes of me? There are whores floating in the river every morning. Nobody ever does owt. Why do you think they keep bringing in more? It's not because our cunnis wear out, you know."

Tears welled on Brinna's pale lashes and splashed down her big, painted face. Wynflaed threw her arms around her and pulled her close. She felt the broad, strong body give way against her, emptying Brinna, the frightened child, on to her breast.

"Let's run away," whispered Wynflaed. "We can find the outlaws and go off with them." The great sobs ended abruptly. "This Rabbian they're all talking about, I think he must be just like us really. They all fear him, but why should we? Why would he hurt us? He might be a runaway slave too. Maybe that's why he hides. And now look - he's the king of the forest. We could do the same. We could join him."

"But he's a murderer," said Brinna, wiping her face on her hands.

"Show me one man here who isn't. Anyway, I don't think he'd kill us. It's the rich he threatens. What can he steal from us? Our chains? Our collars? Huh, he can have mine. What else have we got - nothing but blisters and stripes on our backs."

Brinna grabbed Wynflaed's hands and took a step back to gaze at her, grinning excitedly. "Yes!" she said firmly. "Yes, let's do it. Let's go now while they're all busy. Nobody's watching."

"We can't. We need to do it properly. We must get the things we'll need."

"What things?"

"I don't know exactly, but certainly a knife, a strike-a-light, some food and blankets, and some better clothes, men's clothes maybe. We have to keep warm and dry and be able to feed ourselves. It might be weeks before we find ..."

"I can get all that," said Brinna, excitedly. "What else?"

"A head start," said Wynflaed. "Probably the best time to go is before dawn, while they're all still sleeping. They'd not miss us for ages. By the time they do it'll be too late. They might not even bother to look for us."

Brinna watched Wynflaed intently, hanging on her every word. Her imagination was bounding on towards the freedom Wynflaed had conjured inside her head.

"When can you get the things?"

"Tonight, but what shall I do with 'em?"

"Hide them somewhere safe. We must find a good place." Swinging her gaze about them Wynflaed tried to think what sort of hiding place would be best. "Some place we can get to easily, without waking the guards."

"I'll think of somewhere," Brinna said breathless with anticipation. "How will I know when it's time?"

"You'll have to stay awake. Wait for the fires to die down and then go to the latrine. The guards should be sleeping by then. You just wait for me there. If anybody sees you, squat down as if you're — you know."

Brinna clasped her hands in front of her face and shuddered gleefully. "This time tomorrow, we'll be free and far away."

***

Pedlar Blackbird Dawes lit his campfire for the night. He had collected only the oldest, driest firewood, to limit smoke. With so much of value on his ponies, travelling alone made him nervous. He was beginning to wonder if Wynflaed's gift piece was worth the risk.

Flames began to crackle through the little pile of kindling, but gave barely enough warmth to raise a wisp of steam from the damp soles of his boots. Tension froze his muscles, making him jump at every woodland sound. His old heart was pounding. He peered about fearfully, certain of a robber behind every tree. "Thieves don't usually take a pedlar's pack," he assured himself without the slightest conviction. "They'll rob a rich merchant, but let a poor pedlar pass."

His gaze fell miserably on his three ponies nibbling the grass at the firelight's edge. He had hidden their bulging packs nearby under a veil of branches and leaves.

Jumping suddenly to his feet, he darted to one of the packs and stripped away its binding. Delving inside he found the linen gift piece. He spread it out beneath the curious gaze of his horses, and gently ran his fingers over the fine needlework. "See this. This is worth more than you and everything in them packs put together," he told his animals. "If I'm going to be robbed, I'll make bloody sure they don't get this." He removed his tunic and wound the linen runner around his stomach. When he was done, he put on his tunic again and smoothed it carefully across his broad front. Then, bending and twisting like a dog chasing its tail, he examined his handiwork. With a few minor adjustments, he satisfied himself that there were no tell tale wrinkles to betray the riches his tunic concealed.

"When we catch the others up, we'll be safe enough," he told his animals. "We'll go with 'em to Lundenwic and spend Yule there, but don't say a word of this to nobody." He patted his front. "In spring we'll latch onto a party going north and make our way to Penda's golden vill. It's not far from there to Badecanwell." He rubbed his hands gleefully. "Believe me girls, when I show this to Lady Aenflaed, we'll all be rich."

***

Wynflaed shivered in a dew wet copse as the first glimmer of dawn crept over the horizon. She had a good view of the camp's latrine where she had agreed to meet Brinna. When anyone approached the crude facilities she could pull back into cover. The sentries posted around the camp were dozing peacefully, but their watchdogs remained alert. A couple of them had caught her scent and lifted their big brown heads to peer quizzically in her direction. With her heart in her mouth, she willed them not to betray her. Luckily, they obliged; doubtless her abiding stink as a latrine digger met with their approval.

There was no sign of Brinna. The pink glow in the eastern sky brightened behind distant trees silhouetted along the horizon. Beyond a broad expanse of mere, a blackbird struck up its song, boldly staking claim to the dawn. Somewhere in the murk a mallard's alarm call burst raucously across a black, glassy mere. A brief splashing flurry of beating wings followed, telling of death and a vixen hunting food for her demanding litter. It was a troubling omen, and with every sight and sound of dawn she became more certain that Brinna was not going to show up. Angrily she imagined her too drunk or sleeping.

Like the poor hunted mallard, she felt exposed and vulnerable - prey to every stalking danger.

Disappointed and angry, she returned to the cook's wagon and slipped into her sleeping place beneath it. Escape would have to wait for some other day. "Next time, I'll go alone," she grumbled to herself.

Feelings of despair settled heavily upon her. The truth was that without Brinna's help, escape was probably impossible. It would certainly be more difficult and frightening. And she needed the things Brinna could get for their survival: blankets, food, and a good strong knife. Even more, she wanted Brinna's company. She needed her. She doubted she could do it without someone with her.

"Get the fires lit, you lazy bitch. The sun's almost up."

Wynflaed turned to face the harsh voice. It was the chief cook, his short, round body silhouetted against the lightening sky. Another day had begun.

***

At Badecanwell, Modbert the magistrate listened to Lefric and tried to conceal his rising anger. Somebody was sticking their nose into his business, but who? Otherwise, why was the shire-reeve, after years of careless indolence, suddenly taking an interest in what he did? Lefric had never taken his duties very seriously. He was supposed to be the shire reeve, the second most important man in the Peaklands. But all he had done since his appointment was breed deerhounds and talk to wolves. Now, to Modbert's intense annoyance, he was turning into an attentive, demanding official, and asking him awkward questions.

"Why are you gaping, Modbert? Surely you know what arrangements were made?"

"Of course I know. I'm just a bit puzzled as to why, all of a sudden, you want to know. Usually you don't bother."

Lefric shuffled in his great chair and cast an injured glance around his smoky hall. Modbert could always make him feel uncomfortable, and never missed a chance to remind him of his shortcomings as the Ealdorman's high reeve, a position he knew Modbert coveted. "Well I'm bothering now. So stop gawping like a beached carp and tell me."

Lefric's hall stood on a slightly sloping shelf of land overlooking the settlement of Badecanwell. It was the most southerly of several well-kept farms and houses that occupied the broad valley. Modbert's own fine house was close by.

"Rendil Aelricsunnu is their guardian," Modbert told him in a weary tone. "They live with his wife and daughters. Their aunt."

"Yes but what happened to Wulfric's estate?" Lefric would not be put off.

"It was all dealt with lawfully. As you know the widow couldn't inherit, she was a convicted felon, so after the king took his third the rest was properly assigned." Modbert sat down opposite the big man and poured himself a beaker of ale. The last thing he needed was Lefric getting involved. The deeds he'd drafted for Rendil would not bear close scrutiny by the sort of experts to which Lefric had access. They designated Rendil protector of the estate on Eadric's behalf until the lad came of age. Eadric, however, would not find it easy to shake Rendil's sticky grip from the lands, even when he reached his majority, thanks to a few carefully worded ambiguities that Modbert had included. If the shire-reeve had left Modbert alone to sort it all out as he usually did, then he and Rendil could have quietly divided the spoils between them and nobody would have been any the wiser. At least not until young Eadric came of age and tried to inherit.

"Was this written on lamb skins?"

Modbert was astonished that Lefric should even know of writing let alone comprehend its uses. "Yes. Why?"

"So?"

"So what?"

"Have you got it? I want to know what it says. Matthew can read it to me."

"I — err — it's not here," said Modbert, lying and adding indignantly. "Lefric, why your sudden interest? You know Rendil Bentbeams as well as I do, and you've known me even longer, surely you are not doubting ..."

"Grim's cods Modbert! What the Frigg is wrong with you?" howled Lefric. "I simply want to be assured that the young lad, — err — what's his name, is properly taken care of. His father was a good friend to my nephew and he …,"

"Ah haagh," cried Modbert, suddenly understanding. "So it's Maenche who's been poking his nose in, isn't it?"

Lefric looked surprised. "Well, why not? He was Wulfric's comrade and close friend. He's every right to *'poke his nose in'* to any damn thing he likes. Some might even say it's his duty to help young — what's his name."

"Eadric – Eadric!

"Yes, Eadric. I'm told he's a fine boy. I just need to know that he's been treated fair and square. His father was a brave man. The lad warrants our concern and favour."

Favour, Modbert was thinking, filling with dread. Favour. That was the last thing he had wanted to hear. "Certainly, he's been well cared for," he said, adding with a cheery tone. "His uncle worships him."

"Who Rendil?" Lefric queried doubtfully, "The only thing he worships is his pocket, or I'm no judge of Rendil Bentbeams."

Modbert flinched, then sprang back to recover the initiative. "Aah, but he has no sons of his own, you see. The lad has become the apple of his eye." He saw that Lefric seemed to appreciate how that might be so.

"And the little maid?"

"Wyngifu?" said Modbert, letting a tense sigh slip secretly away. "She's very happy too." He pulled a face as his bowels churned audibly. "She now has three sisters to grow up with."

Lefric appeared puzzled.

Beneath his calm exterior, Modbert was sweating profusely. "I mean that Rendil's daughters are like sisters to her. She lives with them and their mother, you see." He mopped his brow but tried to appear casual. "I can assure you Lefric, neither you nor Maenche need worry. You can tell him his old comrade's children could not be happier, nor their father's estate better managed."

Taking advantage of Lefric's apparent satisfaction, Modbert studied the shire-reeve's demeanour. He prayed he could avoid any discussion of what would really happen when Eadric came of age. Seizing his chance, he excused himself and left sharply before the topic could arise. He was trembling and wet with sweat. His limbs seemed to have lost their strength. Lefric may be a sorry excuse for a shire-reeve, but if he ever found out what Rendil and he had concocted between them their heads would adorn his gateposts.

"Rendil will have to be told," he said to himself, as a wave of nausea swept over him. In the lane leading from Lefric's hall he vomited on his shoes and staggered weakly for the support of a fence rail. Why on earth, he thought miserably, did I let Rendil talk me into it?

Modbert had a good life, wanting for nothing. For years he had been the Ealdorman's magistrate and on the whole considered himself honest. Not until he fell into Rendil's clutches had he wavered. The shire reeve's mention of the word *favour* still rang in his head. If Maenche took a shine to the boy, he might want to become involved with his education and training. To be *favoured* by Maenche would raise the lad up, almost out of Modbert's reach. He would join the richest, most successful warriors. He would be able to count the Ealdorman himself amongst his close associates. This could mean disaster.

Rendil got me into this mess. He'll have to get me out of it.

***

There was no word of Brinna for four days. Wynflaed had waited for her each night, but she never showed up. Now it was too late. The march had taken them away from the forest. They were deep into the fen country. Escape here in these flat, treacherous wetlands was out of the question. Only the main road between treacherous bogs and meres offered safe footing. To stray from it could be fatal. She did not wait again. That night she crawled beneath the cook's wagon and sobbed herself to sleep.

The following morning, Crabhand Connah led Sour Apple, or Emma as Wynflaed now knew her, into the slave camp. Resplendent in a blue woollen gown, trimmed with squirrel fur, she was accompanied by a fat, doting, elderly man of obvious wealth. All work stopped as Emma strode about, peering imperiously into store tents, and carts. At last, she pointed to Wynflaed. "That one," she said grandly.

"Her! But she's the filthiest of the lot," her rich friend cried. "Can't you pick a clean one?"

"I want her," Emma insisted.

"You heard her, but give her a good scrub down first."

Emma turned and strode away, her hips swinging, much to the delight of her ageing escort. Nothing in her manner had betrayed even the slightest hint of recognition of the slaves standing around, gaping at her, even though she had shared the chain and collar with them.

Wynflaed's gaze followed her, lamely wondering what was going on. Connah grabbed her arm. "Don't you fuck this up for me," he said, the stink of wine and onions on his breath. "She's picked you out. I'm getting a good price, so behave yourself. If you mess this up for me, I'll kill you, so-I-will."

....

CHAPTER TWENTY-TWO

Throughout the summer Penda's army ravaged the Lindissi flat lands. There were no major battles. The canny Lindissi stayed out of the way of the great army, leaving little of value behind them. Many buried their portable wealth or carried it away with them. More often than not Penda's frustrated raiders returned empty handed. Eventually they cornered Blecca, the Lindissi's ruler, near his city of Lincoln. He immediately paid Penda a huge tribute in silver and affirmed his allegiance.

As harvest time approached, and with a small profit for his troubles, Penda turned his army homeward. In truth he had little option; numbers were declining as men slipped away to return to their farms and the harvesting that awaited them. The East Anglians could relax for a while, or strengthen their defences and wait for the next war season.

***

In Holmesfelt even a glimpse of Eadric or his little sister Wyngifu could throw Rendil into a fuming rage. Nobody quite understood why. When he first became their guardian he showed little interest in them, but nowadays he followed them about, glaring at them and grumbling. A canny observer might have made a connection between his changed attitude and a recent, frosty visit by Modbert the magistrate.

Modbert was not expected. He turned up catching Rendil unawares. The pair immediately fell into a furious row. Rendil cleared his hall and made sure nobody could get near enough to eavesdrop. But it was obvious to all that the magistrate was deeply upset about something. When they parted, later that same day, Modbert's humour had not improved, and with no offer of hospitality from Rendil, he had to set off in rain and darkness for his home at Badecanwell.

Since then Rendil had been in a foul mood, and even after one of the best harvests Holmesfelt had known in years, he was still so miserable and angry that his family and servants stayed well out of his way.

Goda and the entire homestead were much relieved when he announced that he was going to Badecanwell to see the magistrate. She did not know why his trip was necessary and did not ask. To be rid of him for a few days was good enough. She and the children would get some peace.

***

"I've been sick," Brinna told Wynflaed. "That's why I couldn't come. I tried to get word to you, but I couldn't."

"That was weeks ago. Where've you been hiding?"

"I told you I was sick," she whined. "I'm sorry. I wanted to explain. I tried to get away, but I couldn't."

"You didn't try very hard. Surely you could have done something. I waited every night for a week."

They were sitting alone in the tent where Emma lived with her doting lover. Wynflaed sat on a plain oak chest at the doorway, to get the best light on a hem she was mending.

"Well, I'm sorry," Brinna mumbled, swinging her muddy bare foot. She crossed the tent and flopped down beside Wynflaed and hugged her. "You're not mad at me, are you?"

The dark red tent rocked gently, its frame of saplings creaking as the waxed cloth strained at its guy-ropes. It covered a square of ground about four paces across and was high enough inside for a man to stand. A double palliasse of straw and furs was laid out in the middle of the floor. Beside it was an elaborately carved war-coffer containing the old warrior's weapons and armour. The only other furnishings were a mat of woven sedge laid out as a ground sheet, and the chest upon which the pair now sat.

"Anyway, it wouldn't have worked," mumbled Brinna. "I couldn't get the stuff we needed. And — then I got sick"

"Drunk, you mean!"

A guilty sigh was Brinna's only response. In silence she watched Wynflaed finish the hem on Emma's dress. It was yellow linen, trimmed with embroidered silk at the neck and arm holes. "She gets whatever she wants, doesn't she? She must be a great shag."

"Well, he certainly doesn't love her."

"What do you mean?" Brinna was agog.

"He shouts at her. He won't let her out of his sight, and he slaps her when he's drunk. She's with him now. She has to go with him and stand behind him when he drinks or gambles with the other men."

"Oh, the poor cow!" said Brinna sarcastically. "And all she gets in return is her collar taken off and the moon if she wants it." She rolled her eyes in mock horror.

"She's miserable," said Wynflaed, smoothing out the new hem for closer inspection. "She knows she's not really free, and she's scared he'll tire of her."

"And he will," Brinna said puckering her chubby lips. "They're all the same. Their cocks rule their hearts and their bellies rule their heads. There isn't a man alive who can think straight without considering both. She's lucky that he's an old man. It might take him a bit longer to get fed up with her. She'd better make the most of it while it lasts. She'll soon be back in the king's necklace."

"My, you've got an old cynic's head on your shoulders."

Brinna jumped to her feet alarmed. "Oooh, Frigg!" she cried in panic. "And I should have an old cynic's cock up my love-box. I'm late, I have to run. It's one of my regulars. He brings me food, even a pie sometimes - the silly old sod."

"A lover? You mean like Emma?"

"Mother Frigg, no!" howled Brinna. "Whores like me don't have lovers. It's only fancy pieces like Emma what gets lovers."

"But you said he's a regular?"

"Yeah, but he's just an ordinary man. He's not rich and he's even older than Emma's bloke. The poor old sod can't get it up."

"So why does he come to you, then?"

Brinna gaped. "Holy Frigg! You don't know nothing about men do you? He likes me to tell his friends that he shags like a stallion. He thinks it makes him look good. Sometimes he has a little go, bless him, but it never really works."

Wynflaed laughed and hugged Brinna's shoulders. Clowning and pulling a comic face, Brinna sighed and went on. "Usually we just sit and talk about his dog and his bloody onions. Can you believe it? He grows big onions. This is all I hear every night. Then he has a quick fumble and gives me a meat pie before he toddles off to tell his mates he's shagged me dizzy."

Wynflaed had not laughed so much in months. Tears were rolling down her face. What a joy it was to see Brinna. Life's troubles seemed to roll over her without leaving the slightest scar. To her, everything had fun hidden inside it somewhere. If she could she would dig it out and spread it around for all it was worth. "Oh gods!"

cried Wynflaed. "You're such a tonic. I hope you can find some way to come again. This is usually the best time of day. Emma goes trailing about after him in the afternoons, and I get the chance to do her sewing. He got her some Eastern silk for a new dress; it's as blue as the sky."

"I'll try," promised Brinna. She paused at the tent door and looked back guiltily, her chubby face colouring up. "I'm really sorry about — you know ... I was so scared. And you're right, I was drunk. I meant to come. I just thought a few drinks would give me some courage."

"Go! Or you'll not get your meat pie."

"Oh Frigg! Look, that's him." She pointed out a lean man in the distance. "I'm off, before he drops dead and squashes my pie."

Suddenly she was gone. Wynflaed was alone, staring at the hot day.

***

On the last day of Litha, Penda's army reached the crossing place on the banks of the River Trent. On the far side lay the great shire wood.

"The king's commanders are planning the river crossing," Emma announced regally. "I don't expect my lord until after midnight." She and Wynflaed were standing beside a cart containing her tent, boxes, bedding and clothes-chest.

What's new? Wynflaed wanted to say but remained silent.

"See that the tent is erected somewhere dry and sheltered this time - not in some quagmire. Then get me something to eat. Nothing too heavy."

The following day, as she heard this from Wynflaed, Brinna asked dryly, "And what did you feed her, mouse farts on feathers? Would that be light enough for her?"

The two were sitting on the riverbank with their toes in the water. The sun appeared as a dirty orange disc, slowly slipping behind the trees. There was barely a breath of wind and the air was heavy with the scent of meadow sweet.

"Rabbian is out there somewhere," said Wynflaed, after a long silence. "How about it? We could try again. Will you come with me?"

Brinna did not answer immediately. "Look, I know I'm coarse and foul-mouthed. Everybody thinks I'm brave because of it. But I'm not. You're the brave one. I'm not like you." She tossed a pebble into the river and paused as if waiting for it to reappear. "All that toughness and fighting, it's not me really — not inside. I'm scared, Flaedy. Inside I'm scared of everything. If I stopped to think about things properly, I'd be so scared I'd never move another step. The far side of a fence is something I don't like to think about. I must leap it blindly, and then it's not the far side anymore."

"But you'd have me with you. I'd look after you. I wouldn't let ..."

"Your hair's growing again. When it's fully grown, you'll have a man in a blink," she said, cutting her off. "He'll love you and — and eventually you'll love him. Then what will I have? You can't tie yourself to somebody like me. I'd shame you. You'd get tired of me."

"No, that's rubbish. I love you like a sister. We can be free together."

Brinna climbed to her feet and drew them through the grass to dry them. "Hunwald, you know, the meat pie man?" she reminded Wynflaed. "He wants — well he doesn't know what he wants, but I think he wants me to go with him. He says he's trying to put together enough silver to buy me free. I know he's been talking to Connah and the whoremaster about me. If he could buy me, I'd be free and I could go with him. Oh, I know he's old and certainly not handsome, but I think he cares about me - in his own way. He says he wants a little farm and me to help him with it."

Wynflaed stood up, and took Brinna's hand. She squeezed it in her own. "I know," she said softly. "It doesn't matter." They stood together silently, watching the river slide by, each wishing they could help the other.

"I'll get you what you need to escape," promised Brinna. "As soon as they cross the river I'll start getting it all together. Then, when you're ready, I'll bring it to you, no matter what. I won't let anything stop me this time. But I won't be coming with you. Hunwald wants me. He likes me, Flaedy. I'm sure he does."

"Do you think he can raise enough to buy you?"

"I don't know. He says he's not rich, and Frigg knows, that's obvious enough."

"I've got enough," said Wynflaed. "And you know where it's hidden.

"No! Not the ring. I won't take it. I can't, it was your husband's.'

"You must, Brinna. I'm scared I might lose it soon anyway."

"Why?"

"The other day, Emma saw it. It was an accident. I was washing myself. I didn't know she was there. She was watching me. She didn't say anything, but you know what she's like? I daren't trust her, Brinna. It was in my hand - I know she saw it. I'm scared she'll take it."

"But you could buy yourself free with that," said Brinna.

"No, I couldn't, not even with ten more like it. There's no freedom for me, unless the king grants it.

Anyway, I would never use it for that." She turned her back on Brinna and struggled to release the ring from its hiding place. She rinsed it in the river and dried it on her skirt. "Take it. Give it to Hunwald. Let him use it to buy your freedom. Go with him, Brinna. Start a new life."

"I can't ..."

"You must, Brinna," she insisted. "I'm determined to escape; you know I am. I'll soon be free. And once I'm gone they'll never find me. But I can't go unless I know you'll be free too."

"I can't Flaedy. I can't take it."

"If you don't, I won't try to escape. I'll stay with the column. Emma will probably steal the ring one day soon, and it will all be your fault. I might never get another chance like this. The Shire-wood is the perfect place for me to escape. If I can find this Rabbian they all talk about, I can join his ingas and be free and safe. I might even be able to get my children back." She stared into Brinna's face, her steady gaze hammering home her argument. "But if you don't accept the ring, I won't be able to go. I'll miss my chance."

Later that evening, Brinna met her lover in a stable attached to a house Penda had commandeered from a luckless farmer. As soon as the subject of onions loomed on the horizon, Brinna produced the gold ring and held it up before Hunwald's astonished eyes. The old man's jaw dropped. His fingers reached out unsteadily, but withdrew gingerly, as if touching such richness would harm him. "Grim's teeth, Brinna," he gasped. "Where did you get that?"

"Is this enough for a farm and a wife to care for you for the rest of your life?"

"Of course it is, but how did you get it?" Panic twisted his face into a frown. "You'll have to give it back. Tell them it came off in the bed ..."

"I didn't steal it. It was given to me. It's mine!"

"Yours? How can it be yours? Do you think I'm stupid?"

"I didn't steal it. My friend gave it to me. She wants you to buy my freedom, like you said you would."

"What friends of yours have rings like that?" He tried again to snatch it.

"You've seen her. The woman I visit at the red tent."

Hunwald scratched his bristly chin and lowered himself slowly to sit on a small barrel. "D'you mean the fancy piece in the yellow?"

"No not her, her maid."

"Her maid? Are you mad, woman? How could her maid give it to you? She must have pinched it, and that amounts to the same thing as you pinching it."

"It's not stolen. It's for you to buy my freedom."

"Forget it! If I tried to buy you with that ring, they'd take one look at me and accuse me of stealing it. I'd have to explain how I got it. Can you imagine what they'd say when I told 'em? They wouldn't believe it. I'd be called a thief and strung up to the nearest tree."

"Will you listen to me, for Frigg's sake," yelled Brinna. "I can explain everything. It'll all make sense if you'll just shut your gob for a moment." She sighed crossly and smoothed her skirts over her large thighs. "She's the widow of a great man. The ring was his. He was called Wulfric Aelricsunnu. He gave it to her ..."

"It's a load of horseshit," Hunwald said. "For a start, if she really is who she says, then she's definitely no widow. I know that for a fact." He stuck his chin out and eyed her belligerently. " I know Wulfric. I served under

him, up north. I know him better than I know you. I was at
Bebba's fort. I saw him get wounded there. I was the last
man to pull out when Penda withdrew. There was a great
fire. The Northumbrians rushed out for prisoners. They
took Wulfric and about twenty others. They damn near got
me too."

"Alive?"

"Of course, alive. You don't take dead prisoners."
He paced the barn. "I saw him. He was bleeding, but he
was alive. I saw them take him into the fort. He was
limping and burned. His clothes were scorched. Believe
me, Wulfric Aelricsunnu is very much alive."

"That's wonderful! We've got to tell her," gasped
Brinna, starting for the door. "This changes everything."

Hunwald barred her way. "No, you don't. Give me
that ring," he yelled, snatching it from her fingers. "You'll
tell her nothing."

Brinna gaped at him, shocked to see him suddenly
so changed. He was a different man, a cold, cruel man she
had not seen before. His eyes were quick and sparkling.
They darted around, as if spotting his thoughts flying
about him like wasps. "Stay yourself, woman. Calm
down, while we think this through," he told her. "If people
think Wulfric is dead, then the news of his survival will
be worth a lot of silver to somebody. Probably a lot more
than this ring."

"Give it back to me. It's not yours. It's not mine
either, now. This changes everything."

Hunwald drew away sharply, protecting the ring
from her. He held it up before his eyes, licking his lips.
"Don't you see? If I put this ring alongside everything else
I know about Wulfric, it could be worth ten times the gold
it's made out of."

Brinna pounced and snatched it from him. She turned her bulk and sprinted for the door. Hunwald dived and grabbed her legs, tripping her over. She tumbled heavily, knocking the wind out of her, but still fought to escape him. Hunwald could not hold her, she was too strong for him. She crawled away, kicking and punching him off her as she went. In desperation, he drew a knife and plunged it down into her back. The blade struck her spine and crunched through into her heart. She died instantly, clasping the ring, the golden ring of her freedom.

**

Penda's army crossed the river near Newark and began the march through the Shire-wood towards Nottingham and on to the North-Worthig. Wynflaed's nerves were on edge. She could hardly wait for the night camp to be set up. Shire-wood was at her feet at last. She could smell freedom, taste it on the warm wind blowing in from the west. She felt sure that this time Brinna would bring her the supplies she needed. This time she would seize her freedom.

Squinting into the evening sun, she willed it to set. She felt happy and excited, but frightened too. In a few hours, she told herself, she would be free; slavery, beatings, and the fear and uncertainty Emma's harsh complaining and petulant whims created would all be behind her. Yet it seemed the sun would never set. It hung in the duck egg blue sky, as if held fast by a cloak pin. To take her mind off it, she worked, gathering firewood, fetching water, sweeping the reed floor matting and picking the bits of grass and bracken from Emma's fur bed cover. Even then she could not concentrate on her work. Her gaze wandered repeatedly to the tent door and the horizon beyond it. There sat the sun, defying her, touching the treetops, but refusing to slip behind them.

Emma sat watching her quietly. That at least was diverting, thought Wynflaed. Normally she would be barking orders and complaining about her every move, but this time she seemed oddly withdrawn, even nervous and demure.

Finally she stirred on her seat and made coughing noises, as if to attract Wynflaed's attention. "I'll have my wyrtdrenc now. I've a bit of a headache."

Wynflaed smiled dutifully and went to make the herb and honey drink. Did a woman like Emma really get headaches? It seemed incredible that any sickness would have the courage to intrude upon her.

When she returned to the tent, she found Emma reclining in graceful disarray. "Have you anything for my head?" she asked pitifully.

An axe, Wynflaed wanted to say. "I can make you a willowdrenc. You could take it instead of your honey and wyrts. Willow is good for a headache."

Emma smiled wanly and gave her a sorrowful glance. Wynflaed found it deeply puzzling. She eyed her mistress with suspicion and backed out of her presence, unnerved by her unusual demeanour.

Outside the tent, the warm day was at last turning to purple evening. The sun had almost set, leaving in flames the few straggling clouds in the baked sky. Beneath it, the shire-wood's great oaks stood as black as soot along the western horizon. In the east, Penda's camp, crammed along the north bank of the river appeared gilded like a king's harness. It sparkled like snow melting from a log in a winter fire. Everywhere was movement and noise: traders, horses, cattle, carts, cooks, stockmen and smiths, all milling about endlessly. And everywhere the swaggering warriors, their faces and armour painted orange by the sunset.

Wynflaed peeked back into the tent and saw that Emma had closed her eyes. Perhaps she would soon fall asleep. Now seemed a good time to slip away, she thought. Selecting a wooden bowl from a box of household utensils at the tent door, she set off towards the forest. Nobody would suspect a slave carrying a bowl into the woods. They would simply assume she was going to pick forest fruits or herbs in the dying rays of the sun.

More than two hours would pass before the sky finally darkened, unveiling the moon's bright crescent above the trees. Its pale glow silvered the leaves and brushed ghostly highlights onto the marjoram's clustering pink flowers. Wynflaed hid in a stand of alder. From her secret vantage, she could see the path she expected Brinna to take, and watched it with growing excitement. Her mind raced over the many ideas and plans she had for her new freedom. Uppermost were thoughts of Eadric and little Wyngifu. Somehow, no matter what else she did, she must see her children. Whether she would bring them away with her she still could not decide. It would mean Eadric losing his name and the chance of an honoured place on the king's mead benches. She would try to find some way of seeing them secretly, so that they could remain in society without shame — perhaps this would suffice. She sighed and put her thoughts aside. Always she reached this same point in her planning, and always grounded on the same problems. Frustrated again, she put the idea from her mind. There would be time to think it through later.

The camp was now still and silent. The moon slid behind her back, pushing shadows towards the river. "Oh Brinna, please not again. Please don't let me down," she murmured. Surely, she would not - not after everything they had said. How could she?

Anger rose inside her as her desperation grew. It became obvious that Brinna had let her down again. What should she do now? Should she go alone? How could she without food or even a knife for hunting and protection? How could she hope to survive? But should she abandon the idea? She could always try again later. "I'm having no more to do with Brinna, no matter what excuses she gives me this time." She thought angrily about Wulfric's ring. How could Brinna do such a thing? She would make her give it back.

Time slipped by. The dogs and sentries were sleeping. If Brinna could not get away now, Wynflaed thought, she is definitely not coming.

Her heart leapt as she caught a glimpse of a figure running furtively through the camp. She could not see who, but it was certainly a woman. The figure came closer, darting silently from one shadow to the next, hugging the darkness. A sudden turn of the woman's face caught the moonlight. For the briefest moment, Wynflaed saw it shining from the depths of a cowl drawn about the figure's head. She could not believe her eyes. Dread churned her stomach. It was Emma.

Wynflaed drew back into hiding as Emma approached and then paused near the hazels. She watched her push back her cowl and peer searchingly into the thicket.

"Wynflaed," Emma called in a hoarse whisper. "Where are you?"

Panic rose in Wynflaed's chest but she remained still, not even daring to breathe for fear that Emma might hear her. Everything she knew about this woman, her stony resentment and peevish, tormenting ways, told her to stay hidden. Full of dread, her mind buzzing with questions, she waited, praying desperately that Emma would go away. How had she had found her? She seemed to know exactly where to look, and yet, how typical it was of her. No doubt she had been watching her and Brinna, spying on their every move for the sake of some twisted enjoyment. Why did she do it? What had she ever done to her, to make her so hateful? She had everything a woman like her could hope for, yet she seemed unable to live her life without the perverse satisfaction of spoiling Wynflaed's.

"I know you're here," Emma said into the shadows. "I've got to talk to you. Let me see you. I want to help. Look, I've brought some things." She held out a bulging sack. "I must tell you something important. I know you can hear me. It's about Brinna. We must talk."

Concern for Brinna drew Wynflaed out of hiding. "What about her?"

The two women faced each other in the moonlight. For a moment neither spoke, as if testing the other. "We'd better move away. It's as bright as day here." Emma turned and led Wynflaed back into the shadows.

"What's all this about?" asked Wynflaed, their mistress slave relationship suspended by the meat of the occasion.

Emma blew a sigh and faced her. "It's Brinna. Look, I'm really sorry, but she's dead. They found her in a barn."

"Dead! What ..? How?"

"I don't know. She'd been killed, that's all I know. It's what happens to whores — like Brinna.-. and me."

"Brinna!" Wynflaed stared, searching Emma's face. Could this be true? Surely even Emma would not be so cruel as to lie about such a thing.

"Don't look at me like that," Emma snapped. "I didn't kill her. I'm just telling you." She locked her fingers together and twisted them violently as if unable to pull them apart again. "I'll say I'm sorry again, if it makes you feel better, but it doesn't change anything. The poor drab was murdered. Your little escape is off."

"Where is she?"

"Why do you want to know? Don't expect a funeral. She's probably in the river by now. Anyway, what difference does it make?"

"Don't you feel anything? You were on the chain with her. You slept under the same blanket, shared the same food? Doesn't any of it matter?"

"Why should it? It's too late. They don't come back. They're gone. They've finished with you and everything else, forever. What you feel about them doesn't change that. They never come back. They leave you on your own, no matter how much you love them. They don't care anymore."

"You never liked her."

"So what? Anyway, you're wrong. I did like her. You might not think so, but I did," she said. "It's stupid to get close to people. They always leave you. They die, and that's all. That's the way it is." She tossed her head haughtily. "The sooner you get used to it the better."

Eyeing her obliquely, Wynflaed smiled slowly. "But you can't, can you, Emma? Even you." Tears welled in Wynflaed's eyes a she looked back into Emma's defiant eyes.

They moved apart, facing each other beneath a large tree. "I'm coming with you!" Emma said. "I know what you were planning. I want to come."

"You? What do you mean?"

"I'm not stupid. I know what you and Brinna were doing." Her tone was strident, but there was uncertainty in her delivery. "I've been watching you," she said, "I know all about it. You're running away."

"No!"

"Don't lie. You're hopeless at it." She shrugged her shoulders. "I'm going anyway, with or without you. You can do what you like, but you'll soon be caught on your own. Together we'd stand a better chance."

"But why do you want to leave? You've got everything you ..."

"I've got nothing!" She looked past Wynflaed into the trees, taking a moment to calm herself. "Not that it's any of your business, but he doesn't love me and I hate him." She blew her nose. "I could turn you in," she threatened. "They'd hang you. Or I can help you. You ought to be grateful."

"Why? Because you could get me hung?" Wynflaed asked scornfully. "You think that's a good basis for trusting you?" She squared up to her boldly, their noses almost touching. "Go on then, tell them. I don't care anymore."

Emma backed down a step. "I don't mean it, I just said it. But we should go together because ..." She stopped as if the words had locked in her throat.

"Well, tell me why?"

"I owe it to you."

Wynflaed laughed. "Oh, this is new. I can hardly wait to hear more."

"You made me free, once," cried Emma. "You've forgotten, haven't you?" She stared at her, seeming to recover her sneering confidence. "Did it mean so little?"

"I don't know. I don't know what you're talking about."

"Oh, forget it. We're stuck with each other. You'd never survive on your own. That should be a good enough reason.You haven't the guile to survive on your own. You needed Brinna to lie and steal for you. Now she's dead, so you need me to do it. I'm stronger and cleverer than she ever was. Take it or leave it. I'm going anyway."

For a long time, Wynflaed watched her; half remembering but questioning her memories. "What did you mean, *I made you free*?" she asked, her mind trying to make the scrawny child she recalled from years ago on the road from Uhtredstun match the tough, beautiful woman that now faced her.

Emma leaned back against the oak tree, apparently much amused. "You're remembering, aren't you? I can see it in your face." She straightened her spine and looked at Wynflaed squarely, presenting her face for her scrutiny.

Wynflaed picked at fragments of memory, assembling them into the image of that young girl, her thin body marred by welts and bruises, dragging her chains around the Ceorl's pristine garth. "That was you?" she asked, knowing it was true. "You were so thin and small."

"Now will you come with me?" Emma asked sharply. "Look, I've brought what we'll need, food, blankets ..."

"But you hate me," interrupted Wynflaed, still puzzled and still trying to make sense of what she knew to be true. "You've been awful to me from the start." She stuck out her fingers and began counting off Emma's crimes. "You lied to Connah about me. You made him think I was poisoning the water. You knew what they'd do to me, but you still accused me. And when they kept me away from the others for weeks, you spied on me all the time. Because of you, I was the last to get food, and I had to do all the filthiest jobs. I've been beaten. I've been chained up, more nights than I can recall ..." She had run out of fingers for counting and was using the same one repeatedly. "You did that to me." Wynflaed's mind sped over every wrong Emma had done to her. "You haven't been satisfied with a single thing I've done for you since you made the master buy me." Her frown suddenly deepened and she leaned forward accusingly. "And yes — why did you? You could have picked anybody. Why me? You've hated me from the start, yet you chose me for your maid."

Emma's gaze fell to her hands hanging loosely before her. "I did it for you."

"Oh, that's rich! You'll excuse me if I don't fall on your neck with kisses."

"I did. I was trying to keep you away from the others. If I hadn't done, you'd have been seen by the whore-masters. Even with all that filth you had on your face, any fool could see you're pretty. They'd have taken you and used you up."

"So what?" howled Wynflaed. "It might have been better than sleeping in chains with the dogs and having to share their food."

A hint of impatience flashed across Emma's face. "You couldn't have stood it for a day," she said. "Believe me, the whore tents would have killed you. If not, you would have killed yourself."

"You expect me to believe you were protecting me," Wynflaed scoffed. "You must think I'm ..."

Emma's patience snapped. "Aargh! I don't care what you believe. All I want to know is are we going to stand here all night, or are we going to make a run for it?" She glared hotly at Wynflaed. "You don't have to like me, but you certainly need me."

....

CHAPTER TWENTY-THREE

Hunwald had not slept well. It was not Brinna's murder that kept his thoughts churning; he had barely given her a thought. Neither did he fear being accused. Nobody cared about the death of a slave, except perhaps her owner, but even if he were accused, and proved guilty, he would simply pay her owner the appropriate wergild and that would end the matter. It was the problem of how to best convert Wulfric's gold ring into a more easily transferable asset that was spoiling his sleep. It was only of value if he could trade it without raising suspicion. All he wanted was a nice little retirement farm and enough silver to keep him in his old age. The ring could do that for him, but only if he could exchange it without getting himself hung as a thief.

He could sell it to a comrade; he knew several who would buy it and ask no questions. The trouble was they might soon discover its history, and he'd find himself being turned in as a thief, or worse, they might blackmail him into handing it over for nothing.

"People are such thieving bastards," he said through a despairing sigh.

Selling it to a comrade would be too risky. He must find some other way of wringing a profit from it. It would not be easy, but it would be worth the effort, especially as Brinna had made it clear that Wulfric's widow knew nothing about her husband's situation. This meant that as well as the ring he possessed valuable information that Wulfric's family would pay him dearly for. He wondered briefly about the woman Brinna had got the ring from, but decided she was not his concern. He should concentrate on the ring and those who would pay him the most for it. That would surely be Wulfric's family.

He lay back on his narrow bed and sighed with satisfaction. His mind toyed with warm thoughts of the riches he might soon gain. It seemed so simple. It was obvious that the family would be pleased to pay. What could go wrong?

A chilling thought intruded. He sat upright in bed and stared into the darkness, a cold sweat slicking his brow. Why didn't the family know already? Why hadn't Wulfric been ransomed like the other wealthy prisoners? Hunwald had seen him captured, and although he was bleeding and limping, his wounds did not appear too serious. A rich man such as Wulfric was a valuable prize. The Northumbrians would certainly have patched him up and ransomed him. That was the usual way. So, why was he not safely back in his home? He knew many other rich men who had been returned to their families, several were on this present campaign and had been free almost two years. Prisoners of rank and wealth were always ransomed. Only lesser men, such as Hunwald himself, were executed or sold as slaves - usually across the Frisian sea in Armorica and Gaul.

There were too many unanswered questions. Hunwald would have to be sure of all his facts, and that would take serious investigation. He would be gambling more than just the ring. If he got it wrong he'd find himself at the end of a rope.

He vowed that as soon as he got back to Mercia and collected his share of the booty he would go to Wulfric's home to learn whatever he could about the great man. Perhaps he would find that Wulfric was now safely returned. If he was, he could return his ring to him and expect a rich reward, especially if Wulfric was searching for news of his wife. He now regretted having killed Brinna. She might have been able to add much more to his knowledge of Wulfric's wife.

Staring into the darkness above his sleeping place, he turned over his thoughts, his confidence slowly rebuilding. There were many questions, but at least things seemed to be fitting into place. He would take the ring to Wulfric's home. Whether he found him there or not, he was sure he could make a profit from it.

***

At Badecanwell, Rendil and Modbert the magistrate were met in Modbert's house. At first their discussions had been cool and cautious. They were somewhat over-polite to each other, clearly keen to put behind them the acrimony of their last meeting. They ate a meal of lamb and barley stew, washed down with ale followed by generous cups of mead. Conversation was limited and littered with awkward silences.

"Excellent mead, Modbert, thank you. By the way, has anything more been said about the boy?"

"The boy?"

"Young Eadric. Has Maenche ...?"

"No, not a word. They seem — err ..."

"Content?" suggested Rendil.

"Content," agreed Modbert, wiping a bead of sweat from his temple. "I'm sure they're satisfied with your provisions for the lad," he went on grandly. "I can see no reason why the matter should not be put to rest."

Another awkward silence ensued, during which Rendil stretched for the mead jug and helped himself. "Will they want a new deed, d'you think? I'd like to know what they'll say about the boy's share."

"Rendil, please don't worry. Why would they say anything about it? If you keep quiet they'll want nothing.

By the time the lad comes into his own it will all be forgotten."

"That's easy for you to say. You've nothing to lose. You already have the By Streams farms out of it." He shuffled in his chair, visibly calming himself. "Not that I'm complaining, of course. That is as we agreed. And I'm not saying it's your fault."

"What's my fault? What are you talking about?" Modbert asked.

"I mean their dabbling in the boy's affairs. I know it's not your fault."

"Well of course it's not my fault." Modbert stared hotly.

"But if they do keep meddling, I'll have to give up what I was expecting out of it. If that happens I think we should share any losses equally."

"Why? You didn't want to share the gains equally, so why must we share the losses? I did everything required of me. I was paid no more than I was promised, and I've not asked for more." Modbert reached with trembling hands to pour more mead. When he managed to steady the jug, he found it empty.

"It's empty. You can't get mead from an empty jug," Rendil said icily.

A coughing spasm overtook Modbert. A lusty serving wench brought a large wooden pitcher of ale. " Av yer done?" she asked.

Modbert looked up at her through tear-misted eyes and nodded dumbly.

"Is he staying?" she asked, clearly intent upon discouraging an invitation.

"That's kind of you, Modbert," Rendil said smoothly. "It is getting late, and the nights are drawing in."

"You're welcome, of course," said Modbert, struggling to clear his throat.

"I'm sure," said the big skivvy before stomping away into the shadows.

A long draught of ale calmed Modbert's coughing, though it did nothing to ease the discomfort inside his head. "Rendil, what do you expect me to do?" he asked, leaning across the table. "While the lad lives, things must stay as they are. You know very well that you can never own Wulfric's estate, except in trust for Eadric."

"Can't I?" growled Rendil. "There's one very sure way that I can."

Fear produced strange clucking sounds in Modbert's throat before he managed to answer. "No harm must come to the boy. If anything happens ..."

"May the gods preserve him," Rendil said. "That's the last thing I want, even though I believe I would inherit in that case. That is correct, isn't it?"

"Yes, though there would be another third for the king, but the lad's not going to die, is he? He's a fine healthy boy."

"I absolutely agree, and we must protect him from — err — anything untimely. Don't you have more of that excellent mead?"

"Drink — drink what you like. I'm pleased you're satisfied with something."

"My dear Modbert, surely you can see the wisdom of preparing for the future?"

"It's the lad's future that concerns me. Nothing must happen to him."

"Do not fear for him. Such a strong, healthy lad is unlikely to die of sickness." Rendil waved his empty mead cup at the skivvy lurking in the shadows. "It's most unlikely that anything, except some tragic accident, climbing, or hunting, or some such thing like that, would steal him away from us."

"I'll have nothing to do with it."

"Nor indeed would I, my dear Modbert. Are you sure there's no more mead?"

Modbert stood up and leaned across the table, pushing his face close to Rendil's. "I'm telling you Rendil, and I mean it. I'll have nothing to do with it. The boy must be left alone. If anything happens to him, they'll be sure to suspect ..."

"Nothing!" snapped Rendil. "They'll suspect nothing. Accidents happen. That is what they are — accidental. They are in the hands of Wyrd. We are all subject to her whims. If the lad does have an accident, that is precisely what it will be — an accident. And you, my dear Modbert, will make sure it is thoroughly investigated and recorded as such."

"No! No, I will not. I am not getting involved."

"You are involved. You're involved all the way up to your greedy beak. You seem to forget that you personally handed silver to some of the witnesses. They took it from your hands, Modbert — not mine."

"But it was your silver." Modbert sagged back onto his seat.

"But they took from your hands." Rendil stood up and walked around the table to stand behind Modbert. He rested his hands on the magistrate's trembling shoulders. "You are as guilty as me, no matter what happens." He bent close to whisper in Modbert's ear. "So, if the lad should meet with an unfortunate accident, you will make diligent and thorough enquiries. Your conclusions will record nothing but a tragic and unavoidable accident."

"No! By the gods, Rendil, no. It's too dangerous. That old reeve of yours, what's his name? Manwine. You said yourself that he watches the lad every waking moment. You can't buy off people like him. He won't be silenced."

"Maybe not, but he's old. He can't live forever. Even a nasty shock might kill him."

"Let it go, Rendil. It's over. Maenche will make sure the lad inherits and that's that. You've done well enough out of your brother's estate. Don't spoil it now."

***

Wynflaed had lost count of the days she and Emma had been on the run. They were deep in woodland with no idea of where they were or how far they might yet have to travel to reach safety. They dare not use the footpaths, or tracks where they might be seen, and progress through the dense undergrowth and briars was slow, painful and strenuous.

So far, they had not seen another soul, nor heard sounds of pursuit. They began to wonder if Connah or Penda's men were simply unaware of their escape, or had just not bothered to come after them. As one danger receded, another loomed - hunger. They had flour and pig fat but dare not stop to cook it. The only other food Emma had been able to bring was some cheese and some turnips. They had eaten the cheese and were now crunching on turnips as they pushed on through the tangled briars. The little they could forage as they ran was not enough to sustain them, added to which weariness was making them careless — they tripped, staggered and stumbled as they fled, picking up small injuries that hindered them.

Wynflaed ran a few steps ahead of Emma and flopped down on a grassy hillock. She laid back and tugged at the neck of her dress. "If Weodmonath be dry and warm, comes the harvest to no harm," she sang, as

Emma sat down wearily beside her. "If wheat be wet and lack of dust, it will make a tough bread crust."

"What?" sneered Emma, rubbing the scratches and nettle rash on her legs with dock leaves.

"Haven't you heard that before?" Wynflaed asked. "My father — well, Uhtred, my foster father, always said it on the first day of Weodmonath. It's true too."

"But it's not Weodmonath," Emma said.

Wynflaed peered at her curiously. "You sound as if you're getting a cold."

"I'll survive it."

"We'd better find some yarrow and a decent shelter for you," said Wynflaed undeterred. "A cold can be bad in summer."

"Who are you, Mother Duck? We daren't waste the time. If we don't find this robber soon, a cold will be the least of my worries. It's been three days and we've not even seen a swineherd."

"Do you think we dare light a fire? I'm starving hungry."

"Nobody is after us," said Emma. "They would have caught us up by now, or passed us by. They'd be a lot quicker than us. They don't have to keep off the tracks."

"Yeah, I think you're right. Let's find somewhere and make camp."

Emma clutched her stomach. "Frigg, I'm hungry. Is there anything left that's not a bloody turnip?"

"No, but look, there are some early blackberries over there - let's pick 'em."

They rose wearily and began harvesting the briars. After a while Wynflaed found she had wandered to the edge of a small, sun drenched clearing. At its heart, a dilapidated hovel leaned its turf roof into a tangle of ivy. It was a simple shelter made of roughly split logs, interwoven with willow and hazel and plastered with mud. A curtain of rags between pillars of river stones served as a door. It was typical of the sort of hut a swineherd would build for comfort on the long autumn nights.

"Emma! Come here, look."

Emma gaped at the hut. "Mother Frigg!" she gasped, staggering backwards and struggling to keep on her feet, her face ashen.

"What is it?" Wynflaed threw out a supporting arm and grabbed her. "You look like you've seen old Grim.

Emma calmed herself and recovered her balance. "It's this place. It reminds me of somewhere I once …"

"Where?"

"Never mind, but if this is Rabbian's hall, I'm off back to the army."

"No, it's just an old herder's hut by the look of it. I don't think it's been used for years. We could rest. You need to get over your cold, and besides, I'd like to bathe my poor feet."

"Hum, it should be safe enough for now, I suppose," Emma said, her eyes narrowing to scour the clearing for signs of potential danger.

Wynflaed felt sure they could be safe there, even until late autumn if necessary. "Right, that's it then, we'll stay. You get a fire going. I'll go and look for some yarrow for that cold of yours."

"A fire!" said Emma, wafting her hand before her face, as if to remind Wynflaed that the sun was scorching hot.

"No, not inside, outside. It's to make bread and boil the yarrow. See if you can find a pot."

A little while later, Emma was hanging her face over the steam of boiling yarrow, inhaling noisily.

Wynflaed toasted a rope of bread dough she'd made, wrapped around a stick.

"You're supposed to drink it, not sniff it."

"You said inhale."

"I said inhaling steam was good for a cold, but yarrow is to be drunk."

Emma sniffed huffily and pulled a face.

Wynflaed ignored her and returned to her baking, in between examining her blistered feet. "The trouble is, you don't listen," she said absently. "You're always too busy trying to prove that you don't need anybody's help, so you never listen."

"Oh, and I should heed you, I suppose," Emma said, her face red and dripping.

"Well, at least I know that yarrow is only good for colds if you drink it and not snort it like a pig in mast."

Too wretched to argue, Emma swung venomously onto what she felt would be an easier tack. "So where's this wonderful Rabbian then? What are we doing here?" She sniffed her medicine and frowned. "You said we'd find him. You said he'd take us in. We can't stay long in this spiders' midden, and we can't keep wandering around up to our tits in thorns and stinging nettles with no food and no hope."

"Is there anything more you'd like to say? I don't recall asking you to come with me in the first place?" said Wynflaed. "We might not find him. Maybe he doesn't even exist, but don't forget you came because you wanted to. It's not my fault." She limped up to the hovel door and peered inside. Fingering her slave collar, she leaned back against the doorjamb. "We've got to find some way of getting my necklace off. I daren't show myself with it on, and I can't breathe in this heat if I cover it up."

"We need a smith."

Wynflaed glared at her scornfully. "Oh, that's a good idea. Why didn't I think of that?"

"Is that ready yet?" Emma glared at the bread, pouting.

Wynflaed examined her baking on its stick. "I think so." She took it from the heat and pinched it gently.

She moved into a patch of shade under the wall of the house. "Gods, it's so hot." She began to pick carefully at the high neck of her dress, tearing it open to bare her throat and the swell of her breasts.

"Well, we do need a smith. You can't get that off any other way. And when it's off, what then? This mystical Rabbian was supposed to be our protection." Emma shuffled on her knees to join her in the shade, the pot of steaming yarrow clasped to her face. "And we've no food. We can't live on pignuts and nettles for ever."

"There's bread."

"It looks like cinders." She broke a piece off the loaf and blew to cool it.

Wynflaed leaned back against the shading ivy-covered wall, her legs straight out before her, her eyes closed. "If we stay here a while we can put some snares out. We might catch something."

"It will have to be a blind, one-legged frog," said Emma, nibbling at her bread. "What do you know about snares?"

Wynflaed laughed, mindful that there were odd moments when she felt a growing fondness for Emma, despite everything. Discovering her secret concern for her had been a big surprise and now, sharing the hardships of their journey, its novelty was maturing into affection.

"I know about snares and forest life. I'd no choice when I was a girl," said Emma.

"You were never a girl? You'd be a wasp or a viper?"

Emma turned her head away.

"Oh, I'm sorry. That was too far, wasn't it? Are you crying?" cried Wynflaed, seeing Emma lean away, her shoulders shaking. "No, Gods you're laughing! I made you laugh, didn't I?"

Emma straightened up and faced her gravely. "Of course not. Why don't you go and look for some food."

Wynflaed felt oddly elated. Even though she had tried to hide it from her, she knew she had made Emma smile. Their relationship was taking a quite unexpected turn.

"Maybe there's a farm nearby. I'm sure we'll find one soon. They might let us work for some eggs, or a fowl. I could do some mending or darning for them."

"Oh, what a lovely idea," Emma sang sarcastically. "And I could fuck the farmer legless, all his sons too, if they throw in some dried beans."

Wynflaed's rising spirits crashed. She felt tears welling up behind her eyes. "Well, we have to hope. We have to try. Being sour and moaning all the time won't save us."

Emma sipped her yarrow, her sullen frown betraying the merest hint of apology.

"If we get ourselves organised, we can manage. I know how to make fish traps. You said you can lay snares, and there's plenty of nuts and blackberries."

Emma stared at the ground and mumbled her agreement. "Autumn's not a bad time for traps and snares, and there's fairy club, pignuts, wild turnip. I've seen some anise cap fungus around."

"Drink up," said Wynflaed, putting an encouraging hand to the wyrtdrenc Emma nursed in her palms. "We need you to get well."

Later, inside the hut, Wynflaed searched its corners unearthing its few treasures: a leaky leather bucket, a small iron boiler in which a robin had once nested, a rusty trivet, a few broken pots and a wooden spade. With a good axe and some flour, it was probably all a swineherd would need to survive his annual three-month vigil.

With the old leather bucket serving as her basket, Wynflaed scoured the woods for food. She also looked for rosie-under-the-sun and water cress, so they could wash their hair.

That evening, after washing in a nearby stream, Wynflaed was pleased to note that a mysterious smell had vanished. As she sat, shivering pleasantly inside her blanket and watched her clothes drying before the fire, Emma tried to complete the transformation by teasing Wynflaed's ill-shorn hair with her fingers. Wynflaed sat quietly, enjoying the attention and welcoming her first stirrings of vanity in months. She felt as if she was approaching a door beyond which lay her old life, ready and waiting for her to pick it up and swing it round her shoulders like a warm, comfortable cloak.

"Just think, Emma," she said dreamily. "If we can find Rabbian or somebody to help us and get this collar off, I might be able to see my children. I could even let them see me if my hair is grown back. We might talk and touch and I can hold them and smell them again. I've dreamed of it so many times. I'm sure Manwine or Gutty would find a way to let me see ..." She stopped suddenly and clutched miserably at the clothes drying before her. "Oh, but Gods! Not in these rags."

"Yeah, not exactly the great lady is it? You can't let them see you like that. I mean, even a good homespun wouldn't be good enough. They'll expect to see you looking like a lady, with linen and silk trimmings. We'll have to find you a fine dress. Don't worry. Nothing's impossible, especially on a good drying day."

Three days later, Emma was getting over her cold and was more like her old self. They had decided that they should move on. The following day they took a last look around the little hut. Wynflaed smiled at Emma. "I shan't forget this place. Our first taste of freedom," she said wistfully. "Almost home sweet home — eh?"

"This dump! Good riddance to it."

"Thank you, hut," Wynflaed said, teasing Emma by defying her surly glare. "Thank you, hearth, and you too, old crocks."

Emma's stoicism weakened, she giggled and pushed Wynflaed towards the door. "Get going before you name every damned spider and flea."

Beyond the curtained door a bearded, muscular man barred their way. Wynflaed jumped back, and pulled the ragged curtain across it, as if it would somehow keep him out. The man tore it aside. "Now, now!" he said, his voice a mocking sneer. "That's not very friendly, is it?"

"We're going," Wynflaed cried. "We didn't take anything. We just sheltered."

The man unhitched a circular, lime wood shield from his shoulder and rested it against the doorjamb. He was richly clad, though his arrogance was that of a common ruffian rather than a wealthy warrior. His ornate leather armour was haphazardly festooned with more than twenty glittering cloak pin brooches. At his waist, a broad belt of silver plates supported a jewelled sword and seax.

His muscular arms carried numerous battle scars, as well as the fresh red slash of briars.

Wynflaed felt the strength melting in her legs. She knew that if she did not act now, she never would. "Stand aside!" she said, her voice clear and steady, "We've done no harm here. We demand that you let us pass." A glint of admiration flickered briefly in the man's pale blue eyes, but he did not move.

Wynflaed stared defiantly into his face, and edged forward, feeling the comforting presence of Emma at her shoulder. The man smiled, showing a row of small, perfect teeth, but still he did not move. Running his eyes over her body, pausing appreciatively where she had opened the neck of her dress, one hand loosed the chinstrap of his iron helmet, allowing his wiry beard to burst out from beneath silver cheek plates. The other hand rose slowly to touch Wynflaed on the cheek. "Proud-headed. I like that in a woman," he said.

She leaned away, glaring defiantly. She saw there were several other men behind him, all well armed. They crowded forward to peer through the narrow doorway, grinning and leering from beneath their helmets. Swords, axes and spears flashed and shook in their scarred fists.

"You've a proud head, woman ..."

"And a king for a jeweller," said another man from the group.

Wynflaed's hand rose to the slave collar at her neck. "Stand aside. I'm — I'm on the king's business," she said, desperately hoping it might make a difference.

"Bollocks! Let's see her tits," some man cried.

Emma secretly tapped Wynflaed's thigh with a heavy stick of fire wood. Wynflaed accepted it unseen and prepared to use it as a club.

Unfortunately, the man had spotted it. He looked down at it trembling in the white knuckled grip of her fist and smiled. "You've got courage too," he said. "So, you're on the king's business are you? I don't think so, lass. So what are you - a couple of cods-queens on the run?" He bent close to peer past Wynflaed at Emma. "Aaah, sisters, eh? Just like two peas, but where's your pod, I wonder?"

"Come on Theel, stop jabbering," one of the men cried impatiently. "Let's fuck 'em and be on our way."

***

Two charred corpses were found in the ashes of the old reeve's cottage at Holmesfelt. Rendil spared no expense on their burial. Old Manwine's remains were laid to rest with the shield and spears he had carried as a young man. The notched tally sticks, worn and shiny from many years of use, were also laid at his side. His grieving sons, with their wives and bewildered children, placed food in the grave for his journey to the hall of the dead. Holmesfelt's cottars and bonded servants watched with surprise as even Rendil contributed salt and a kidskin purse, said to contain silver coins, to the burial.

Many found Rendil's reactions to the tragedy puzzling. On receiving the news, he had flown into a hysterical rage and wept openly. Even weeks later, he could not speak of it without raging tearfully. Some said it was only to be expected, since his wife Goda had perished in the flames too. Cynics sneered at this, arguing that Goda and Rendil had hardly exchanged a word of friendship in years. It was widely known that he had a mistress with whom he spent weeks on end; something he had made no attempt to conceal.

Goda had refused to move into the hall with him after Aelric's death. Contact with each other had been confined to the minimum necessary for raising their own children and Wulfric's.

Goda was laid to rest the day after Manwine. It was done with the solemn ceremonial befitting her station as the wife of a wealthy landowner. Her remains were lowered into the ground, wrapped in a linen sheet, scattered with flowers. The symbolic iron keys of her office, as the lady of Rendil's house hung from a belt about her waist. A hastily made horsehair wig covered her fleshless, cinder of a skull. A necklace of red glass beads was placed round the charred sticks of bone that had once been her elegant neck. Before shovelling in the earth, salt, loaves of bread and a bowl of apples were put beside her.

At the graveside, Rendil spoke of how blessed they were that little Eadric had survived the blaze. He reminded everybody that Eadric's narrow escape was entirely due to Goda's selfless sacrifice. "If she had not gone into that burning house and brought the lad out, we would have lost him too."

People noticed how Rendil had seemed so moved by this that he could barely bring himself to look upon the little survivor. The cause of the fire was never discovered.

....

CHAPTER TWENTY-FOUR

It was dark by the time Wynflaed and Emma arrived at their captor's camp. For most of the journey, Theel and his handful of lusty men had joked and teased them, promising them all manner of sexual abuse. Wynflaed did not know what to expect of their destination, but soon formed the impression that the men were more boisterous than dangerous. The worst she could accuse them of was ribaldry and joyful exaggeration. There lewd joking had even brought a smile to Emma's face.

The first sign of journey's end was their arrival at a robust ring of sharpened spikes, concealed in the underbrush at the edge of a clearing. Beyond the clearing a deep ditch bristled with more defensive spikes and hideous sprung-sapling traps, ready to impale intruders. An earth rampart rose up from the ditch to twice the height of a man. It was topped off with a timber palisade from which spearmen and archers peered down, their helmets and weapons glittering in the light of flaming torches.

One of Theel's men blew two blasts on a cow-horn. Immediately, a narrow section of palisade seemed to break free from the rest and transform itself into a gate. From inside it men rolled out a long runway to bridge the spike-filled ditch. Although barely wide enough for a hand cart to cross safely, some of Theel's men danced and leapfrogged over each other, whooping and shouting, contemptuous of the danger.

Wynflaed was jostled across onto the worn, patchy grass of a large compound. It was bright with fires and guttering torches. Dozens of armed men milled about, greeting the return of their comrades with bawdy cries and jokes. A large hall stood at the middle of the enclosure. Wynflaed could see it was being modified or extended. Some of its beech timbers glowed pink with newness. Despite the late hour, thatchers were still working on its enlarged roof, part of which had a makeshift, tent-like structure over it. A ramshackle assortment of houses, huts, tents and shanties jostled for space beneath the hall's stout walls. A few grander, high-roofed buildings stood off at a distance, some had ornately carved porches, door posts and shutters, but most were small, windowless dugouts or mean lean-to frames of branches, roofed with bracken or turf. The biggest structure was a great barn surrounded by a clutter of lean-to hovels and animal pens. Against the inside of the palisade, more pens held goats, sheep and cattle. Squawking flocks of hens and geese rushed about freely, trying to avoid the feet of carousing warriors and their women and children.

The jostling, giddy crowd pressed around the two women. Wynflaed struggled to keep sight of Emma as unseen hands prodded and pushed her through the throng. Somebody grabbed her slave collar and steered her into an unlit lean-to in the lea of the great barn. Emma tumbled in behind her, spitting and fighting. The door slammed shut, plunging the cramped space into gloom.

For several long moments they pressed themselves back against the walls in fearful silence, hardly daring to breath as their eyes became accustomed to the dark. Throughout their ordeal they had been unable to speak to each other. Now, alone, bruised, and frightened, they sought each others touch, wondering what would be next.

Emma spoke first, her voice seeming oddly small. "Do you think this is it?" She made a slashing gesture across her throat.

Wynflaed had no idea, though she felt it seemed likely. "I don't think so," she replied forcing cheerfulness.

"Oh, shit!" Emma cried. "You do, don't you? I can tell. That's your little cuddly sunbeam voice. I always know we're in trouble - you start with that."

Wynflaed felt hopeless. "Well, what else can I say? How do I know?"

"Are we at Rabbian's? Do you think this's his camp? You said he'd help us. They don't look helpful."

Wynflaed blew a tense sigh and slid slowly down the wall to sit on the straw covered ground. She drew her knees up to her chin. "I don't know who they are. They're obviously rustlers and thieves. That much is plain."

"Why is it?"

"All those pens full of sheep and cattle, yet there's not enough pasture for granny's old goat. I'd guess this is some sort of collecting point on the way to a market somewhere." A thought interrupted her and she released a mournful groan.

"What?" gasped Emma.

"If it is, they'll not be keen to let us go now that we've seen it."

"Bloody marvellous," said Emma. "So in other words, we've been rescued by bloodthirsty murderers who'll kill us. Bloody marvellous." She stomped about the small space, smashing her fist into her palm. "How did I let myself get into this? I should have known. What sort of mad man gives himself a name like Rabbian anyway? The *rage of devils*! Huh! He has to be some sort of mad wild killer." She gazed about desperately. "They must be just waiting for fools like us to wander in to their trap. And now they've got us; a bunch of bloody rustlers, thieves, rapists and murderers. Well, we're certainly moving up in the world."

"It might not be like that," Wynflaed said. "I mean, they could be runaways like us. They're bound to have some sympathy for us. And anyway, don't try blaming me for everything. I didn't make you come. And if this is Rabbian's camp, don't forget that most of what we've heard about him is just kitchen talk. He might be ..."

"What, a really nice man?" said Emma. "Good to his mother and little furry things? Good! You can try your little miss sunbeam voice on him when you're begging him not to tear your head off."

"Well at least I try to look for the good. All you do is pour gloom on everything."

"Frigg's tits! You make me sick," cried Emma. "Even when you see pig shit you say, ooooh, that'll be good on the bean strip."

"Well what's wrong with that?" Wynflaed asked. She moved to the door and spied out through a gap in its timbers. "At least I'm not lost before I start, like you."

"Shit is shit!" Emma yelled, exasperated. "And that's what you're in now, right up to your pretty little nose. We could have our throats cut or be hung or disembowelled, or worse."

Wynflaed turned from the spy hole and cast her an astonished look. "Worse? Gods Emma, isn't disembowelment bad enough?"

"Oh don't worry, little fairy child, that's nothing," Emma said. "I know things that'd make having your throat cut seem like a harvest feste."

Wynflaed abandoned the spy hole and sat back against the wall. "Spare me the details."

Emma scrambled to the door. "Let me have a look. I think you're blind anyway unless something is right under your nose. That's probably why you stitch so well. I haven't made a decent stitch since my close-up eyesight went with my virginity." She put her eye to the peephole and wriggled into position for spying out.

"Really? I didn't know you ..."

"What? Are not a virgin?" she interrupted. "No, sorry sweet thing, but I've been well and truly tampered with."

Wynflaed laughed. "No, I mean, I didn't know you sewed."

"Oh, I see," said Emma. "You're happy to believe I fuck like a frog, but you think sewing is beyond me?"

"No, I didn't mean ..."

"Of course I can sew," Emma snapped. "I'm quite good at it, as a matter of fact. I'd easily be as good as you, if I could see right."

Wynflaed sighed, wondering if she would ever have a straight conversation with Emma, or would she always have to be on her guard?

"Who taught you?"

"Granny Ettith. Well that's only what I called her. She was ..." Emma stopped and glared sourly.

Wynflaed sensed she was about to retreat behind her chilly defences again. "Tell me," she urged. "I'd like to hear."

"No! I don't feel like chit chat. Some bastard has locked me up and he's probably going to rape me and kill me. I'm never at my best before that."

"No time is ever right with you. You're scared of giving anything away. You can't talk to anybody. You even try to hide things from yourself. I feel sorry for you. You can't ever ..."

"Keep your sympathy for others. I don't need it. I don't need anything, and certainly not you."

"No, you don't, do you? You're so strong and independent. Well I'm not. I do need things, Emma,"

Wynflaed cried. "I need you for a start. And whether you like it or not, I've grown very fond of you."

Emma turned her face from her, pouting thoughtfully. "That's your problem."

Wynflaed gave up. Leaning her head back against the wooden wall, she closed her eyes and tried to bring Eadric and Wyngifu to mind, hoping she might sleep and dream of them.

Some time later the whimper of reluctant leather hinges startled her out of a fitful sleep. It was almost pitch black, but she sensed the door being jerked open. A flaming brand was thrust inside, illuminating the face of the man holding it. She recognised Theel, grinning at her.

"Come on then, my two little peas," he said cheerfully. "The master wants to see you. Behave yourselves like good little huswifs and he might not eat you."

"Fuck him!" cried Emma defiantly, rising stiffly and stretching her cramped limbs. "He'll find me hard to chew on." She glared at Theel. "Who is he anyway, this master of yours, another shit-head like you?"

Theel's initial shock shifted to amusement. "You'll never win my heart like that, my little love-chick," he said, setting them walking towards the great hall. "Flattery doesn't work on me. I'm a man of action? Deeds are what I respond to."

"Really, well remind me to kick you in the balls then," said Emma.

Wynflaed grabbed Emma by the arm and spun her round to face her. "Shut up! You'll get us killed. Try to be respectful for once. It might save your stupid neck."

"They don't scare me," said Emma.

Theel turned to Wynflaed. "She's a fearsome pup, your sister," he said. "She could freeze a lamp flame with that frown. Thank Old Grim I'm not travelling with her. I'd rather carry a dead horse up a wet hill."

"We're not sisters," Wynflaed said.

Theel nodded understandingly. "Lucky for you." Casting Emma a wary glance, he picked up his step and led them past a clutter of thatchers' ladders and scaffolding to the hall's half-built porch. As they approached it, an iron-studded door swung open. Two women, one quite old and clinging tearfully to her younger companion, came out.

The older woman looked up at Theel and reached out her scrawny arms to him. "Oh, thank you, thank you. May the gods bless you. I don't know what I can ever do to thank you."

Theel stepped back, looking embarrassed, as the old woman embraced him, spilling tears on his chest. He pushed her gently back into the arms of the younger woman.

"We can never thank you enough," the young woman said, embracing the older.

Wynflaed watched the pair leave, wondering what was happening. The old woman turned back to Theel and continued to thank him through her tears as she was led away.

"What was that about?" asked Wynflaed.

Theel appeared quietly moved as he watched the pair leave. "We found her missing son for her. He was taken prisoner more than two years ago. He was sold across the sea in Gaul. The young one's his sister. She asked my brother if we could find him and bring him back."

"You can do that? How?"

"Humm sometimes. We've got a few friends over there. We trade with the Gauls and the Armoricans, so we've got contacts. Sometimes they can find people; runaways, exiles, slaves. It took about six months to find her son. The Gauls make us pay of course. It's good business for them. I'm sure that sometimes we finish up paying the very same people who stole them in the first place. Of course, we can't ever say that to them."

He started towards the iron-studded door but paused and turned to Emma, wagging a warning finger in her face. "Try not to be so sour," he said. "They don't call him Rabbian for nothing."

The heavy door swung on its hinges, releasing a puff of warm air smelling of wood smoke, dusty earth and bracken litter.

Theel caught Wynflaed's arm and nodded towards a man seated in a high backed chair at a long table at the top of the hall. "Take my advice, love-chick. Don't try to be clever. You could do much worse than have my brother for a friend."

"What should I say?" she asked, almost choking with nervousness.

"Just tell the truth. He's not Grendel."

Without taking her eyes off the seated figure, Wynflaed reached back and grabbed Emma's hand. They started towards him, nervously stealing an occasional glance about them. Somewhere behind them, in the gloom of lower hall, a couple of servants talked softly to each other as they worked. Sparrows, disturbed by the lamplight, twittered in the rafters. The voices of the men working outside filtered in through the unfinished thatch. Wynflaed thought how eerily disembodied their voices seemed in the naked austerity of the huge, barn-like building.

The man at the table did not look up as they approached. Wynflaed took the chance to look around her with more care. A drift of cold, white ash lay upon a raised bed of hearthstones. Along each side of the room, the earthen floor bore the imprint of long tables. She surmised that the tables had been moved outside, either because of the hot summer weather or the new building work. She had seen merrymakers at tables outside as they had approached the hall. She wondered why Rabbian was not out there too, dining with his friends. She hoped it was not because of her and Emma. But no, it could not be, she realised. That would be giving themselves too much importance. Although why was he sitting alone in the stale, exhausted air of his unfinished hall, instead of with his friends in the balmy, forest-scented evening?

He was fondling the head of a hunting dog. She heard him speak to it in a strange, squeaky whisper, as one might to a babe in arms. Seizing on his distraction, she studied him closely. He had a tangle of hair the colour of sun-bleached leather. It brushed the shoulders of his brown linen tunic. His face was partially hidden as he bent over the dog. His athletic physique and what little she could see of his face, suggested he was about twenty-five.

Mounting the plinth upon which his table stood, she announced herself with a cough. He turned instantly, surprising her, forcing her to retreat a step.

"Aah, there you are," he said swivelling to face her in his wide, high-backed chair. His smile was warm, though slightly self-conscious, almost apologetic, she thought. It revealed a chipped front tooth in an otherwise faultless array. Blue eyes peered out from a square, cheerful face that was tanned and clean-shaven. She saw him run his gaze over her body with a look of nervous appreciation, as though unable to help himself but nevertheless enjoying what he saw. Thick golden eyebrows trapped wayward strands of his hair, giving him an almost feminine look at times. He certainly did not look much like the Devil's Rage, Wynflaed thought. More like somebody's big-soft brother.

"I'm sorry," he said. "I don't get much time with this old girl." He cast a fond glance at the dog and stroked its head. "She's more than twelve, you know. That's a very good age for a dog who's fought wolves and bears and run her heart out for you a thousand times. I keep her by the hearth nowadays. She'd still go chasing if I'd let her, but it'd kill her of course."

Wynflaed eyed the dog doubtfully, desperately foraging for an appropriate response. Regrettably, the hound's appearance suggested nothing even remotely complimentary. It had only one eye, an ugly scarred muzzle and ears as tattered as a beggar's shirt.

"Fancy," she heard herself say, bereft of inspiration. The beast eyed her dolefully, as Rabbian enthused about its head.

"You don't like dogs?" he queried, looking distraught. "They're the most loving and faithful ..." He stopped in mid sentence and peered past Wynflaed, his face contorted into an expression of mystified shock. "What is she doing?"

Wynflaed turned to see Emma coupling unflattering facial expressions to his gushing observations on dogs. "What're you doing? For Grim's sake, at least show some common courtesy."

"I hate dogs." Emma said.

Rabbian sank back into his chair. "You must be the Sour Pea," he said with a scowl. "My brother named you well: Sweet Pea and Sour Pea."

"This is Emma, your honour. Please don't be angry," Wynflaed said, adding quickly, "We're not sisters. I'm — I'm Wynflaed Alfwalddohtor, widow of Wulfric

Aelricsunnu of the Peakland Cenwulfingas. We seek your honour's protection."

Rabbian was still looking at Emma, his eyebrows knitted in doubt. "I think it's me who needs the protection," he said. Then, standing, he strode past them into the well of his hall, not taking his eyes off Emma.

Wynflaed watched him. He had a tall athletic figure. His legs, tanned and scarred, were naked to the thigh. As he moved his tunic fell open, revealing a tanned, hairless chest and a pair of short, brown woollen brecs belted with a chain of silver plaques. He passed by her with easy strides, his bare feet hardly disturbing the floor litter of bracken. Turning to face her, he sat down on the edge of the stone hearth and indicated that she and Emma might sit opposite on stools that seemed to anticipate them.

"You don't *have* to tell your stories here," he told them. "Your past life is your own. We don't ask questions. No matter what you've done, you'll be welcome. We have a few rules – not many. Just the ones that make sense. Basically, respect people and help them."

"Are we prisoners?" asked Wynflaed.

"You can leave whenever you like. There are no prisoners or slaves here. There aren't even any servants, except those who choose to serve others."

"We want to be free," Emma said, her sincerity smothering all cynicism.

"Freedom? Aahh, yes. I'm afraid that's not mine to give you. I can't ..."

"Why not?"

He studied her curiously. "Freedom is not real unless you take it by your own two hands. Freedom can't be given." he told her quietly. "Freedom that is given is illusory."

"But we're runaways."

"Then you've already seized your freedom. I can take your collar off, if that's what you mean, but that's just iron-smithing."

"What — what do you do here?" Wynflaed asked.

"The same as any other place, I expect." He shrugged his shoulders with an air of inevitability. "We do whatever's necessary: plant, reap, raid, fight, take, give away. People bring us their animals to sell for them. Others we occasionally might steal. Mainly we just live our lives like everybody else, only here we don't pay gafol or tribute to any man." He smiled at her, sensing his answer was less than she had expected. "I expect you've heard that we're a vicious, murdering rabble; spirit beings that kill and rob and then melt into the trees like mist." He laughed. "That's my brother, Theel. He spreads wild stories about us to keep people away."

"They are precisely why we searched you out," said Wynflaed.

He chuckled. "You must tell him that. He'll be distraught, but on the whole it does seem to work. People leave us alone. Personally, I think it has more to do with the fact that we don't threaten anybody, and we don't have much that's worth stealing. Now, if this was rich pasture around here, instead of useless forest, we might have more trouble than we do. Besides, our presence here is useful to the kings and chieftains around us. We help to keep them apart, like a living barrier." He stood up and stretched his spine. "Let's go and eat, and then we'll find somewhere to sleep. Tomorrow, if you decide to stay with us, you can start building a house."

"But how will we live?" Wynflaed asked, put out by his easy ways and careless faith in the generosity of Wyrd.

He gave her a slightly pitying smile. Taking a step towards her he took her hand and held it gently. "Oh don't worry, something's sure to turn up. Life is nothing if not full of opportunity. Just do whatever you do best and try to enjoy yourselves a little. Make choices. That's what free people do."

***

The dusty summer days were shortening, sliding hazily towards autumn. As Wynflaed accustomed herself to her new surroundings, far off in the south of Britain, Pedlar Dawes was growing impatient with his. He was in the country of the Middle Saxons, peddling his wares to the Ciltern Saetan. Business was poor. The long dry summer which had blessed Mercia with a rich harvest, had been too long and too dry further south. Crop yields were low and pastures exhausted. Forest fires raged unchecked, wiping out villages and farms. The dispossessed, with neither food nor shelter, had taken to the roads, begging, raiding and robbing other farms for the means of survival.

Some families chose to abandon their farms and move north in search of a new start. Dawes joined one of these groups of refugees. There was safety in numbers on the parched, robber infested roads. With trade so bad, he saw no profit in waiting for spring before travelling to the Peakland. He might as well go now, before he too fell victim to the knives and clubs of starving, burnt out farmers.

***

Rabbian and his men were often away for days or even weeks at a time. Their comings and goings swung the settlement between extremes of frantic festivity and careless indolence. Emma quickly put the life-style to profitable use. She solved the question of her subsistence by attracting a wealthy lover. He was a vain young man with little ambition and less intelligence. He housed, fed, clothed and bejewelled her like a queen, adoring her with a constancy even she found touching. She repaid him with frequent and meticulous attention to his nether regions.

As Emma worked on her indispensability to her lover, Wynflaed spent her days working with the women of Rabbian's household. They were civil, though slightly grudging to start with, so she worked quietly, trying not to get in their way. She studied their customs and conventions, to learn where she might eventually fit in. Her needlecraft soon attracted attention, breaking down barriers. After a week or so, when the women were happy that she had little interest in any of their men folk, their regard for her ripened into respect and even affection. Little by little, they allowed her into their company, and finally the secrets of their inner circle.

Within a month, she had repaired or replaced much of Rabbian's meagre wardrobe and subjected him to bed-curtains. She came to see that Rabbian was a kind and gentle man. He was fond of music and dancing, and could easily be brought to tears by a sad song.

She was also pleased to learn that the blood of others was not paying for the life and security she enjoyed at the fort; at least, no more so than at many a so-called legal ruler's settlement. The fort was well-defended, and for the most part as peaceful as any place in Penda's Mercia. Women had their babies and brought them up in relative calm and safety. There were no robbers or rustlers powerful enough to threaten them, and no border disputes, since thick, impenetrable forest has no internal borders. There were no raids or warfare. Neighbouring kingdoms considered the forest a useless wilderness where they could not marshal an army.

When Rabbian was not off hunting, rustling or trading, his presence around the place seemed huge, as though he was everywhere at once. Everything she saw around the fort was invariably for him, or by him, or because of him. His existence touched everything, like blood powering muscles.

In his treatment of her, he was shy and unsure of himself, though it was clear that he thought of her with growing fondness. He was always inventing reasons to seek her out. Often he would bring some little gift: a brooch, a smoked ham, a bone needle or length of cloth, He always claimed they were merely unwanted items that he would have discarded, but for her.

Little by little, she began telling him her story, exposing her fears and entrusting him with her most secret desires. He was a good listener, easy to confide in. He seemed to see things from precisely her perspective.

Wynflaed had enjoyed a stroll in the evenings for as long as she could remember. Lately, Rabbian had taken to the same habit and would often meet her - *accidentally*. They would laugh and agree that they might as well walk together. She told him about her children, and of her wish to be with them. He understood exactly, and not merely on an emotional level. He did not immediately say, as others did, that she should bring them to the settlement. He understood that would be impossible. He and his ingas were outlaws. If Eadric and Wyngifu joined Wynflaed there, they too would become outlaws. The rights and privileges of their birth would be forfeit. What she did not realise was that Rabbian's understanding went even deeper, clamping his heart in the icy grip of a new reality, for he saw that she would never feel able to make her home with him. She would eventually leave him to be with her children, no matter what the risks.

For a long time the two were silent. Wynflaed was lost in thoughts of her children, but Rabbian's thoughts lay scattered in the ruins of secret plans and desires that he had hardly dared to admit to himself.

A few days later Wynflaed and Emma were seated on leather stools outside the great hall, enjoying the late autumn sunshine. Wynflaed suddenly thought of Buhe and a wave of sadness swept over her. Emma saw her look and frowned. "What's up? You look ealf-touched."

Wynflaed collected her thoughts. "If only Buhe had thought …"

"Oh, Frigg!" cried Emma, cutting her off sharply. "That spoilt cow! You haven't mentioned her for weeks. I thought you'd come to your senses."

"But we were like sisters," said Wynflaed. "I never had a sister. We were even better than sisters in so many ways."

"She's a spoilt, vindictive little cow. How can you feel fondly for her? You could never have done what she did to you."

"She was upset and confused. She believed what her husband said. What could she do? She must be so miserable now."

"She's miserable!" said Emma, incredulity sending her eyebrows skyward. "Grim's cods, that's rich. You're the one who's suffered, not her. She's at home enjoying an easy life. In my opinion, she deserves all the trouble she gets."

"No — oh no, Emma," Wynflaed said. "I know what she's like. She'll be heartbroken. She was always the main victim of her outbursts. She trusted Colnoth. I don't know what she ever saw in him, but she loved him. She could never see malice in him."

"All she ever saw was her own selfish desire. I know that sort very well."

"No, she loved him. It tore her apart finding him with me." She turned to Emma, willing her to understand. "Don't you see? On that night she lost the two people whom she loved most in the world. Now she's alone and in pain."

Emma glared pityingly. "I think you're soft in the head."

. . . .

CHAPTER TWENTY-FIVE

Ealdorman Cenwulf, leader of the Peakland folk, was well known for celebrating Yuletide at his Badecanwell hall with infectious zeal. For him it was the most sacred and joyous of all the seasons. Ever since he had led his people to settle beside the warm, chalybeate waters of Beadaca's well, Yuletide, the first important feast they had celebrated together in their new land, had been a most special time. Badecanwell's famed Yule feasts attracted crowds of visitors. They came to trade or sample the entertainments, or simply to gape at the grand folk feasting on the Ealdorman's benches. Many simply sought relief from the grinding oppression of winter, for Modrenacht, on midwinter's night, represented the turning point of the season.

Pedlar Blackbird Dawes arrived too late; Modrenacht had passed. The king and many of the great families who had spent several days in the Ealdorman's hall were already gone. So too were most of the traders, plegerers and song makers. A few stragglers were all Badecanwell had left to show for its famed festivities, apart from over flowing latrines, lanes impassable with churned up mud, and the scarred ground and cold hearths of many abandoned camp sites. Not that any of this bothered Dawes. On the contrary, he was relieved to find the crowds gone. It served him better. All he wanted was an audience with the Lady Aenflaed, the Ealdorman's sister. He prayed that she would still be in residence and not driven away by the litter and rubbish the crowds had left behind them. Even so, he would not attempt to contact her until he had learned all that might be useful to know of her. He was a wily old bird and well knew that the true value of anything can only be determined by knowing precisely what the buyer is prepared to pay for it. Therefore he would listen, observe and learn all he could before he met her.

Aenflaed's large house stood on a steep hill overlooking the fording place on the river. Her land adjoined a glade of sacred yew trees where offerings were made to the gods. Beadaca's spring bubbled up into a stone-paved basin at the foot of the path that led to her front porch. The ford, where the river meandered through level pastures, was about a hundred paces beyond it.

Aenflaed ran her house as a refuge, a place where orphans, widows and distressed women could find peace and sanctuary. Dawes had heard that she was a follower of the new religion, a worshipper of the Roman Christ child. If that's true, he thought, she would be almost the only woman in Mercia able to get away with such a thing. King Penda disapproved of Christians, and although he claimed that his people were free to worship whatever gods they cared to, he did not waste favour on those who turned their backs on the Old Ones.

Dawes was doubtful. He had seen Christians in Cantwarre and Lundenwic. There, they put up stone crosses and temples, and burned candles and incense. He had also seen the dark robed foreigners, the drinkers of blood, who were their priests.

Dawes was relieved to find that no Christian signs adorned Aenflaed's house, but who was to say what vile practices she and her women were up to inside? He shuddered, and tried to smother his fear that behind the door and shutters they might all be Christian blood-drinkers.

He bent down at Badecanwell's tepid spring to drink and wash away his superstitions, but the water, being slightly chalybeate, tasted like blood. It made him retch. It was a bad omen. "The sooner I get away from here, the better," he told himself and stomped back up the slope from the well, warily eyeing Aenflaed's house.

It looked innocent enough, a mixture of dry stone walls and a sturdy timber frame with lathe and daub between, under a thatch of reeds. Its ridge was sealed with living turf, blackened with soot around the smoke holes. Narrow window slits in the walls also let smoke out, as well as light in. Each had sturdy, iron bound shutters which could be closed against the weather. A porch, roomy enough for a tinker's family, stood at one end of the south facing wall. A broad pavement of flat river stones lay before it. These were scattered with gravel and straw to help prevent mud from the yard being carried inside the house.

A small tower stood at the west end of the building. It was a simple framework of timbers, jointed and pegged together. It rose to about three times the height of a man. A bronze bell hung at the top, under an iron gibbet where an alarm beacon could be hoisted. Kindling for the beacon was kept dry in a lean-to at the foot of the tower.

Dawes wasted three days in superstitious fear and dread before giving himself a severe talking to and resolving to get on with his purpose. With his chin stuck out in determination he climbed the path to Lady Aenflaed's door, tied his pack mules to the gate post and unloaded his trading pack. He kicked the mud off his boots against a tethering post, blew out his nostrils and relieved himself against a tree; a precaution against an untimely interruption by the call of nature which might sour an important deal.

He was glad to find a corn doll and a posy of dried flowers, honouring Nerthus, nailed to the door. These showed that the real gods were respected in the house after all, and not, as he had heard, the blood drinking upstart from Rome. He thumped on the door with renewed spirit, the linen gift piece still wound safely about his stomach. He planned to show Aenflaed his trade pack first, to win her over with a few worthy bargains. Then, when she was relaxed and more trusting, he would unwind the linen piece and lay it out before her.

He took a deep breath, knocked on the door again and looked back nervously to his pack animals. This was his big chance. He had waited a year for this moment. His whole life may be about to change.

***

When Penda's army had returned to Mercia, Hunwald, to his fury and frustration, was detained for a few months of extra duty. Wealh cattle rustlers had been taking advantage of the king's absence by raiding English farms along Mercia's western marches. Hunwald was one of twenty spearmen sent to deliver a sharp reminder to them that King Penda was back and would not idly stand by while his people were robbed. To ensure the continued loyalty of his weary warriors, Penda withheld their share of the Lindissi booty until the job was done. He also promised them a bonus of Wealish gold when the last rustler's head was spiked at the roadside. Hunwald and his comrades resigned themselves to a miserable winter - slaughtering Wealhs.

It was spring before he eventually returned to the Tame-Worthig. He had lost a piece of his left ear and gained only a twelfth part of a poor gold torc for his troubles. His bones ached with the damp, his piles were a curse, and his stomach burned with acid for want of decent food. He swore that he never wanted to see another army as long as he lived. Limping and sullen, he collected his bonus and his paltry share of the Lindissi booty and headed for his home village, barely taking the time to complain about the pittance doled out to him. All he could think of was selling Wulfric's gold ring. That, he swore, would make up for all his disappointments.

He still expected to be dealing with Wulfric, the ring's true owner. More than two and half years had passed since the Northumbrian wars and Penda's humiliating withdrawal from Bebba's smoking walls. Wulfric's family would surely have ransomed him by now. Hunwald hoped so. Wulfric's reputation for generosity was well known, but even if he had not yet returned, Hunwald felt sure that the family would reward him for the ring, and also for news he could give them of Wulfric's wife, assuming she really was the filthy slave he had seen at Penda's camp.

Shutting his eyes tightly, he rubbed his hands together greedily and thought of the farm he would buy with his reward. He had dreamed of it for so long. It seemed almost close enough to touch. All he had to do was present himself at Wulfric's door and collect his reward. Added to his piece of Welsh torc and his pitiful share of the Lindissi booty, he would have enough for a nice farm. There would even be sufficient for a strong young bride to bring him comfort and pleasure in his old age. If she had a strong back and some property too, it would be no hardship to marry even an ugly woman.

***

The folk of Rabbian's worthig had settled to the dull routine of post equinoctial winter, urged on by harsh necessity and the cheering prospect of Eostre-tide. For Wynflaed and Emma, Yuletide in their new surroundings had seemed to speed by. For weeks they had prepared for it, and then, in the blink of an eye, it was over. Now spring approached. Farmers fettled ploughs, repaired pens and smoked bees. The winds grew kinder and on the forest floor butter yellow celandine were soon joined by pearly white wood anemones.

On the occasional sunny afternoon, Emma and Wynflaed would meet to stroll beside the nearby stream that fed the settlement's wells. They were greatly at ease together, and gossiped and laughed, comparing notes about their new lives. For Wynflaed it was always a time to voice her thoughts about her children. There was never a day that she did not think of them. As they strolled one particularly spring-like afternoon, a long pause in their conversation caused Emma to glance inquiringly. "You could bring them here now," she suggested, not for the first time. "Now that you know this place and its folk; they're good people. It's safe and prosperous. They could have good lives here."

"I know," Wynflaed replied, "and I'd love to, but ..."

Emma frowned and stayed her with a firm hand on her forearm. "You like it here, don't you? You like Rabbian? What's wrong then?"

Wynflaed sighed and looked up at the sky as if asking the gods for the answer. Turning back to Emma, she patted her hand gratefully. "I expect I want too much," she said, her tone full of self-recrimination. "I want what I suppose is impossible."

"Nothing is impossible."

"Some things are I'm afraid." They walked on a few more paces before she spoke again. "When Eadric grows up he'll be master of his father's lands. He'll have a place on the King's mead-benches. He can be a great man, like his father was." She paused and looked round at the hazy green of the budding woodland. "To bring him here would be to rob him of all that. I'd be making him an outlaw, stripping him of the life and status his father died for."

"Maybe, but you'd be giving him a proper home with his mother and all. And what about Wyngifu, doesn't she deserve a better life?"

"Of course she does, but how can I be sure that I'd be doing it for their sakes" she cried, "and not just for my own happiness?"

"Nonsense! Bairns need their mothers. Bairns need love and care." Emma eyed her scornfully. "Holy Frigg, if anybody should know that it's we who never had mothers."

"Yes, but I'd be denying them so much. Things that you or I could never have had. If I stay out of their lives their future is assured. They'll have rank and wealth; something that was never mine to lose."

Emma pinched her lower lip thoughtfully. "You do realise you're entrusting all this to Rendil?"

"What?"

"You're expecting him to do what's right." She paused, letting her point sink in. "Why should he? Why should he let such wealth go to Eadric? You don't know what lies Rendil might have told. From what you've said about him he seems capable of doing anything to cheat Eadric out of his inheritance."

Wynflaed's brow furrowed and she chewed on her cheek, but then shook her head dismissively. "No, he daren't. Everybody will expect Eadric to follow his father. My disgrace has nothing to do with him. No stain attaches to him. He's the son of a great warrior, a hero, and even Penda respects that."

"Maybe, but does Rendil?"

***

At her home in Badecanwell, Lady Aenflaed gasped at the beauty and quality of the linen runner. She recognised it instantly as Wynflaed's work and reacted with such interest and emotion that pedlar Dawes abandoned his carefully rehearsed sales pitch. Instead he found himself submitting to her close interrogation. She wanted to know how he had come by it, and why it was unfinished.

He told her of Wynflaed's disappearance from Uhtredstun. She was puzzled and clearly uncomfortable about what she heard. She questioned him closely. His prodigious powers of persuasion were ripped ragged as he struggled to convince her that he had neither stolen it nor been part of some plot against Wynflaed. Things were not going well for him. He even began to wish he had never seen the thread-work.

Aenflaed's scornful disapproval was frightening. Blackbird Dawes' ambitions for making his fortune wilted under her questions. He began to believe that he would be lucky to get away from her without being arrested by her brother. Like a whipped dog, he sat at the foot of her stool, listening to her bitter opinions of all those whom she accused of letting Wynflaed down. Her accusations included Lefric, the shire reeve, Modbert the magistrate and even her brother Cenwulf, the Ealdorman, who, she said, "Was too preoccupied with his reproductive organs to notice if his feet were on fire."

Pedlar Dawes groaned despairingly. He felt sure that one could be hanged for even hearing such talk, let alone being its instigation.

Aenflaed ploughed on, careless of his discomfort. She told him that in her opinion Wynflaed's trial had been a wicked lie from start to finish. She said she had tried to persuade her brother to overrule the magistrate, but because Modbert was an old and trusted friend he believed him incapable of deceit. Dawes hid his fears behind a carefully modelled sympathetic frown. He was good at that sort of thing. Years of pretending to agree with buyers had all but destroyed his ability to display any facial expressions but admiration and wonder, and his best one of all, sympathy.

By the time he got away from the great lady and headed out of Badecanwell he felt drained and miserable. After all his trouble, his poke was much lighter than he had hoped. Aenflaed had parted with her gold with all the enthusiasm of a starving dog relinquishing a bone. He felt compelled to peep into his purse to check that the gold coins she had handed over were still there, or had she magically spirited them back into the oyster like grip of her pearly trimmed fist.

With a subtlety and cunning that would have done credit to a wolf, she had made him feel guilt-ridden and miserable for offering the linen piece for sale. Then, while he bumbled around in that unfamiliar emotional territory, she had pummelled him soundly on the matter of price, giving him no chance to mention a figure of his own.

The ears of his horses twitched as he related the whole sad tale to them. They seemed understanding, he thought, though they kept their opinions to themselves. Or did they? Dawes bent to peer close. Did their eyes, those deep windows on their patient natures, glow with just a little amusement?

***

As winter edged towards spring, Eadwin the muler's thoughts turned homeward. Homesickness had weighed on him for months, even though, as he led Snowflake along the road from the Tame-worthig, he knew that he was missing people long gone and places changed beyond recognition. Time had moved on. Everything was different; nothing would ever be the same.

Driving mules could often be a lonely business. He was used to that, but at least in his own country, among familiar hills and dales, being alone had never meant being lonely. The familiar roads and sights had always held a promise, or stirred a memory to keep him company. Working for the King's reeve however, had put him with strangers in unfamiliar lands. And although people were friendly, he often felt alone - an outsider. Even the landscape had nothing to say to him. So it was, on a day of rainbows and showers, that he took his leave of the royal worthig by the River Tame and headed north, homeward to the Peaklands.

Beyond the certainty that he wanted nothing to do with his brother, he had no idea what he would do there. He thought of Wynflaed, remembering their journeys across the Peak and later through the great forest to Uhtredstun. He longed to see her again. She had seldom been out if his thoughts. He could easily go by Uhtredstun on his way to the Peakland, but would it be fitting, he wondered, for him to just drop in on her on some pretext or other? He had no reason to believe that she would not be pleased to see him. In fact, he dared to hope the opposite. Maybe she could suggest some ideas for his future. In any case, it would be so good to see her again. He had missed her more than he could ever tell her.

***

Rabbian's shyness with Wynflaed seemed to increase in direct proportion to his growing affection for her. Emma summed it up with her usual dryness by saying, "By the time he finally gets round to proposing marriage, he'll have stopped seeing you altogether."

To compensate for his inability to face her, he sent her gifts and did things for her all the time. He and his men had built her a fine little house with a window shutter and a wooden floor. It was soon crowded with the gifts he sent her. They occupied every chest, shelf and recess. Over the weeks, he had given her as many needles and silks as any merchant would be proud to call his stock. She had seven glass goblets and three white, fox-fur bedcovers.

One day, as the nymphs of spring took hold of the forest, he appeared unexpectedly at her door.

"Rabbian! Hello — err — oh, is that for me? What a lovely glass goblet. That makes eight now." He gaped at her, his face bright red, a bunch of primroses wilting in his trembling fist. "Do you want to come inside?" she asked.

"It — it don't make sense, us — you — being alone."

Wynflaed stepped back, realising that something of considerable moment was about to occur. She looked him up and down as if she was not entirely able to believe her eyes. "What do you mean?"

"I mean, I think we should marry. I'm fed up of all this."

"Of all what?"

"Of — of all of it. Everything."

"Are they for me?" she asked, fearing he would grind the heads of the flowers to pulp against his chest.

"A man in my position should have a wife." He handed her the drooping posy.

"Yes, but I ..."

"It's not right that I should be alone over there, with you alone over here. You have nobody to care for you, or anything." He tried to ignore the small crowd of curious onlookers, craning behind him.

Blushing hotly, Wynflaed reached out, grabbed his tunic and yanked him inside. "Everybody's looking at you."

"I don't care," he said, his voice taking on the tone of a public announcement. He struggled to remain on view in her doorway. "I came here for you and I'm not leaving without …" At this point his confidence seemed to falter slightly. He quickly stepped inside and shut the door. "I love you. It's driving me mad. I never felt like this before. It's awful — well not awful — I don't mean it's awful. I mean it's ..."

Wynflaed sat him on her bed. She kept her gaze on him as she dropped the primroses into her latest blue glass goblet, teased them briskly into a display and gave them water from a pitcher.

"I shouldn't have come, should I?" Rabbian said. "You're going to be upset, aren't you? I've got it all wrong, haven't I?"

Wynflaed gathered up a cup and a flask of ale from a side table. She put the cup in his hand and filled it to the brim, her face taking on a despairing frown. "What in Thunner's name do you think you're doing?" she asked him, adding flatly. "Are you hungry?"

"It's Theel's fault. He keeps on at me to wed you. I knew you didn't want..."

"Didn't what?" she snapped. "You don't know anything of the sort. I asked if you were hungry."

"I've eaten," he told her, miserably. "I knew you'd be all — all — like this."

"Like what?" she cried. "You come swanning up to my door, a gaping audience behind you, and demand we get married. I'm supposed to be swept off my feet like a little virgin. Then you have the damn cheek to tell me it wasn't even your idea."

"Now look here!" he said. "You're supposed to say yes — or even bloody no. I don't have to hear this. I love you. I want to marry you. You don't have ..."

"It's no, then." she shouted, tears suddenly flowing down her cheeks. She began to cry, shaking out great sobs as she tried to speak. "There, feel better now? You've got your answer, so you can stop sending me damn glass goblets. The house is full of the things."

"Goblets!"

"I can't marry you," she wailed, falling into his arms, her face streaked with tears. "I thought you understood."

"Why not? And don't say, your children. I know you're worried about them, but you love me. I'm sure of it."

"Who says I do?"

"You do. I know it," he said, holding her at arms length. "I say that you love me, so does Emma, so does Theel, so does half the fort besides. Tell me you don't." He glared defiantly into her face. "Go on, deny it."

Wynflaed's body sagged against him. She pressed her face into the soft leather of his tunic and let her arms encircle him lightly. "It's not just about me and you," she said softly, her misery catching in her throat. "If it were that simple, I'd marry you or be your mistress, or anything you wanted. I wouldn't care what."

"Do it then," he whispered, burying his face in her hair. "We can overcome anything, if we try. Your life is for more than just your children, it's for you too. I know you want to do your best for them, and that's wonderful, but you have a life too."

"I can't. My husband fought and died for his bench-place. His name means something, and when the time comes his son's name must count for something too." She looked up into his face, her eyes red. "I do love you. I want you too, and if you'll have me without marriage, I'll gladly come to your bed, but one day I will leave it. I can never marry you, nor bring my children into your house."

Rabbian pushed her away gently and stepped back from her. For several long moments he studied her thoughtfully, disappointment carved into his face. Then, turning slowly, he left without a word.

**

Sighting Uhtredstun through a sunlit haze of spring buds and pussy willows struck Eadwin like a home coming. Memories crowded in on him, bringing a sparkle to his eyes. His heart soared as he saw old Horse Ebell leading a foal to the pond near the spot where he had camped so long ago. The old horsener greeted him as though he had never been away. "Well give us an 'and, then. Don't just stand there gawping. Fetch yonder cob over here."

"Aye — and it's nice to see you too, Ebell," Eadwin said wryly. "Thanks for the welcome."

"You'll think a lot less of your welcome, when I tells you all."

"What?"

"She did for 'erself," he said, a tear rolling down his grizzled cheek. "Poor little mare. She were out of her mind with grief and guilt."

"What? Who?"

"Little Buhe, bless her heart. She hung 'er self."

Eadwin felt his legs give way beneath him. He grabbed his mule's neck and steadied himself. "Holy Mother Frigg bless us. Is Wynflaed all right?"

"Wynflaed? She's been gone two years. That's what it were all about." He released the foal and began coiling its lunge with exaggerated care. The animal stamped and splashed playfully across the gravel bed of the pond. "Come on, lad, I'll tell thee all about it. Old Grim knows how tired I am of saying nothing to nobody everyday."

***

Emma was furious with Wynflaed when she learned what had happened between her and Rabbian. As the days passed, fury became despair, enveloping them both in its gloom. Even the best of the season could not lift their heads. On every side the forest glowed with vibrant greens and fresh new blossoms. Birdsong at each day's dawning made even the most sluggardly eager to rise. Around the fort, Rabbian's ingas went about their daily chores with a new spirit, ready to break into song or laughter at the merest provocation. All save Wynflaed and Emma. They slunk about as if yoked to winter.

Their heads finally lifted when they heard the curious news that Rabbian had stripped his treasury and marched off with his brother and a dozen of his most trusted hearth companions. Speculation was rife, though no one knew what to make of the news. Had he left for good? Why had he taken his silver and valuables? Had he sailed across the Frisian Sea to his Frankish trading partners? No one knew. Reactions varied from disbelief to fury. Warriors he had left behind gathered at the heorden's iron bound doors, now hanging wide open, and stared inside at the empty floor and shelves.

***

Eadwin did not linger at Uhtredstun. The mental image he had treasured of Wynflaed, safe and comfortable with her friends, lay shattered. While he had complained and felt sorry for himself, she had been betrayed and dragged into slavery. He had eaten in the king's kitchen, lived on the best and slept in the warmth of well-thatched halls. She, he guessed, would have been lucky to live in as much comfort as a stray dog. He knew that wite-theow were less than dogs. Nobody cared if they lived or died. Whatever else he did with his life, he told himself, he had to find her and rescue her. There was now nothing uncertain or pointless about his life. He had a new purpose. It would be difficult and dangerous, but he would find Wynflaed and somehow lift her out of slavery.

Bidding goodbye to old Ebell, he set off for the Peakland, his mind sifting ideas. He would start by going to By-Streams. If Maud was still there, she might have news of Wynflaed, or know of others who had seen or heard of her.

Darkness crept up on him unnoticed, forcing him to stop for the night when the road vanished into the Peak forest. He unyoked Snowflake and let her wander to nibble the spring grass. Absently, he watched her shadowy shape as he unwound his bedroll and settled down for the night. For hours, he lay tormented by images of the horrors he imagined Wynflaed subject too. The suffering of convict slaves was well known. He had seen the wretches beaten and brutalised, shuffling along, roped together, or digging latrines and ditches. At crossroads' gibbets he had heard the cries of recaptured runaways, hung up to die slowly.

He had to find her, but he would need silver to buy her freedom. Sebbi would help, and Eofar must be made to. He thought of selling Snowflake. He could also sell himself into bonded service for a few years, or better still he could secretly smelt out some silver from the lead at By-Streams. He knew how it was done; he would make Eofar help him.

....

CHAPTER TWENTY-SIX

Gutty did not like her new lodger. After only one night under her roof, she regretted allowing him bed and board. Her other paying guests, a garrulous horse healer and couple of fleece buyers, were a good-hearted trio. They had little on their minds but profit and a good time. The newcomer, however, was shifty, sour and secretive. She soon decided he was up to no good. Even so, she felt a slight twinge of guilt for taking a dislike to him so hastily. After all, she reminded herself reproachfully, everybody is entitled to keep their business to themselves, if they must. And, if they did not want to be drinking, dancing and singing, they should be free to choose. No woman in her right mind, and certainly not Gutty, would claim that an attachment to such diversions was necessarily the mark of a good man. She had known fine-voiced drinkers, as light on their feet as a king's fool, who punched their wives senseless after a few drinks. A good man, she had learned, was hard to spot, drunk or sober. As her late mother had put it, "Even the best-looking cloak can have a rotten lining.".

Finding nothing she liked about him, she contented herself by listing his failings. The most annoying was his mystery. His refusal to disclose anything about himself, let alone his purpose in Holmesfelt she found intensely galling. Despite teasing, wheedling and probing, she had learned only that his name was Hunwald, and he could not enjoy fatty food because of heartburn. He had told her that he expected to be lodging with her for two days — no longer.

From his manner and dress it was easy to spot that he was an old soldier. She guessed he was waiting to see

Rendil, having noticed how he constantly watched the comings and goings at the hall. Judging by his eagerness and impatience, she assumed that he expected to do well from his visit. That just made her doubly determined to solve the mystery of his purpose. Exasperated, she waited until he sat down for his evening meal. In her typically forthright manner, she put her suspicions to him. "You're waiting for Rendil, aren't you? He could be away another two or three days yet. What do you want with him? I might be able to help you. I know everybody."

The old soldier did not lift his eyes from his non-fat broth. Leaving her fuming with frustration, he carried on eating as if she were not even in the room.

***

Eadwin's heart sank when he arrived at By-Streams. He found it deserted. Only ghosts and memories occupied its houses. Little more than two years had passed since Wynflaed had been taken away, yet the atmosphere of neglect and abandonment was all-pervading. At the top of the village, he found the hall stripped of its hangings, lamps and hearth wares. Benches and trestles lay upturned and broken, Wynflaed's loom stood unthreaded, like a gaping gate to nowhere. The chests that had lined the walls were gone, leaving only their imprints on the earth floor.

Angry and fighting off a growing sense of uselessness, he turned away and took the stony path down to Bell Delfan. Near its entrance, where once gossiping groups of women and children had dressed the lead ore, a green haze of weeds coated the striking floor. All was now silent, save for the calls of whirling jackdaws. Looking about, sickened and dismayed, he wondered why Rendil had gone to such trouble to get By-Streams if only to kill it. It made no sense.

Unknown to him, the rag-tag families illegally working the mine and its spoil heaps, had run off and hidden at his approach. They began drifting back to their gleaning when they saw that he too was probably just another trespasser, like them. Eadwin sauntered over to them, hiding all signs of urgency and purpose so as not to scare them off. They eyed him sullenly.

"Where'd they all go?" he asked, casually waving at the deserted village. "I was looking for the house-keeper, the one called Maud."

A young woman with shining red hair squinted up at him against the sunlight. She was pretty and fully aware of the power of her charms on men. Sitting on the ground, her naked legs spread wide either side of a small pile of undressed ore, she made no effort to cover herself. "You used to live here, didn't you?" she said.

Trying not to look at her shapely thighs, Eadwin studied her face, wondering how she had recognised him. He did not know her. "Do you know where Maud is?" he asked, adding, "You do know her?"

The woman's dirt-smudged face was spattered with freckles. She smiled and shrugged, making her plump breasts wobble invitingly against her threadbare woollen shift. "You did, didn't you? You were one of them who lived here. I seen you and that old white mule afore."

"Yes, I did - ages ago."

The young woman seemed satisfied. She climbed to her feet and moved close to him. "They've all gone. There isn't nobody here now but us."

"And Maud? Where'd she go? Do you know the woman I mean?"

She tilted her head and reaching inside her dress slid a hand across her breast into her armpit. Eadwin briefly imagined the damp warmth of that soft, downy place and felt a stirring in his groin. "Are you her man?" she asked.

He nodded.

The young woman squirmed with delight. "Some went with the new master, you know, the limping misery with the stick," she said, adding vaguely, "At least, I think so. I don't know if she did or not."

"A limping man? Does he still come here?"

"Not for a year or more," she said. "There's only that big fellow what comes now. I seen you here with him once. He's big and hunched over. He comes all the time. He's always creeping about in the caves and popping up out of the ground all over the place."

Eadwin was sure she meant Eofar, and a chilling sense of things unfinished washed over him. "Does he speak to you? Do you know what he comes for?"

The woman eyed him curiously. "No, he just creeps about," she said.

Eadwin thanked her and headed down into the stony dale below By-Streams. At the river, he took the road east, towards Rendil's homestead at Holmesfelt. The image of his brother wandering forlornly through the desolation that his greed and treachery had brought about played in his mind.

Eadwin had decided to seek out Gutty. Perhaps she would know where Maud was. She might even have word of Wynflaed. A surge of anticipation welled up inside him, and despite the risk of being caught by Rendil the thought of seeing Gutty again cheered him.

"Good old Gutty," he murmured to himself. She would help him. She was sure to join him in any scheme to up-end Rendil. He could ask for no better ally. Although, he acknowledged with a lascivious chuckle, she would exact her price. Prurient warmth flooded over him as he thought of it - quite unlike his cold terror the first time Guthrum's widow had dragged him to her bed.

***

Rabbian returned after three weeks, though without his treasure. Wynflaed watched him march through the narrow gate at the head of his hearth troops. He looked grim-faced and determined, and though he dutifully acknowledged the welcome of his ingas, there a steely preoccupation to his manner.

Wynflaed studied his face, but she was unable to decide what his mood or motive might be. Instead of going straight to his hall as he usually did after a trip, he strode up the gentle rise towards her house with the entire settlement in train. Wynflaed felt suddenly conspicuous, as if her clothes had fallen off and she was standing naked on her threshold. She tried to look unperturbed, but her hands fluttered awkwardly in front of her as if wondering which bits of her person to conceal from public gaze.

Rabbian came up to her and stopped. At his shoulder the crowd clattered to a whispering standstill. "You look lovely — like the spring." He spoke without a hint of romance in his tone.

For the briefest moment Wynflaed hung her head coyly then, lifting her face, looked him in the eye. "We've — I've — missed you. I'm glad you're back - safe."

"Aye safe — and different too," he replied smiling.

"Different?"

"You are now addressing a loyal thegn of Penda, my lord king of Mercia."

"You!" She gasped in disbelief. "How?" The answer struck her even as she asked him. "You paid tribute to him. That's why you emptied your treasury."

"Aye, and he was mighty glad to recognise me too." He pulled a roll of vellum from inside his tunic and waved it aloft for everyone to see. "King Penda conferred full and legal title to all that I asked for, all the lands and woods about here. Furthermore, I am made his high reeve of these parts and protector of his roads and the travellers upon them. All who call yourselves my people are hereby made free and shriven of all past deeds and misdeeds, all indictments are remitted."

"You said you would never kneel to a king. You said you loved being your own man."

"True, I did, but now there's something I love even more." He looked at her, his eyes full of longing. "I'm no longer outside the law," he whispered. "I have a place on Penda's benches. Perhaps it's not quite as elevated as your husband's was, but it's a place of honour, nonetheless." He stepped forward and gently took her into his arms. "Marry me, Flaedy. Your bairns can live with us now and no shame on them. They will never want for anything. My name is as good as any in Mercia." He clutched her hands to his lips. "I love you more than a man can stand. Marry me. I know you loved Wulfric, and maybe you can never love me as much. But I don't care, I'll take what I can get."

* * *

Gutty shrugged off her shift and dived naked into bed beside Eadwin. "Oh, you're a welcome sight, young Eadwin. I'm ready for a good man. It's been too long."

"Have you had no handsome lodgers then?"

Gutty fetched him a hefty clout to the head. "Don't be cheeky," she said, giggling. "I've had my chances, but despite what you may have heard, I don't just leap into bed with anybody."

"What about that old boy I saw earlier, is he staying tonight?"

Gutty's face darkened. "That's a queer body that one. I'd like to see the back of him. He's from somewhere south. He's all secrets and scheming and skulking." She stretched over him to snuff out the lamp with her fingers and snuggled closer. Eadwin's penis proudly pushed against the bedclothes. He wished she would stop talking and grab hold of it.

"He won't say a thing," Gutty said. "All I know is he's called Hunwald and he's an old soldier – one of Penda's."

She took a firm hold of Eadwin's rampant organ and squeezed it angrily, venting her disapproval of her secretive lodger. "He's the most, tight lipped, miserable old sod I've ever known. He's been here a week, and I know no more about him now than when he arrived."

Eadwin winced and struggled to peel her fingers from his member. "Grim's cods, Gutty!"

She laughed apologetically and cooed into his ear. "Momma kiss it better."

Eadwin sighed happily as she slid under the covers. At least she'll stop talking for a while, he thought, squirming ecstatically.

In the darkness, the outer door scraped across the earthen floor. A figure was dimly silhouetted by starlight in the doorway. It vanished as the door closed again. "Grim's balls! Haven't you no lamps, woman? I can't see a bloody thing."

"I've got company, you old sour puss," yelled Gutty, spitting out Eadwin's penis. "Can't you show some fucking manners?"

***

At dawn the following morning Eadwin woke to find Gutty curled in his arms, her cheek on his chest, her hair, free of its braids, spilling across his stomach. He squinted down at her fondly, and decided to leave her undisturbed a little while longer. He thought how sweet she looked in the filtered glow of morning that lit the room. So different from the strong, confident woman she portrayed in the full light of day. It tugged at his heart, seeing her so vulnerable. He wondered if perhaps, in some strange way, he did love her after all. And what did she think of him? She made no secret of her liking for sex with him. That was what she enjoyed. She never spoke tenderly, yet he had the feeling that she would probably sacrifice a great deal to help him if he needed it. Wasn't that a sort of love? Maybe under all that brash and bawdy toughness she felt much more for him than she was willing to admit. Was such a thing possible? And what of him being half her age, could he really love her in that way?

At the far side of the room, Hunwald was stirring. He raised his head, mumbling unintelligibly, broke wind and started coughing. Peering sourly at Gutty's great bed, he tried to focus as his cough subsided. "You were at it long enough last night. I thought I'd never get no sleep."

"Yeah, me too, but good work can't be rushed."

"Huh, well she'd be a good judge of that sort of work," Hunwald said. "From what I hear, she sees more cocks than a pissing stone."

Eadwin glared, but smothered his annoyance. He slipped out of bed, trying not to disturb Gutty. Hunwald ran his gaze quickly over the younger man's hard, muscular body, absently comparing the size of his penis with his own ragged organ, and then dragged himself out of bed. Like a pair of sleepwalkers, they stumbled out to the yard and relieved themselves. Eadwin then staggered to the yard cistern, ducked his head in it and swilled his face.

"I'm Eadwin."

Hunwald splashed his face and shivered, pinching dripping water from his nose. "Hunwald," he growled and limped indoors over the sharp gravel yard to dry and dress himself.

Eadwin followed, hugging himself against the morning chill. "Are you just passing through or what?" he asked, adding with a chuckle, "I suppose you know that you're driving her mad because you won't tell her anything."

Hunwald grimaced, his chin on his chest as he belted his brecs. "It's got nowt to do with her, nor you neither for that matter." He looked up defiantly. "Not that it's a big secret. I just don't like women who think they can waggle their tits and make you do anything they want."

"Not even hers," joked Eadwin, feeling ashamed of the remark, even as he said it. But he had hoped it might help to ease him into Hunwald's confidence.

"Aghh, a tit's a tit," Hunwald snarled. "When you've seen one, you've seen 'em both." He grinned at Eadwin and went on, "When you've had as many women as me they can't ring my nose like some dozy ox. I can get a woman anytime, do whatever I want with her, and then leave her when I feel like it."

Eadwin looked up pityingly from fastening his boots. "But surely you've been touched at some time? I mean, some woman must 'ave ..."

"Nah, not likely," sneered Hunwald. "But no, I tell a lie, there once was a woman who changed my life."

Gutty sat up sleepily in her bed. "I hope she did it with a gelding thong," she said, rubbing her eyes vigorously, making her naked breasts wobble. "Your trouble is you've never known goodness from a woman," she went, "and that's because you're the sort of arsehole women hide it from. No woman in her right mind would want you for longer than it takes."

"Yeah well, fuck you too," Hunwald said. "You see what I mean?" He turned to Eadwin, his palms up. "I always winkle out the truth of their natures."

Gutty expressed herself by farting. Eadwin laughed and sat on the end of her bed wafting a hand before his face. "But what about this woman who changed your life?" he asked, steering Hunwald back to his point.

"Well, she's not quite done it yet, but with Wyrd's favour she soon will."

Gutty was pulling on her day shift, only her bottom and legs were visible as she asked, "Where is she then? How's she going to do all this?"

Hunwald grinned, and carefully unrolled the top of his brecs. He unpinned a small fold of cloth from the waist band and slipped his hand into a secret pocket. A look of triumph lit his face as he gripped something and withdrew his hand. "With this," he announced, opening his hand to reveal a gold ring.

Colour drained from Gutty's face. She moved stiffly towards his upturned palm, her eyes fixed on the ring. Eadwin's jaw dropped too. He had seen barely half a dozen finger-rings in his life and could probably recall what each of them looked like, but none more vividly than this one. It was given to Wulfric by his father. On the day he had received it, Wulfric had proudly showed it off to him. He had even let Eadwin try it on his finger. The memory of that moment crashed into his mind with such force that he had to stop himself from vomiting.

Gutty knew the ring too. She recalled that the old master had bespoke one for each of his sons. Rendil still wore his. How did Hunwald come to have Wulfric's?

Eadwin's mind was racing. He was remembering the day Wulfric had given the ring to Wynflaed to hold for little Eadric. She had kept it on a cord around her neck and given Wulfric her blue-gem stone in exchange, the one he had brought from the little slave girl years before. Dozens of possibilities of how it could have come into Hunwald's possession flashed through his mind, none making any sense. Fury rose inside him. His emotions suddenly snapped. He pounced on the old soldier and grabbed his throat. They rolled around on the floor in a riot of tumbling furniture, bedding and flailing fists.

"You bastard!" Eadwin screamed. "You thieving bastard. Where did you get it?"

Despite his youth, Eadwin was no match for the old warrior's practised moves. Hunwald's surprising speed enabled him to twist free and turn, pinning Eadwin firmly. A knife blade flashed in his hand. Hunwald pressed it with seeming ease through Eadwin's struggling fingers and pushed the blade towards his throat. Cold terror quenched Eadwin's rage. Death was only an instant away. He was at his mercy, but then he groaned and slumped like an empty sack. Eadwin saw Gutty standing over him, white faced, her eyes wide and wild. In her hand was an iron trivet from the hearth. A trickle of blood ran from Hunwald's hair and splashed onto Eadwin's forehead.

"Holy Mother! I think I killed him."

By mid morning, Gutty had bathed and bandaged Hunwald's head. Despite lots of blood and a great deal of fuss, he had suffered only a flesh wound.

"I don't know why you waste your salves on the old turd," said Eadwin. "He was gunna slit my throat."

"You were trying to kill me." Hunwald winced at the effort of speaking.

Gutty pulled a face, showing her impatience. "Shut up the pair of you. It's over and nobody killed nobody, thank Frigg, but I'll kill both of you if I don't get some answers. Where did you get that ring?"

Hunwald panicked and grabbed at his secret pocket. In all the excitement, he had forgotten about the ring. He rummaged frantically but failed to find it. Scowling, Gutty handed it to him. He nodded, breathing a sigh of relief.

"I don't think he trusts us," Eadwin said.

"I don't! Why should I? You tried to steal it" He glared at them in turn, his bristly chin jutting pugnaciously. "And I don't have to tell you nothing, neither. I came by it fair and square," he said. He held it up before their eyes, before slipping it admiringly onto his finger.

"Well, if that's true, you won't mind telling us all about it," said Eadwin. "Only the crooked are scared to speak."

"I'm not crooked and I don't have to tell you nothing, neither."

Impatience gnawed at Gutty's insides. She saw that Eadwin's approach was just annoying Hunwald. If she left it to him, the old rogue would never talk. She decided that a little tongue loosening was called for. With a disapproving glance for Eadwin, she fetched a flask of mead to the hearth. With various facial contortions, she mimed that Eadwin should leave matters to her. Eadwin got the message, and scowling sullenly, fell silent. Gutty poured Hunwald a large cup of the sweet, heady mead.

"I think we all need this," she said, handing Eadwin an almost empty horn beaker and taking a similar one for herself. Hunwald snatched up his brimming cup and drank deeply, with neither grace nor gratitude. Gutty and Eadwin pretended to do the same. Hunwald drained his cup and smacking his lips, held it out for more.

Gutty obliged and watched him drain that just as quickly. Before long he was talking freely. He explained how he expected to get a generous cache of silver for the ring from Wulfric himself. When Gutty told him Wulfric was dead, he rose triumphantly from his stool and swaying like a great tree told her that he was not. "I saw him taken prisoner at Bebba's city."

"You can't have," Gutty cried. "He would've been ransomed by now, if he'd lived."

"Look, woman! I know Wulfric like I know my own hand," Hunwald said. "I saw him taken. He was alive."

Eadwin's heart was racing joyfully at the news, but he was still confused; it did not explain how Hunwald came to have the ring. "But Wulfric didn't have the ring. He gave it to his son, I saw him do it …"

"I don't know about that. I got it from a slave -an army whore. I don't know nothing about how she got it."

"You stole it from her?"

"No, I didn't. She gave it to me."

"Oh yeah, we're supposed to believe that. Why would she?"

"Because I'd bought her freedom and she was grateful. We were going to be married after the campaign," he said, enjoying the generosity of spirit his lies implied. "She wanted me to buy a farm with the ring. You see, she was having my child."

"Where did she get it?"

"I don't know. Unfortunately she died. The bairn too."

"I'm sorry …," said Eadwin. "Wyrd can be cruel."

Gutty did not believe his story, though she saw that Eadwin was almost in tears. "How did she get the ring? She must have told you. Nobody gets a ring like that without some sort of explanation."

"All I can say is that I took it from her – the woman I was to marry. How she got it, I don't know, but I recognised it as Wulfric's as soon as I saw it. That's why I came here. I thought he'd be here. I'm amazed that you think he's dead."

Eadwin was stunned. Was the dead woman Wynflaed? It could be no other. This sickening realisation flung his mind into turmoil. In an instant he had been faced with a completely new and terrible reality. Wynflaed was now dead and Wulfric was evidently alive. The world was tossed on its head. Hunwald's words, truth, lies or half-truths, were incredible. They jumbled and shattered joy and grief in a storm of confusion, setting up a completely new set of possibilities.

Gutty was devastated. She sat on her bed in a daze. Could it really have been Wynflaed? How had she died? Did Hunwald have any part in her death? And what of Wulfric? Hunwald's words had the ring of truth about them. It made absolute sense that the Northumbrians would snatch a rich man if they could. Such a man's ransom would be worth a hundred times his slave price. Wulfric was well-known. He'd be a rich prize. But if so, why hadn't he come home?

The notion that Rendil might have received a ransom demand and deliberately ignored it flashed into Gutty's mind. He was certainly capable of it. But where was Wulfric now?

Eadwin leaned forward, his head in his hands, as the weight of his new knowledge pressed down on him. Beside him sat Gutty, staring dumbly at the floor. Wynflaed's death, seemingly at the very moment of Wulfric's rebirth, had bounced them from joy to sorrow. And as if to emphasise her contempt for them, Wyrd had ensured that just as enslavement in some far, unknown place had been Wynflaed's lot, it might now be Wulfric's. The exchange was brutally symmetrical. The dead were the living, the living were dead. Hunwald watched them through a drunken haze, unaware and too drunk to comprehend the vicious twist he had dealt them.

Vengeance pulled at Eadwin's heart, as his shock gradually subsided. Was Hunwald Wynflaed's killer? He watched him leering drunkenly from a stool opposite him. In a blinding fury Eadwin suddenly leapt at him and clamped his fingers around his throat. He squeezed on the old soldier's windpipe, choking off his air. Shocked and drunk, Hunwald struggled weakly, his hands clawing ineffectively. Gutty watched unmoved at first, her heart and mind closed to the older man's drunken struggle, but then she jumped up and pulled Eadwin from him. "No! No, let him go! Don't make a murderer of yourself. Besides, there's more to do. We need him alive."

Eadwin allowed Gutty to push him aside, as Hunwald dropped to his knees, coughing and spluttering.

"Why? What more have we to do with him?"

"If Wulfric really is alive somewhere, we might be the only ones who can help him."

Eadwin sat on the bed, gaping at her in disbelief. "Can you hear yourself, woman?" he cried. "Help Wulfric. Huh, have you any idea how much gold that would take? When I set out to come here, all I was looking for was enough silver to buy Wynflaed's freedom - a convict slave. If I wasn't being so stupid, I would have realised that even that is more silver than a man like me can hope to raise in several lifetimes. What you are talking about now is completely different. Ransoming a high-ranking warrior will need a mountain of gold. Even his wergild is a hundred times that of an ordinary warrior. How do you expect us to get that much gold, even if we knew where he was?"

Gutty stared back at him solemnly. "A lot easier than raising the paltry price for a convict slave," she replied. "Don't you see?"

Eadwin stared blankly. "All I can see is that we need a heap of gold, not far short of a king's ransom, and even that is useless if nobody knows where he is."

"Wulfric's a rich warrior. He can repay his own ransom once he's free. His old friends and comrades will gladly put up the gold, and even the worst of them will know they'll get it back. Even the Ealdorman will pay." She jabbed Hunwald with her foot. "We need to keep this slimy old sod alive. He's got to tell his story to the Shire Reeve." She put her hand fondly on Eadwin's arm. "Seeing that gold ring in his greasy hands proves it's too late for Wynflaed. She must surely be dead, and we'll probably never know how she died. You may be right that he killed her, but I don't think so. Now, we must concentrate on finding Wulfric. When he comes home, he'll clear her name and make Rendil pay for what he's done. We owe Wynflaed that much at least."

Eadwin flashed a worried glance. "But that means going to the shire reeve. How do we know he'll believe us?"

"He'll believe us, don't fear, especially when he sees the ring and hears what this slimy little sod has to say." She paused and looked at him, a sly smile coming to her face. "Anyway, the shire reeve won't eat you. Old Lefric is a friend of mine. He's a very nice man too, especially if I jog his memory a little bit."

Eadwin frowned. "Don't tell me you ..."

"Maybe I did, maybe I didn't," she said coyly. "But I'll make damn sure he thinks he did."

***

A festive atmosphere put a smile on every face at Rabbian's settlement. The contents of his treasury had made legitimate freemen of every soul there, even the lowliest. Only Wynflaed was not smiling. "You shouldn't have made it all so public," she sobbed. "No matter what I do or say now, everybody will blame me."

"I've done everything you wanted," said Rabbian. "I have a good name at Penda's tables. I can give you security and position." He gazed skyward, as if at some distant deity and wove his fingers together in frustration. "Gods show me what more can I do."

"You could have talked to me first. I could have saved you all this."

"You said you loved me. You said you've not been happier since ..."

"I do love you. I meant every word," she said. "But it's not about love. It never was." She stamped about her tiny house, wringing her hands. Rabbian sat on the bed. There was not room enough for both of them to pace.

"But you know I'll have to go soon. I have to face Rendil and win back what he took from me. You've known this from the start. Do you expect me to abandon my children, my dreams?"

"Of course not, but now, your children can come here. I can fetch them and teach Rendil a lesson at the same time."

"No, it can't be done that way. It must be done properly — legally. I want the Shire Reeve to deal with him. I want him to stand before the bench with everyone watching, exactly as he made me do. I want the full weight of the law bearing down on him. I know force of arms would get me my children back in an instant, but it would leave too much unfinished. There must be no doubts, no stain on their names. Rendil must not be physically harmed, not a hair of his head. Believe me, Rabbian, I've thought this through a thousand times. The worst I can do to him is to beat him with the law."

"But I could crush him."

"No! He won't get off that easy," she said. "For the rest of his life I want him to face each day knowing that I beat him. I can only do that with the law. If I let you deal with him, he would just say I was your whore, paying you a whore's services. That would suit him perfectly. He'd be able to claim that I was no better than he said I was. That would soil Wulfric's memory and Eadric's name. She reached for his hand and pulled him down to sit beside her. "But I do love you, and I have been happier with you than I thought I could ever be again."

"That sounds like an ending," he said, pulling his hand away from hers. "You're leaving me. I've gone too far, haven't I? I've chased you away."

"No, it's not that."

"Asking you to marry me has forced you to make up your mind. Instead of winning a wife, I'm losing you altogether."

"No! When it's done I'll come back here. I love you. I need you, and I do want to marry you. Please believe me."

Moisture sparkled in his eyes. He hugged her close, his arms enfolding her gently. "I wish I could be sure, but life has taught me to always expect less."

"I will come back," she promised. "I want you as much as you want me. I've felt it from the start. When I'm not with you I feel such longings. When we're together I want it to go on forever. I will come back."

He hung his head sadly. "I know you mean it now, Flaedy," he told her. "The trouble is life often gets in the way."

"Let's go somewhere," she said. "That hut where Theel found Emma and I. We could be alone for a few days. We could dream and make some new memories that are purely ours alone."

***

Hunwald sat astride Snowflake, his hands tied behind his back. Gutty rode her own mount, a large red mare with a wall eye and a permanently startled expression on its broad face. Eadwin found himself aroused by the sight of her, her thighs occasionally coming into view as the breeze played with the hem of her dress. It made it worthwhile, having to follow her on a skittish pony she had borrowed for him.

The journey to the shire reeve's house at Badecanwell would take a long day. They would arrive much too late to petition, and so would have to spend a night on the road, so as to be early the following morning. The prospect of being in Badecanwell troubled Eadwin. He decided he'd try to avoid his family, partly because he did not want to risk involving them, but mostly because he could still not bring himself to face Eofar, especially in light of Wynflaed's death.

***

As she and Rabbian crept from the settlement and headed into the woods, Wynflaed felt light and as gay as a child at play. Her heart was racing madly and she giggled for no apparent reason. Trotting breathlessly beside him she tried not to laugh, relishing the sense of mischief which flooded over her.

It was dawn. The birds were waking to fill the air with their crystal music. Everything was perfect, she thought, and glancing up at Rabbian shot him a mischievous grin. "What a dawn. I've never heard so many birds."

"It's wonderful. And so are you. You look lovely. I can hardly believe we're doing this. I feel as if I don't deserve it."

She craned up to kiss his cheek. "I know, but you were all I could get," she joked, giggling and running off.

He chased her, feeling childishly free. She had arrived in his life just at a point when he had thought he was satisfied; he was successful, and surrounded by friends and folk who needed and respected him. But she had opened his life up to so much more, he could barely believe all he now wanted from it. Everything seemed new and interesting, colours brighter, birdsong more musical. It was as if she had stripped a veil from his senses, awakening thoughts and emotions he had long let slumber. He felt he was the luckiest of men and could wish for nothing more. She was everything. Her happiness was all there was. And now, for a little while at least, she was entirely his.

They talked endlessly as they walked, hardly noticing anything but each other. After a while they stopped and looked around. Apart from birdsong there was no sound. In every direction huge trees moved gently in a soft breeze beneath a cloudless sky. The sun had climbed towards noon, spreading deep green shadows at the foot of every tree.

Wynflaed ran ahead to a sheltered spot beside a stream. She threw herself down in the long grass and let her feet touch the water's rippling surface. Rabbian stretched out beside her. He kicked off his boots and splashed his feet in the water. Wynflaed took off her shoes and dangled her feet next to his. Dappled sunlight filled the woods with emerald shadows and flitting green ghosts. Gem-like flowers splashed across the forest floor in brilliant pools of light. The warm, scented air vibrated with the buzz of insects, their wings sparkling in the sunlight.

"What are you thinking?" he asked, his voice softened by agreeable weariness.

She seemed to hear his question from a great distance. It surprised her, so that she found herself wondering what indeed had she been thinking. "I don't know — nothing I think. I can't remember." She was not being entirely truthful. It was the memory of a hot summer's day at By-Streams. She and Wulfric had paddled in a noisy brook and made love beneath gently swaying lime trees.

"Planning for Eadric and Wyngifu coming?" Rabbian said, wishing he could read her mind.

She rolled onto her stomach so that she could look down into his face. "Won't it be wonderful?" she said. "We'll be a family again. Well not again — I mean not you — oh gods! I'm sorry. I mean – well you know what I mean. We'll become a family and you will be its head."

The slip of the tongue did not offend him. Such things were inevitable, he thought. Indeed, he found comfort in it. It showed she was thinking of him as her husband. She was already sewing him into the continuous tapestry of her life. He kissed her forehead. "If I'm its head, you will be its heart and soul."

She buried her face in his neck and clung to him. "We must have a baby straight away. I want to give you a son. You do want children, don't you? We've never talked about it."

"Hey slow down. We've got the rest of our lives," he said laughing softly. "Of course I want children, but I'm getting two to start with, aren't I? We should give them a chance to settle first. It will be a lot for them to get used to."

His thoughtfulness filled her with emotion. "You're such a lovely man." She clambered on top of him and kissed him firmly on the mouth.

"You missed out handsome and virile," he joked, as the kiss ended.

"You're certainly handsome," she replied. "In fact you're even pretty in a womanish sort of way, but that's the problem." She bit her lip looking suddenly stricken by worry. "You don't look very virile. Perhaps you can't ..."

"Well in that case, my lady ..." He rolled her onto her back and threw his leg across her. "The least I can do is put my lady's mind at rest." He kissed her lightly at first, chuckling softly as she laughed, allowing him to pull clumsily at her clothes. But his passion quickly rose as he felt the warmth and generosity of her response. She pressed up to meet his mouth, her hands pulling him down to her, her tongue forcefully caressing his.

"I love you, Flaedy. You have made me so happy."

"I love you — I do — I really do," she said, releasing the cord at her waist and freeing her shift. "I'm sure now. I want you. I think I'm sure now."

Sliding his arm beneath her, he lifted her slightly to pull up her dress and push it off over her head. As it fell away she smiled and relaxed across his arm, offering herself unconditionally. He looked down upon the flawless, honeyed pink of her skin and let his reverent gaze wander over her beauty. She was the loveliest thing he had ever seen. His mind traced over the smooth, silky swells of her breasts, ornamented with tiny sunlit beads of sweat, and across the golden filaments of hair on the soft contours of her belly down to the long tapering loveliness of her legs and rose-pink feet.

Lowering her gently into the sun warmed grass, he kissed her on the temple and brushed his lips across her cheeks, her eyelids and nose, and onto her waiting mouth. He pressed his lips gently upon hers, letting them sink into their softness like hands into blood-warm dough. Her tongue moved around his, caressing it slowly, sensually, rolling with his like magical sea-borne lovers.

She helped him to shake off his tunic and loose the belt at his waist so he could kick his legs free of his brecs. He felt the hot sun on his buttocks, and the soft breeze stirring the hairs on his legs. His shins bathed in the cool, moist grass, contrasting with the warm, silky dampness of her skin against his thighs and stomach. Moving his mouth across her breasts, he nibbled gently at her hardening nipples. Soft new grasses, sticky with sap, brushed against his balls and thighs. He buried one hand deep in her hair as he slid the other behind her waist and lifted her pelvis. Her fingers had found his penis and were working it firmly, guiding it towards the hunger in her groin. As he felt her thighs lift to his hips he pushed his buttocks forward, penetrating her with powerful smoothness. She gasped beside his ear, releasing a little whimpering sound and clung to him, pulling him down into her. He moved his hands to her buttocks and thrust into her, grinding his hips searchingly until he felt her shudder. He moved on her, slowly at first, but gradually quickening as she pulled at his shoulders and back, urging him on. She panted and groaned, letting out small random cries and thrusting her whole body this way and that as if first to escape him but then to draw him deeper inside herself. As he reached his own climax, an agony of delight, he clung onto it, smothering it for several more powerful thrusts of his hips. Her whole body quivered beneath him. She sobbed ecstatically and with a final, almost unbearable thrust, he released his sweet, pent-up pain. He clung to her tightly, as together they rode down from the dizzy heights of their delight, hugging and kissing as it slipped pleasantly away from them.

He rolled off her, his heart singing, his spirit soaring. They lay side-by-side in silence, letting the sunlight bathe them and the breeze tickle them playfully. Rabbian was the first to move. He sat up and propelled himself on his buttocks toward the stream. Whooping and laughing he slipped into the chilly waters.

Wynflaed did not move. She remained in that hot island of sunlight, lapped by waves of Forget-Me-Not, Campion and Dog Violet. From the stream Rabbian gazed at her, in awe of her beauty, emotion welling up inside him, tightening his throat and misting his eyes. She was all that he could ever have dreamed — and more. Her skin glowed as if it had an inner light, her limbs gleamed like silk, and the sunlight seemed to alchemize in her hair. He watched her cross her legs tightly and fold her arms across her breasts, as if sealing in the tenderness they had shared.

At least, that was how it seemed. That was how he hoped it was, though he knew he could not be sure, and perhaps never would be. The fear that she was remembering her dead husband slid over him, like the shadow of a cloud crossing a sunlit landscape. If only he could be inside her mind and know with absolute certainty that she loved him. He was so filled with love for her. It was as if his life had only now begun. But love brought with it a new and terrifying reality; the thought that he might lose her. How easily he could now be hurt.

He had never feared losing anything, not even his life, but now there was Wynflaed, and he could not bear to think of losing her. In the past he had always taken the time to study things carefully, so as to understand them and know their ways. That was how he had survived and prospered. He could not do that with her. Her thoughts and longings were locked away inside a life he knew almost nothing about. She had children he had never seen, and a husband who was supposed to be dead, though when she had talked about him, he had sensed her forlorn hope that he was not. He could easily understand that — she had loved him completely, added to which nobody had seen him die. It was only natural that she should nurse that thin sliver of doubt in her mind. But, like corn cockle in a wheat field, would it spoil the whole?

He felt sick, as if suddenly wrenched outside her life, separated and removed from it. She had said that she loved him, and he was sure she believed it, but one day, would that tiny, gnawing doubt spoil everything? Could he really get into her life? It would have to be a slow and careful progress. Too much haste might turn her away from him. Was this how love was? Would he ever feel at ease again?

***

Wynflaed watched the sky through lowered lashes and let the heat of the sun soak deep into her flesh. She crossed her legs tightly and folded her arms across her breasts. A chilling truth had gripped her, one which prevented her from turning her head to look upon the face of the man who now looked upon hers.

"Do you see that swan out there?" asked Rabbian.

"I love it here. We must remember this place and find it again."

"Where is its mate, d'you think?"

Wynflaed sat up and ran her gaze along the river, searching. "Someone told me — a long time ago, that swans mate for life."

....

CHAPTER TWENTY-SEVEN

What Eadwin and Gutty had to say impressed neither Lefric, the high reeve of the Peakland shire, nor Modbert his magistrate. Apparently theirs was not the first report of Wulfric's alleged survival. Lefric assured them that he had investigated every reported sighting, no matter how far-fetched. He was most sympathetic and greatly appreciated their loyalty to Wulfric. As a mark of his respect, he invited them to join him at his table and explained his reasons for believing further investigations would be fruitless.

"Northumbria now bends the knee to Penda," he said, addressing Eadwin, never Gutty. "Their tribute is not only gold and silver. It also comes as respect and goodwill. For example, they returned all our men to us. They cancelled all ransom demands and returned any that were already paid. In addition, they completed an accounting we demanded of all those who had died in captivity. Wergild was paid for every man lost." He laughed at some inner secret thought and leaned close to Eadwin's ear. "They say Lord Penda has sleepless nights over the Northumbrian gold booty he's buried around his kingdom. I've heard he walks the nights like a ghost, to see if any has been dug up yet by thieves – that's assuming he can remember where he's buried it."

Lefric leaned back in his huge chair and took a deep swig of wine from a gold-rimmed horn beaker. "Perhaps you can understand why I think further investigations would be wasted. I wish it were not so, but I'm certain Wulfric is dead. His wergild was paid. It was the biggest of course, because he was the highest-ranking officer they captured. It was paid in silver, months ago. His brother

Rendil accepted it on behalf of the boy – err – Eadric. In time it will be passed on to him."

Gutty and Eadwin sat in silence, bitterly disappointed. Such assured confirmation of Wulfric's death extinguished all their hopes. Seeing their distress, Lefric insisted they should stay the night and ordered a room prepared for them. Hunwald was chased out of the hall at a whip's end, though without Wulfric's ring. Lefric kept that for young Eadric as his father had intended.

It was a terribly disappointing outcome for everybody, but at least Eadwin and Gutty now knew that everything that could be done had been done. They had seen Lefric's honest diligence and energy for themselves. It was obvious he had tried to find Wulfric, though one curious development which nagged at the back of Gutty's mind was Lefric's reluctance to discuss Rendil in any detail. She told Eadwin she was encouraged by this. To her it was a sign that Lefric too had concerns about Rendil, but did not want to discuss them with them.

The following morning brought another unexpected development. Lady Aenflaed sent word that she wanted to see them.

"Aenflaed!" The name rang like a great bell inside Eadwin's head. He gulped with apprehension as if he had just heard that old Grim was at the gate, calling him out. He gaped at Gutty, his face riven with worry. "Aenflaed? What does she want?"

"How would I know?" Gutty snapped. "That's all the messenger said."

"When?"

"Now!"

"But I'm not dressed."

"Then get dressed, you dumb ox! And be quick. She's the Ealdorman's sister; she'll not expect to be kept waiting by mulers and lodging-house keepers."

Eadwin gazed at her, distraught. Gutty smiled back at him and lifting his sagging jaw with her thumb closed his mouth. "I'm just kidding. She's only a woman after all. You're very good with women, aren't you?" She winked at him and stroked his crotch briefly before mincing back to the rumpled bed in which they had spent the night. "Come here, my little stallion," she called. "There's just time for a quick one before we go."

It was some time later that Eadwin emerged stiffly into the enclosure before Lefric's hall. Gutty followed, blinking in the bright daylight and occasionally prodding him onward, as his pace faltered. "And remember," she told him sternly, "we've got nothing to fear. We've done nowt wrong."

Eadwin tugged at the neck of his woollen shirt. "But why does she want to see us? I mean, how does she even know who we are?"

Gutty grinned at him. "Perhaps she's heard what a stallion you are."

He grinned weakly, and taking Gutty's hand in his own set off towards Lady Aenflaed's house. No matter what Gutty said, he felt far more like a sick sheep than a horny stallion.

Aenflaed's house was about a mile away, across the river. Behind it, a bosky hillside glowed with drifts of wildflowers. A warm southerly wind stroked the trees. Despite the glories of such a fine summer's day, optimism and self confidence eluded Eadwin. He worried that he might lose his ability to speak and imagined himself standing before the great lady and honking like a goose. Thank the gods Gutty would be with him.

They found a small crowd in the porch of Aenflaed's house, mainly young, pregnant girls, ragged and tearful. It was well known that Aenflaed helped such women, especially those cast out by their families, or with no man to support them through their ordeal. Gutty gave them all a polite smile as she pushed Eadwin through their midst with firm determination.

Eadwin was terrified. The women glared hostilely. Some looked ready to tear him apart. It seemed no surprise to him that their men folk had abandoned them. He hammered on the door with his fist. The door swung back with barely a creak. Gutty pushed him towards it, her reassuring warmth pressing against him.

"The lady sent for us," Gutty announced to a small, round faced woman.

"Yes, come inside." The woman stood back from the door and beckoned them inside. Eadwin breathed in deeply and stepped tentatively from the cobbled porch into a small reception area. The house was dark and cool after the bright heat of the morning. For a moment, he could see no more than his shadow, laid out across a scatter of dried flowers on the floor. He smelled beeswax, lanolin and dusty meadowsweet on the silent air. The woman closed the door behind them, sealing them off from the sunlight.

Richly embroidered hangings separated them from the rest of the large house. The only furniture they could see was a small oak table upon which was a hand bell. The woman parted the hangings and stood aside, motioning that they should enter. Eadwin stepped through into a high roofed, barn-like room. He found Lady Aenflaed seated at a large embroidery frame beside an open window. Sunlight streamed in on her, gilding her eyebrows and lashes. As she saw him she smiled warmly.

The sun's rays seemed to light her teeth from inside, making them glow like the wax tops of lighted candles. Even in her undyed, coarse-spun gown and wimple, he could see she was a beautiful woman. Several other women wearing similar drab sat or knelt at her feet. Eadwin saw how her beauty surpassed them all, like a polished jewel shining out from dead coals.

"I'm so glad you came," she said, appealing to her women, with a polite tilt of head, to leave her alone with her visitors. Amid the muted chink of hidden keys and jewellery and the rustling swish of their heavy garments, the women rose as one and melted into the shadows. Aenflaed stood and took Gutty's hand. She led her to a stool at the shaded side of the window. "Guthrum's widow, Hilda" she said, with seemingly genuine admiration. "I've heard much good about you, Hilda. I'm so glad to meet you at last. Sit my dear, be comfortable."

Gutty moved like an overawed child and sank slowly onto the stool. Eadwin looked round for a seat, but not finding one, stood awkwardly and waited for the great lady to return to him.

"I heard all about your visit to Lefric. There's little I don't get to hear in this place," she said unashamedly. "My brother tells me nothing, so I make a point of knowing more than him. I am afraid it is making me into a nosy woman. I find that these days I enjoy gossip much more than I should, but then there are such dreadful things happening in the world nowadays. I think it is one's duty to take an interest, otherwise chaos and injustice will overrun us. The cheats and liars of this world will get away with it, and that must not be allowed."

Eadwin could not form one word of reply. He nodded dumb agreement, and decided it was best to remain silent until he had some hint of what Aenflaed wanted. Gutty, he noticed, was wide-eyed and gaping. She seemed to have taken on the startled look of a painted mask, such as a child might make with an old rag and elderberry juice. When he turned back to Aenflaed, he found her studying him curiously. He tried again to speak, but failed.

"Well, Eadwin the muler," she said brightly. "We share a common cause."

"We do, my lady?"

"Oh yes, we most certainly do."

"I would be honoured to know what it is, my lady," he said, surprising himself with both his eloquence and manners.

"You will, but first," she said, turning to Gutty, "I have something for you." She summoned her servant, with a slight motion of her hand, and whispered something to her. The woman smiled and slid away into the gloom. She returned bearing an extravagant flourish of colour across her outstretched arms.

Gutty jumped to her feet in astonishment. "Wynflaed's work!" she cried. "I'd know her needle anywhere." It was the linen runner Aenflaed had bought from Pedlar Dawes.

"I'd like you to have it. Such a piece should be kept by those who loved its creator."

Eadwin peered over the servant's shoulder. Even his untrained eye could see the work was extraordinary. It lay across the woman's arms like a jewelled stream. The fresh, wet colours of spring seemed to trail to the floor from one arm. The middle part showed children playing at a holy well, the very water falling like drops of brilliant sunlight from their pink, incandescent fingers. At the other end, the golden harvest reached through autumn to merge with the icy blue and white of yuletide. Over all shone the sun, lighting the boughs of the great ash tree of the world, with its three giant roots reaching out like serpents to the holy yew, the rowan and the birch.

"I see its beauty," he said in awe. "Only a blind man would not. How could the woman who did this have done the things they said at her trial?"

Aenflaed took the linen from her servant and passed it reverently to Gutty. "And there you have it," she said, turning back to Eadwin. "That is our common cause. Even though we now know she is dead, it is not too late to clear her name. That's why I wanted to see you." She turned to Gutty and leaned towards her, resting her hand lightly on the embroidered linen. "To entrust her work to you, Hilda, and ask you both never to stop looking for the truth."

"We won't."

"My lady, I don't want to give up," said Gutty, "but what can we do? Rendil has won. With both of them dead, there's nobody to challenge him."

"But there is, Hilda. There's the three of us. And as long as we believe in her, evil cannot win. We must never give up. Somehow, we must find the way. I will do whatever you want to help and I will see that you do not lose."

"But why you, my lady?" asked Eadwin. "Forgive me, but I think you were not close friends, surely — just acquaintances?"

"Yes, I know, Eadwin. I can't really explain it to you." She reached out a hand and patted the linen piece reverently. "All I can say is, if you knew what I feel about this work, perhaps you'd understand me better," she told him. "I have some very skilful needlewomen here, perhaps the finest, but there is something special about this. It speaks of the woman behind it and I simply can't believe what was said of her."

***

For Rabbian, the days and nights spent in the forest with Wynflaed were perfect; idle days of play and peaceful wanderings. They fixed up the herder's hut, set fish traps together, made love in the afternoons in the long, scented grass. And in the evenings, as the sun slipped behind the trees and bats skimmed across the purple sky, they cooked their supper over a fire and chatted quietly as they ate it.

For Wynflaed too, the time was full of joyful, loving moments, though doubt still gnawed at her complete happiness. As time went on though, her doubts grew. After a while she was overcome by the feeling that the happiness she so badly wanted would always be impossible. She would be stranded at the edge of their lovemaking like a watcher, no longer part of it and powerless to change things. She could not get Wulfric out of her mind. It was the exquisite weight of his ghost pressing down upon her when she whimpered and clawed at Rabbian's back. They were Wulfric's kisses filling her head and robbing her senses. And when she cried out in passion she could not be sure that it was Rabbian's name she called and not that of her beloved phantom.

Rabbian deserved so much better and she knew that somehow, no matter how painful it would be, she would have to rid herself of the past, even that most cherished spirit, before she could give him the future he deserved.

She looked at Rabbian as he lay dozing beside her and felt her love for him well up inside her. She vowed he would never learn that they were not his kisses that had fired her so. After all, she had wanted them to be. Whatever she felt, and however her doubts might gnaw at her, she loved Rabbian — she did truly love him.

Two days later, back at the settlement, Wynflaed woke in her own bed. The now familiar sounds of

Rabbian's ingas going about their daily chores filtered in through the open shutter. She and Rabbian had returned late the previous night, too late for explanations for their friends. They had gone to their own beds, having decided that in the circumstances it would be best. "There'll be more than enough explaining to do," Wynflaed had said. "We'd better not make things more difficult."

Living together as man and wife was a simple enough formality, but for a man of Rabbian's standing there were estates and property to be considered. It was usual to consult hearth companions and families first, if only to make clear who the heirs would be and what role and property would fall to the huswif.

Wynflaed felt hungry, but as she lay in her bed, gazing up at the smoked meats and bunches of drying herbs that haphazardly festooned the rafters, she was remembering pleasantly the very different place she had awoken in for the past few days. Emma's explosive arrival collided with her thoughts, knocking them clean out of her head. "You look like the bitch that stole the umbles," she cried. "Gods! I've never seen you look so well. You see, I told you, it does you the world of good."

"Emma! Must you?"

"Where's lover boy, then? I can see I needn't ask if he's any good."

Wynflaed climbed out of bed. "He slept in his own bed last night," she said, thinking, what in holy Frigg's name does it have to do with you?

"I know that," Emma said sharply. "I mean, where is he now, not where did he sleep? He's gone off somewhere. Some foreigner, a shipmaster, came and he went with him."

"Went where?"

"I knew it," she squealed. "I knew you wouldn't know." She flopped onto the bed beside her and began helping her to fasten her dress. "They all buggered off at the crack of dawn. He didn't tell you, did he?"

"I'm sure he did, I — I just can't remember ..."

"Remember, my arse!" sneered Emma. "He didn't tell you. You've had a fight haven't you? Ho-ho, trouble in lovey-dovey land already. Oh well, never mind, there are plenty more ready to jump all over you. Especially now that you're one of his cast offs."

Frowning dismissively, Wynflaed flapped a hand in front of Emma's face, hoping to silence her. "We didn't quarrel. We had a lovely time and we got on very well. In fact everything's wonderful. I expect he'll soon be back, wherever he's gone."

"Not according to my man. He thinks they've all gone to the trader's ship at the coast. He says they do this twice a year. Usually lover boy sails back with it to some foreign place – Armorica or some such." Emma studied her closely. "According to my man he says he won't be back for a couple of months, maybe longer."

"Armorica? Where's that?"

"How do I know? Somewhere across the Frisian Sea, I suppose. My man says it's where they get the wine from."

"He'll be gone for two months? I don't understand …"

"Face it, love. That's men all over. They just do what they want when it suits them and sod everybody else."

***

Ten days later, it was Theel, not Rabbian, who returned at the head of a train of carts and pack ponies. They were loaded with wine, spices, silks and luxury wares. Full of eager anticipation, Wynflaed watched with the other women as the returning men led the pack animals and carts into the settlement. She counted them in, smiling expectantly into the men's faces as they laughed and called to their loved ones. Rabbian was not among them.

Theel approached her and nervously explained. "He's sorry, but we had a problem with the merchants. He has had to go back with them. It's only about trade. This sometimes happens. While he's over there, he'll look for new things to bring back. It's something that has to be done from time to time."

"Trade! You think this is about trade?"

"Of course it is. How do you think we prosper here?"

"No! He's running away from me," she cried. "This is not about trade."

"No! You make too much of it, woman," Theel said sharply. "This is our way. He's been making these trips for years. Sometimes I go too."

Wynflaed would like to have believed him, but she kept thinking that if it were true, why had he slipped away without even saying goodbye? "Didn't he have any word for me?"

"Of course he did. I already told you. He was upset about going — leaving you. He hoped that you would understand. He said something about swans."

"Swans?"

"Yes, he said swans mate for life, and one day you would know what it meant."

"One day I'd …"

Theel shrugged and swung his foot at the ground. "Look, I'm sorry. I wish I could put things better. I'm useless in these situations, but I really think you make too much of it all. It's not what you think — whatever that might be. I've known him most of his life and I've never seen him like this. He loves you, more than life itself."

She gave him a forgiving smile. "You're very good to him, and to me too."

Theel hung his head and shrugged before looking up at her. "What will you do now?" His question and tone spoke with a chilling, far-reaching eloquence. It seemed to confirm that Rabbian was not coming back for quite some time.

Her stomach churned and her throat tightened as she tried to answer him. "I don't know. Am I to stay here? Do you know what he expects of me?"

"Well, he told me that whatever you decide, I am to help you and protect you. If you want your children, I am to see that you have a strong escort. He wants me to fix up the hall anyway you'd like it done. He would like you to be living there. He said something about you needing more room for your glassware. He made me promise."

***

Eadwin took Gutty back to Holmesfelt and stayed with her until word of Rendil's imminent return obliged him to make a swift departure. With no desire to face his brother at Badecanwell and no work for him at By-Streams, he was at a loss where to go. He set off towards the west, not sure where he was headed. Perhaps he should look for work on the salt trail, or go to the royal worthigs in the south of Mercia. Penda's volatile, insecure nature kept him constantly at war with somebody, so there was always work with the army for a muler.

Leaving Gutty proved more of a wrench than he expected. In their weeks together he had grown increasingly fond of her, and were it not for Rendil's certain vengeance, he was beginning to feel he could happily spend the rest of his life with her at Holmesfelt.

***

After three months with still no word of Rabbian, Wynflaed decided she could wait no longer. She wanted her children and bitterly regretted every day that passed without them. The harvest was in and stored away. In a couple of months it would be winter. Rivers would swell and burst their banks making the roads impassable. If she did not fetch them soon, she would have to wait another six months for Eostre's time.

She spoke to Theel about her intentions. He chose ten of his bravest, most trusted hearth warriors for her escort and provisioned her with all that she could possibly need for the journey. Her plan was quite simply to confront Rendil and demand that he give up her children to her, together with all documents of title and deed concerning their inheritance. She would arrange for this to be done before witnesses of good standing. She wanted them to see that her children had no choice in the matter. She believed this would undermine or negate any future counterclaim by Rendil, or any interference with their title, should she meet an early death.

Rendil had no warriors in his hall. His labourers would be thinly scattered about the homestead, so there would be few men he could call upon to stop her taking the children. Theel's warriors would be more than enough to overcome whatever resistance Rendil could put up.

In the vigour and distraction of decision and planning, Wynflaed was able to concern herself only with the logistics of her journey. Her doubts and concerns for what might follow were easy to put aside. However, there comes a time when preparations must end. Cost-free anticipation becomes price-loaded commitment. Action, with all its unknowable consequences, takes over. So, when the pack animals were loaded and her escort lined up ready for the road, it was with deep foreboding that she took her leave of Rabbian's ingas.

Emma walked with her for half a mile or so, then stood aside. "I expect you'll go crawling to Buhe, on your way," Emma said, sniffing back a tear. "I hope you tell her what she did to you."

"I'll say you sent your love," teased Wynflaed.

"I'd not waste my ..."

Wynflaed touched Emma's arm. "Please look after yourself," she begged. "I will need your friendship so much when I get back. I want to find you strong and well." She hugged her close. "And maybe even pregnant too."

"Like you, you mean?"

Wynflaed blushed and looked about her to see if anyone else had heard her. "I might have known you'd guess," she hissed. "For Grim's sake don't tell anybody, especially not Rabbian, if he shows his face."

"Who's the father?" Emma joked.

Wynflaed laughed and pushed her away with a playful punch. "Oh, I'm going to miss you," she said fondly, "but only Holy Mother Frigg knows what I'm going to do when I have to introduce my children to you, especially poor little Eadric."

....

CHAPTER TWENTY-EIGHT

After five days and nights, including the briefest of stops at Uhtredstun, Wynflaed laid eyes on Holmesfelt for the first time in nearly three years. If the place had changed much, she probably would not have noticed. The discoveries she had made at Uhtredstun along the way, although in some strange way half expected, weighed her down. Horse Ebell's loving account of Buhe's decline and last days was heartbreaking. As Wynflaed had listened to the old horsener and watched his rheumy eyes move sadly about him, her mind had turned to happier days, seeing Buhe as the giddy, golden child who had accepted her and made of her a loyal and loving sister. She had long since forgiven Buhe. And despite all, she held her tenderly in her memory. As she bid farewell to Horse Ebell and to Uhtredstun for the last time, she vowed to remember Buhe in only those long ago days; days of play and make do and mend dresses.

At Holmesfelt, Gutty swooned when she saw Wynflaed, and had to be carried to her bed. When she was finally persuaded that she was not seeing a ghostly apparition, she was ecstatic and took some time to calm down.

They sat by the hearth, talking for hours. Wynflaed kept much to herself about her time in the king's necklace but spared little when she spoke of Rabbian. Gutty barely paused for breath. Her animated chatter rolled back the years of separation, filling in the details of all that had happened and drawing to the front of Wynflaed's memory names and faces she had all but forgotten. Except for the occasional point of clarification, Wynflaed listened in silence. Her children, she learned, were strong and healthy. Since Goda's death in the fire at Manwine's cottage they had lived at the hall, sharing their lives with Rendil's daughters.

Rendil, Gutty told her with relish, was away up country. "He's always away since Goda was killed," she said scornfully. "He's got some widow woman up there; some poor demented cow he's apparently known for years."

"Good, I'm glad he's not here yet. Let's hope she can keep him occupied a few days more." She paused and looked her friend in the eye. "Gutty, there's something I have to do. I will need your help."

Guthrum's widow nodded enthusiastically. "Of course."

"I shall be taking the children back with me, but I want it all to seem quite normal to them. I shall just ask them quietly if they want to come with me. I don't want any sudden changes or difficulties to worry them." She paused, thinking for a moment. "I shall go and see them now - in a moment. I can't wait, but I want it all to be calm and quiet. I just hope I don't weep all over them."

"Don't worry, I can fix that. It's Maud, your old housemaid, who takes care of 'em nowadays. She'll help us."

"Maud. Oh wonderful. She's a good woman. When I was in the collar, I always prayed it would be her. I'm sure she would have never let Rendil's lies about me go unchallenged. She would tell them the truth." She stood up suddenly and dusted down her dress. "How do I look? I made this especially. I can't wait to see them.

Gutty cast a critical eye over the dark green woollen dress. "When were you going to tell me?"

"About the dress?"

"No, about what's under it. You're pregnant, my girl; about three months I should say."

Wynflaed smiled. "I never have the chance to tell anyone. They all seem to know first."

"Don't tell anybody else," Gutty advised. "I don't think you should let Rendil find out until you are well away from here."

"How long do you think he'll be away?"

"I don't know." Gutty wrinkled her brow, thoughtful. "He comes and goes all the time. He could be back anytime, I suppose."

"He must be here when I take the children. I want witnesses in good standing to see me take them. That way the shire will hear of it from honest men and not just Rendil's lying mouth. It must be done proper and legal, for Eadric's sake."

"I'll send word out. Don't worry, I can guarantee you will have your witnesses. I'll make sure they're here, whether Rendil is or not. He doesn't have to be, does he?"

"Not really, but it would be better if he was; just so long as the witnesses see me and hear what I have to say." She kissed Gutty on the cheek. "What would I do without you?"

Gutty laughed and hugged her again. "I'll send out word for Eadwin too. He ought to be here. The poor boy was searching for you all over the place, but now he thinks you're dead - like I did."

Wynflaed walked to the door of Gutty's house and looked out at the hall. Her escort were lounging in the shade of an apple tree. A small circle of admirers had gathered and were giving them food and ale. A couple of little boys were wearing the warriors' iron helmets, staggering about and giggling under the weight of them.

She still thought of it as the old master's hall. And even despite the horrors of her trial and everything that had happened there, what she recalled of the place were mostly pleasant memories of Wulfric and his father.

"Shut the door and come away. I've got something to show you." Gutty stood on a stool and reached up high to take down a leather wrapped parcel from a beam above their heads. "You will never believe who gave me this." She jumped down, beaming impishly.

Wynflaed followed her to a table, where Gutty carefully unrolled the leather, revealing Wynflaed's embroidered linen gift piece.

"Buhe?"

"No."

Wynflaed tried to think how it came into Gutty's hands, if not from Buhe. "Did Eadwin get it from Buhe?"

"It was Aenflaed, the Ealdorman's sister — she gave it to me."

"Aenflaed, but how?"

"She got it from ..." Gutty suddenly thought of all that Buhe had once meant to Wynflaed and stopped in mid-sentence. On this occasion, the truth would do no good, she decided. "Buhe apparently sent it to her for you."

***

When she was not playing with her children, Wynflaed used Rendil's absence to gossip with old friends, filling in the gaps in her knowledge. They talked about By Streams and all those who had been forced to leave when Rendil closed Bell Delfan.

Gutty sent word to her three most influential and respected friends, asking them to come and bear witness to "important deeds".

When all was ready and the formal witnesses were gathered, they first announced their names before the assembled crowd, even though everybody knew very well who they were. Wynflaed then took her children by the hand and with great theatricality pulled them from the hall, declaring that she was taking them without leave of the magistrate and against the children's will. Wyngifu giggled and clung to her mother's waist.

When it was done Wynflaed breathed a sigh of relief and hugged her children amid the cheering crowd. She took them off to Gutty's house where they immediately began planning her return journey to Rabbian's worthig. She thought how, once they were safely back in its leafy security, she would be free to raise Eadric and Wyngifu as their father would have wished. She intended that when Eadric came of age he would return to Holmesfelt with the might of Rabbian behind him, to claim from Rendil all that was rightfully his.

Perhaps she had succeeded after all, she thought. And even though Rendil's absence denied her the pleasure of confronting him personally with his humiliation, she knew him well enough to picture it clearly in her mind.

From the start, she had been careful not to say where she was taking her children. Rabbian, and the location of his settlement were never mentioned. She wanted no possibility of Rendil finding her. Not even Gutty knew. Fortunately Maud, who had eagerly agreed to return with her, did not care where it was. She was just happy to be reunited with Wynflaed, though her lusty brood of disparate offspring found this harder to take. They wept and argued with their mother about leaving. Maud quickly wearied of their noisy opposition. Wynflaed began to worry that her enthusiasm for the move might wither too. One of Wynflaed's escorts however, a young man with an imaginative turn of phrase, saved the day. He told Maud's brood of the settlement's many attractions. These, Wynflaed later learned to her amusement, included not having to get up in the mornings, never having to work, and being close to a warm water spring-fed pool frequented by naked virgins.

After several gloriously happy days, Wynflaed sent Maud's children off to their new home, safe in the charge of four of her escort. She had decided that Eadric and Wyngifu should see By-Streams and Bell Delfan one last time before taking the road south to Rabbian's. Maud was remaining with her to look after them. Perhaps Wynflaed also delayed her departure in the hope that Eadwin might hear of her from Gutty's messengers and return in time to see her. It would be good to see him. She wanted to thank him and tell him the secret location of her new home.

Eadwin had still not been seen by the tenth day. Little Wyngifu and Eadric were restless, and Maud was increasingly bad-tempered as they waited. Even Wynflaed's remaining guards had become jumpy and sour faced.

Under a bright autumnal sky, having tearfully taken her leave of Gutty and the others, Wynflaed led her little procession out on the road to By-Streams. Eadric marched beside her, eager for his new adventure. Wyngifu sat on one of the pack ponies. Maud walked beside it holding its bridle. The guards, with three more packhorses loaded with tents and supplies, brought up the rear. Looking back, she waved again to Gutty and the others at the edge of the village, and remembered the many times she had made this journey with Wulfric. She prayed that one day she would be able to visit Gutty without fear or threat.

***

Little more than a few hours separated Wynflaed's departure and Rendil's frantic arrival at his homestead. Word that she was at his hall had eventually reached him. One of Gutty's chosen witnesses, no doubt anxious to keep in with his rich and powerful neighbour, had provided him with a full account. Rendil was furious. He had recruited a dozen mercenaries and raced back to Holmesfelt at their head.

He raged and bullied his household until he had learned all they could tell him about Wynflaed's departure. Once he knew which road she had taken, it was not difficult for him to guess where she was headed. He quickly readied himself for the road, promising his mercenaries extra silver when they caught her.

***

It was late afternoon when Wynflaed reached By-Streams. The autumn sun was still warm, though in the shade of the limestone hills over Bell Delfan the day felt chilly and warned of approaching winter.

The children were bored, tired and hungry. They ate cold meat and bread from a linen bag provided by Gutty and drank the sweet water of the village spring. Wynflaed tried not to notice the decay and neglect smothering the lanes and houses. As soon as they had eaten, she got her children to their feet and led them towards the mine. At Bell Delfan's entrance, Maud shivered and indicated to the guards that they should wait while Wynflaed went inside. The men unloaded the pack horses to rest them and lit a fire.

"You don't want me with you do you?" Maud asked.

Wynflaed knew Maud was uneasy about Bell Delfan. She smiled, "Don't worry," she said lightly. "Eadric will look after me, won't you?"

Eadric beamed and boldly stepped up to the entrance. His little sister ran after him excitedly.

"I'll wait up on the hill, in the sunlight," said Maud, rubbing her scrawny arms and shivering.

Wynflaed reached for Maud's shoulders and embraced her. "Oh Maud, I'm so glad you're coming with me. I've missed you." She kissed her on the cheek. "Go and sun yourself. We won't be long. I just want them to see what's theirs by right. They must see it and remember it, and know what it means. They may have to fight for it one day. They must know why it matters."

Maud nodded and set off up the steep path to cross above the mouth of the cave. It was a fine day and the sun was warm on her shoulders as she climbed out of the shaded valley. About half way up the steep hill, she stopped in a little clearing, sat down and waved to Wynflaed, who was watching her from below.

Wynflaed waved back, hugged her children to reassure them and then set off with them towards the cave. She could not remember how many times she had approached Bell Delfan's great sightless eye. Firmly gripping Gifi's little hand, she led her into the blackness. The light faded as she stepped inside. Eadric skipped past her into the gloom.

"Wait, we must make a light. There used to be a strike-a-light and tinder here somewhere," she told him. She reached into a niche in the rock and found the same fat candle, tinder and flint. Soon she had a spluttering flame. Its unsteady glow added sparkle to the children's eyes as they watched her coax it to a bright flame.

"This is Bell Delfan. One day Gifi, when you are a big girl, it will belong to you. You will see to that, Eadric, won't you?" The boy nodded, as if the task were no more difficult than squashing a fly. "It's a magic place where lead and silver come from," she told them, adding emotionally, "You can make wishes here."

A hundred feet above their heads, in the open air above Bell Delfan, Maud lay back in the springy grass, enjoying the sunshine. She basked in the autumn warmth, feeling that at last her life was changing for the better. She was happy to be working for Wynflaed again, and wondered excitedly what her mysterious new man would be like. Her own children had finally accepted the idea of moving to a new home; of going to a country they had never seen, or even heard of. What would it be like? Would she like it? Yes, of course she would.

Shading her eyes, she peered out across the valley. Below her, Wynflaed's guards were chatting by their fire and cooking something on a spit. Beside them their pack animals browsed, content to be free of their heavy loads for a while. A pair of woodcocks burst noisily out of the brush startling her. The flash of sunlight on metal drew her eyes to the bosky hillside beyond the mine entrance. There was something, or someone, down there, but she could not see clearly. She jumped to her feet and scanned the scrub and bushes, trying to make out what had disturbed the woodcocks and flashed in the sunlight.

Her heart sank as she spotted several armed men stalking silently towards the escort at the cave-mouth. From her lofty vantage, she could now clearly see their leader urging them forward. It was Rendil.

Panic gripped her. She could not think what to do. She had to warn the guards. If she tried to climb down to them she would never make it in time. Rendil's men would see to that. She scraped a few small stones from the worn path and flung them down at the guards, shouting a warning to them. Thankfully, they heard her and sprang up, readying themselves for a fight.

Next she must somehow warn Wynflaed. It would be impossible to reach the cave entrance before Rendil's men. She looked around in panic, trying to think. She thought of shouting down to tell the guards to run and warn her. But if she did, Rendil would hear her too. If she kept quiet there was a slim chance they might not look for her in the mine.

She knew there were plenty of other ways into the mine. Eofar used to pop out of the ground all over the place in the old days, but she didn't know those passages.

"The Ealfen Pipes!" she cried, remembering the three strange stones high on the brow of the hill above her. She could shout down from there. The stones were said to be magical. Voices near them were said to carry deep down into the cave below. If that was true, she could make Wynflaed hear her. She and the children would be able to hide before Rendil and his men got to her.

She saw that down below, Rabbian's men were putting up a brave fight, but were outnumbered. Rendil's mercenaries soon had the upper hand, and after a bloody struggle they overwhelmed them. Rendil, who had taken no part in the fighting, finished them off with an axe as they lay wounded. Maud began the steep climb up to the ealfen pipes.

***

Rendil dismissed his men and limped towards the mine entrance alone. He hated the cave. All his life he had hated and feared its darkness. No matter how he tried, he could not stop thinking what horrors might be lurking there. This time however, he had no choice. He had to go inside. This was his chance to finally end it. He could get rid of Wynflaed, and her children, in Bell Delfan's endless maze of tunnels. Nobody would see, nobody would ever know.

Wynflaed reached Belle Earegasp deep inside the cave at the same moment that Rendil began feeling his way along the smooth, damp walls at the entrance. In the huge bell shaped chamber, unaware of the danger, she searched about on the ground near the cave wall, collecting up the lamps and candles she knew were kept there, and began lighting them. Eadric and Wyngifu joined in excitedly, setting them around the Bell's polished walls.

She led her children to the middle of the slightly sloping floor. They whispered and gazed about in wonder. Wynflaed then took them by the hands and led them to the cave wall. "Put your ear to the stone and listen. Tell me what you hear."

Eadric had done this once before and obeyed immediately, fearing nothing. Wyngifu was slightly nervous and puzzled. Her brow knitted doubtfully. "Listen, birds," Eadric told her.

Wyngifu's little face lit with delight as she too heard them. "Birds. I can hear birds," she cried.

Eadric pressed his ear closer to the limestone, his face a mask of concentration. "It's as if this rock is just a curtain and the birds are on the other side."

Wynflaed giggled, delighted to see them sharing something that had thrilled and mystified her. She told them about the magical cave and how their father had revealed its mysteries to her.

"And did your wishes come true, Mother?" asked Eadric, a note of cynicism in his voice well beyond his years.

"If I tell you that, I might spoil their magic," said Wynflaed "You must never reveal your wishes."

"Pooh! They only say that so that nobody knows if they come true or not," said Eadric.

"Blessed Frigg, but you've become a proper little sour puss since you lived with your uncle Rendil. We will soon change that when we get you home."

Belle Earegasp suddenly filled with loud scraping and rustling noises. Rendil burst into the light. "You'll be seeing no home but this," he said, his voice echoing round the great chamber. "You've done a perfect job for me, sister. I could not have wished for better."

"Rendil!" Wynflaed reached into emptiness to steady herself. She regained her footing and pulled her children behind her. "How ..? It's too late, Rendil. I've got men outside and more not far away."

"You have nothing. Your men are dead. How do you think I got past them? As for any others, where are they?" He laughed and moved towards her. "You've done me a great service, sister. You let the whole village see you leave but told nobody where you were going. You have played into my hands. I knew you'd come here. It was not difficult to work it out."

He waved a hand at the walls, fixing Eadric with a sneering gaze. "Look around, boy. This is your new home – for all eternity. You'll never leave it. You can thank your mother for that."

Wynflaed rushed towards Rendil. "You can't mean to harm the children," she whispered.

"Can't I? It's your fault. You forced my hand. You have left me with no choice. I can't leave them alive to tell the world where your bones lay, can I?"

"Then let us all go. I'll give up my claims, all of them. We'll disappear. You'll never hear of us again." She clasped her hands before her, tears glistening on her face.

For a moment Rendil seemed unsure. He shrugged regretfully, glancing at the children. "I can't. It's gone too far. Only one of us will leave this serpent's pit."

"It hasn't gone too far, Rendil. We can stop it here, right now."

"It's too late." He stared about angrily. "This shouldn't be happening," he cried, almost sobbing with rage. "You wouldn't let me help you. I could have helped you. We could have got Wulfric back and everything would have …"

"Got him back, what do you mean?" Wynflaed cried.

Rendil was sobbing. Great tears streamed down his face. "He's alive," he wailed. "My brother lives."

Wynflaed gasped, "He can't be." She felt sick and weak. "Alive? Where? How?"

Rendil wiped his face, misery written in every pore as he stared back at her. "They wanted a ransom, but I couldn't …"

"But He's your brother."

"I couldn't let him come back – not after … It was because of you. It's all your fault."

"Does gold mean so much to you? Surely even you're not that greedy."

"It's not about gold, you stupid bitch! You pushed me too hard. You made me fight you. You only had to let me help you, but no, you fought me about everything. Wulfric didn't want that. You even killed his baby. How could I let him come back after that? You and your stubborn, stupid ways spoiled everything."

Her legs buckled beneath her. She sank to the ground. "You mean you condemned him to death, rather than let him find out what you'd done?"

"What you'd done. Not me. I only tried to help you." He drew a knife from his belt. "You spoilt everything."

On the sunlit hill, high above the cave, Maud struggled to climb up to the Ealfen Pipes. As she finally reached the hilltop, she fell to her knees exhausted. Her lungs felt as if they would burst, but she started to crawl towards the great stones. Beyond them she saw a blurred shape coming towards her. Tears filled her eyes, distorting the image so that she could not make it out. She straightened up and wiped her face, squinting at the apparition. Her heart raced with joy as she began to make out the familiar shape of a man leading a white mule. It was Eadwin, coming across the moor towards her. Snowflake wearily plodded behind. She struggled to her feet and rushed towards him yelling and breathlessly gabbling her story.

Eadwin dropped Snowflake's reins and ran to the Ealfan Pipes even before Maud had finished telling him. He dived headlong into the tight space where the three great stones were jammed into the ground. He could hear Rendil and Wynflaed shouting at each other. Panic flooded over him. He gaped back to Maud, speechless. She caught up, gasping for breath. "What is it?"

"They're down there. I can hear them. It's too late," he cried, looking about in anguish. "What can we do?"

Maud's mind was racing, her heart thumping. She could think of nothing. She was helpless. Wynflaed could be killed and she could do nothing to stop it. Eadwin suddenly grabbed a clod of grass from between the stones and heaved it out. "I've got to get down there. Help me," he yelled, scratching at the ground like a digging terrier.

"You can't do that. Even if you could dig your way in it's too far down. The drop would kill you."

Eadwin lifted his eyes to hers. "I have to do something."

Maud knelt beside him and began digging with her bare hands.

In the cave below Wynflaed was pleading with Rendil, unaware of Maud's efforts. Rendil took a step towards her, his knife raised. A scatter of small stones fell noisily onto the cave floor, distracting him. His old fear of caves welled up inside him. Fleetingly he imagined some beast stalking him. He looked up, terrified that the whole cave roof was about to collapse on him. He peered around to see where the sound was coming from. More earth and gravel fell, and he crouched down frightened, watching the little stones scud across the smooth rock floor.

Wynflaed seized the moment and ducked away. Grabbing her children she ran round the walls, kicking over the lamps to extinguish them as she went. Steering them carefully past the rim of the swallow pit, she dived into a gallery and pressed into a niche behind some large rocks. Huddling there, she hugged her sobbing children to quiet them, and tried to collect her thoughts. One of the toppled candles still burned dimly in the vast cavern. Looking back from her hiding place, she saw Rendil had started to follow her, but he was slow and unsteady in the darkness. He looked terrified and flinched fearfully at every flicker of light and shadow. More earth and grit trickled down from the Whispering Bell's great dome.

Wynflaed waited no longer. She seized her children's hands intending to lead them deeper through the pitch blackness, to a safer hiding place. Sounds of a scuffle caused her to stop and look back. As she did, a narrow shaft of sunlight from high in the dome speared the blackness. It struck Rendil full in the face. Blinded, he staggered back trying to shield his eyes.

The brilliant shaft of light dazzled her too, so she could barely see. She thought she saw a large, hulking figure struggling with Rendil. Then, without a sound, Rendil disappeared, as if swallowed up by the ground. She peered into the blinding light, straining to make some sense of what her streaming eyes were telling her. Rendil had vanished, and the monstrous bear-like creature seemed to melt away into the limestone wall.

Slowly emerging from hiding, she walked into the shaft of sunlight. The Whispering Bell's walls glittered and sparkled in reflected sunlight. Feeling awed and exhausted she sank to her knees and hugged her children.

"It's over. Belle Earegasp has made everything all right again. Perhaps even ..." She dare not utter the words, but Rendil had said that Wulfric was alive. Could it be?

Moments later they were outside the mine in the full glare of day. Maud and Eadwin were running down the steep path from above the cave entrance. Snowflake picked her way down slowly with surer steps. Rendil's men had run off, unwilling to face a gathering, boisterous crowd of squatters, making ready to stone them. The squatters' leader told Wynflaed they had come because the big man asked them to.

Wynflaed entrusted her children to Maud. "It's over Maud. It's really over." She held out her arms and looked at them. "No chains, Maud. No chains."

Maud did not understand. She took a deep breath, stretched her bony shoulders decisively, and then led Wynflaed and the children through the lanes to the old hall. As they neared the door she stopped and turning to her mistress, smiled at her. "I can feel it too, now," she said. "It is over, isn't it?"

....

CHAPTER TWENTY-NINE

From the longboat's deck, the flimsy wharf now seemed to have risen to eye level. The tide was ebbing fast, and Rabbian paced impatiently around the ship's central mast. Occasionally, he gave the Frankish skipper an apologetic glance. A thin covering of trampled snow lay on the wharf. Dirty icicles festooned its timbers. The sky pressed down on the little harbour, leaden over muddied seawater. More snowfall threatened, and Rabbian feared the skipper might yet refuse to set sail.

The prospect of another night's delay did not appeal. He was tired of travel, of sleeping in uncomfortable inns, barns and stables. He had searched every market and chased every rumour. He had followed up the reports of every ship that was said to have carried English prisoners and slaves from Northumbria's war. Five months had passed since he had last walked in his own country. He was desperate to get home. He had found what he came for, though it was not what he wanted. It was time to go.

"I hope it is worth all zis trouble," the skipper said. "What a slave he must be — err — to have you do all zis for him."

Rabbian ignored him, distracted by the sight of a solitary swan swimming across the river that flowed past the wharf into the sea. The clatter of a horse's hooves and the rumble of cartwheels on the wooden wharf drew his attention. He watched the cart draw to a stop. Two porters climbed out and began to unload a litter. At last, what had cost him so much time and silver had arrived. The litter bearers edged their way gingerly down the gangplank towards him. The skipper barked orders at them in his strange language, his voice oddly light and musical.

Rabbian moved to help them as they lowered the litter onto the deck. Its occupant smiled up weakly, no doubt relieved to be off the swaying gangplank.

Rabbian stepped off the ship with the porters and shook hands with them. He gave their foreman a small leather bag of coin and waited as the man opened it and peered inside. He bit into a couple of the old Roman coins and then weighed the pouch on his palm. Finally, he beamed a gap-toothed grin of satisfaction.

Back on board, Rabbian eyed the man on the litter and signalled to the captain that he could cast off. All was in order.

"Are you the one who paid my ransom?" asked the man. "Who sent you? Is it my wife — my father?"

Rabbian shook his head and turned to the Frankish sea captain. "Cast off, skipper. Let's not miss the tide."

"Where are we going?" asked the new passenger. "This is not an English ship."

"Be quiet. You're free," said Rabbian. "Be satisfied with that for now."

"Who are you? At least tell me your name. I want to repay you."

A tear clouded Rabbian's eye. He turned and swatted it away. "Get some sleep."

Reaching inside his ragged tunic the injured man struggled to remove a leather cord from around his neck. "Here, take this," he said, holding it out to him.

Rabbian looked at the thong threaded through a small purple and blue gemstone, and sneered.

"I know it's not worth anything, but it's all I have. My wife gave it to me for luck. It seems to have worked."

"Your wife? It was hers?" asked Rabbian

"Yes, she loved it more than even gold. Please take it. She would want me to give it to you. I only managed to keep it because it's so obviously worthless. But if you bring it to me one day when I'm at my home and safe with my family, I'll load you with as much silver as I have."

Rabbian stared at the little blue gemstone hanging from its leather thong. He took it gently, folding his fingers over it. The man was still talking, but Rabbian did not hear him.

Out on the river a swan flew in and landed on the water near its mate.

THE END

GLOSSARY

Armorica	Brittany
Barmote	Lead miners' court
Badecanwell	Bakewell, Derbyshire.
Bebba's fort	Bamburgh Northumberland. Comes from Bebbanburh, meaning Bebba's fort. King Aethelfirth 592-616, nicknamed his queen Bebba. The fort was probably her morgengifu. See note below.
Belle Earegasp	o.e. Whispering Bell
Blotmonath	o.e. Blood-month, November
Bouse	Rubble containing lead ore
By Streams	Eyam, Derbyshire
Ceorl	o.e. pron. churl. Minor land-owning freeman allowed to bear arms
Coffer bed	Crib-like bed. The raised sides kept draughts out and bedding in.
Cyste	o.e. pron. chist. Storage chest
Delfan	o.e. Dig, digging
Ealf	o.e. A sprite, not usually helpful
East wixna	Melton Mowbray/Newark area
Elmet	Celtic kingdom in South Yorkshire. Sherburn-in-Elmet preserves the name.
Eorforwic	York (Eorfor viccus or boar city) The boar symbol had great significance. Its use here means much more than simply a place to buy a pig. It means military might and power.)
Eostre	o.e. Goddess of spring
Flesherer	o.e. Butcher
Francisca	Battle axe of Frankish influence
Frigg	Fertility goddess, Woden's wife (Feast day Friday)
Frisian Sea	The North Sea
Gafol	o.e. Taxes, dues
Gesithas	o.e. Comrades/friends
Gewissa	o.e. Saxons settled around Oxford and the Thames Valley
Grendel	The monster in Beowulf

Grim	Woden in earthly guise of a ragged old man
Heahrune	o.e. Holy man, priest
Handfast	A marriage or other important legal agreement
Holmesfelt	Holmesfield near Sheffield
Hordeon	o.e. Strong-room
Horsener	o.e. Ostler/groom
Huswif	o.e. Married woman
Ingas	o.e. Clan or "the people of" some person or place. A modern survival is "ing" at the end of earthling.
Jagger	Driver of pack horse or mule
Lindissi	People of Lincolnshire
Litha	o.e. The months of June and July
Lundenwic	London
Mercia	English West Midlands region. Like the River Mersey, the name comes from border region or marches.
Modrenacht	o.e. Night of mothers (circa 25th Dec. Midwinter feast)
Morgengifu	o.e. Morning gift. See note below.
Mydercan	o.e. Box to hold weaving and sewing equipment
North-worthig	o.e. North Enclosure. The Vikings later re-named it Derby.
Peakland	Now the Peak National Park in the Derbyshire/Yorkshire region. Still a beautiful wilderness.
Plegerer	o.e Player, actor
Portcwene	o.e Prostitute (port queen)
Quern	o.e Manual grain-grinding stone
Querner	o.e One who grinds flour
Seax	o.e Single-edged knife
Shire	A defined region or county from the o.e. root scir. Derivatives include Sherwood and, from Shire reeve we get Sheriff.
Skep	Straw rope beehive
Slaen	o.e Brightness
Solmonath	o.e February (month of cakes)
Sough	(pron. Suff) adit to drain a mine
Spalda	People of the area around Spalding, Lincs

Spinwif	o.e Female weaver/spinner
Stodlan	o.e Upstanding loom posts
Tame-worthig	Tamworth Enclosure by the River Tame
Teag	o.e Jewellery box
Thegn	o.e Sort of baron; king's warrior servant
Theow	o.e Slave
Tiw	o.e God of war (Feast day Tuesday)
Thunner	o.e God of thunder (Feast day Thursday)
Torc	Celtic gold neck ring,
Tun	o.e. Farm or settlement
Waelcyrge	o.e. form of Valkyri, the gatherers of the slain.
Wealheal	o.e. form of Valhalla, the hall of the dead.
Wealh	o.e Anglo-Saxon word for foreigner, from which comes Wales/Welsh
Weodmonath	o.e August. (month of weeds)
Wirgeld	o.e "Man-gold" Compensation due to murder victim's family. Intended to stop blood feuds. 40 shillings for a slave, 1200 for an earl.
Wite-theow	o.e Convict slave
Woden	Father of the gods. Ruler of the slain. (Feast day Wednesday)
Wyrd	o.e One of the three witches of fate — the goddesses who looked after the ash-tree of the world, spinning the threads of people's lives and snapping them off at their pleasure.
Wyrtcyste	o.e Medicinal herb box
Wyrtdrenc	o.e Herbal infusion, herb tea
Wyrts	o.e Plants useful for healing

Morgengifu

Morgengifu is an Old English word meaning "morning gift". Christine Fell, in her excellent book, Women in Anglo-Saxon England, published by The British Museum, points to extensive evidence suggesting that this was a payment made by a bridegroom to his bride, the purpose of which seems to have been to assure her financial independence within the marriage.

As the term suggests, the gift was made on the morning after the marriage, presumably conditional upon its successful consummation. Generally, it seems to have comprised land or property with revenue-generating potential. It is probable that the details of a morgengifu were widely publicised. There are numerous field, farm and place names extant to support this. Only a cynic would suggest that such publicity was to make it difficult for the groom to sneakily recover what he had so publicly bestowed, should the marriage cool off.

Apart from a few wise precautions to discourage professional merry-widowism, once given the morning gift could not be withdrawn. Women had the right to sell or otherwise dispose of their morgengifu without the interference of their husbands. To put this slightly more into context, it is perhaps helpful to remember that both Christianity and the Norman Conquest grossly undermined women's rights. On the whole women in Anglo-Saxon England were the hardy recipients of much greater fairness and equality than at any time from 1066 until the early twentieth century.

www.briansellars.com

Lightning Source UK Ltd.
Milton Keynes UK
UKOW02f1849300914

239443UK00001B/2/P